the
sight

the sight

2 NOVELS: PREMONITIONS AND DISAPPEARANCE

JUDY BLUNDELL

WINNER OF THE NATIONAL BOOK AWARD

WRITING AS JUDE WATSON

SCHOLASTIC INC.

New York   Toronto   London   Auckland
Sydney   Mexico City   New Delhi   Hong Kong

Premonitions was originally published by Scholastic in 2004.
Disappearance was originally published by Scholastic in 2005.

ISBN-13 978-0-545-20647-1

12 11 10 9 8 7 6 5 4 3 2 1   10 11 12 13 14 15/0

Printed in the U.S.A.   40
This edition first printing, March 2010

the
sight

PREMONITIONS

In a vision, I saw blood explode
over my uncle's heart.
Two days later, he nearly died.

I knew something would
happen to my mother.
It did.

People talk, and I hear
what they're saying.
But I also know what
they wish they could say.

I see flashes of Emily
somewhere else.
And then she disappears.

What if you saw what
was going to happen,
and you couldn't stop it?

ONE

I think I was a nice person before my mom died. I have a hard time connecting that person to the person I am now.

It's going on a year and a half since the accident, and I think I'm running out of leeway. People, like teachers, aren't giving me slack anymore.

One of these days, I'm going to have to decide on a personality.

I am mean to my best friend, Emily Carbonel, that day. And no, it isn't the first time. But I'm not the first person in her life to let her down.

So that's not why she disappears.

In Washington State it doesn't usually get hot in June, but today, the temperature is smack on ninety and the heat is making the air bounce. I just moved here from Maryland five months ago, so I'm used to humidity. I don't get why everyone is suddenly fainting from heat exhaustion. It just feels like summer to me. No school, and a bunch of people in shorts who really shouldn't be wearing them.

The only trouble is, my aunt Shay doesn't have air-conditioning. Most people don't on Beewick

Island. So I try to cool off the old-fashioned way —
with a hose on my feet, in a shady spot in the backyard. When Emily drifts in and starts talking to me,
it's too hot to make an excuse and go back inside,
but it's too hot to listen to her, either.

It's one of the first days of summer vacation.
Shay had suggested all sorts of fun summer programs to organize me, but I said no to all of them.
She must have put in a secret call to my grandparents, because she targeted what used to be my in-
terests before the accident. Photography camp?
Swim club? Writing workshop? Summer job teach-
ing art to kids?

No. No. No. No.

She gave up.

Emily doesn't have summer plans, either. Her
parents haven't been able to get it together to do
much for her this summer. They recently separated, and the whole thing is still pretty ugly. Emily
had been accepted to a highly competitive computer camp in Seattle, but her parents fought over
who would pay for it and if she'd live at her dad's
full-time for the summer. They were so busy fighting that the deadline passed. So Emily's stuck with
nothing to do all summer but pretend not to hear
them fight on the phone and blame each other for
the fact that Emily has nothing to do.

Emily must have some sort of built-in misery
meter, because she attached herself to me the very

first week I arrived on Beewick Island. I could tell she thought we were soul mates, since our parents had abandoned us. I wanted to scream at her that she was lucky her parents are still around and in her face. I wanted to point out that considering what had happened to me, *I* should have been the needy one. Instead, I just let her sit down at my table at lunch and unwrap her sprout sandwiches. I let us become friends.

I never would have picked Emily for a friend. First of all, we look stupid together. Emily is your standard tall blond, partial to tiny T-shirts and low-slung pants. I'm short, with acorn-color hair, and whatever interest in clothes I used to have has funneled down to finding jeans that are clean. Emily is practically plugged into her computer, and I don't even go online anymore because she's always messaging me when I just want to hang out and download some music. Her mode is permanently set on mope, and I don't need more depression in my life. She has a habit of not listening to you when you're talking, and this really pisses me off. I don't talk very much, and you'd think she'd make an effort to listen when I do.

Even though I have some sympathy for her, being with her sometimes just makes my brain scream for mercy. I consider myself in default mode, and she just happens to pop up in the friend department.

Like today. We sit on Shay's pink Adirondack chairs in the backyard, and I wait for her to get bored and go home.

"It is *so* hot," Emily says for about the thirty-sixth time. "Why don't we go into town? We could get ice cream and go to the library."

"I don't think I can handle the excitement," I reply.

Emily takes a swig of her Orangina. The smell of it makes my stomach turn. It is so hot. I lower my head and rest my cheek on my knees. I turn on the hose nozzle again and let the water wash over my bare toes. If we were really friends, I'd turn it on Emily, too. She's kicked off her sandals and even her little frosted toenails look sweaty.

"So will you come?" she asks.

I'm smelling orange soda and I feel woozy. "No. It's too hot."

"Maybe Diego would drive us."

I don't ask Diego for favors. "He's busy."

"Why don't you ask him?"

I think Emily has a secret crush on my cousin. There's probably some little old lady somewhere on Beewick Island who's the only one who doesn't, but I haven't met her yet.

Maybe Emily is trolling for a new boyfriend. One of the reasons she attached herself to me is because her old friends put her in cold storage. She'd dated Will Stein almost all of last year and dropped her friends like hot fries to spend every minute with him. Not that Emily told me this version, but the truth was pretty obvious. Then when Will broke up with her, they wanted to teach her a lesson, so they didn't take her back. They would have eventually, but Emily has a thing about rejection and just got frosty instead of wooing them back. Instead, she hung around me to show them she didn't care. Somehow, our friendship stuck, despite the fact that there was basically no reason for it to exist.

"Gracie?"

"What?"

"Are you my friend?"

It's the kind of question I hate. I look up at her, and that's when something happens. At first, I think it's just the heat playing tricks on me. It starts with something in the corner of my eye, a shadow that grows on the lawn. My heart starts to speed up, to patter in my chest like a hard rain. Because I know what's coming.

Suddenly, Emily looks different. Her short blond hair isn't swept back with clips anymore. It's matted to her forehead with sweat. The trees and lawn fade behind her, all the greens and blues, and I see her against a white background. I feel fear shimmer off her body in ripples. Then I can hear the sound of breathing in my ears. Only it's not mine, and it's not Emily's. It's someone else's.

Someone is looking at Emily.

She hears the breathing, but she doesn't look. She is afraid . . .

I close my eyes and tell the image to go away. *Go away. Go away.*

"All right."

Emily sounds hurt. I must have said the words out loud. When I open my eyes, she is clutching the Orangina bottle between her fingers and biting her lip. The sky is the same whitish blue, and the pine branches still look like they're drooping in the heat. The clips in her hair are yellow and pink. Shay's small house hunkers down on the hill, white clapboard and the windows with twelve tiny frames painted green. Everything is exactly the way it was.

Before I can say anything, Emily is walking away. She's really hurt and angry, but she keeps the empty Orangina bottle in her hand. She doesn't drop it on the lawn, like I would have done. Emily is a nice person.

I watch her cross the lawn. I should call her back, but I don't. She vanishes around the corner of the house and I put on my headphones. Within thirty seconds, I've forgotten about her.

I'm the last one to see her before she disappears.

TWO

You can drive from one tip of Beewick Island to the other in about an hour and across it in fifteen minutes. It's long and skinny, like the finger of a witch in a fairy tale. On a map, one skinny end is close to the mainland, and the other looks like it's making a break for Canada. The Olympic Mountains loom in the distance, blue and purple, their peaks snow-capped even in summer. The water in the bays is the color of blueberries, and there are fields of lavender that perfume the air if the wind is right. Seattle is about an hour away with no traffic, but there's always traffic.

It's not a bad place to live. Unless it's completely different from everything you've known, and you were never looking for a change.

So how did I end up here?

I don't think most impulses when you're fifteen are necessarily stupid, but sometimes it feels that way. Back in Maryland, I offered Jake Buscemi, who got the nickname "Scarface" in the sixth grade, twenty dollars to punch me. I really didn't expect him to take it. And I didn't expect the whole school to find out.

Oh, and another thing I didn't expect?

How much the punch would hurt.

The school called my grandparents, and they were a tad upset at the situation. I expected to be slammed right back into therapy, where I'd spent almost a year being coaxed by Dr. "Call Me Julie" Politsky to hug a stuffed panda. This was supposed to allow me to express my grief in a healthy, non-threatening, accepting atmosphere. The fact that I refused to make out with a stuffed animal indicated that I hadn't "fully processed my grief."

Oh, excuse me, Dr. Politsky. The next time your mom gets swiped by a jackknifing semi that turns her car into an accordion, I'll just toss a coot widdle stuffed panda in your lap.

So all my friends were really nice at first, and they were afraid to even mention my mom's name. In the beginning, that was a big relief. Then they started blushing whenever they mentioned their *own* moms, and they'd change the subject really fast. And soon I guess I was just too big of a drag to be around, because I started spending a lot of time in my room.

I could tell that everyone was waiting for me to *get on with it* and *process* and *find closure.* I tuned them out. I plugged into my headphones and filled up the empty space in my head with music. I didn't bother to listen to anyone anymore. I listened to songs instead, the same ones, over and over, until they made a groove in my mind that I could depend on.

But I guess I spooked my grandparents. Instead of more therapy, Mimi and Pop-Pop had a family conference and decided to follow through on my mom's original intention in her will, which was to have Aunt Shay be my guardian. The next thing I knew, I was yanked out of school during the midterm February break. The situation was deemed too serious to wait until June. I blinked, and suddenly I was on a plane to Seattle, clutching a roll of Tums and a noisy box of Tic Tacs, my grandmother's remedy for motion sickness.

My grandparents cried a bucket of tears at the airport, but I knew they were secretly happy that they could now return to playing golf all day instead of nagging me about my math homework. They'd raised three kids. They were done. It was apparent within weeks of their moving in with me — because the family agreed that after the tragedy I shouldn't be uprooted — that they realized they'd made a big mistake. There was even some attempt to find my father, which shows how seriously weird everything was at the time. My dad was a perfectly respectable D.C. lawyer before he went on a solo vacation to Santa Fe when I was three years old and never came back. He told my mom that he needed to "get clear." He promised to send child support. He sent one check. Then we never heard from him again.

Oh, sorry to interfere with your life crisis, Dad. Have a good one until you're dead.

So my dad was as gone as it gets, and my grandparents weren't equipped to handle me. They deserved to focus on nine-irons at this stage of their life, I guess. Uncle Owen lives half the time in D.C. and half the time in London. So that left Shay.

I'd only met Shay maybe a half-dozen times in my life, usually at some big, corny family reunion. She had a son, Diego, who was two years older than I was and completely uninterested in developing a cousinly relationship. It wasn't like we bonded over burgers on my mom's back porch, or kept up with each other on e-mail.

Once I moved to Beewick Island and into Shay's house, I was positive that if Mom had really known her sister instead of relying on telephone sisterly bonding and some hazy childhood memories, she would have changed her mind.

Shay is the complete opposite of Mom. For a scientist, she's an incredible dimwit. She's some kind of expert on wild grasses. *Very* exciting. She makes lists on Post-its that constantly fly off counters and flutter around the house like little fluorescent pink and yellow birds. They always get stuck on the bottom of your shoe. You peel them off and read things like *Buy oranges!* or *Learn Italian!*

She eats muffins the size of hats for breakfast. She cooks with butter. I can't count how many times she's yelled at dinner, "Oh, I forgot to make salad!"

Shay is round and curly-haired. She is a big fan of the drawstring-pants look. Her legs are strong from all the hiking she does, but she has a belly and flabby upper arms. She's always saying, "Oh, those extra ten pounds just turned into fifteen when I wasn't looking," or, "Help! I'm out of my fat pants and into my gross pants!" You'd think she'd stop baking muffins and cookies on Saturday mornings, wouldn't you?

Mom was a fresh-vegetable person. She was extremely healthy. She never embarrassed me. She never complained about something if she didn't plan to fix it.

I know that if this were a TV movie, I would fall into Shay's flabby upper arms and eat her blueberry muffins slathered with butter. I would take comfort from Shay's nurturing personality, her large breasts concealed in a series of Gap denim shirts, her insistence on calling me "sweetie" no matter how much I wince. I would tumble for her warmth, and slowly, painstakingly, find myself beginning to come alive again. Can't you see the misty reconciliation scene? Sob.

But this is real life, and I just feel pissed off.

I'm just about to go to sleep when the phone rings. I can hear Shay pick it up in the hallway.

I'm too tired at first to listen to what Shay's saying, but something about her voice wakes me up.

"I'll ask her. Hold on, sweetie," Shay says. Her voice has a gentleness to it, like she'd be holding the person's hand if she could.

A quick knock and she opens my door and stands in the doorway, the phone pressed against her chest. "Gracie, it's Emily's mom. Did you see Emily today?"

I know it immediately. It's like being hit in the chest with a baseball.

I know this question is not an opening into good news.

"We hung out for a while in the backyard," I say.

The answer sounds empty.

I feel empty. Everything has drained out of me.

Because I know what's coming.

"Do you remember what time it was?" Shay asks.

I think back. "After lunch. About two o'clock, I guess."

"Did she say where she was going?"

Remember. You have to remember.

But I remember stupid details, like the smell of oranges, and Emily's toenail polish, and her finger tapping against the glass of the bottle. I hear that tap in my head, and it grows, and it drowns everything out.

"I think she wanted to get ice cream, but I didn't want to go to town."

Shay looks more concerned, if that's possible. "Did Emily walk to town?"

"I don't know. She just left."

I know that's not the answer anyone wants to hear.

It's not the one I want to say.

But it's all I have.

I know Emily's mother isn't panicking for nothing. It isn't like Emily to stay out late. I know why her mother is worried. She should be worried. We should all be worried.

Shay listens on the phone, then says, "Of course, right away." She hangs up but doesn't put down the phone. She grips it and takes a breath.

"The Carbonels want us to come over. They want to talk to you about Emily. They think you're the last person to talk to her. She hasn't come home."

The night is warm. The windows are open. I'm shivering, and trying to hide it from Shay.

Emily's eyes shut tight.

The sound of someone breathing.

Shay is waiting for me to move, and I'm not moving, because I know with cold certainty that everything I saw was true.

It's happening again, and I can't stop it.

I don't want this. I never wanted this. I just want it to go away.

I didn't want to see a red bloom of a stain spreading on my Uncle Owen's chest, on his white shirt. Two days later, he had a tear in his aorta and almost died. In eighth grade, I didn't want to see that Hannah Bascomb was afraid of her own father, or the reasons she was. I didn't want to know the results of our neighbor Mrs. Shale's biopsy before she did.

It's like people are bleeding in front of me, and I can't move to help them.

I have too much sorrow crowding my heart as it is.

The worst possible thing has happened to me. I don't have room inside me to care about it happening to anybody else.

But I get up and get dressed.

THREE

Every light in Emily's house must be on, as if all that light could shine out to tell her it's okay to come home. I'm surprised when Mr. Carbonel answers the door. He hasn't stepped foot in the house in months. He must have driven from Seattle as soon as they decided Emily was missing. It must be really bad if both of Emily's parents are willing to be in the same room together.

Shay gives him a hug, patting his shoulder like he's a kid. She's known both Carbonels for years, and I think she's even closer to Emily's dad than her mom. Emily's mom is something of a head case.

We walk into the living room. I've never actually sat down in the living room before; it's just a pass-through on the way to the kitchen for Emily and me. It doesn't invite lounging, anyway. There's a 1950s-style orange couch that looks toxic, and a coffee table shaped like a surfboard. Mrs. Carbonel painted one of the walls violet and another wall pink. It doesn't work.

Mrs. Carbonel sits on the couch. She's perched on the edge, as if the phone will ring any second and she'll need to answer it. The phone is lying right next to her on the cushion. Even though it's almost midnight, everybody is still dressed, down to their shoes.

A stranger is sitting in the only comfortable chair in the room, an armchair upholstered in maroon leather. He rises when we come in. Mrs. Carbonel introduces him as Detective Joe Fusilli. He has a big nose and dark eyes that don't seem to have any expression at all. The bags underneath them look like suitcases packed for a six-week trip.

I get a quick flash from him. Sometimes this happens. I get sadness from him, sadness that lies buried underneath everything that's inside him that has to do with the job. I see him bending over someone, someone he loves, who stares blankly out the window.

Shay nods a hello. I think she might have smiled at his name if the situation had been different. It isn't often you meet a detective named after corkscrew pasta.

Shay and I sit down on the couch. Mrs. Carbonel leans forward, her hands clasped between her legs. Every so often, she catches them between her knees and squeezes. Mr. Carbonel sits on the other chair. He's a stocky man with big shoulders and arms and a silver beard. I've met him maybe four times, and each time, I've picked up waves of guilt when he looked at Emily. Now I notice that he never looks at his ex-wife.

The worry in this room is like a heavy blanket on a warm day. I can feel it pressing against me, and I want to kick it free.

"Gracie, did Emily seem upset today?" Mrs. Carbonel asks.

I remembered her face as she walked away. "No."

Joe Fusilli's dark eyes are on me. I decide to break my usual habit and tell the truth. It seems called for.

"Well, I wouldn't say she was really upset. But she wasn't happy when I wouldn't go to town with her. It was too hot."

"Do you think she went by herself?" Mrs. Carbonel continues.

"I don't know," I say. "I'm sorry."

Mrs. Carbonel's mouth twists, and she looks away.

Detective Fusilli speaks up. "Gracie, do you remember what Emily was wearing?"

"Sure. A white T-shirt and yellow capri pants. They have tiny pink flowers on them. And brown sandals. The kind you can hike in. Merrell's."

Mrs. Carbonel nods at the detective like a good student, as if that's what she's told him, too. As if we all give him the right answers, he'll find her.

He writes in his notebook. "Did Emily seem to have anything special on her mind?"

"Nothing in particular," I say.

"What did you talk about?"

"How hot it was, basically," I say.

"What about other times?" Detective Fusilli asks. "Did Emily ever talk about running away?"

"No."

I was sure of that. No matter how much she trashed her parents, she never talked about leaving.

"How about a boyfriend?"

I shake my head.

"A crush?"

I shake my head again. "Emily never talked about boys."

Detective Fusilli looks skeptical. "Oh?"

"Really," I say. I'm seriously annoyed now. I want to tell him to think about it a minute. Doesn't it occur to him that Emily and I might have other things on our minds? Like the fact that her parents are flakes and I don't have any?

"Did Emily ever mention having a Net buddy? Someone she met on the Internet?"

"She e-mailed some people, sure," I say. "I don't know who they are, though."

"Do you think she'd meet one of them without telling you, or her parents?"

I think about this. One thing about Emily, she follows the rules. "I don't know. I don't think so."

Mrs. Carbonel squeezes her hands between her knees again. "We can't find her laptop," she says to Shay. "She took it."

"Did she have the laptop when you saw her, Gracie?" Detective Fusilli asks.

I shake my head. So Emily must have gone home to get it.

"Is anything else missing?" Shay asks.

"No. No clothes or anything." Mrs. Carbonel starts to cry. "She was upset that she didn't get to go to that camp . . ." She looks at Mr. Carbonel for the first time. "If you would have agreed to exchange summer for school breaks —"

"I *did* agree," Mr. Carbonel says. "You wouldn't agree to Christmas —"

"You know we were planning a trip to Arizona!"

"I was going to send the check!"

"After the deadline!" Mrs. Carbonel's voice rises sharply and ends on a sob. She looks at Mr. Carbonel as if she hates him, and I guess she does. The anger between them could fill up six houses. No wonder he had to move out. There's no room to live in this house. I'm finding it hard to breathe. Had all this anger squeezed Emily out, too?

"Let's try to calm down," Detective Fusilli says. "She's only been gone eleven hours. She could come home."

I know he doesn't believe it. I can see the dread. It is his enemy. It is lead in his bones. The feeling is familiar to him, it is part of the job, but he hates it.

"It's midnight and she's out there somewhere," Mrs. Carbonel says. "Can't you do something?"

"We're on alert," Detective Fusilli says. He stands up. "What that means is that every cop in the state is looking. If you think of anything, call me. If she gets home, call me. If you remember anything, call me. Even if it's the middle of the night."

"You're leaving?" Mrs. Carbonel asks, her voice rising in panic. "You're just going to leave?"

"I'm going to get to work and find your daughter." The detective's voice is soft now. He feels the dread moving up to his throat, and he wants out of here, he wants to find the kid, and he's saying, *Please, let her be alive.*

Mr. and Mrs. Carbonel nod. I can see they want to believe in Detective Fusilli's competence so badly. Mr. Carbonel rises and shows the detective to the door.

We all stare at the carpet. "Why don't I make some tea?" Shay asks. No one answers, so she goes in the kitchen. I hear her filling the kettle.

"We did this to her, Rocky," Mrs. Carbonel says. She doesn't sound angry anymore. She sounds worse.

"Yeah," Mr. Carbonel says. "I know."

It's like I'm not in the room.

Joe Fusilli left some of his dread behind. I can

feel the weight of it settle inside me, anchor me to the chair.

Emily's parents feel guilty. But they weren't the one who could have stopped her.

I was the one who could have done that.

I was the one who saw her future.

I was the one who let her go.

FOUR

We don't talk on the ride home. I'm thinking about my answers to the detective's questions. How many times had I said *I don't know*? Had I really known Emily all that well? Had I ever really listened to her? Or was I too busy listening to my own head?

I wish I'd turned the hose on her feet, too.

Shay pulls into the driveway. She turns off the car, but she doesn't move. "Gracie, is there anything you didn't want to say in front of Emily's parents?"

"What do you mean?"

"I don't know. Something Emily might have said, or done, and you don't want to get her in trouble."

"That would be pretty stupid of me," I say. "She's pretty much in the worst trouble I can imagine right now."

"Yeah. If you want to talk —"

"There's nothing to talk about," I say, shouldering open my door. Which, I admit, is a pretty stupid thing to say, considering my best-friend-by-default is missing. But what's the good of talking about anything? Adults just don't get it. They think that expressing your feelings makes them go away.

Next, Shay would be tossing stuffed animals at me to hug.

Shay gets out of the car. It's cooler now. The heat of the day has dissolved into a breeze that makes the pines whisper.

"I don't think I can sleep yet," Shay says as she opens the front door. "Do you want to share some cookies and milk? Or I could make omelettes."

"Do you always think you can fix things with food?" I ask. I'm tired, and the question comes out snottier than I meant it to. The truth is, I'm so stuffed full of the emotion I felt at the Carbonel house I feel sick.

Shay looks hurt for a minute. She runs a hand through her springy hair and takes a breath. I can tell she's searching for the right thing to say. "No," she says finally.

"I think I'll just go to bed," I say.

"All right, sweetie," Shay says, but I'm already walking down the hall.

I pull on a big T-shirt and climb into bed. My room is tiny, but I don't mind. There's something about it that makes me feel safe. My mom used to say, "Climb into your nest," when I was a little kid, and pull up the blankets and mound the pillows and stuffed animals around me. This room reminds me of that, in a way.

It used to be a mud room, a sort of summer porch in the back of the house. Shay and Diego went to some trouble to fix it up, I guess. Shay had winterized it. They painted the floor dark blue and the windowsills yellow. Shay bought an old dresser and painted it white. My bed has a patchwork quilt with moons on it. White gauzy curtains hang at the windows now, because it's summer, but in winter Shay had hung thick velvet drapes to keep out drafts. Now that's it's warm I can open the windows all the way, and hear all the night noises outside. I can smell the Sound and hear the foghorns. Sometimes I feel I'm on a big liner, out in the middle of the ocean. That's how far away I feel.

I reach for my mp3 player. I've filled it with songs my mom loved, dopey songs I never listened to when she was around. We used to have a serious difference in musical tastes. But now when my head is full of things I don't want to think about, which is most of the time, I just drown them out. If something plays in my head, I can't hear what I'm thinking. Tonight I listen to Boy George singing "Karma Chameleon."

But I can't stop thinking about the dread I'd seen in Joe Fusilli. It wasn't in his eyes, or his face, or things he said. It was there inside him.

He doesn't think Emily is coming home tonight. I don't think so, either.

This is how it started.
When I was ten, I went to the shore with my

best friend, Annie Keegan, and her three brothers. Her mom set up the cooler and blanket and the chairs, and we all ran into the ocean. Mrs. Keegan yelled for us to wait for her, but we pretended we didn't hear her over the wind and the seagulls.

I remember how high the waves were, but I didn't want Annie's brothers to tease me about being a wimp, so I waded right in. I was doing okay until I misjudged a wave. I remember being taken over by the wave, how I tumbled and tumbled, how I tried to swim and couldn't. The force of the wave was incredible. I couldn't get my head above water. Then when I did, another wave was coming, and that one hit me, too. I swallowed water and I suddenly knew I was drowning. I don't remember that part very clearly, just that things slowed down, but I still couldn't get out of the grip of the wave.

The next thing I knew, I was on the beach. I heard a voice clearly in my head, a voice I didn't recognize. It was saying, *Come on, come on, come on, come on.* I opened my eyes. A lifeguard was looking down at me. *Oh please oh please oh please . . .* She had blue eyes that were filled with fear. Her freckles stood out against her tan like blotches.

I saw the relief on her face and I also *felt* it. It flooded my body, like it was inside me. Then I started to cough and threw up on her leg.

Mrs. Keegan wrapped me in a towel and hugged me. I remember that so clearly. How scared everyone looked, how the lifeguard sagged down on the sand, how the other lifeguards clustered around her and me. I remember Mrs. Keegan's hair blowing into my mouth, and that it tasted like salt. Everything looked different, somehow, like the world was sharper than it had been. Everything was louder. I could feel the day like it had weight, like I could feel seconds passing like air currents, like I could cup my hands and collect moments like water.

Then I sat on the blanket for a while, and drank some water, and ate a chocolate chip cookie, and things shifted again, and I felt normal.

Mrs. Keegan asked me if I was still scared. I said no. Mrs. Keegan smiled and said she thought the lifeguard had been more scared than I was. She said the lifeguard had to go home — it had been her first day on the job.

Somehow I'd already known that. I figured I'd overheard someone saying it. I said something about how her voice had called me back, saying, *come on, come on* and *please please please . . .*

Mrs. Keegan shook her head. "The lifeguard never said anything. She was trying to resuscitate you. Nobody said anything. We were all frozen. Everything went very quiet. I think even the seagulls stopped squawking."

I stopped asking questions and chewed on this along with my cookie. The lifeguard hadn't spoken, but I'd heard her voice. I didn't know what to make of that, so I just hoped I wouldn't get in trouble when I got home for not listening to Mrs. Keegan and running into the surf.

I didn't realize everything that had changed until later, until after I began to see things and feel things. It's hard to explain. People talk, and I hear what they're saying, but I also see something in a flash, like a digital photograph starting out jagged and then filling in.

I finally told Mom. It took her a while to accept it. Then after I told her that something was wrong in Uncle Owen's chest and two days later he was in the ER, she got serious. She called a couple of places and thought about getting me tested, but neither of us wanted to do that. I didn't want it to be real, somehow. I don't think Mom did, either. She was a very practical person. I think she just wanted it to go away. I couldn't blame her. So did I.

I still do.

I turn up the music. I don't want to think about where Emily is. I don't want to know what's happening to her. It will be a long time before I'm able to close my eyes.

I'm afraid of what I'll see if I do.

FIVE

I don't remember falling asleep, but when I wake up at five A.M., I know I'm not getting back to sleep. I never do. My face is wet, and so are the ends of my hair, which is clinging to the back of my neck. I know I've been crying in my dreams again. I'm shaking and I pull a sweater on over my T-shirt.

I asked her not to go.

She said, *Did you see something?*

No, I said. *Not like that. It's just . . . a feeling. I'm afraid something will happen.*

She had smiled. *I'll be back tomorrow. I'm just flying down to take a deposition.*

I didn't say anything. That was the moment. That was when I could have said, *don't go.* I could have begged. I could have pitched a fit. I could have lied and said I saw a vision of her plane crashing.

I'll call you when I land, she said.

She called from her cell phone, right from the plane while it was on the runway. She'd landed safely. The weather was clear in West Palm. After the deposition, she was hoping to take a walk on the beach. She wished I was with her — it was December, and it was seventy-five degrees. She wanted pompano for dinner. She'd never had pompano.

And key lime pie, I said.

I had hung up the phone, feeling relieved. And then I couldn't seem to figure out what to do with the day. Rosie, the friend of my mom's who was staying with me, made me a sandwich. I sat in front of the TV and ate it. It stuck in my throat and it was hard to swallow.

I started to choke. I choked and choked. I couldn't breathe. Rosie came running to help.

There was nothing in my mouth to choke on.

I ran to the phone. I called her cell, my fingers stabbing the buttons. Her cell phone had no service.

For the next four hours, I kept dialing the number, over and over and over. I just sat on the couch, dialing, while Rosie peeked in the room at me, a worried expression on her face. She kept saying, *I'm sure everything is fine,* and I kept dialing, not even bothering to answer her.

The next thing I knew, my grandparents were at the door. They lived two hours away, and as soon as I saw them, I knew. I put my hands over my ears and screamed. I screamed and screamed.

I am still, somewhere in my head, screaming.

They tried to keep the details from me, but you find out. A bit here, a bit there, a question you don't want to ask but do.

PREMONITIONS

Don't think about it. Don't think about how it happened. Don't think about it.

I turn on all the lights. Better.

I tiptoe out into the short hallway. The house is so quiet. Even the birds haven't woken up yet. I push open the door to the kitchen. I know just how much to push the door so that it doesn't squeak. I squeeze in through the gap.

I turn on the kitchen light and sit at the table. It's an old wood table, with knotholes and wide planks. I put my hands on the wood. I stick my fingers in the knotholes. Sometimes feeling things helps. After Mom died, I couldn't understand how a table could still feel so solid. I felt like the whole world was dissolving and I would fall through the edges of things. Nothing had seemed real.

I rest my cheek against the table. It is so strange to live without touch. Mom touched my hair as she walked by. She hugged me. She scratched my feet while we watched TV. She kissed my forehead. Shay doesn't touch me much because I flinch when she does.

If only, I think, the missing her would go away. Then maybe I could figure out how to live with everything else. The fear that I'll always be like this is the worst.

The door squeaks behind me. I don't know how she does it. But Shay always knows when I'm up. I sit up straight, but I don't turn to face her. I don't want to see anyone, not yet, not while I'm afraid.

I hear her get out the milk and pour it into a pan. I hear her rummage for cups. I hear the paper rattling as she unwraps the chocolate.

By the time I can smell the milk, I'm calmer. Shay puts a cup down in front of me. It is a blue cup with a green dot on the handle for my thumb to rest on. It's my favorite. I haven't told her that, but she knows.

She breaks off a piece of chocolate and puts it in the bottom of the cup. She puts a spoon and a napkin near my hand. Then she pours the frothy warm milk into my cup. I watch the milk swirl around the chocolate. Within a few seconds, I can see curls of melted chocolate in the milk.

Shay pours her own milk. We stir, the spoons tinkling softly. We take our first sip. The warmth and the sweetness fill my mouth.

The first time Shay made me hot chocolate her way, I had been shaking and crying. It's hard to describe the feeling — it's panic and pain and rage all mixed together, and it sent me shooting from my bed without thought, moving anywhere to get rid of what I was feeling. She had put a hand on my shoulder, and I had jerked my shoulder away. She had asked me if I wanted to talk, and I had said no, said it very loud and very strong and very mean. I had told her to go away and leave me alone.

When she didn't leave, when I heard her rustling around the kitchen, I didn't turn around. I wouldn't give an inch. I didn't care what she was doing, I didn't want anything she had to give. I almost didn't drink what she put down in front of me. Then I had taken the tiniest of sips, resolving not to finish it, not to give her the satisfaction. But there was something about the way she sat there, sipping her own drink, that had calmed me. She hadn't tried to talk. She hadn't looked at me. She had looked out at the gathering light. I had finished the hot chocolate. I was suddenly grateful for the kitchen lights, the blue cup, the silence.

I didn't know how to say thank you. So I washed the cups instead, and the milk pan. She waited at the table. And then we went back to our beds, where I guess we both stared into space until it was time to get up.

That had set the pattern. Shay doesn't try to touch me. She doesn't speak. She just comes and keeps me company until morning starts.

The birds start to make a racket. The light starts out black and turns blue. I've never seen anything like it before. In Maryland, the day just gets lighter. Here, it gets bluer. I wonder where Emily is.

I drain the chocolate, feeling guilty at how good it tastes. And I wonder if I can stand one more death.

SIX

No news?

No news.

It goes on like that for days.

I have nothing to do but wait. Shay goes to work. There's a line between her eyebrows now when she looks at me. I know that she wants to sit down and have a talk. I know exactly what she's thinking, and it's not because I can read her mind.

I do a lot of loud dishwashing, so Shay can't start a conversation. I clean my closet and rearrange my bookshelves. I appear busy whenever she's home, and I lay around when she's gone.

I try to remember something else — anything else — about Emily.

I get nothing.

Sometimes all I remember is how much I wanted her to go away.

I do everything in a Novocaine-type way that I remember from the period right after Mom's funeral. Someone dies, and for a while you do nothing. You don't even notice anything except pain. You see strangers, people on the street, people passing in cars, and you feel like screaming at them. *What are you doing? My mother is dead!*

But then, incredibly, days follow each other, and there is life-stuff to do. My grandparents moved into the house so that I could finish out my freshman year. That was really nice of them. But the only bedroom they could use was Mom's, so we had to pack some of her things away. They were careful to leave plenty of her things around — I'm sure that was Dr. Politsky's advice, because she counseled us during the "transitions." So they cleaned out drawers and closets, but they left Mom's perfume bottles on the dresser and her jewelry in the little blue-and-white bowls she used to hold her earrings. That was nice of them, too, I guess. I guess I would have felt worse if they gave everything away, right away, or put things into storage. That came later.

So they moved in, and there were groceries to buy, and I had to show them where the recycling went, and how to use the washing machine, and which place had the good bread and which place had the good tomatoes. I had to do these things, so I did them. But I felt like everything was frozen, and every little act took way too much energy. I took tiny steps and moved in small ways. I tried not to speak.

My freshman year ended, and my grandparents decided that since I still wasn't doing so well, they should move to my town permanently so I could finish out high school. But it didn't matter if I stayed where I was. Nobody seemed to realize that.

Christmas was the worst. We put up a tree and we gave one another presents. When it got really unbearable, we mutually agreed without speaking that we would watch TV constantly instead of trying to communicate. And I slid, from December to January, into a black place that seemed worse than the first days after the accident.

It was a bad place to be.

Now reminds me of then, and that scares me. It should make me feel better, it should make me see how far I've come in only five months. I didn't realize I'd gotten better, but I had. Instead it just shows me that I can slide backward so easily, right down the slope, back into where I was — a wasteland of ice.

"Hey," Diego says.

"Hey," I say.

This counts as a typical conversation with Diego. When I think of my cousin, I picture the back of his head. Usually because he's heading out the door. I've lived here for almost five months, and he's gone through a string of girlfriends, all of them named Jessica. Or maybe it just seems that way. Currently he's engaged in marathon phone sessions with a girl named Marigold. Yes, Marigold.

I'm sitting between my bed and the wall. I heard the screen door slam, and I knew Diego was home from his summer job with a landscaping crew. I was hoping that he'd figure no one was home and leave me alone, but for some reason Diego always seeks me out to say hello before he disappears into the glow of his laptop. Shay probably makes him.

To my surprise, Diego crouches down beside me and slides into a sitting position. His legs are too long, so he props them up against the wall. He smells like freshly mown grass, and I see a few stray green spears on his bare shins. I notice that Diego is already tan. He's got dark skin, inherited from his Spanish father, I guess. I never asked him about his father, and I haven't asked Shay. No one in the family knows anything about what happened to Shay in Spain. They only know that she lived in Spain for a year and came back pregnant.

Shay told everyone she didn't want to discuss it and didn't want to answer questions. She instructed them that they were to accept and love her baby. Everyone in the family kept their mouths shut for once, and obeyed.

I wonder if even Diego knows the story. In a way, his father is even more of a mystery than mine.

Diego gives me a sidelong look. He is incredibly handsome. He's got those dark eyes that stupid girls call "soulful." No wonder he has a string of Jessicas.

I guess I'm staring, because Diego inches back a little, like I have something contagious. Then he drums his fingers on the floor.

"I got something for you," he says. He sounds nervous.

"Okay," I say cautiously.

He slides a book over. He was keeping it hidden by his side. I lean over and read the title: *Psychic Power Points: How to Nurture, Develop, and Utilize Your Own Hidden Intuitive Abilities.*

My blood pounds in my head. I can feel my face turning red. I didn't know that Diego knew about me. His big-mouth mother must have told him.

By the way, your cousin Gracie is going to move in with us. We'll have to feed her, clothe her, give up our summer porch, and include her in dinner-table conversation. And did I mention this? She's a wacko.

I slide the book back across the floorboards at him with such force it hits his leg harder than I meant it to. He looks at me, shocked. He's pissed off, too, I can tell. We stare at each other for a minute. After having basically no contact except "please pass the salt" for five months, it's hard to handle our first fight.

"Don't tell me," Diego says with a twist to his mouth. "You've read it already?"

"This," I say, putting my fist on the book, "is none of your business."

"Okay," Diego says. He's nodding, but I can tell

it's not because he's agreeing, he's just trying to figure out the next thing to say. "That's fine. Nothing about you is my business, right? Except that you live in my house and are in my face."

I draw up my knees against my chest. For some reason, what he says hurts me. I didn't think I knew Diego well enough to allow him to hurt my feelings. "It's not my choice, in case you haven't noticed," I throw back at him.

"Gracie," he says in a nicer tone. It's weird to hear my name come out of his mouth. He never uses my name. He just says "hey."

"What I mean is," he continues, "ever since Emily disappeared, you've been holed up in here, and it's obvious that you're spooked about something."

"Maybe I'm spooked because she disappeared into thin air?" I suggest.

"Mom thinks you might know something about it," Diego says, which makes me furious again, just when I'm starting to calm down. "I don't mean you're hiding something," he says quickly. "She thinks maybe you saw something . . . I mean, in your head."

"Well, I didn't."

"Whatever." I can't tell whether Diego doesn't believe me, or whether he really doesn't care. "But if that's true, I thought maybe if you knew how to access that, you could learn something that could help Emily. Or not be scared anymore, at least."

My head jerks up. *Scared.* How had Diego known that?

Diego sighs, like this conversation is just too heavy for him to process. He gets up and walks out. No doubt Marigold is panting for his attention. After I'm sure he's gone all the way down the hall, I pick up the book.

When a kid disappears, your town gets smaller. Neighbors bring things and leave them on the doorstep. People tie yellow ribbons on trees. Posters go up in every shop. Strangers hit their knees at night with one name on their lips. In every gaze, there is that awareness, that shock that a kid has been lured and taken, in the middle of a slow summer day. Your town becomes better than it was, and everyone says, *how could it happen here?* Forgetting the things that happen all the time — the divorces, the dad who hits mom, the depressions, the alcoholics who send their kids to school with a bag of popcorn instead of a sandwich. It happens everywhere, but suddenly, how could it happen here?

I think of the strain on the faces of Emily's parents. I think of how that phone sat on the cushion. How Emily's mother's hands kept kneading the material of her pants. How Emily's father's broad chest seemed to have caved in.

I think of Emily against that white background, sweaty and scared.

I look at the book in my lap.

I don't want to open myself up to this darkness, this dread. I don't want to see any further, any deeper, than I already have.

But since I can't do nothing, this is the least I can do.

SEVEN

The next morning is Saturday, Diego's day off. He's at the breakfast table, chomping his way through Shay's homemade granola, when I stop in front of him. I put the book down on the table.

"It says that psychics can get flashes from touching things that a missing person owned," I say. "I've never actually tried to *get* the visions. I've always tried to *avoid* them."

He nods slowly, still chewing, his liquid eyes on my face.

"I was wondering if you'd give me a ride to Emily's house," I say really fast, before I lose my nerve.

He stands up, still shoveling the last of his cereal in his mouth. The spoon hits his bowl with a loud clang. "Let's go."

Diego must have taken a page from Shay's rule book, because he doesn't say anything on the drive to Emily's. He's probably waiting for me to say something. I'm sure an apology is in order, for example, but I'm too nervous to give one, and I'm not sure what I'd be apologizing for, anyway. For hitting him with a book? For moving into his house in the first place?

We don't have to knock on the door. It opens immediately, and Mrs. Carbonel practically grabs us by our collars.

"Do you know anything?" she asks.

Quickly, we shake our heads. The disappointment on her face is so painful to see that I actually take a step back. Her eyes have purple smudges under them, and her hair is completely matted on one side. Mrs. Carbonel always looked a little sad to me. Now she looks insane. She was always thin, but her khaki shorts are hanging off her hips. I think she's wearing the T-shirt she slept in. It looks creased, and there's a stain on it that looks like coffee.

She steps away from the door listlessly, as if it doesn't matter why we're here now. She goes right to the sofa and sits. The phone still lies on the cushion next to her.

"I was wondering if I could see Emily's room," I say. I've been trying to think of a reason the whole way over. I don't want to tell Mrs. Carbonel why I want to. I can't imagine what she'd think if I told her the truth. I can't imagine how furious she'd be at me. I would be furious at me, if I were her.

"Why?" Mrs. Carbonel asks. I'm not sure if she really is interested in the answer. Even though we're in the room, she's busy listening to something else going on in her head. I know that look.

The world isn't real to her now. It won't be real to her until her daughter walks through the door.

I'd thought on the way over to say that I wanted to borrow something of Emily's, something to remember her, but suddenly, that seems really stupid. It would seem like I was thinking she was dead.

Then I thought I'd say I'd left something of mine in her room. But suddenly that seems awful, too. How could I be thinking about a missing T-shirt or a CD when Emily is gone?

So instead I just stand there like an idiot.

That's when Diego steps in. "Gracie misses Emily," he says. "Would you mind if she just spent a little time in Emily's room?"

Mrs. Carbonel's eyes fill with tears. "Oh, sweetheart." She leaps up from the sofa and hugs me. She rocks me back and forth. "Oh, sweetheart," she says again, this time into my hair. "Of course you miss her, too."

Mrs. Carbonel hugs me really hard, so hard I can feel her breastbone. It almost hurts, but I don't move. I hug her back, swallowing against a huge lump in my throat. The only thing that keeps me from crying along with her is not wanting Diego to see it. I wish I could pass just a little relief from my body into hers, but I don't have any to give.

Mrs. Carbonel turns away, rubbing at her eyes with a tissue. "Go ahead," she says.

"Can I make you some tea?" Diego asks. His

mother's son, that's for sure. If I leave him in the kitchen too long, he'll be baking muffins.

I walk into Emily's room. I've been here plenty of times. Without Emily, it's just a room. A bed with a pink quilt. A dresser, a chair, a bookcase.

What should I pick? I'm not sure it matters. I pick up her hairbrush and put it down. I open the closet, but nothing seems right. I run my fingers along her clothes.

I move to her dresser and pick up a bracelet. I don't think I've ever seen her wear it. Then I see a framed photograph. It is of Emily at the beach, probably taken just this past winter, because she's wearing a jacket and a bright striped wool scarf that I recognize. She's grinning at whoever is behind the camera, and somehow I know it's her father, on one of the weekends they spend together, because there is something a little too giddy about her smile. The light is just perfect. It's one of those shots, one out of twenty-six on the roll, that you just get right. The light in Emily's eyes, the light on the water, the striped scarf against the gray sky and rocks on the beach.

I pick it up and run my finger along Emily's cheek.

The images come at first in pieces that shimmer. Somehow this time I can remain outside of the fear I feel. I know what I'm seeing, and I can concentrate enough so I can see it clearly, or as clearly as I can.

Emily. Emily and water.

Emily is moving, up and down. A boat. The boat is hitting waves, hard, ramming down in a trough of a wave and then grinding up a curl.

Emily is not afraid. She is laughing at the bucking boat.

Then the water changes.

It is a waterfall I see now, a beautiful blue waterfall with sunlight glinting on the spray. It is the biggest waterfall I've ever seen, but oddly, there is no sound now, where before I could hear the slam of the boat and hear Emily's laughter.

Then I see something I don't understand. Quick flashes of an object. It is cubelike, white, and flames shoot out of it. It frightens me. Fear settles in my bones and I feel it grow. It expands to fill the space between my ribs and my stomach and my throat. I feel the scream in my throat.

"Gracie!"

Diego is kneeling in front of me, and I'm sitting on the floor. It takes what feels like long seconds to focus on his face.

"What is it?" he asks. "What did you see?"

"What?" I croak.

"We heard you yell," he says.

Mrs. Carbonel is holding a mug of tea. "What's going on?" she asks, frowning.

I drop my head in my hands. I need to make sense of this before I say anything. But Mrs. Carbonel drops down on the rug and leans toward me. "Gracie, tell me what's happening this instant."

I hear the panic in her voice, and the fear, and I say in a voice that doesn't sound like me, "Sometimes I see things."

I lift my head. Mrs. Carbonel looks at Diego.

"Gracie has psychic abilities," he says. "We thought maybe she could help. I'm sorry, we didn't —"

Mrs. Carbonel's eyes widen as she takes this in. Then she leans forward. Her gaze is burning with hunger.

"Tell me." Mrs. Carbonel grabs my knee with her free hand. "Tell me what you saw."

I tell her the best news I can. "She's alive," I say.

Mrs. Carbonel jerks and cries out. The tea spills on her bare knee. She begins to sob. Her face is so open, so naked. She sits perfectly still, but her whole body shakes with each violent sob.

Diego disappears, running. He comes back in a few seconds with a washcloth. He takes the mug of tea out of Mrs. Carbonel's hand and presses the cold washcloth on her leg where the hot tea had spilled. Mrs. Carbonel doesn't even notice.

"Tell me," she says.

"She left with someone she trusts," I say. "She

wasn't afraid. She was in a boat. Then I saw a water-fall."

"What else?" Mrs. Carbonel asks, her voice urgent now.

I can't tell her about the white cube and the flames. I know it would be too much. I just can't do it.

"That's all," I say.

Rocky Carbonel is suddenly in the doorway. "What's going on?"

Mrs. Carbonel stands up. Her skin is so tight against her bones. It's the oddest smile I've ever seen, ecstatic, delivered. "She's alive, Rocky."

She walks across the room and grabs his hands. "She's alive. Gracie saw her . . . in a vision . . . Gracie saw her in a boat. She saw her! And she isn't afraid! That's what broke me, Rocky, the thought of her being afraid. . . ."

I feel cold inside. Emily *is* afraid. I remember back to the first vision. However she left, things are different now.

Slowly, Rocky Carbonel's face changes. Hardens. He looks at me with such anger it feels as though he's shoved me up against a wall.

"What are you doing to her?" he says to me. "Get out."

I reach out a hand to Diego. "Mr. Carbonel, Gracie is just trying to help," Diego says.

"Get her out of here," Mr. Carbonel says, each word a rock thrown at my head. He looks at his ex-wife. "What's the matter with you?"

"She's alive," Mrs. Carbonel says, her face set in the same smiling grimace, tears running down her face. "She's alive."

Gently, as though I'm a newborn colt, Diego helps me up from the floor. My legs don't work right. He leads me out of Emily's bedroom, Rocky Carbonel's furious gaze following us.

The front door shuts quietly behind us. I remember why I hate having what some people call a gift. It is not a gift and never has been. It is ten tons of concrete on my back. It is every misery in the world. It's inside of me, and I can never get rid of it.

It will never go away.

EIGHT

Diego and Shay have this whole shared language that I'm not part of, a shorthand I remember from my relationship with my mom. All Mom had to do was say, "I'll take a Pooka-sized slice," and I'd know that she meant an extra-big piece of cake. Our old dog, Pooka, was about the size of a handbag, but she could eat twice her weight in one sitting.

In other words, a family has shorthand. When you lose your family, you lose that. You just can't walk into another family and pick it up, either. Shay bent over backward to include me. If she and Diego said something I didn't get, she'd tell this anecdote about how it came about, and I'd listen politely, but the whole explanation is so lame, because the thing about family shorthand is, you had to be there. I wasn't there with Shay and Diego. And the person I was there with once, through a million memories, isn't with me anymore. So I don't have a shorthand I can ever say out loud, ever again. You would think when you lose your family, you just lose love, but guess what? You lose a whole vocabulary.

In other words, Diego and Shay are close. So I'm surprised when Diego doesn't tell Shay what happened at the Carbonels. I can tell because there's nothing in the air between us, no more than usual, anyway.

Shay makes pasta with broccoli that night. She puts the bowl on the table and leans over to smell it. Then she takes a piece of broccoli in her fingers and eats it. I don't know why she can't wait until she puts it on a plate.

"Geesh," she says. "It's a good thing we're not having visitors tonight. I might have overdone the garlic."

Just then, the doorbell rings. Shay and Diego laugh.

"Just don't exhale," Diego says.

It's Detective Fusilli. He tries to keep this cordial expression on his face, especially when he sees that we're eating, but it is obvious that he is steamed, and I think I know the particular object of his rage. Still, he gives an appreciative glance at the pasta and grilled bread with olive oil and garlic, the green salad gleaming with dressing. Suddenly, he looks hungry as well as tired and angry.

Shay pushes away her glass of wine nervously, as if Joe Fusilli was doing a spot check for Mothers Who Drink and Cook. "Can I help you, Detective?" she asks.

Detective Fusilli tears his gaze away from the pasta. I exchange a glance with Diego. It's the first time we've found something funny at the same moment. I wonder if Joe Fusilli is just dying to take off his jacket, hang up his gun (I can't see it, but I know it's there), and sit down for a bowl of linguine.

"I need to talk to you and your daughter," he says.

"I'm her niece," I correct quickly, before Shay has a chance to.

"My sister died a year and a half ago," Shay explains.

"I'm sorry." For a moment, Detective Fusilli looks human. But then something else kicks in behind his eyes, and he gives me a quick glance. It's only a flicker, but I'm beginning to read Joe Fusilli like *Green Eggs and Ham.* He's thinking, *motherless girl, orphan, possible emotional problems, stirring up trouble for attention.*

Shay covers the bowl with a plate, and we all troop out to the living room. Everyone sits except for Diego, who lurks in the doorway. It's still light out, the long light of a Northwest summer. The sun shines right in my face, and I consider changing my seat, but I wonder if that would make me look guilty.

"Are you aware that your niece went to the Carbonel house this afternoon and told them she had a vision about their daughter?" Detective Fusilli asks Shay.

Surprised, Shay looks at me.

"I drove her over," Diego says. "I thought it might help."

Shay looks at Diego now. She turns back to Detective Fusilli and doesn't say anything.

He leans forward. "She told them Emily was still alive. Can you imagine how much damage she did to those people?"

"By giving them hope?" Shay asks.

He leans back again, but he keeps his eyes on Shay. "What if it's false hope?"

"What difference does it make?" Shay asks, surprising me.

That takes Joe Fusilli aback. I can see it. He turns the question over in his mind.

"Well, let me start with this," he says. "Your niece here —"

"Her name is Gracie," Shay interrupts tartly. Her skin is flushed.

"— told them that she saw a waterfall. Mrs. Carbonel wants us to check out every single waterfall in Washington State because your niece — Gracie here, saw one in a vision. Don't you think that might be an incredible waste of resources? And don't you think, if we don't do what Mrs. Carbonel wants, she's going to think that no matter what we do, it isn't enough?"

"Hey," Diego says, "what if Gracie's vision is true?"

The detective sighs. He runs a hand through his hair. There is a bottle of antacids in his car, and he wishes it was in his pocket.

"Too much TV," he says tiredly. "Too many movies. People think that psychics help cops out. They think psychics can find people. It just doesn't happen that way."

"Cops do use psychics," I say. "I read about it."

They all look at me, as if they're startled I can speak.

Joe Fusilli's gaze is especially intent. It's like he's a tracking device, and now he's totally focused on me. His voice is soft. "So you read about it, Gracie?" he asks, and I realize that I've made a big mistake. *So that's where you got the idea to make things up?* I can't read his mind, but I know what he's thinking.

I feel my face flush, and I hate myself for showing him he's caught me off guard. "It happens," I say. "It *has* happened. I've read the cases."

"So you thought you could help us with Emily," Joe Fusilli says. "Let me go over what you told Mrs. Carbonel." He reaches into his breast pocket and takes out a small pad. He starts to read. "Gracie was transported over water on a boat."

I realize this is a show he's putting on. He's deliberately trying to embarrass me. We live on an island. Lots of people have boats. There is a bridge about fifty miles north of us, but the ferry gets more traffic, because it's the quickest way to Seattle. There is a better than fifty-fifty chance that Emily left by boat.

"Was it the ferry?" he asks me.

I shake my head. "It was some kind of powerboat. It was going very fast."

"Ah, a new detail." He makes a show of writing this down. "And you say Emily was with someone she trusts. How do you know that?"

"She was laughing."

"You saw that in your vision?"

I nod.

"Why was she laughing?"

"Because the boat was going fast, and she was having fun." That was very clear to me. Emily had felt free.

"Did you see her by the waterfall?"

"No. I just saw a waterfall. But it was weird." I'm trying to remember now. I know the detective isn't really interested in this. But I know something wasn't right about that waterfall. I just can't figure out what.

"Weird?"

"No sound," I say. "But it wasn't just that. I don't know," I say finally, unable to put it into words.

"All right, then, Gracie. I have copied down everything you remember. Is that all you remember?"

"Yes," I say, because there is no way I'm telling him any more than I have already. He's going to walk out the door, tear out the page he's written on, ball it up, and throw it on the floor of his car, along with what I'm sure are crumpled fast-food wrappers, a sweaty T-shirt, and crumpled cans of diet Sprite.

And because I want to get back at him, I say, "I'm sorry about your mother."

He goes still. "My mother."

"She has Alzheimer's. You're always able to help people. And now you can't. When it's most important."

Everybody kind of freezes for a minute. Detective Fusilli's face doesn't reveal what he's thinking, but he's furious and not happy to find himself just a little confused. He takes a breath and casually puts his pad back into his pocket.

"I was the chairman of the annual Alzheimer's fundraiser. It was in the paper last month."

"I don't read the paper."

He dismisses this. He had been off his stride for a moment, but now he's figured out an explanation, so he can dismiss what I say. He leans forward, resting his elbows on his knees. "Tell me something, Gracie. You say that Emily was with someone she trusts. You know this because of your vision."

I wait.

"Is that the only reason you know it, Gracie?" Joe Fusilli asks. His voice is very soft now.

"Yes," I say. "I told you that already."

"Are you sure?"

"Do you want to hear it three times?"

"Because if there's something you have to tell me, now would be a good time. A very good time." There is something threatening in his voice now. He's leaning on me, hard.

Shay suddenly bounds to her feet. "That's enough," she says. "You are harassing my niece."

"I just want the truth," Detective Fusilli says, his eyes still on me. "There's a young girl out there we're trying to find."

"Gracie's a minor, I'm her guardian," Shay says, not giving an inch. "So get out."

Joe Fusilli gives Shay a cool look, as though her anger doesn't affect him in the least. "I was just leaving," he says, standing up. "You might want to have a talk with your niece, Ms. Kenzie. If she knows more than she's telling —"

"She told you she doesn't!" Shay snaps, her eyes blazing.

"Let's keep our focus here," Joe Fusilli says. "Our focus is Emily."

Now Shay *really* gets angry. Her hands actually curl into fists, and for a moment I'm afraid she'll haul off and land one on the detective.

Instead she whirls around and heads for the front door. She opens it with such force it bangs against the wall. "I haven't forgotten about Emily for one *second* since this happened," she spits out. "Her parents are close friends of mine. I've known her since she was born. We are all living with this, Detective. We are all in our separate hells about it." Suddenly, it's like Shay's throat closes over the words. "Now get out of my house."

He looks at Shay for a moment, then walks out the door. Shay closes the door very gently. She composes herself, still facing the door, before she turns back to us.

There is a long pause. Then Diego speaks.

"Detective Pasta sure knows how to push your buttons," he says.

We hear Detective Pasta start his car and take off.

He thinks I know something more than I'm telling. And I do. I'm just not sure what it is, and he is not the person I can tell it to. Nobody is. I'm alone. This is not in any way news to me.

But now being alone in the world has a new weight. Somebody has to find Emily Carbonel.

That someone, I now realize, is me.

NINE

From the very first week I arrived, Shay had declared that Sunday was Field Trip Day. *It will be fun!* she said. *Gracie needs to have a sense of place! And it will give us a chance to explore!*

Subtext: *I Don't Care If You Have Plans, Diego, We Are Going To Bond With Gracie Even If It Kills Us.*

So we got in the car, and I wore my headphones, and after trying to get me to "contribute," Shay pretty much left me alone, and she and Diego talked in the front seat. I saw Seattle, I saw Bainbridge Island, I saw Mount Rainier, I saw La Conner, I saw Desolation Pass. I was one big, walking Pacific Northwest bumper sticker.

Today, the sightseeing has to fit around our mission. Shay wants to drop by Rocky's studio in Seattle and leave a food basket. She's baked bread, made a marinara sauce, put some pasta and cheeses and a salami in there. As if Rocky couldn't walk out his front door and buy all those things in two blocks. As if eating pasta would make him forget that his daughter is missing.

And, not incidentally, as if I want to see him again. I am currently far from his favorite person.

"I spoke to Rocky," Shay says, not looking at me as she packs the basket. "He's sorry about the way he reacted. He knows you're just trying to help. We're all doing the best we can."

She closes the basket and sighs. "I know bringing food won't make a difference. I just have to do something."

In other words, I want to say, *you're doing this for you, not him.*

I remember casseroles rolling through the door after Mom's funeral. Little cards would be pinned to them. *Bake at 375° for one hour.* As if macaroni and cheese could matter. Could make a difference. As if eating food wasn't some gray experience, a forkful here and there of something you don't even taste, because someone says, "You have to eat," so you eat, just so they'll stop talking to you.

Thinking of that makes my throat feel tight, so I pull my headphones on and go out to wait in the car.

We take the ferry over to the mainland, and Shay drives to Rocky's studio, a restored boat factory on Lake Union. I know that Rocky has moved into his studio until he can find a house. Emily used to come here for weekends. She'd said the place spooked her because it got so empty at night. The neighborhood is still partly industrial.

Shay squeezes her old Saab into a space behind

a boat trailer, and we all pile out, Shay grabbing the food basket. She knocks on the door of the studio. After about a full minute, we hear footsteps clomping on the floor. The door opens, and a guy a little older than Diego stands there, squinting at us. He's slim, with sleek dark hair to his shoulders and eyes like chips of gray ice. His jeans are spotted with paint and his blue plaid flannel shirt has been laundered so many times it's almost white. Underneath it, he wears a T-shirt that was once black and is now almost green. Together with those pale gray eyes, he certainly looks well-washed.

"Hi, Zed," Shay says. "How're you doing?"

"What's up?" Which is not really an answer, I note. This guy is too cool to even say, "Okay."

"Is . . ."

"He went for a walk up at Green Lake. I kicked him out, actually. He needed some air, man."

Shay nods sympathetically.

"He's got his cell on, though, if you —"

"It's okay," Shay says. "I just wanted to drop this off." She points to the basket and shrugs. "Just some food. Do you know my son, Diego? And this is my niece, Gracie."

Zed's pale eyes flick over me. It is the shortest of glances, but I feel my face heat up. He doesn't say hello, or even nod, just stands aside to let us in. Thanks for making an effort, Mr. Handsome.

As I brush by him, I pick up an emotion. Worry.

Worry about Rocky? Worry about something else? I don't know, but I know he chews on that worry like a cow on grass.

We walk into a sort of living room, with a cushy couch and a long table with some of Rocky's glass pieces on it. They're big vases shaped like chrome kitchen garbage cans. There's even black shiny stuff that's supposed to look like a Hefty bag rolled over the top of the rim. I'd seen Rocky's work in Emily's house — well, I passed by some vases and things on the way to the refrigerator — but these were big and different and kind of cool.

Zed passes them by without a look and pushes open another door that leads into the studio area. It's just one huge room. One wall is full of books on metal shelves. Long tables are in the middle of the open space, with paper and pastel crayons scattered on them. Big drawings of vases and vessels are drawn with huge loopy lines. The drawings are in black and white and blocks of bright color are in the margins, as if Rocky is trying to figure out what color they should be.

A couch that matches the one in the other room is against one wall and has sheets and a blanket neatly draped over one arm. There's a wooden screen in the other corner with a map painted on it. I realize that it's a cartoony version of Beewick Island. Behind the screen is a rolled-up futon and a small table. Wooden cubes with clothes in them are stacked next to the bed, and I recognize some T-shirts of Emily's. So that's where she slept when she visited. Some dried lavender is stuck in a pretty yellow vase on the table. That makes me feel sad, because I see that Rocky had tried to make the place sort of homey for Emily, and I know it hadn't worked.

"Are you blowing today?" Shay asks.

Zed nods. "Going to try, anyway. Work might help."

Shay puts the basket down. "How is Rocky doing?"

Zed leans over and shuts the lid of the computer. "I don't think he sleeps."

I drift away, over toward Emily's corner. Shay is moving over to look at a table with some sketches. She is talking to Zed about Rocky, who, according to Zed, is a "freaking mess."

I see a T-shirt, neatly folded in one of the cubes, and pick it up. It's from the computer camp that Emily never got a chance to go to this summer. She was so proud of getting into that camp. It's a bright red shirt — not Emily's best color, but she wore it a lot at the end of school. Then she stopped wearing it.

The room fades suddenly, the gray walls rushing toward me like a waterfall. Then the water is like a wave, a gentle wave splashing against a beach full of pebbles. The pebbles are grayish, opalescent.

Then the gray bleaches to white, and I'm looking at a bed. Light sweeps across it, and then darkness comes again.

I'm standing in a doorway, looking down at Emily on a white bed.

I'm angry at her.

I'm angry at all of them.

It's all their fault, and they won't try hard enough, and it's all about that, isn't it?

If only they would listen to me. If only they would see that we have to share. That we have to love one another.

If only they could see that.

How much harder can I try?

They make me sick, they make me so mad . . .

The walls move back again, and I'm in the studio. The fear starts from the ground up. I feel it surge through me and I want to scream. I want to run outside and gulp air. My mouth tastes like greasy coins.

I've been in his head.

I've been in the kidnapper's head.

I've seen through his eyes. I've felt what he's been feeling.

He's on the edge of something. It's like he's holding back a great torrent of black emotion, holding it back with the fraying ribbons of his control.

And Emily was there. I saw Emily.

But this time, I didn't really register her. I was too overwhelmed by the thoughts. Emily hadn't been a real person to me.

Because I was looking at her through his eyes.

I sink onto the futon.

She's not a real person to him.

It makes me feel sick to my stomach.

She existed *for* him. She wasn't *Emily* to him.

How could someone look at someone else and be so detached, so . . . *wrong*?

I realize that I've crushed Emily's T-shirt in my hands. They feel stiff as I try to smooth out the shirt. Something tells me to act normal, not to call attention to what just happened.

I get up and walk toward Diego, who has wandered over to another door. I just need somewhere to move. As he opens the door, I see something. Flames.

I shake my head. Is that something I see, or something I imagine?

I walk quickly to the doorway, my heart pounding now. I stand in the doorway and see the ovens. The opening of the oven is square, and flames are shooting up, burning hot and orange.

A white square with flames shooting out . . .

"What is it?" I ask.

Diego turns slightly. "It's called the glory hole. It's where the glass is kept hot before it's shaped."

I'm so confused I can't think clearly. There's too much information flooding me at once. I can't pick up one single thread. When I hear Shay's voice behind me, I jump.

"Time to go," she says.

I turn automatically. We walk toward the door.

"I'll stop by the Harborside soon," Shay says to Zed. "You working tonight?"

"No, next weekend." Zed nods for a good-bye. His eyes meet mine for a brief second. I don't know whether I'm chilled or attracted. There is so much that is wrong here that I can't pick out what is important, what I need to know.

The door closes behind us. I take a breath of fresh air, but it feels thick and humid and doesn't help to clear my head.

The beach. The light, then darkness. The man standing in the doorway. The flames.

What does it have to do with Emily? Are they clues I can follow? How can I find Emily based on flashes that come in bursts of light and then go before I really *see* anything?

I'm so balled up with frustration I want to howl and kick the car door.

I am sick inside, and afraid.

What I really want to do is walk away. Walk away from all of them, from all of this.

But I'm trapped, and I know it. I push away the

panic, grind it down with my foot. I try to hone in on the first thing I can. Zed's worry. What was it about?

"The Harborside?" I ask as we walk toward the car.

"Zed's father owns a restaurant on Beewick Island. Zed cooks there on the weekends. He stays in a fishing shack near the place," Shay explains. "Zed became a gaffer for Rocky just recently, when he got out of college. He also happens to be the fastest oyster-shucker on Beewick Island. Which means he's probably the fastest oyster shucker just about anywhere."

Shay opens the car doors, and we pile in.

Oysters.

Those weren't beach pebbles I saw, they were *shells*. Oyster shells.

I look down and realize that Emily's shirt is still bunched up in my hand. I put it down carefully and buckle my seat belt. "Where's the Harborside?"

"In Greystone Harbor," Shay says, pulling out of the parking spot.

Greystone Harbor is the next town over on Beewick. It's where the tourists go. The town is pretty, white houses and flowering bushes, all built around a horseshoe-shaped cove. Very postcardy. There's even a lighthouse.

Light sweeping, then darkness. Was that a lighthouse in my vision?

Let's get ice cream, Emily had said. The ice cream place is in Greystone Harbor.

A long, hot walk on the hottest day of the year. She couldn't have wanted ice cream *that* badly.

I remember Zed's silver eyes, the way he looked at me. Had Emily ever mentioned him?

I remember asking her how her weekends were in Seattle. She'd said they were grim. She said Rocky trying to please her made her feel strange. Usually, the weekend would disintegrate somehow, and Emily would suggest that Rocky go to work. She liked to watch him blow glass.

And she'd said, *But the sightseeing is pretty fine, if you know what I mean.*

Clueless me thought she was talking about . . . sightseeing. But I think back on the way she said it now, and I realize what she meant. She'd been talking about Zed. Zed in his faded jeans, his tight T-shirts, his cool, silvery eyes.

Zed with the worry inside that doesn't go away, no matter how much he tries to bury it.

TEN

Shay takes us out for an afternoon of fun, she says. We watch them throw salmon for the tourists in the Public Market. We have an early dinner at Etta's, and then we go to a big, old bookstore in Pioneer Square, which Shay calls a Seattle landmark. I lose Shay in Cooking and Diego in History.

I wish I could lose myself.

It's like this thing with Emily has cracked me open, and I don't want to say *like a nut*. But suddenly, it's like I can read what other people are feeling. Not Shay, and not Diego. Not everyone I see. But sometimes, a wave hits me, and I *know*.

I know that the fat man in Travel is worried about his daughter's marriage.

The woman in head-to-toe Gore-Tex just threw up in the bathroom. She's pregnant.

It's a girl, I want to tell her. *Don't worry so much.*

The man in the green shirt taking down a book in Fiction wonders why books can't save him from falling in love with women who hurt him.

The woman with the long silver ponytail has a doctor's appointment tomorrow. She's worrying about cancer as she chooses a book called *Living Simply in an Age of Stress.*

You're okay, I want to tell her.

But what good would it do? She'd think I was just another passing lunatic.

Emily isn't okay.

I've got to screen everything else out. I've got to figure it out, I've got to decipher it.

I've got to break it down.

I go downstairs to this little café they have. They're out of soda, and the girl behind the counter suggests coffee.

"I don't drink coffee," I say, which I realize is enough to get me deported from the city of Seattle.

"We have juice," the girl behind the counter says. She has a pierced eyebrow and a seriously punked-out haircut. Her gaze is somewhere between hostile and bored. She hates her job and pretty much hates her life, but I'm relieved that I get no insight, no flash into why.

"I don't like juice," I say.

She shrugs. I finally ask for tea, which I don't really want. I find a table and start dunking the teabag like I'm trying to wash it clean.

Forget about the visions, I tell myself. What else did you see?

Detective Fusilli had asked me if Emily had a crush, and I'd said that Emily never talked about.

boys. I thought I'd been telling the truth. But what if she'd been *trying* to talk to me about a crush, only I was too dense, too locked in my own head, too busy trying to hear music that I wanted always, always playing? I wanted the music to block out everything in my head, and it wound up blocking someone talking just a couple of feet away.

I remember Zed closing the laptop as Shay moved toward the table. Had he been hiding something? How could I get back into the studio and find out? I couldn't drive, which was a serious handicap. I discovered something essential: Detectives need cars.

Maybe I could talk Shay into going back so that she could see Rocky. Why was she taking him food, anyway? Why wasn't she taking food to Mrs. Carbonel? Did Shay have a crush on Rocky? Was she using this as an opportunity to move in on him? That would be totally snaky of her, but I really don't know how Shay operates in her love life. All I know is that for an overweight middle-aged woman, she has plenty of dates. You'd think on an island you'd run out of men at some point.

Maybe I'm wrong. Maybe Shay and Rocky are *already* involved. Maybe Shay is the reason the Carbonel marriage broke up. I try to think back about that night we went over there. Mrs. Carbonel hadn't even said hello to Shay.

Shay plunks down a bag of books on the table,

making me jump. She points to the tea with her chin.

"I didn't know you liked tea."

I push the tea away. She sits down. I look at her sandaled feet, then look away. Shay has feet like a hobbit. Her toes are chunky and round. You'd think that if you had toes like that, you wouldn't want to call attention to them. You'd be too embarrassed to get pedicures. Not Shay. Her toenails are bright red.

"Don't you want to buy a book or two? I'm treating," Shay says.

I shake my head.

Shay looks distracted. She lifts her hair off her neck and lets it fall again. Her hair is thick like my mom's, but it's brown, not blond. Not that my mom's was natural. Mom used to call me her "tell," which meant that because I have brown hair, everyone would know her blond hair was fake. She used to ruffle my hair when she said it; she really didn't care, she was making a joke. I feel anger grip me in a fist and squeeze. Shay's feet, her hair, annoy me. Her breath, the fact that she's breathing. The fact that I'm sitting here, in a strange place, with a stranger, miles away from what I know. What I've loved.

"Are you after Rocky?" I ask her.

Shay looks confused for a minute. "Am I . . ."

"Are you trying to move in on him?" I ask. "Is that why you're bringing him food?"

Knowledge floods Shay's eyes. I see it happen, filling her brain as the blush fills her cheeks. So it's true.

"That's a horrible thing to say," she says.

She is furious. I've never seen her angry, at least at me. Only at Detective Fusilli, or at a driver going too fast on a country road.

"You think I'm using Emily's disappearance to spice up my *love life*?" she asks. Her green eyes are intense, watching my face.

I shrug. I press my finger on the teabag on the table and watch the brown stain spread out.

Shay stands up. "I'll meet you at the car," she says.

I sit there for a few minutes. I'm not feeling too great about myself. I tell myself that detectives have to ask questions that people don't want to answer, but deep down, I know something that I'm afraid to admit. I *enjoyed* asking the question.

Finally, I stand up. Diego is coming down the stairs to get me. He waits while I wipe up the tea and throw the napkin and cup away. We walk to the car without saying anything. I can tell he knows Shay is upset, but I'm not sure if he knows why.

Shay is sitting in the driver's seat. "I hope we don't hit traffic," she says in a neutral voice. "There's a Mariners game letting out."

We do hit traffic, but I think she's relieved, because she gets to concentrate on driving. I want to say something, but I don't know what. So I start thinking about how to investigate Zed. It's up to me, and I know it. If I go to the police and babble about oyster shells and feelings, they'll laugh me out the door.

Shay had said that he stays in a shack on the beach. If I could get inside, maybe I could find something.

Or maybe *Emily* could be inside. Maybe Zed got her to go away with him, but then she changed her mind. Maybe he's keeping her there, and that's what I saw in the vision.

"Why don't we stop for ice cream on the way home?" I suggest.

Diego turns from the front seat and looks at me, surprised. Shay glances in the rearview mirror. It's the first time I have ever suggested prolonging an outing. It could be the first time I've suggested doing *anything* together.

"How about that place in Greystone Harbor?" I say.

I see how Shay's face relaxes. I realize that she thinks that this is my way to apologize. I'm embarrassed. I should have thought of it as an apology. Instead, it's just a ruse. But at least it gets me somewhere closer to Emily.

ELEVEN

Diego gets vanilla, which is weird, because I'd never peg him for a vanilla person. Shay gets chocolate, which is not a surprise. I get toasted coconut. Diego knows the pretty girl who serves the ice cream, of course, since he knows every pretty girl on Beewick. So he hangs out at the counter, licking his cone, while she giggles and pretends to fill napkin containers.

I've got news for Diego. She likes him, but she's using him. She's overdoing the giggles, hoping her boyfriend comes early to pick her up so she can make him jealous.

Shay and I head for a table. The silence is awkward, at least for me. Shay licks her cone and looks out the window. The sun has already set, and we're getting the last of the light. Across the street from us are the restaurants and shops at the harbor's edge. They're built up on a kind of pier over the beach. I can see the lights of the Harborside, which looks like the kind of place Bluebeard's pirates might hang out in. Creaky wood siding and lanterns outside casting dim pools of light into the dusk. Fishnets hung on the siding. All for the benefit of the tourists.

Emily, where are you?

If I can pick up the feelings of strangers, why can't I feel you here?

I saw the house in the dunes as we drove down the harbor road, but I can't see it from here, it's around the point. It looks like an old fisherman's shack. It couldn't be more than one room.

"I'm sorry I got up and left," Shay says finally. She still looks out at the fading light. "I was just so *mad.*"

"I was just asking," I said.

"But you thought it might be true."

"I don't know you," I blurt out.

She looks at me.

"I don't know what kind of person you are," I say. "So I don't know if you would be the kind of person to have a crush on Rocky, and bring him food, and think that comforting him would . . ."

Shay's mouth twists. "Get me what I want?"

I don't answer.

"Okay," Shay says. "I'm not that kind of person, first of all. I'm more the kind of person that does dumb things like bring people food when I don't know what else to do. I was a friend of both Rocky and Laura when they were together and I'm still a friend. Not a close friend, but a friend. I'm not attracted to Rocky. He's a piece of work, if you want to know the truth. I like him, I just wouldn't want to be involved with him. Okay?"

"Okay," I say. The ice cream is melting on my hand, and I lick it off.

Shay takes a breath. "What hurts me," she says in a slow, careful voice, "is that I felt like you *wanted* it to be true."

I think about this and realize that she's right.

Mostly, I don't want to be having this conversation. The light is going, and I need to find a way to leave and prowl around that shack. But it would be too weird to get up now.

"I don't want to get all psychodrama-ish about this," Shay says, "but has it occurred to you that resenting me for not being your mother is a waste of time?"

"You're just so not like her," I say. "Like you're from a different family."

She grins and takes a lick of her cone. "True. We were always opposites. Your mom knew what she wanted to do, and she did it. She was on the debating team in, like, fifth grade. She always knew she wanted to be a lawyer. Graduated from college right before her twentieth birthday. I was on the five-year plan. Me, I just wanted to sleep at the beach, tool around in a boat, go crabbing. It wasn't until I was thirty that I realized that loving water could be a profession. That's when I went back to school to study wetlands. You should have seen your grand-parents. They turned cartwheels. They thought I'd end up, I don't know," and Shay waves her ice-cream cone to take in the shop, "dishing up ice cream on the boardwalk in New Jersey."

Shay crunches on her cone. "Carrie was a force of nature, that's for sure. She never let up; she never gave in. You should have seen her on the swim team in high school." She smiles. "You should have seen that water churn."

I didn't ask for a eulogy, I want to say. But I'd said enough mean things to Shay already that day.

"Being opposites doesn't mean you can't be close," Shay says. "Look at you and Emily."

Everyone thinks I'm Emily's best friend. The truth is, I care about her more now that she's miss-ing.

Guilt may be a pathetic propellant, but it works. I want so badly to get up from the table that my knees are shaking.

"One time, your mom and I decided to become blonds together," Shay says, a smile on her face. "We had to hide the box from your grandmother. Carrie went first. She —"

But I switch her off. I don't want to hear Shay's memories. I can't handle the memories I have. I sure don't need anybody else's.

I don't care how weird it looks. I have to get out of here.

I stand up. "I need to take a walk."

Shay's face flushes. She's not angry. She's kicking herself because she thinks she's handled this badly. "I'll come with you," she says, starting to stand.

"That's okay. I just want some air."

I leave her there, her chocolate ice cream dripping down her hand, staring after me.

The air is cooler off the water. I walk down the street, away from Shay's sight line. I'll have to double back, go under the piers so she won't see me. I don't have much time. As soon as I'm out of sight, I start to jog.

There's no moon tonight. The lights from the restaurants don't penetrate the dark of the beach. The sand sucks at my shoes. I begin to feel something skitter along my skin, ruffle the hairs on my arms. If I'm right, what will I find in that shack?

Emily wasn't moving in my vision. She was so still.

For the first time, it occurs to me that Emily could be dead.

TWELVE

Dark . . . light. Dark . . . light. The beam from the lighthouse sweeps the harbor. As I walk, it sweeps over me. Every few seconds, I feel exposed, even though I'm walking up near the dunes and there are scrubby pine trees here for cover.

There are curtains at the windows of the shack, and no light seeps out through the cracks. I leave the shelter of the trees and walk toward it.

When I'm up against the wall of the shack, I try to peer into the window. Not only does it have a curtain, the windowpane is frosted with salt. I can't see a thing.

As I try to peer in, the window moves slightly, and I realize that it's hinged on top. All I have to do is pull the bottom out, which I do. I look around. The beach is deserted. I pull the window open and put in my foot.

It's hard to climb in a window, especially when you're so scared your muscles aren't working right. I manage to slither inside, still holding the window out. I let it fall behind me.

It's too dark inside to see more than shapes at first.

"Emily?" I whisper. My heart is booming, rushing in my ears.

I am able to make out now that the shape in the corner is a bed. There's one chair, one small table. A few books are stacked on the floor. There's no sink, no bathroom. Just a bottle of water by the bed.

No Emily.

My heart is beginning to slow down. I start to explore what little there is. I go through his books, which are mostly art books, with some fiction by young male writers thrown in.

I flip through the books, and a piece of paper flies out of one and slowly wafts downward, where it hits my shoe. I pick it up.

It's a copy of an e-mail.

To: glazboy
From: eminel
Subject: book
Z,
This was life-changing. Which means you are, too, I guess. Too much pressure? Sorry. Only I'm not.
E

Emily.

I stare at the paper, knowing what it means. It means Emily and Zed had something going on.

Then something touches my ankle.

I scream. I leap off the bed and land on the other side of the room. I'm backing up toward the window when a gray cat pokes its nose out from under the bed.

I put my hand on my chest and beg my heart not to explode. I bend down and look. The cat's yellow eyes shine out at me.

"Hey, cat," I say softly.

She stretches, then steps out daintily a few inches, just like cats do, telling me that she's not in the mood to socialize, but she'll endure me.

I tuck the note into my pocket and replace the book on the floor with the others. That's when I notice a small dish of dry cat food in the corner, along with a bowl of water. If I'd seen it on my first inspection of the room, I would have spared myself a major heart attack.

As I stare at the cat food, it occurs to me that if there is a cat here, with a full bowl of food, it stands to reason that the cat's owner is currently in residence, and not an hour away in Seattle. He's here, now. Somewhere.

Crunch, crunch.

It isn't the cat, munching on her kibble. It's footsteps. On the beach. Coming closer.

I peer out the window. It's Zed.

I jump back, even though I know he can't see me. There is nowhere to hide in a one-room shack.

The door and only window face the beach, where Zed is. There is nowhere to go.

I touch the paper in my pocket. I have proof that Zed had some kind of relationship with Emily, something he'd hidden from Rocky. That doesn't make him guilty, but it does make him a suspect. Which means he could be dangerous.

I look outside again and see Zed trudging toward the shack. And then suddenly the moon comes out, and I see that it's raining.

Zed is carrying a body in his arms.

A girl.

She's wearing a nightgown, and the rain is starting to plaster it to her legs.

Her head lolls back, and he tries to keep it up.

I feel cold, frozen to the bone.

I know that the girl is dead.

Then something happens — I blink, or the world shifts and turns a fraction — and it's Zed again, just trudging across the sand, tired after a long day.

It was a vision. Of the future? Of the past?

Of Zed carrying Emily.

And Emily is dead.

But had it really been Zed? Had it been Emily?

Now I'm not so sure.

Enough! I want to scream. I can't figure it out, I can never figure it out, and yet the visions keep on coming. And Emily is getting farther and farther away.

I won't be able to find her, I won't be able to interpret what I see, and it will be too late, and all my life I will know that I could have saved her, could have done something, only I was *just too stupid to figure it out!*

I am shivering now, shaking. The cat jumps back down and scoots under the bed.

I have a more immediate problem. Zed is going to arrive any minute and find me.

I hear someone calling Zed's name. Even through the closed window, I can hear it.

I see Diego running down the beach, running fast, calling as he runs. Zed stops and waits for Diego to catch up. Diego says something I can't hear, waving his arms, pointing. Zed shrugs. Diego talks again.

Zed has turned his back to the shack to talk to Diego. I push the window open and climb out, managing to do it without falling or making noise. My legs are shaking as I run around the back of the shack and into the dark pools of shadows from the pines. I can't get to the road from here; I have to walk down to the beach and retrace my steps. I start to walk along the dunes, hoping that it's too dark for Diego and Zed to see me.

I could wait in the shelter of the pines, but I have a feeling that if I'm gone much longer, Shay will be calling Detective Pasta. I walk quickly across the pebbly part of the dunes. It's really awkward trying to walk quickly and quietly on rocky sand.

"Gracie!"

I want to keep walking, but I turn. Diego is waving at me, with a big, stupid grin on his face. I've never seen him direct that grin toward me before.

Zed looks at me. It's too dark to see what his expression is. I walk slowly toward them, wishing with every step I was walking the other way.

"Hi," I chirp. Once, a mouse got in our kitchen and climbed into the trash can and started squeaking. Our dog, Pooka, went over, jumped up on the can, looked in, and barked at the mouse, which promptly dropped dead of a heart attack.

I feel like that mouse. My teeth are chattering, and I grind them into a smile. I feel like I might pass out. I can't look at Zed. I can only remember him walking with a dead girl in his arms. I can only push back the fear that it was Emily.

"Where've you been?" Diego asks amiably. "Shay is about to call in the FBI."

"I told her I was going for a walk," I say.

"Did you get lost?"

I realize he's given me a great save. "Just a little."

He reaches out and knocks my head with his knuckles. "D'oh." What is this big-brother act he's putting on?

"Thanks, anyway," he says to Zed. "I guess we found her without looking."

Zed's eyes are the color of the moon, and just as remote. "See you, then."

"See ya," Diego calls, already walking without waiting for me to catch up. Which I do. I run. I'm glad of the company, even if it's Diego.

For a while I just hear the soft slap of the water and the scrunch of our footsteps in the damp sand.

Then Diego explodes. His voice hisses like the waves. "Are you nuts? Who do you think you are, Nancy Drew?"

"I don't know what you're . . ."

"I saw you come out of Zed's shack, Gracie, okay? I had a feeling that's where you were heading. If you want to be a detective, get a new face. I saw how you were looking at Zed at Rocky's studio. At first, I thought you were into him, but then I realized you were after him. It's insane to investigate on your own. Whoever took Emily . . . she could . . . *anything* could have happened, okay?"

It's the longest speech Diego has ever given. He's really steamed.

We're under the piers now. It's a creepy place to be, in the dark. I look over my shoulder. The beach is deserted. No one is behind us. But the pillars make me nervous. There are so many places to hide.

"Could we just get to the sidewalk, please?" I ask.

He shoots me a look. Then he does a nice thing. He takes my hand and helps me up the slope of sand. He practically hauls me up onto the sidewalk.

"Explain," he says. "Here. Now. Shay can't see us. We have about thirty seconds before she freaks."

I hand him the note. He reads it.

"I found it in one of Zed's books," I say. "In the shack. Eminel is Emily's screen name."

Diego still stares at the note.

"When I was at Rocky's, I had a vision," I add. "I saw the light from a lighthouse sweeping over a bed. Emily was in the bed."

Diego looks up, out to the bay.

"The *lighthouse,*" I say, even though I know he gets it. "And I saw oyster shells, lots of them. Shay said Zed was the champion oyster shucker. And I remembered something Emily said about weekends at Rocky's. I think she had a crush on Zed, and that note proves there was something between them."

"What else?" Diego asks.

I shake my head and turn away.

"Something spooked you, and it wasn't this note," Diego says. "You've got to trust someone, Gracie. Don't you see that this is too big for you to handle alone?"

Fury balls up like a fist inside my throat. Who does he think he is? I've handled the biggest thing in the *world* all alone. "I *am* alone," I say coldly.

"You're *not* alone," Diego says.

I don't say anything, I just look out at the water.

"When you first came to live with us, I was scared of you," Diego says. "Shay told me that you had some psychic experiences. I was scared that having some spook-doozy living with me would invade my privacy or something. Or that you'd see things about me, and they'd be all bad."

"It doesn't work that way," I say defensively. "I'm not an X-ray machine."

"I'm just saying, that's one reason why I didn't talk to you much."

"That's really stupid."

"Yeah, well, the other reason is that you're really a pain."

I laugh. I can't help it. Diego calling me spook-doozy helps somehow.

"So I just wanted to say that," he says.

"Okay."

"So tell me what else you saw."

I look at him and I see kindness in his face. He wants to help, and at least he doesn't think I'm crazy. "I saw a vision when Zed was crossing the beach," I tell him. "He was carrying a girl. A dead body. In the rain."

Diego sucks in his breath. "Was it Emily?"

"I *assumed* it was," I admit. "But I don't know for sure. I didn't see her face. I'm not even sure I saw his face."

"You know what we have to do, don't you?" Diego says.

I am already shaking my head, but I know I'll lose.

"The police have to know," Diego says. "That means we have to tell Shay first."

I just look at the sidewalk.

"She'll be cool," Diego assures me. "C'mon."

We start to walk back toward the ice cream parlor. I'm not too thrilled about the prospect of seeing Joe Fusilli again. But I'd much rather face the police than Shay.

THIRTEEN

One of Dr. Politsky's questions in therapy was "Can you name one thing that made you happy today?" I don't know why a question that always really bugged me won't get out of my head. So if I have to find a ray of sunshine in my current state, I'd have to say that after all, it is a relief to tell Shay that I've had a little episode of breaking and entering.

She doesn't yell. She doesn't move. She listens without talking, which is a highly unusual trait in a person, if you ask me. Diego is there for support. We sit in the living room, which feels weird and formal, because we're always in the kitchen. And after I am through and Shay looks sort of pale and shaken, she says we need to go to the police, which is exactly what Diego said would happen.

But she doesn't get up. She looks at me. "You have to trust me," she says. "You *have* to now, Gracie. It's too dangerous for you not to. You have to tell me what you know, and even what you suspect. Do you understand?"

I nod.

"I can't believe that Zed has anything to do with this," Shay says, shaking her head. "I've known him since he was a boy."

"You have to admit he's a weird guy, Mom," Diego says.

Shay looks reluctant to call anyone weird. "He's . . . different, okay," she says. "He's had it tough. His mother died when he was seven, and his dad works all night at the restaurant. He was raised by his dad's girlfriends. I can't imagine him kidnapping Emily, or being involved somehow." She shakes her head. "I hate going to the police, but we have to. This could be all my fault."

"What do you mean?" Diego asks, because Shay looks stricken. I see a vein throb in her forehead I'd never noticed before.

"Don't you remember?" Shay looks at Diego. "I'm the one who recommended that Rocky hire Zed in the first place."

We must have interrupted Detective Fusilli's late dinner, because there's a plastic bowl half-filled with salad on his desk. I see slivered chicken, I see noodles, I see red pepper, I see green beans. I thought police detectives were supposed to live on junk food.

He looks up and meets Shay's eyes. I feel the surge that he feels. I could have lived without knowing that Detective Joe Fusilli thinks that, if this were a different time and a different place, and he wasn't in charge of a missing-child case, he would like to experience what it would be like to really kiss Shay Kenzie.

You would never know it by his face, or his voice, or the way he looks at Shay, but the feeling is so strong I can pick it up like a megawatt radio station on a clear night. I also pick up that although he is glad to see Shay again, he is not particularly happy to see me.

We sit. Shay very calmly hands him the copy of the e-mail I found at Zed's shack, explaining that I, well, climbed inside.

"I can't take this," he says. "If it's evidence, it will be thrown out. I can't even read it," he says, reading it. He rubs his forehead.

"Did you know that Emily had a relationship with Zed Allen?" he asks.

"No," I say. "She never mentioned him. But thinking back, I remember something she said . . ."

"What?" Obviously, Detective Pasta is not one of those listeners who doesn't interrupt with questions.

"That she liked the sightseeing at her father's studio," I say. "I didn't pick it up at the time. I thought she was talking about boats. You can see boats from the windows," I add lamely. "But I think she was talking about Zed."

He taps the paper against the desk.

"He might still have the original on his computer," I say.

"I realize that," he says. "There's this thing I need called probable cause. Is there anything else you can give me to go on?" He speaks gently now. "I know it's not easy, Gracie. But just now, you told me something that's important, something you remembered and saw in a different light. Can you think of anything else like that?"

At first, I'm impatient with this question. I don't see how I can reinterpret something that didn't stick in my mind. I can't just pluck a sentence from my memory that Emily has said and shout, "That's it!"

But suddenly, I *do* remember something.

"The library," I blurt out. "Emily wanted to go to the library that day, the day she disappeared."

"Yes?" Detective Fusilli said.

"Emily wasn't a reader," I say.

"And? You think she was meeting someone?"

"I don't know," I say. "But the library has computers. If she wanted to send a message that she didn't want traced, she could go there."

Joe Fusilli nods slowly. I can see two things — frustration that he didn't think of this already, and relief that he has something to go on now.

I've given him a lead.

FOURTEEN

The police search Zed's computer. It's been wiped. There's no trace of e-mails or websites visited, not even buried in the hard drive. When they search the library computers, they find the same thing on two of them.

They want to talk to him, but Zed disappears.

The days pass, and they can't find him. Shay tells me all this after she gets home from work. Her head is in the refrigerator while she roots around for something to cook for dinner. I can see that she can't really focus on food, and for Shay, that's saying something. She takes out a lemon, a head of cabbage, and a cantaloupe.

She stares at them on the counter.

"There's always pizza," I say.

"I need to cook. Want to go to the grocery store?" she says.

I know she doesn't want to leave me alone. Diego didn't go to work today. He hung around the house, which he never does. We weeded the garden together, just because I couldn't stand to see him out there doing it by himself. I felt too guilty. We watched some lame afternoon TV. Diego chatted on the computer while I stared out the window and wished I'd have another vision that would clear everything up, even if I was too scared to try. Shay got home and released Diego from Gracie duty. He scooted out to see Marigold.

She tells me that they are checking out all the websites visited from the library on the afternoon Emily left, but so far it didn't sound like they'd found anything. The librarian remembered seeing her, but she doesn't remember if it was that day. If she had, she would have gone to the police already.

Another dead end. Another day.

But it's just us for dinner, and it will feel good to take a drive.

Shay grabs the keys, and I follow. We roll down all the windows and the blast of air is warm and smells like summer. I like the early evenings here best, when the sun is liquid and pours over the fields. The sky turns this incredible color, a blue so deep that it seems to vibrate, and the shadows of the pines are purple.

"The blue hour," Shay says. She smiles, loving it, too.

We drive to Greystone Harbor, where the good grocery store is. I trail along behind Shay as she buys salmon and greens for a salad. She picks up a tub of freshly baked cookies from the local bakery. When I used to go grocery shopping with Mom, she tossed things into the cart quickly, consulting her list. Shay never makes a list. She inhales, she peers, she talks to the fish man and the wine lady. I'm mildly bored, but the music is catchy. I hum along to "Secret Agent Man."

He's giving you a number, and taking away your name . . .

. . . taking away your name . . .

I go away and come back. I don't know how else to describe it. Something gray drops over me, like fuzz on a TV screen, and I hear Emily's voice in my head, and she says, "He took away our *names,*" and when I'm there next, I'm still standing next to the freezer section. My fingertips are against the glass. But that's not why I'm cold.

Fear again. I feel it. Multiplied.

Emily isn't the only one. There are others there with her.

Shay is wheeling the cart toward the cashier. I hurry toward her. I'm tired of visions. I'm tired of fear. I'm afraid of being here, in this grocery store, where visions can come as you're staring at packages of frozen French bread pizza.

I want to go home.

Shay pays for the groceries. She came for just a couple of things, but the cart is full. A man walks over to her with a smile and starts to talk to her. I slow down.

I walk up to them. Shay absentmindedly puts

her hand on my shoulder as the man finishes his sentence, something about a memo at work that everyone got that day, and Roger fouling things up again.

Shay introduces me to the co-worker, whose name I immediately forget. I need to be outside. I want to be home like a two-year-old.

"I'll load everything in the car," I say.

"Be right behind you," Shay says, handing me the keys. I can tell now that she really doesn't want to discuss Roger or the memo, but she's stuck.

I push the cart out into the parking lot. The lights are on now, and the blue has turned inky. The lot is almost empty now. I put the grocery bags in the trunk.

I hear the footsteps before I see anything, even a shadow. Someone is running, a whispery sound on the asphalt. I'm just turning to see, trying to get out of the way of the trunk lid, when something slams into my body. I start to fall, but I feel hands grab me.

I can't see behind me, but I feel his breath. He is very strong. The force of the slam carries us both over the side of the car and, before I know what is happening, he pulls me down the slope of the grass. We roll together, over the rocks and the roots, grunting, me trying to scream. But the breath has been knocked out of me, and we spill out together underneath the dark, dark trees.

No light overhead, no moon.

And yet I can see him.

I know him, his face over mine, his body pinning me down.

Zed.

FIFTEEN

"Just . . . don't . . . scream," he says. He puts his hand over my mouth.

I nod jerkily, quickly.

"What do they know?" he asks, his voice a hurtling ball of fury, fear. "What did you tell them?"

I think the word *who,* but I can't say it. My throat has closed from fear.

"The police!" he yells into my face. "I know you were in my place. Don't lie to me!"

The fear inside me has drained me of everything I have — bones, muscles, will. His eyes are chips of moon. I am falling into the earth underneath me.

I hear the noise of something falling down the slope, rocks sliding, someone breathing. Zed whips his head around, straining in the darkness.

She slams into him headfirst, using her body to push him off me. I hear the thud of their bodies connecting.

"Get off her!" Shay shouts, and she pummels him until he rolls away. She kneels next to me and scoops me up and holds me. Her eyes are wide and frightened. "Gracie?"

I nod to show I'm okay. She turns, holding me against her and faces off against Zed. But he doesn't give her time to say or do anything. He's scrambling up the hill on all fours, grabbing chunks of dirt and rocks and sliding down, then gaining a few inches. Finally, he finds his feet and scoots the rest of the way, over the lip of the hill, and we lose sight of him. Then I realize that the high-pitched noise I've been hearing hasn't been my breathing. Sirens.

Shay is hugging me, rocking me. In the past, when she hugged me, I was repulsed by her softness. This time, all I feel is muscle. I lean into it, glad of it.

"I'm sorry, I'm sorry," she is saying. "I never should have let you go into the parking lot like that. Alone."

I find my voice at last. "It's okay," I croak.

"I'm sorry," she keeps saying, crying into my hair.

We hear the sounds above in the parking lot but can't see it. The squeal of tires. Someone yelling.

"Nice and easy!" someone shouts.

Shay looks up. "They got him," she whispers.

My legs are shaking badly, but Shay helps me, and we get up the hill and back to the parking lot. Zed is being frisked, his legs out, his hands on the police car. Under the streetlights and next to the uniformed cops, he just looks like a skinny kid in a torn T-shirt and dirty jeans.

Joe Fusilli is there, in another car. He sees us and hurries toward us. "What are you doing here?" he bellows.

Shay's worry for me now moves into a channel she can groove on — irritation at Detective Pasta. She waves at the grocery store. "Maybe, like, buying food? Until Zed grabbed Gracie and tried to kidnap her! Where were you?"

Joe's gaze makes that abrupt turn into concentration, and he focuses on me. "What happened?"

I explain how I was putting the groceries in the car, and Zed tackled me. Then Shay says that she came out and saw the trunk open and got scared, and started to look around. She saw me down in the grove of trees and came after Zed.

"We had a report he was down in Greystone Harbor," Joe Fusilli says. "We were cruising and just happened to spot him. Can you come down to the station? Now we have him for attempted kidnapping and assault, too. Come on, I'll drive."

"I have my car —"

"I'll drive," Detective Fusilli says firmly.

As we get into his car, we draw closer to Zed. The police are doing that weird thing where they sort of help him into the car so that he won't bump his head. The gesture always seems tender to me, like what a mother would do.

I can see his face now. He doesn't look angry anymore. Just lost. He has a tattoo on his arm of a lily of the valley. The most delicate of flowers, little white bells.

The image of the tattoo and Zed's lost face fill me up with a gully wash of guilt that cuts a whole new stream of knowledge inside my brain.

His mother's name was Lily. I know that somehow. And I also know something else. The worry that fills him up isn't about Emily, it's about everything. It's about being a loser, it's about being lost. He is angry, withdrawn. But he didn't take Emily.

And there's another thing. The guy in my vision didn't have a tattoo.

I stop in my tracks as Joe Fusilli holds open the car door.

"He didn't do it," I say.

Joe Fusilli looks at me. I can tell I just got to the end of his last nerve. He sighs a sigh that seems to sum up every sleepless night he's had since this began. "Just get in the car," he says.

SIXTEEN

"She really tackled him?" Diego asks me the next morning.

We're in the kitchen. Diego is emptying the dishwasher. I am wiping down the counters. We occasionally intersect and do a neat dance, Diego's arms holding a plate over my head, my bumping closed a drawer for him with my hip. Disco chores.

"Like Boo Radley jumping the bad guy in *To Kill a Mockingbird,*" I say.

"Hey, Boo," Diego says, and we giggle. Well. I giggle. Diego laughs.

"There's only one problem," I say. "Zed didn't do it."

Diego is stooping over the dishwasher. He straightens up. "What?"

"For one thing, he has a tattoo," I say. "In the vision, the guy carrying the dead girl doesn't have one."

"You said you didn't see him clearly."

"There were parts I saw clearly," I explain. "And I know there was no tattoo."

"So maybe the vision doesn't have to do with

Emily at all," Diego says. "You didn't recognize the girl."

"It may not be Emily, but I know it has to do with her," I say. "I just know it. It doesn't add up, Diego. Zed says that Emily had a crush on him, and he tolerated it. She was his boss's daughter. He loaned her a book. She's the one who made more out of it than there was."

"He says."

"I think she would have told me if there was something between her and Zed," I say. I stop wiping the counter, because I just might grind away the Formica. I turn and lean against it. "She might not have told me about a crush, but she would have told me about a thing."

"What about his computer?" Diego asks.

"He says he doesn't know how it got wiped," I explain. "And his dad says Zed doesn't know enough about computers to do it. Even *Rocky* has his doubts. He told Shay he can't believe it. Zed swore to him he doesn't know anything about Emily's disappearance."

"Are you forgetting that he tried to kidnap you?" Diego asks. He shuts the empty dishwasher.

"I don't know that." I've thought about what happened all last night. "He tackled me, and we fell down the hill. He wanted to know what the police had on him. He was *scared.* Angry, too, sure. Because I was the one who led them to him. I'd be plenty pissed, too, if I was innocent."

Diego doesn't try to argue with me. "So what should we do?"

"I don't know," I say. "I told Detective Fusilli all this, but he didn't care. The police think they have their guy. It's just a matter of getting more evidence."

"What does Shay think?"

"She saw him attacking me, or at least that's certainly the way it looked. The book is closed for her, too."

"Well, until we can figure out who did it, Zed is in trouble," Diego says.

"Well, Emily is in worse trouble. But finding her will help Zed."

"Exactly." He drums his fingers on the counter. "What about the oven? You saw that in your vision."

"Sort of."

"What about Rocky?"

"Emily's dad?"

Diego shrugs. "Nasty custody battle. It happens. Emily could be in another country by now, and Rocky is just cooling his heels, waiting to go."

"I hadn't thought of that."

"I bet the police have."

I shake my head. "This is all so confusing. I'm not a detective. But thanks."

"For . . ."

"Taking me seriously."

"No problem," Diego says. "Spook-doozy."

We hear Shay's footsteps. She walks into the kitchen, holding up a credit card. "Retail therapy," she says. "Anyone interested?"

"Mom," Diego says, "can I remind you of something? I'm a guy."

"Not tempting?"

"Not tempting."

"So what will you do today? It's Saturday."

"Guy things."

I watch them together. It's like I zoom backward, out of their space. There is something easy about the way they are together. Diego is seventeen. He has a relationship with Shay that I'll never have with my mother. I'll never have a relationship with Mom at seventeen, or nineteen, or twenty-three. We were just starting to have that thing where you're friends, when it's not just me looking up to her, but us looking at each other. I'll never get there. I'll never have the pleasure of watching us change. I'll be locked into Mom and me at fifteen.

Still grinning at Diego, Shay turns to me. "What do you say? Seattle? New clothes? I know all the cool stores in the U district."

What would Shay, Woman of Gauze, know about cool stores?

"Yes," Shay intones, noting my look of surprise, "I am a woman of fashion and mystery. Come."

The heat wave has broken, and the temperature is in the seventies when we hit the streets of Seattle. It's T-shirt weather, blue-sky weather, and everyone is out and grooving on it, because Satellites (which is what I call Seattle-ites) see most of the winter days through a frizzly, drizzly curtain of gray rain. Then mold starts growing on their sport mocs, and boom, it's summer.

I try to be enthusiastic about shopping, but I've got things on my mind. I can tell Shay does, too. We flip through racks of clothes but we can't get up the necessary self-interest to try anything on.

"This was a bad idea," Shay says finally.

I don't bother denying it. It feels weird to think about clothes when Emily is still missing.

"Let's go to Ballard and get Sno-Cones and look at the salmon ladder," Shay suggests. "That always makes me feel better."

"Okay," I agree, even though I have no idea what she's talking about. Motion seems like a good idea, though.

We're right near the University of Washington, the school everyone calls "U-Dub," which always sounds like the beginning of a nursery rhyme to me. We start walking down 45th Street, back toward the car. Students swirl around us, eating burritos as they walk, shouldering backpacks, talking about keg parties instead of chemistry. Shay suddenly stops outside a housewares store.

"Oh, I just remembered, I need a new cheese grater. Mine imploded the other day. Do you mind if we —"

"I'll wait outside." I'd much rather watch people than browse for cheese graters.

"It's a great store —"

"Shay? Not tempting."

She grins and goes inside.

I study the posters glued to the streetlamp. Concerts, yoga classes, a lecture on "The Porpoise-Driven Life: Lessons From Our Marine Friends," a night of "macrobiotic stand-up" at the Oat Harvest Health Restaurant.

And I think high school is wacky.

Behind the Oat Harvest flyer I see something. It's like I'm dreaming. It's a drawing. It's half of a white square, and flames are coming out of it.

Slowly, I tear off the Oat Harvest flyer. Underneath it, there is a logo. It is a computer monitor with flames licking out the top.

It is what I saw in my vision. I hadn't seen an oven. I had seen this.

COMPUTER CAMP FOR HIGH SCHOOL STUDENTS
SPONSORED BY MEGAWALL

I suddenly feel shaky. The day shifts, just like that, and the sidewalk seems to move under my feet. Suddenly, nothing seems as solid as it did a few seconds ago.

I read the flyer, faded from the weather and tattered from having other flyers tacked on top of it. It's the camp Emily got into, but couldn't attend.

I read the address, and it's only a few blocks away. And the camp is taking place now. I rip off the flyer and shove it in my pocket. Then I go into the store to find Shay.

She's got a grater tucked under her arm while she contemplates a roasting pan.

"Oh, Gracie, sorry, I get lost in these stores, I'll pay for this right —"

"No, it's okay," I say, trying to make my voice sound normal. "I found a store with some cool stuff. Can I meet you back here?"

"Ten minutes," Shay says.

"Fifteen?"

Her eye wanders and settles on something called a *bain-marie*. She holds it up. "Do I need this? I would feel very French if I had this."

"You could need it," I say. "That's what I'm thinking."

"Fifteen minutes," Shay says.

I walk out of the store.

I am thinking about the T-shirt I found in

Rocky's studio. I was holding the T-shirt when I got the vision of him. When I was inside his head. The T-shirt gave me the way in.

He had touched that shirt.

I start to run.

SEVENTEEN

I had promised Shay to tell her if I suspected anything, but that was before Zed was arrested. I know Shay wants to believe that the kidnapper has been caught, and she'll argue with me if I want to keep looking. After what happened in the parking lot, I know she'd tell me to let the police handle it.

But the police aren't handling it. They have Zed, and they're done. Besides, what kind of trouble could I get into at a computer camp full of kids?

What kind of trouble could you get into in a supermarket parking lot?

I tell myself to shut up and keep walking. The building is close to campus, one of those renovated warehouses with wood floors and big windows. I'm reassured at the sunlight pouring through the skylights as I step into the lobby.

The camp has taken over a suite of rooms on the second floor. I peek into the different rooms, which all empty out onto the hallway that winds around the building and overlooks the lobby. Kids are at computers while cool geeks stand over them or sit at their own computers. It's hard to tell the high school kids from the instructors, who look mostly college-age or a little older. There are tons of soda cans and balled-up bags of potato chips scattered on the long tables. There's a scoreboard for some kind of team game, divided into Team Rant and Team Rave. Pinned up on long bulletin boards are digitized photographs of President Bush with various vegetables on his shoulders instead of a head, and long sheets of code.

I'm not sure what I'm doing here, and I'm not sure what I'm looking for. All I know is that I have exactly twelve minutes to find it.

A tall boy with red hair stretches and cracks his knuckles like rifle shots, then pushes off from his computer. His wheeled chair shoots straight back into my knees.

"Ow!" I jump back and rub the area where two functional knees used to be.

He scrambles off the chair, almost falling in his eagerness. "Oh, man, I'm so fantastically sorry, are you okay?" He peers at me. His eyes are green behind his wire-rimmed glasses. Cute nerd. "File me under Idiot."

"No worries," I say. "Just a couple of knee replacements and I'll be fine."

"Can I help you, like, limp to a chair or something?"

"That's okay," I say. "I'm not staying. Just spying.

My friend got into this camp, but she wasn't able to come after all. I just wanted to check it out in case I want to apply next year."

"That would be awesome. I'm Ryan, by the way. Who's your friend?"

"I'm Gracie. My friend's name is Emily Carbonel."

"I thought so. When you said she couldn't come after all." Ryan looks eager. His breath smells like orange juice, and I see a carton of Tropicana on his desk. I step back a half-step. "How is Emily? I've e-mailed her a bunch of times, but I guess she got tired of my constant worship."

"She's missing," I say.

Ryan frowns. "Missing? Like, right now? You were supposed to meet her here?"

"No, I mean she's *missing*," I say. "The police think she was kidnapped."

"She didn't run away?" Ryan asks. "She was seriously bummed about her folks, I know that for sure."

"How do you know her so well?" I ask. "She wasn't able to come to the camp."

He nods. "Yeah, but I met her during the sign-up process, when a bunch of us came to check out the computers and stuff. And she came with her mom for orientation. That's when they found out that Emily's dad hadn't sent the check. Man, it was embarrassing. Emily was all teary, and it's lucky her mom couldn't get her hands on a ballistic missile. They left, and I found out on e-mail that her dad had spaced out and her mom didn't have the money to cover the cost, so they fought about it, and they missed the deadline, and somebody else got Em's slot. Major bummer for me."

"So you were friends with Emily?"

"Well, if you factor in my huge crush and her complete indifference to the basic fact of my existence," Ryan says. "She had a thing for somebody else."

I try not to pounce on this too obviously. "Do you know who?"

"No idea," Ryan says. "I didn't exactly press for romantic details."

A singsong voice comes from behind me. "I bet it's Mar-cus."

I turn around. A girl about my age is tilting a Diet Coke back to get the very last drop. She has cropped, sleek black hair and is wearing a tight T-shirt that says WHOA BABY. Her taut belly is already tan. It makes a long, slow slide into the low waistband of her jeans. I take an instant dislike to her belly button.

"Why do you think it's Marcus, Dora?" Ryan asks resentfully.

"Well, *ding-dong*. Obviously you haven't looked very hard."

"Who's Marcus?" I ask.

"She didn't even *know* Marcus," Ryan says. "She met him, like, maybe twice."

"Who's Marcus?"

"And how many times did you meet sweet Emily?" Dora cocks her head and widens her eyes at Ryan, and not in a nice way. She's making it clear that he's not in her league. I'm starting to like her less than her navel. "I've got a tip for you about your technique, Rye-bread. You're supposed to make the girl want to come to you, not run away. First Kendall, now Emma."

"Emily," I say.

Dora ignores me. I know she's needling Ryan because I'm there, but she's pretending I don't exist. Freeze the competition, humiliate the guy just for fun.

Ryan's cheeks are flushed. I feel sorry for him. He's no match for Dora. I have a feeling that neither am I.

"Emily and I talked online all the time," Ryan says defensively.

"So how do you know she didn't do that with Marcus, too?"

This stops Ryan for a moment, so I get in the question for the tenth time. "Who is Marcus?"

"He's one of the instructors," Ryan says glumly. "He's a sophomore at U-Dub. He's over there." He points with his chin.

I see a guy, maybe nineteen, sitting at a computer. He's got blond hair shaved down to stubble and a pair of black-framed glasses. He's wearing a white T-shirt that hugs his body *very* well. He looks like he has muscles on his cheekbones. I see what Dora means. He's good-looking, but he looks like Intenso Boy.

As if he's felt my gaze, he turns and sees me looking at him. He gives me a hard stare, then gets up and leaves the room.

"Ooooh, " Dora says. "See what I mean? Definitely hot."

Ryan gives the girl a sour look. "Not the kind of guy a girl like Emily would go for, Dora."

She crunches the can, and I notice that her navy-polished fingernails are bitten down, her cuticles red and angry-looking. "Right. Whatever you say. Anyway, what a waste of time. Why go for minnows when you have sharks? If you ask me, Jonah is the catch around here."

"Jonah? Jonah Castle?" Ryan breathes the name. "Are you delirious?"

Dora laughs.

"You haven't even met him. You didn't come on tour day."

"Who's . . ." I try.

Dora rolls her eyes. "I've seen his bank account."

"Who's Jonah Castle?" I ask.

"Who's Jonah Castle?" Ryan repeats, shocked.

I'm beginning to wonder if too much time in a digital mode makes for an inability to communicate with real people.

"Just your average unattached twenty-five-year-old dot-com billionaire," Dora-the-Ignorer says, finally acknowledging my existence. She walks off, tossing her can toward a trash can. Naturally, it goes in.

Ryan looks after Dora with, I'm sure, loathing in his heart. Who wouldn't?

He turns back to me. "Jonah Castle is a genius. He practically invented firewall software. At seventeen, he hacked into the top twenty of the Fortune 500, just to show them he could do it. They ended up buying firewall software from him. Megawall is his company."

"The sponsor of the camp."

"Right. Oh, that reminds me. Hang on." Ryan reaches for a backpack and rummages through it. He comes out with a photograph and shows it to me.

It's a photo of a group of kids, all wearing the red computer-camp T-shirt. They must have just gotten them, because I can see that most of them are wearing the shirt over their clothes. I spot Emily off to the left, next to Ryan. She has a big smile on her face, and she looks pretty. Marcus is there, on the other side of the group, looking aloof. He's standing next to a young-looking guy wearing a polo shirt and a tweed jacket. "That's Jonah Castle," Ryan says reverently, pointing to the man in the jacket. "This was taken on the tour day."

I take the photograph and stare at it. I feel my concentration slip from Ryan *into* the picture. I can feel Emily's happiness on that day, but I can feel other things, too, things that when I brush against them I'm afraid.

"Can I keep this?"

"I guess," he says reluctantly. "Just be sure and give it to Emily when she turns up. Hey, let me write my phone number on the back." Ryan takes the photograph and quickly scrawls on the back of it. He hands it back. "Listen, let me know if there's anything I can do, okay?" He fidgets, hands in his pockets, as if he's unused to offering help.

"Sure." I put the photograph carefully in my purse. I feel it there, weighing me down, as I walk out.

That photograph is like a rock in my purse for the rest of the afternoon. I can feel it with every step. We drive to the park by the locks and buy Sno-Cones from an Indian woman in a white truck. Then we cross over the locks and pause to look down, eating our Sno-Cones. We watch the water flood in as the boat slowly rises toward us, and Shay waves at the couple leaning against the stern rail.

Here is where the freshwater lake empties into the bay. We let the sea and the salt tangle in our lungs and our hair, and I know Shay feels her spirits lift, but she can't pull me along with her.

I stare down into the deck of the rising boat. It fills my vision, blocking everything out. Sound fades.

Hands are at the cabin window, beating against it.

First the palms slapping, then fists.

Trying to get out.

Have to get *out.*

No one will hear, no one saw

help me help me help me help me

"Gracie?"

The boat is level with us now. The curtains are parted, and I can see into the cabin. It is empty. A box of cookies sits on the dinette table. A sweatshirt is tossed on the seat.

"Gracie?" Shay's curls are blowing crazily. "You dropped your Sno-Cone."

I look down. The Sno-Cone has inverted and is sticking up like a pup tent.

The liquid oozes out on the concrete.

I reach out for the rail. It feels as though the ground is moving under my feet, and I'm dizzy.

Something is here, something I need to know, something I need to grasp.

It's gone.

It slips through my fingers, it sluices out through the locks. I lose it.

"Come on," Shay says. "Let's look at some fish."

We walk down the sloping lawn toward the salmon ladder. I see the flash of the fish even as we approach. We walk down the stairs and we're plunged into a gloomy dankness. We're surrounded by glass, and behind it, fish are swimming, slithering, battling the current. Some of them are cut and bloody. They throw themselves at a small opening, trying to get up into the sea. Again and again they make the leap, sometimes falling back, and always trying again.

I watch the salmon fight and flop their way upstream toward their eventual fate of being roasted or smoked or grilled on a cedar plank. I know I'm supposed to admire their determination, but they just seem so sad to me. Somewhere wired into their DNA is a memory of fresh water, smooth rocks, a still bay, and they'll fight their way past cities and chemicals and dams to find home. Instead they'll meet the hook and the net and be pulled, gasping, water streaming down their silvery gills, into the relentless air.

EIGHTEEN

The next morning in my room, I stare at the photograph for long periods of time, time enough to note that Emily's smile is a little too radiant, certainly more than a tour of computers would warrant, that Marcus is uncomfortable, that Jonah Castle has a cell phone in his left hand, like a busy executive making a dutiful visit to his charitable cause.

Something is wrong with this picture. I don't know what. Which gets me exactly nowhere.

Sunlight floods my room. Diego is in his bedroom, close by. There's nothing to be afraid of, and I'm afraid. There's a darkness in this photo. There's something there, just out of reach. I don't know what it is, but it has everything to do with Emily.

Lying with her eyes shut, afraid to move.

Someone standing in a doorway looking down at her, not caring who she is, only that she belongs with him.

Fists pounding against the cabin window of a boat.

help me help me help me

Who is the darkness coming from? Marcus?

He seems the obvious candidate, but maybe I'm making too many assumptions based on a shaved head and a bad attitude. Ryan? He admitted having a huge crush on Emily — are geeks capable of criminal activity more serious than shoplifting a six-pack of Mountain Dew? Even Jonah Castle could be a suspect, I guess, though I can't quite imagine a billionaire taking time out from running a company to kidnap a teenager. It just doesn't make sense.

I fire up the online search engines. First I look up the website for the computer camp. There are several links, and they list each year's students, as well as the instructors. I see that Marcus Heffernan taught last year as well, and that he's a student at the University of Washington, just as Ryan said. Ryan attended the camp the year before, too. I scroll through the other names of the students, but nothing rings a bell. And then I see the name *Kendall Farmer.*

What about Kendall? You're supposed to make the girl want to come to you, not run away.

I click back on the search engine. I type in Kendall Farmer.

Article from the *Seattle Times,* October of last year.

Runaway Lead Turns Out False, Distraught Parents Report

I click on it and read the article, my eyes darting, wanting to pick up every piece of information.

I have to remind myself to slow down so I can absorb what I'm reading. Kendall Farmer disappeared last November, leaving a note for her parents that she was off to "find a family who cares." The police thought they had picked her up in San Diego, but it turned out to be a different kid.

Two missing girls, both of them connected to the computer camp. What were the odds of that?

I scroll through the rest of the results, reading everything. It's funny what oddball stuff comes up on a web search.

Kendall Farmer is mentioned in an article in the local paper of her hometown on Bainbridge Island. She'd played Marian in her school's production of *The Music Man,* and the reviewer praises her "lovely singing voice and stage presence."

Her parents gave a pot luck on August 17th of last year to benefit the library. Kendall presented the proceeds of the annual Car Wash Jive from her high school.

She won second prize on Get Up and Prove It Night at the Smells Like Good Coffee Café in Seattle.

She sounds like a normal kid. She is still missing. She is sixteen.

I look back at the photograph. In Marcus's neutral face, I think I read obsession. Is the darkness I feel coming from him?

I have to find out.

I cross through the kitchen and then mosey down the hall. Diego's door is open, and I hover in the doorway until he notices me. He's listening to music on his headphones and chatting online.

He lifts one earphone when he sees me.

"Want to go on a stakeout?" I ask.

Marcus Heffernan turns out to be a rich kid. He lives in a million-dollarish house that backs onto Lake Washington. We park the car outside and wait. The only problem is, I have no idea what we're waiting for. But we do it for an hour. We finish a bag of donuts ("for atmosphere," Diego says) and put the CD player on random.

"This is fun," Diego says. His voice doesn't exactly ring with sincerity.

Okay, so stakeouts are boring. Who knew? They go by so fast on TV.

I feel responsible for Diego's boredom, but I have no idea how to entertain him. I had to talk him into coming. First of all, he's not allowed to drive to Seattle without permission, but I point out that Shay is in meetings all day and can't talk to us anyway. It's pretty lame, but it eases his conscience a little bit. Then it turns out that he doesn't *want* to drive to Seattle. He has an intermediate license, which means if he gets even two tickets, his license is suspended. I don't think Diego is afraid of anything, but if he is, it's of not having a car.

He drums his fingers on the dash. He shifts in his seat. He clears his throat.

"So . . ." he says.

"So . . ."

"So why did you hire that guy to punch you?"

I look out the window. It's funny. My life here seemed so unreal to me for so long. But Diego's question takes me by surprise, because suddenly *that* life seems far away, my life in Maryland after Mom died, when every day I woke up and had to talk myself into swinging my legs over the side of the bed.

"Because I wanted to feel pain that wasn't inside me," I say. "I thought if I could focus on a different kind of pain, even for a few minutes, I could feel . . . I don't know, relief. I could be the me I was before, even temporarily."

"Did it work?" He asks the question so delicately, as though he were a doctor probing a wound, which I guess he is.

"No," I say. "I just felt pretty stupid, basically. And Jake Buscemi just felt really bad. I think he was surprised that he actually did it. Me, too."

"You freaked everyone out," Diego says.

"Yeah." Myself included, actually. That was one bad day.

"They wanted to maybe put you somewhere for a while," Diego says.

This gets my attention. "What? Like a mental institution?"

Diego nods. "Mom talked them out of it. She put her foot down. Threatened to call in lawyers and everything. They had talked her out of taking you right after . . . right after, and she gave in because she thought they might be right. That it wasn't a good idea to remove you from everything you knew."

I thought Shay hadn't wanted me. I thought she'd refused. Maybe they'd told me the way it really was. I couldn't remember. I wasn't listening to anyone then.

"So anyway, you know Pop-Pop and Mimi, they always get their way. And Uncle Owen always sides with them, so Mom was outgunned. But after that thing happened, and they were all wondering what to do, Mom called and told them she wouldn't take no for an answer, that your mom had wanted you to come live with us, and that's how it had to be. We'd already redone the room, that summer."

"You did my room last summer?"

"Yeah. In case you ever wanted to come. Anyway, they caved."

"I thought I was too much for Mimi and Pop-Pop."

"Well, you were." Diego chuckled. "That's for sure. They freak when they get rained out of the ninth hole, so you can imagine."

It was true. My grandparents are seriously stuck in their ways. If they run out of seven-grain bread at the supermarket, my grandfather wants to file a lawsuit. And everything has to be just so. Spoons go handle *down* in the dishwasher, forks go handle *up*. Shoes *off* when you come in the door. Wipe the cast-iron frying pan with paper towel *only*. Up, down, top, bottom, off, on, only, never, always. I never understood their rules, and they tried to be nice, but they were always redoing everything I did. Maybe it added to my craziness then, I don't know. But I never felt right. It was the first time in my life I realized that love wasn't enough to help somebody.

"They are serious about toilet paper," I say. "At first, I didn't notice. It took me weeks to get it. If I put it on the roll with the paper coming from the bottom of the roll, they'd flip it over. Toilet paper has to come from the *top* of the roll."

"When I visited them, I used to keep switching it back, just to drive them nuts," Diego says.

We burst out laughing.

With Diego poking fun at them in that genial way, I realize for the first time that flunking out of the grandparent living situation wasn't totally my fault. They *are* kind of nuts. It wasn't my fault that I couldn't fit into their particular brand of craziness. Each family is weird in its own way, I guess, which makes it hard to find your way in a new one.

"There's our boy," Diego says. He starts the engine.

Marcus walks out of the house, jingling car keys. He's wearing a gray T-shirt with lettering I can't read and khaki shorts and boots. If I weren't a detective, I would notice his legs in a much less clinical way. He hops into a Volkswagen Beetle and backs out of the driveway.

I duck my head down until Diego says it's okay. Then we proceed to tail Marcus through the unfamiliar streets of Seattle, through stop signs and red lights. I learn that Diego knows how to curse.

Marcus stops at a gas station (I duck; Diego curses and keeps going, turns right; it's a one-way street; we have to circle and get back, hoping Marcus needs a full tank of gas; we spot him as he zooms through a yellow light . . .), gets caught in a traffic jam (we keep four cars back), and then cruises in the U district, looking for a parking space. He finds one and pulls in.

"What now?" I ask. I look around, but there are no spaces. Marcus is already getting out of the driver's seat.

"Follow him," Diego says.

"But how will you find me?"

"Send me a text message. If I don't find you or hear from you in fifteen minutes, I'm calling Detective Pasta. Now *go.*"

I scoot out the door and bound onto the sidewalk. I keep well behind Marcus. It's easy to keep him in sight. He's tall and he's not walking very fast, chugging on a bottle of sports drink as he goes.

He disappears into the doorway of a restaurant. My palms are wet. I wipe them on my jeans, then walk slowly up to the window. I give a quick look in.

Marcus has his back to me. He stops and reads a blackboard with the specials on it. Then he walks behind the counter and picks up an apron, which he ties around his waist. I don't know how he manages it, but he looks pretty macho in it.

He's a waiter. I watch him for a few minutes. He says something to the waitress that makes her smile. He disappears into the kitchen and comes back out. I study his face. I wait for something to break inside me, some kind of flash that will tell me what I need to know.

When Diego's hand hits my shoulder, I jump about six inches.

"Whoa. What's going on?"

"He went to work," I say. "I guess we can go home. He'll be here for a while." I feel discouraged. This isn't getting me anywhere. I have a sense of urgency now, that Emily is in trouble, that she needs me. I've got to find a way to link Marcus to Emily, or I have to find another suspect.

"Come on," Diego says. "We'll think of something else. This smells like teen washout." He points overhead.

"What?" I look up at the sign hanging overhead.

The name of the café is Smells Like Good Coffee. I had been concentrating so hard on Marcus, I hadn't noticed it.

The Smells Like Good Coffee Café. Where Kendall Farmer won second prize on Get Up and Prove It Night.

"It's him," I say, latching onto Diego's arm. "He's our guy."

NINETEEN

"Let's not jump to conclusions," Diego says, after I explain the connection. "Emily and Kendall both knew Marcus. So what?"

"The coincidences are piling up," I argue. "What are the odds of two girls disappearing when they know the same guy? And the person who wiped those computers was an expert. It went way beyond sending stuff to the recycle bin."

Diego sighs. "We have to be careful, Gracie. You were certain about Zed."

He's right. But that doesn't mean I like hearing it. Time is running out for Emily. I can feel it now, and I realize it's been there the whole day. While we were driving to Seattle, while we were talking in the car, I was feeling it.

She's giving up.

She's slipping away.

And the answers are in front of me. I've seen the clues.

I've been inside his head.

"She's given up trying to be brave," I say. "She's given up waiting to be rescued. She's . . . fading."

"What?" Diego asks.

"Emily. I feel her emptying out. So that" — my mouth is dry — "so that when the worst happens, she won't feel it."

Diego looks shaken. "Maybe if you had something of Marcus's, something he owned . . ."

"Maybe I'd get a vision!" I say. "It's worth a shot."

We're only blocks from the computer camp, and I know they don't start until noon. Diego and I hurry toward it. We push through the doors and run up the stairs to the second floor. All the classrooms are locked.

"What now?" I ask, frustrated. "Should we try to break in?"

Diego sighs. He raises his hand and knocks.

"Or I guess we could try knocking," I say.

The door opens. Ryan's head appears. He brightens when he sees me, then frowns when he sees Diego standing next to me.

"This is my cousin Diego," I say.

Ryan brightens again. "I came in early to get some work done. Come on in."

"How come you have a key?" I ask.

"The instructors give us one if we ask," Ryan explains. "You have to sign in and stuff. Hey, what brings you here?"

I hadn't had much time to prepare a story, so I thought a mixture of truth and fiction was best. "I'm really worried about Emily," I tell him. Truth.

"I guess I was kind of distracted yesterday. I think I left my sunglasses here." Fiction. "Can I look around?"

"Sure. Can I help?"

Diego smiles at Ryan. "That's okay. We don't want to interrupt." He says this firmly, and disappointed, Ryan sits back down at his computer.

I pretend to look around, and Diego stays between me and Ryan so Ryan won't have a good sight line. I drift toward the desk where Marcus had been working, but it's clear of anything, even empty soda cans. Then I see a row of mailboxes with names on them — the names of the instructors. Marcus's is full to overflowing.

Bending down and pretending to look on the floor, I rifle through the pages. Memos, mostly, and takeout menus, and assignments handed in by the students. Then I see a corner of a photograph. I slide it out. It's the same photograph Ryan had given me.

Something clangs in my head. Something's wrong. Somewhere behind me, I can hear Diego sneezing, and I wish he'd stop, because I can't concentrate.

Suddenly, Ryan reaches down and takes the photograph.

"It was on the floor," I say.

His face is red, as though he's angry. "Jonah Castle gave us each a copy," he says. "This must belong to Marcus." He quickly stuffs it back in the mailbox.

Diego knocks over a pile of circuits, and Ryan yells, "Hey!" and runs over. Quickly, I stuff the photograph in my purse. I dig out my sunglasses.

"Found them! I must have kicked them under the desk. Thanks so much, Ryan." I pour as much flirtatiousness as I can manage into my thank-you, but Ryan doesn't respond. His head is down as he reassembles the circuits, and he mumbles a good-bye.

As soon as we're outside, I turn to Diego. "You could have warned me Ryan was coming."

"I did! I sneezed!"

"What kind of a signal is a sneeze?"

"A *clever* one."

"A sneeze isn't a signal; it's an allergic reaction."

"Great. Next time I'll fart."

Suddenly, I realize what it must be like to grow up with an older brother. I take out the photograph.

There's something different about it. What?

And then I get it.

"Emily's not here," I say. I shake my head, confused. "She's gone."

Diego looks over my shoulder. "Where was she?"

"Here, next to Ryan. Now there's just empty space."

"So they took two photographs that day," Diego says.

"But everyone has the same expression. And Jonah Castle is still holding the cell phone in the same position. No, this is the same one." I look up at Diego. "Someone digitally altered it. They *removed* her." I shivered.

"The question is, who?" Diego says.

"It was in Marcus's box."

"But Ryan looked really freaked."

"He always looks freaked."

We walk to the car and get in. Diego starts the engine. I stare back down at the photograph. The absence of Emily registers as a presence. It's like the ghost of her is there, the ghost of the Emily that is fading, and it's saying, *find me.*

TWENTY

Shay makes spinach lasagna that night. I eat two helpings and then drag myself to my room, ready to fire up Google once again.

Shay appears in my doorway. "Want to catch some mindless TV for the masses?"

"No thanks," I say. "I'd rather use the computer."

"Okay." Shay smiles, but I can tell she's disappointed. I almost feel like changing my mind and losing myself in a laugh track, but my brain is burning to hit the Internet for info, and I just can't take a detour. The feeling I got today about Emily pushes out everything except this need to find her.

I've turned Shay down for so many things over the past months. TV, movies, Scrabble, hikes, pedicures at the day spa. I don't know why tonight I feel badly about saying no. I guess it's because she keeps trying.

I log online and plug Marcus into the search engine. I don't exactly hit paydirt. I get the website of the computer camp, but I knew that already. And apparently, Marcus writes for the campus newspaper, because a bunch of articles pop up, but none of them look as though they have even a remote connection to Emily or Kendall, dull stuff about school policy, off-campus lectures, and a couple of film reviews.

Then, back in July of last year, I see something interesting.

Interview with Jonah Castle.

At least I might learn more about the computer camp. I click on the link.

I quickly scan the article. It's all about how Jonah Castle funded the computer camp to help gifted students. Out of all his charities, this is the one close to his heart. He was a prodigy and he knows how lonely it can be. Blah, blah, blah. It all sounds so canned. Potential. Encouragement. Leadership. Synergy. Dreams. Values. The usual.

Q: You had an unusual childhood. You were home-schooled, you had eleven brothers and sisters, and your family lived on a private island in Puget Sound. Has your upbringing influenced the way you look at education today?

A: It's funny. I don't see my childhood as unusual. Does anyone? It's your reality, and you don't have anything to compare it to. I consider myself lucky to have been homeschooled by my parents, who were brilliant scholars and imaginative teachers. Each of my siblings was encour-

aged to develop a specific skill. My sister Frances was an accomplished vocalist. My brother Tate was an outstanding mathematician. Another sister played the clarinet. Our playtime always involved our studies, and our family fun always had an educational element.

Q: In other words, you weren't hanging out watching South Park.

A: No, we were reading aloud, or putting on our own entertainments. We were off the grid, anyway.

Q: Sounds like a pretty cool childhood.

A: It was.

Sorry, Jonah Castle, but your childhood sounds like a snooze fest.

Diego pops his head in the doorway. "Eureka, I found it."

"Found what?"

"The original photograph. Megawall has its company newsletter archived online. I printed it out. Here."

He hands me the photograph. It's identical to the one I took from Marcus's mailbox. No Emily.

"So what does it mean?" I wonder. "Did someone scan Emily *in* or scan her *out?*"

"I've got one way to find out." Diego hands me the phone. "Call Ryan."

"But if he's involved, he'll lie."

"We've got to take that chance. At least, we'll be doing *something.*"

I read Ryan's number off the back of the photo he gave me and punch it out. He answers on the first ring. When I explain who I am, he says, "Wow, I never thought you'd call. I mean, I hoped you'd call. But I never —"

"Ryan, I saw the photograph today in Marcus's box."

"Yeah," he says cautiously.

"Emily isn't in it, but she's in the one you gave me."

"Yeah."

I wait.

"Okay. We got a pile of photos from Megawall? And they had edited out Emily because she wasn't in the camp after all? The photo goes out for publicity and everything, so I guess they wanted it to be accurate. So that made me feel bad, and I thought that it would be a nice present if I gave her a photograph with her in it. I'd taken a photo of her that day wearing the shirt. So I scanned the photo and scanned her in. It was just to make her happy, okay?"

"Oh. Okay. I was just wondering. So, she was in the original picture?"

"Yeah, she was standing on the right, next to Marcus. I just moved her over next to me. You know, I don't want you to think that I'm still in heavy crush over Emily. I'm, you know, available."

"That's great, Ryan." I make a sign to Diego that we're back at square one. Emily's disappearance from the photo has nothing to do with the fact that she's missing. It was just a publicity decision.

"What I mean is, we could have coffee or something."

"Great. I'll call you." I hang up. I toss the photo on my desk and tell Diego about the conversation.

"I guess it's slightly demented, but normal," Diego says. "He's a geek with a crush. That's why he flamed out when you found it — he was embarrassed, that's all. We just need to keep digging. Something will turn up." Diego ducks out again.

I reach over for the photograph again. I stare hard at Marcus. Emily had been standing next to him in the original. Now she was gone. Could Marcus have had something to do with it, despite what Ryan said? I wish I could get a feeling that was true. All I feel is confusion.

I try to walk my brain outside what I know. I try to tune into what I feel, or rather, what's *beyond* what I feel. I have to get control of the visions. I'm tired of them sneaking up on me and giving me a wallop. I have to make it happen, not wait for it to happen.

I stop staring at the photograph. I just look at it. I push every fear, every thought out of my mind and replace it with . . . nothing. Not even static.

The photograph doesn't make sense anymore as people and desks, just as shapes and colors.

The photograph dissolves into dots. The dots jiggle and swim. It's a jarring thing, and nothing comes into focus for a moment.

Then I'm walking on a beach. I'm surrounded by mist. I am carrying something. It is heavy.

It is a body.

I am chilled to the bone. I look down at the face of the girl.

She is sleeping. Please let her be sleeping.

Then the girl sits up and smiles. Blood drips from her mouth.

I scream and drop her on the shells. The sharp edges cut her skin. She bleeds and smiles.

And then the scene shifts, and the shells turn into grass, and I see small children running. They are bending to look at things: flowers and bugs. There is a garden, and a bench. It's like I'm watching from a distance this time. A girl is sitting on the bench. Not Emily, but someone I know. I can't see her face, but she is familiar to me. She is waiting for someone. I see the shadows of the trees fall on the grass. There is something white on the bench next to her — it looks like a party hat.

He is watching her, too. He is waiting.

Footsteps approach her.

Run, I tell her. *Run.*

I know something terrible will happen. I am watching now, but I can't move. She sees someone coming.

Run. Get out of there!

But she doesn't move, and then suddenly I see water churning, close-up, and I smell gasoline, heavy and sweet. I feel sick, and my face is wet and my hands are wet. I touch my tongue to my lip and taste blood . . .

"Gracie."

The word penetrates the mist. I grab onto the word as if it is a grasping hand and can pull me up. "Gracie!"

I am looking up at Diego's face. He is directly over me. His eyes are so black, so dark. I am afraid I will fall into them the way I fell into the mist. I'm afraid I will never come back from his gaze.

He grips my arms. "You scared me. What happened? What did you see?"

I realize I am lying back on my bed. My face is wet with perspiration. My neck is wet. I touch my lip and then look at my fingers, but there is no blood, of course. I shakily try to sit. Diego helps me.

"What did you see?" he asks urgently again. There is fear on his face.

I tell him what I saw, trying to remember every detail.

"You couldn't see the guy's face, or anything? Think. His shoes? His hands?"

"Nothing. Just his shadow." I cover my face with my hands. "When I saw the girl, the dead one, on the beach, I was seeing through his eyes. It was horrible. I think he killed her, Diego!"

He bites his lip. "Was it . . ."

"It wasn't Emily. It could have been Kendall. I don't know!"

"Was it the future, or the past?"

"I don't know."

"What about when you smelled gas, and you touched your lip . . . who were you then? Emily?"

"I don't know," I say, shaking my head. "I don't know!" I tell him about the other vision, about the fists beating against the window of the boat.

"Was that Emily? Remember, you saw her on the boat."

I'm tired of saying "I don't know." So I just look at him helplessly.

"It's okay. It's okay." Diego pats my shoulder lamely. "It's just in your head."

"Isn't that where all the bad stuff is?" I whisper. "Just in our heads?"

Diego clears his throat. "Let's analyze what you saw. What about the party hat? What could that mean?"

"Who knows? I just know that she's his next victim, whoever she is. He's going to take another girl. I saw her." Diego is trying to be logical, but I'm frantic. Panic thrums inside me like vibrating strings. I clutch his arm. "We have to stop him. It's up to us."

"We'll go to the police . . ."

"With what? A vision? A photograph?" I shake my head. "We have to get to the girl before he does."

Diego shakes his head. "Gracie, I don't know. This has gone far enough. We should . . . tell someone again. Shay . . ."

"They won't listen to me! And I know it's going to happen again."

"But you don't know where or when."

But even as he says this, the knowledge roars into my brain. "Yes I do. It wasn't a party hat," I say. "It was a Sno-Cone."

"A Sno-Cone?"

I am already reaching for the computer, typing fast. I run the search engine and find the site I'm looking for.

"Gracie —"

The official website of Seattle Parks and Recreation. I quickly click and scroll. Then I push the computer toward him so he can read what's on the screen.

Toddler Nature Hunt. 11 A.M. Saturday. Commodore Park.

"The park by the fish ladder," I tell Diego. "That's the place. They sell Sno-Cones there. It's going to happen this Saturday. That's where he'll be. I know it, Diego. I know it."

This time I am certain. And I know I have to be there, too.

TWENTY-ONE

I don't know how I talk Diego into it, but I do. There's no danger, I tell him. It's a public park! There will be two- and three-year-olds running around with their parents! It will be broad daylight! And most of all, I tell him, hammering the point home until he begs for mercy, we *know* what we're heading into. Whoever that girl is that I saw on the bench — she doesn't have a clue.

Technically, Shay hasn't given Diego permission to take the car to Seattle. Okay, *definitely,* Shay hasn't given permission. Diego isn't crazy about not telling her again. He got away with it once, but he doesn't want to push it. That's the toughest part of convincing him. He just doesn't lie to his mom. Ever. I'm not sure why he gives in, but he does.

We don't say much on the drive. Even though there's nothing to be nervous about in a certain way, there's everything to be nervous about in an-other way, so we just sit, listening to the radio and vibrating along with the tunes and our nerves.

We park. We hang out by the Sno-Cones for a while, seeing if a young girl buys one, but only a couple of people come by.

"Let's scout out the bench," Diego says.

We walk through the gardens, looking at the benches. When I see the one that was in my vision, I stop dead. There's something so real about it. I've never been in this part of the park with Shay, but I know this bench. I know the texture of the wood and the curve of the slats. This is the first time that something in my vision really comes true, something I can see. The pattern of the leaves overhead, the trampling of the grass in front, everything is just as I had seen it. It spooks me.

"This one?" Diego asks. He looks kind of spooked, too.

I nod.

Toddlers are beginning to arrive in the gardens, along with their parents. A pair of guides appear and start talking about "nature's marvelous wonders." They speak in that overly animated way that people do when they're around kids, and most of the toddlers are ignoring them while their parents are enthralled. The parents keep trying to drum up their kid's enthusiasm, saying, "Listen to the nice man, Dylan!" and "Remember how much you like ladybugs, Marina!" The sun is filtering through the leaves, and suddenly it seems like the worst thing that could possibly happen here would be a two-year-old throwing a tantrum.

The toddler pack moves off down the path, but

we can hear them. We stand there for a moment, but it's obvious that we can't remain.

We can't scare off whoever is coming.

"We'd better keep moving," Diego says. "If we stay between here and the entrance to the garden, nobody can get around us. If only we had a toddler for protective coloration."

I bend down and pick up one of the brochures that a parent had dropped. I hand it to Diego. "Try this. At least you don't have to buy it ice cream."

There's a place to hang by the entrance where we can stay behind some trees. I fidget. The shadows on the ground are telling me that this is it, this is the time my vision took place.

I see someone familiar heading toward us.

To my surprise, it's Dora.

I elbow Diego and point.

"She's in the computer camp," I say.

I notice now that she's eating a Sno-Cone. I feel a shiver rise all along my body.

We're on the right track after all.

Dora doesn't notice me. She walks past us, looking at her watch.

She is meeting someone.

Diego and I give each other a "what should we do now" look.

"I'll go scope out Dora," I say. "You stay here. If you see Marcus or Ryan, follow him."

Diego frowns. "Be careful. Is your cell phone on?"

"It's on." We've already decided to call each other only in an emergency. I take off down the path.

Dora sits on the bench, eating her Sno-Cone. I stop. She hasn't seen me yet, and I could keep going and pass her by, but I can't.

I tell myself Dora can take care of herself.

I tell myself that the important thing is to wait to see who shows up.

But I see her bitten fingernails around the white cone, how her toes are dirty in her sandals, and suddenly I can *feel* her as well as I see her.

I know her unhappiness is deep and wide.

I know that her mother is an alcoholic.

I see Dora, wearing a short nightgown, pick her mother off the floor and put her to bed.

I know that she thinks she's at a dead end, and this is her only way out.

She spots me. I could have waved and walked away, but I come forward.

"Hi."

"Hey."

Not a promising start. I sit on the bench. "Nice day."

She half-turns. "Look, hello and everything, but I'm meeting someone, so if you don't mind?"

"Who are you meeting?"

"Excuse me, are you my mother?" Dora asks nastily.

"Just making conversation."

"Don't bother. Do you *mind*?"

Dora leans over and dumps out the rest of her Sno-Cone. I am not surprised when she doesn't crumple it up. She puts the empty cone down on the bench upside down, like a tent, just the way it was in my vision. She slams it down as though she's marking her territory, making a kind of barrier between us.

I look down at the cherry ice seeping into the ground. The red color is so intense. The stain grows in my mind and I flash into the vision of the blood on the beach.

And suddenly, I know this:

Dora has to get out of here.

"You've got to go," I say.

Dora narrows her eyes. She has lined them with black pencil, and she's wearing lipstick. She has fixed herself up.

"Is it Marcus? Is it Ryan? Who is it?"

"What is *wrong* with you?" she asks, leaning back to put distance between us.

"Tell me who it is!"

"It's Marcus," she says. "Jealous?"

Marcus. It is Marcus.

"Listen, I'm psychic," I say. "Really. And I see things."

She smirks. "You see dead people?"

"I see your mother lying on the kitchen floor," I say. "She needs help, and you can't give it. You can't save her. You tried and now you're just angry."

Her expression changes. "Hey . . ."

"Your kitchen has an orange sink," I say. "Your nightgown has yellow flowers. You have a birthmark on your knee. A butterfly tattoo in the small of your back. Once your mother left you alone for two weeks, and you didn't tell anyone because you were afraid she was dead."

"Nobody knows that," Dora says, a look of fear on her face. *"Nobody knows that."*

"Your dishtowels have green stripes," I say. "Your dish drainer is white. Your mother's blanket is blue."

She is pressed back against the bench now. "What do you want?"

"Get out of here," I say. "Run. What do you think happened to Kendall and Emily? If you see him, don't stop." The danger is like the roar of surf in my ears. *"Get out of here!"*

Dora shoots to her feet. She gives me a last look, and then she takes off. Running. I don't know if she's spooked by me, or my warning. It doesn't matter.

I notice that my hands are trembling. I tuck them in my armpits. I expect Diego to show up at any moment, running, to tell me that Marcus has entered the park.

But instead, Jonah Castle rounds the bend, sees me, and smiles.

"Dora?" he says.

TWENTY-TWO

"I thought Marcus was coming," I say.

"He's at the party," he says.

"Oh," I say. What party?

He settles down on the bench next to me, giving the empty cone a brief, puzzled glance. "It's good to meet you. Marcus says you might need help."

My brain is buzzing like a hive. I've got to keep following this, but I'm lost. I try to come up with Dora's defensive attitude. "Not really."

He smiles pleasantly. He's got a narrow face, and his eyes are bright blue and interested behind his wire rims. He's wearing a polo shirt and pleated khakis, standard nerd attire. Boat shoes and white socks. I try to get something from him, some kind of wave, the way I've done with strangers. Sometimes people have something that is so present on their minds that I can just pick it up like a radio station. But Jonah Castle is a blank. I can't get anything from him.

"Oh, okay," he says genially. "I guess he got it wrong. Marcus is a mysterious guy."

"I'll say."

"He said you were upset at camp the other day," he says. "He wants to help, that's all."

"The way he helped Kendall Farmer?"

He looks blank. "Kendall Farmer? Should I know her?"

"She was in the camp last year," I say. "She ran away."

"Oh. And Marcus tried to help her? I'm not surprised, he's such a good guy."

You think so?

"I'm sorry, I didn't know. Marcus never mentioned her to me." He hooks two hands around a knee. "I lost a sister, you know. So I know about loss. Guilt. All that stuff. I know how bad feelings can grow inside you until they feel like they can eat you alive. I know how scary that can be, and how the fear can add to it until you just want to run and run to get away. But there's no place to run to. You know that saying, 'Wherever you go, there you are'?"

No, I don't know it. But I like how true it is. I'm listening now.

"So I started this thing, this focus group foundation. I mean, Megawall has the computer camp, and other charities, but my foundation doesn't get any publicity. I don't want reporters around, poking into people's privacy. I'm out to revolutionize how social services treat at-risk kids. I've got scholars and shrinks on the payroll, but mostly it's the kids themselves who have come up with the ideas.

Bright kids like you. When I asked Marcus if he knew anyone I could talk to, he mentioned you. I hope you don't mind."

"My life is none of his business," I say.

"No, it isn't. And if you don't want to get involved, I'd appreciate it if you didn't get mad at Marcus. Remember, I'm his boss, in a way." Jonah Castle smiles. "I can't deny that even if I don't use my leverage, it's there."

I can't get a read on this guy. Never mind the paranormal, the normal me can't read him, either. I feel apprehensive, but I don't know if I can connect the feeling to Jonah Castle. Everything about him tells me that he's an ordinary mega-billionaire looking to unload some millions on charity so he can sleep at night. But somehow he's connected to Marcus, and Marcus asked Dora to meet him here.

Could Jonah Castle's foundation be the key? Marcus directs troubled kids to the foundation. But not all of them. Some of them, he keeps for himself. Maybe he'd targeted Dora, only Jonah Castle got in his way.

It's hard to think and carry on a conversation at the same time. I focus back on Jonah Castle. "I don't think of myself as an at-risk kid," I say. "At risk for what?"

He laughs. "Yeah, here I am saying social services is messed up, and I'm using their terms. Let's just say this: You need a home where you can feel safe."

That breaks like a wave of longing inside me. Those two words. *Home. Safe.* When those two things get taken away from you, there's no other feeling more desolate. Maybe Jonah Castle knows what he's talking about.

"Listen," he says. "We're having a party for the third anniversary of the foundation. Most of the kids we've helped will be there. It's right in the park — that's why Marcus suggested this place to meet. Would you like to come?"

My antenna is up, but it's not picking up danger. There will be plenty of people there. Jonah Castle will be there, other adults. Diego is nearby.

My cover will be blown if Marcus sees me, but I don't care. I'll make something up. I'll say I pretended to be Dora so I could go to the party.

"I just need to call my cousin and tell him," I say.

"Sure. Ask him if he wants to come."

I flip open my cell, but I get NO SERVICE on the screen. We hadn't checked our phones when we arrived. Stupid.

He peers over. "Happens all the time. If we walk a bit, you can try again."

"Okay." I get up. Diego is probably watching us right now. And I can call again. I can hear the children running through the grass, and I can see the parents now, chasing after them. I'm fine, I'm safe, Diego would tell me to keep going.

"Great." He stands up and starts down the path.

We'll pass right by Diego, but that's good. Diego can tail us.

We get to the entrance of the gardens, and Jonah looks around. I do, too, but I don't see Diego. I figure he's lurking behind a lilac bush, watching.

"Shoot," Jonah says, and looks at his watch. "It's later than I thought. They must be on the boat already."

"Boat?" Everything lights up now. I'm close. I'm so close.

"Marcus has a boat. Well, his parents do."

Marcus has a boat. *That's it,* I think. *That's how he gets them away.* Marcus invited her out on the boat. At first, she's happy, he's going fast, and the wind is whipping her hair. But something happens, somehow he gets her down in the cabin, and she panics.

I have to see the boat. I have to get on board. If I can just touch it, see it, be in that space, I can pick up something. I know it.

"Do you know the marina? It's a short walk from here."

"Let's go." I don't have a real feeling about what is going to happen, but I do have a real feeling. It is that somehow Emily is calling me. She's telling me, *follow.*

So I follow. It's almost as though I don't care what's at the end.

I just have to find it.

TWENTY-THREE

We cross the locks, and then the parking lot. We start up Seaview Avenue. Jonah Castle tells me about the park, how it started, how a group of neighborhood people got together and made it happen. That's what he believes in, he says. A group of people with a common bond get together and things happen. It's how he built his company, he says. Just a bunch of friends fooling around in a garage with some software. Just to see what would happen.

I guess it's kind of cool, talking to a major cyber-pioneer, a legend. I'm thinking that the Maryland friends I'm not so in touch with anymore deserve an e-mail about this.

We get to the marina. The sunlight scampers on the water. We walk down toward the docks. There are people here, sitting on their boats. They wave at us and smile.

We walk down a dock all the way to the end. He stops in front of a big cabin cruiser, about forty feet long. "I think this is it. Let me check it out." He jumps aboard while I wait on the dock. I look behind me, but I don't see Diego.

He disappears inside the cabin. Then he pokes his head out. "Marcus isn't here. But . . ."

"What?" I ask. Jonah looks worried.

"It looks like the boat has been broken into or something," he says. "There's stuff all over the floor, and —"

He stops.

"What?"

"You'd just better stay there. I'll call Marcus. No, I'll call 911." He takes out his cell phone, then slaps the side of the canvas flap in frustration. "No service. Let's walk back to . . ."

I'm not waiting for the police. I have to get aboard. I have to feel the space, touch it. The police can find clues. But they can't find what I can *feel*.

I spring onto the boat.

"Don't," he warns, taking a step toward me. "They won't want anyone else aboard."

But I evade him. I have to look. He doesn't want to tell me what he saw, but I have to see it. I know that a thief didn't break in. I know that Jonah has seen signs of a struggle. Something happened on this boat.

I had seen the fists pounding.

I had felt her panic like it was my own.

It's as if I'm in a dream, a dream that someone else has dreamed. I can see the white deck, the bright snapping blue flag. And Emily is saying, *keep going. Help me, help me.*

I bend forward to look into the cabin. The surprise that it is neat, nothing out of place, is still registering dully in my head when I feel his hands on my back, when the push sends me down the stairs.

I land on my hands and knees, but I bite my lip hard.

I hear the *thunk* of the door.

My face is in the carpet. I am stunned. My lip is bleeding. I touch my tongue to the blood.

No.

Under my cheek, I feel the engines start up.

No.

I run to the window. I can't open it.

I smell gasoline and see churning foam.

I pound on the window with my palms, slap them against the window. Then I use my fists.

"Help me, help me, help me!" I scream the words, over and over.

No one can hear.

My vision swims into focus. The girl on the bench, waiting.

I had been right all along about the danger.

Now I see it clearly.

The girl I had seen on the bench wasn't Dora at all.

The girl I had seen on the bench was me.

TWENTY-FOUR

When we are far out on the Puget Sound, he comes downstairs. By now I am sitting at the table in the dining area. My lip is swollen, and I haven't wiped off the blood. Somehow I want him to see it. I want him to see what he's done.

I've tried my cell phone a hundred times. No Service.

I am so afraid that my body is rigid. I am so afraid that I don't think I can speak. I am sick with anger at myself for being so stupid. Marcus was in my head, Marcus with his shaved head and his scowl.

Jonah has cut the engines and the boat sits, water slapping against the sides. I know we are in the middle of the Sound, no land in sight. He goes to the sink, takes a washcloth, and wets it. He hands it to me.

"I'm sorry you got hurt," he says. "I'm not going to hurt you."

I press the washcloth against my lip.

"I'm going to save you," he says. "I'm going to give you a home."

He sits across the table from me. "Are you hungry? Thirsty?"

I don't answer.

"Your cell phone won't work," he says. "I have a blocker. A device that disrupts the signal. One of the advantages of being a techno-wizard." He smiles, but it dims when I don't respond. "It's just that I need a chance to talk to you," he says. "It takes time for you to understand, for you to see. I wasn't lying to you. I do have a foundation. It's just a little . . . unconventional, and I needed to get you away so you could really listen to me and not walk away. But if you want to leave, I'll take you back."

I seize on this, a tiny flame of hope. "I want to leave."

He smiles slightly. "But you haven't heard me yet."

This is crazy. It's like the guy is selling real estate.

He spreads his hands on the table and looks down at them. His fingers are long and slender. "People have it all wrong about families. Families don't work the way they are. All we hear about is 'family values, family values,' and I'm not even sure what that means. Loyalty? Love? Is that a blood connection or a value? Values aren't tied to blood. They're tied to brains. Everyday decisions that you make. That's values."

I'm trying to follow him, but it's hard. He's almost making sense, but not quite.

"So our families let us down, say. They demean us, or they desert us, or they just can't cope. There comes a point where you make your own family with your friends. But that doesn't work, either, because friendships have different boundaries. You don't share a life with your friends. You're not forced to live with them and deal with them. You can just walk away."

"I thought you had a happy childhood," I say.

He looks startled. "I did. Oh, I did. I'm talking about *other people.* I'm talking about the things I learned. Okay? Okay? Just *listen.*"

There's perspiration on his forehead, and his eyes are damp. There is a flash of something in his eyes that frightens me.

I swallow against the knot of fear that rises in my throat. I put my hands under the table and squeeze them together. I will get through this. I will find a way out. I will find Emily. He didn't bring me out here to throw me overboard. I tell myself this very firmly. I don't know what's in store for me, but it isn't drowning. I will take this one step at a time. Diego knows where I am. He might have seen the boat take off. At the very least, he knows I was investigating Marcus and Ryan. The trail will lead to Jonah Castle eventually.

"I know what you're thinking," he interrupts.

"You can walk away from your family, too. But if you do, there's a *hole*. You fall into it, you can never climb out of it, it's just there. The problem is that people walk away from their family, but they don't replace it with something real. Okay?"

I nod, because it seems he needs encouragement.

"So I came up with this idea. We remake our family. We choose the people we want in it. And then we make a bond. Family values, okay? We support each other. We love each other. We're loyal."

"Like a commune?" I ask.

"No! Not like a commune!" He looks angrily at me, and the terror rises again.

"Like a real family," I say quickly. "Like the family you want, but thought you could never have."

"Exactly!" He looks eager now. "I have everything you need. You'll have brothers and sisters who will love you. I have a great house, and games, and books, and DVDs, and all the food you want, everything, everything! If you want to learn you can learn, if you want to play you can play, you can develop your specialness within this group that supports and loves you!" He leans forward. "Do you understand, Dora? I chose you!"

"What about Marcus?" I ask.

He waves a hand. "Marcus was useful, but not suitable. Too independent. But I told him I had this foundation, and he recommended kids he thought could benefit from internships and things . . ."

So Marcus had no idea what he was doing. He probably recommended Kendall, and then Emily. He never connected Kendall running away with Jonah Castle. And he might not even know that Emily is missing.

I've been wrong about everything. This kind of failure is colossal. It is beyond stupid. It is unforgivable.

But I know somehow I can't sink into the swamp of shame, because then I'll never get out, I'll never find Emily. I have a sudden instinct that hating myself will only help Jonah Castle.

"So where is your house?" I ask.

He springs up, happy. "You want to see it? It's solar-powered!"

"Where is it?" I ask.

"You'll see! You'll love it. Everyone does. I'm so glad you'll come over!"

He starts to spring up the steps.

"Jonah?"

He stops, looks at me.

"I'm not Dora," I say.

"I know," he says serenely, and continues up the stairs.

TWENTY-FIVE

The island is small, a gray smudge against the gray sea. Fog has rolled in, and gusts of wind send rolling slabs of it across the water. We have been traveling for hours. I don't wear a watch, and the fog obscures the sun, so I can't be sure, but it has to be at least three hours since we left Seattle.

"Come on up on deck!" Jonah yells down to me. "It's a beautiful sight!"

I climb up to the deck. Small droplets of mist hit my cheeks along with spray. A small boathouse looms ahead. I'm cold. It had been sunny in Seattle. I feel as though we are as far away as we can get, that we've passed beyond the boundary of the map and are in a gray wasteland of water that has yet to be discovered.

Jonah steers the boat into the boathouse and cuts the engine. He ties the lines and jumps up on deck, holding out a hand for me. I ignore him and jump onto the deck myself.

Nothing can dampen his enthusiasm. "Wait until you meet the others, Lizbet."

"What?"

"Come on." Jonah swipes a card through the

lock and opens the boathouse door for me to step through.

I walk out onto a beach. His eagerness seems eerie. Up beyond the beach is a high wall that crosses the beach and disappears into the trees. The door in the wall looks like steel. My footsteps crunch as I walk, and I realize I'm walking on oyster shells.

Sorry, Zed. I'll get out and clear you. I will.

He walks up to the wall and flips open a panel. He swipes a card, and the steel door opens.

Ahead, a long, low house hugs the ground. It's built of stone and wood, gray and brown, merging with the colors of the beach. It takes a moment for me to realize what is strange about it. The windows are sealed with metal shutters, like hurricane shutters.

My footsteps falter, and I am afraid.

I picture dead people inside the house, propped up like dolls.

The perspiration is gathering on my neck, under my arms, and I'm starting to shake uncontrollably.

He swipes the door frame with a card. A disembodied voice says, *Welcome home, Jonah.* The door swings open. He steps forward expectantly, happily.

The hallway floor is made of slabs of gray stone. There's a small bonsai tree on a graceful wood table to our right.

"Frances is our green thumb," he says.

He looks around. "It's activity time. Everyone's in the playroom. They'll all be dying to meet you."

Dying. I wish he hadn't used that word.

He swipes another keypad and pushes open the door directly in front of us. We step into the living area. It is a large open space scattered with three overstuffed sofas and at least a half-dozen big cushioned armchairs. The colors are the same as the island, bone, gray, black, dark green. Skylights let in a bit of light, and I can see the fog blowing overhead. The interior looks like a mountain cabin that's been blown up to three times its size. There is a large blank screen on one wall. DVDs and books line the shelves.

Emily is here. I can feel her now. She's close.

I get a flash of her, taking a book down from the shelves in this room.

She puts it back.

The repetition of the movement soothes her.

She does it again, sliding the book into the empty space.

"You see, Lizbet? Anything you want. You have it." He gestures toward the shelves. "All the latest movies. And TV, too! I select the programs, and you just have to scroll through the menu. This is where we have family time after supper."

"My name isn't Lizbet," I say.

"I know that," he says gently. "I'm not crazy."

"I'm not Dora, either."

He looks surprised. "What?"

"I'm Gracie."

He regards me for a moment, weighing something. "You belong," he says finally. "You still belong. I have an instinct about this stuff. Anyway, you'll want a new name to go with your new life soon. Names have associations."

"I don't want a new name."

He looks hurt. "Well, you don't have to."

He took away our names! Emily's voice screams in my head.

The house is so quiet. I don't even hear our footsteps.

"This is the site of the house I grew up in," Jonah says. "The same footprint, anyway. I loved that house and I tried to build a replica, but it was hard, you know. You can't build something exactly. Materials are harder to get, and, well, I had different needs. You can't blame me for modifying the design just a little bit. But it's essentially the same. I need to do it over again, okay? Nothing wrong with that. Anybody would say that, right?"

I blink. His words had started to echo. Suddenly, I see a different house. It's only a flash. The ceiling is low. There is a mattress on the floor with a baby on it. The baby is crying. A young boy sits nearby, reading, ignoring the baby.

Somewhere, another kid is screaming.

"And, of course, I had to wire it for digital controls. It's a smart house, do you know what that is?"

I shake my head, still reeling over my flash. Had I seen what is in Jonah's mind? Had I seen the reality of what it used to be? It was as though time was leaking inside me, forming a pool that contained present and past and future, and I had no control when I dipped into it what I would find.

"I can operate everything from one central panel," Jonah says. "Oven, generator, security, music, you name it. I control it, but you can ask me to do things. I mean, turn up the heat, whatever. The thing is, we have to accept the reality of the hierarchy. The hierarchy is good. The oldest takes care of the next oldest. And so on. And so that leaves me as the head of the house. So I make sure everyone is warm and fed and safe. I can do that. But we all take care of each other, too." He peers at me. "You understand? We all protect each other. That's the most important thing. That's what I learned about family. Here's where we eat. All together, of course, for the evening meal. That's fun, right?"

He pushes open double doors to a dining area. The table is long and can easily fit fourteen or more. There are benches instead of chairs, except at one of the ends, where a straight-backed wooden chair sits.

The room flashes again, and I see a smaller table, crowded with children. They sit on long benches on either side of the table. A man at the head, a thin man with a long beard. A woman at the other end, her eyes downcast. The children eating, silently, staring down at their plates.

I see the man's mouth move. A tall boy, thin as a pencil, looks up. He appears transfixed by his father's gaze. It is Jonah as a boy, I realize. I see the same blue eyes, but they are glassy with fear. I see that he is holding himself so still that his shoulders ache.

The dread at the table gathers. The other children continue to eat, continue to chew, but I can tell they aren't tasting their food. They are afraid to stop.

In a gesture stunning in its casualness, the man takes the boy's plate and sweeps it to the ground. The mother begins to run around the table to get it.

The father stops her.

Slowly, Jonah leans over to pick up the food.

"Meals are bonding time," Jonah is saying to me. I see him now, grown up, a man. I can't see the child behind his eyes. "I know, it's a cliché, bonding, right? But that's exactly what we do. Share our day and our food."

He hesitates. "There's only one rule. You have to stay inside the compound. That's what the wall is for. It's for your protection, you see. When I'm not here, I have to make sure you're safe. But that's not so bad, when there's so much to do inside our walls! I think traveling is overrated, don't you? Now. Let's meet the others."

He swipes a card and a door swings back. He waits impatiently for me to walk in, and I take baby steps, afraid of what I'll find.

It is a long room that ends in double doors at both ends. There are computers set up in different nooks. Sofas and chairs. More books and DVDs. Huge screens fill the walls, projecting images of nature. One whole wall is made up of a waterfall. The waterfall I'd seen in my vision. No wonder it hadn't seemed right. It had been a projection. The room is unnaturally bright, track lights on the ceiling mimicking a sunny day. It's so normal it's spooky.

There are kids here, dressed in jeans and sweatpants and T-shirts. None of them is talking to one another or working together. That's what's so strange — the silence. They are in their separate niches. One girl is potting a plant. One is playing with a Game Boy. A boy is reading a book. The rest are at computers. My gaze roams restlessly, anxiously, searching for Emily.

I spot her in a corner, at a computer, staring at the screen, and my heart leaps. At least I have found her. At least I have done that. And she is alive, and looks okay. Relief warms me instantly.

Jonah follows my gaze, then walks over, and I follow. She glances up furtively, then hunches her shoulders. In that quick glance, I try to convey to her to not reveal that we know each other. I'm not sure if she gets it. All I can see in her gaze is blankness.

Alarm clangs inside me.

This is not the Emily I know.

This is the Emily I sensed.

The one who wants to disappear inside herself so she can escape the fear.

"That's our Nell, always working."

He touches her, and I can see how she shrinks against the touch of his fingers, long and supple, on her shoulder.

She hates and fears him.

He singles her out. The pressure of that is too much for her.

It is crushing her.

Jonah turns away and takes my arm to bring me to the center of the room. "Meet your brothers and sisters." There is just the hint of an eye roll from a girl slouched on a sofa, watching TV. She had once been a blond, but now black roots extended three inches into her hair.

Jonah whistles through his teeth. "New member of the family has arrived. Do you remember the procedure?"

Suddenly, the kids move. Even the black-rooted surly girl on the sofa snaps to. They line up, ten girls and boys. Emily is four down from the top. I feel completely surreal, like I'm Maria the nun and Jonah is Captain Von Trapp in *The Sound of Music*.

As he calls out the names, each girl or boy raises a hand. It is amazing how much they give away by this simple gesture.

"Susannah." Barely raises her fingers, pushing insolence as far as she dares for me.

"Edwin." Blond boy, Susannah's height, jerks hand up, giving me an assessing stare.

"Frances. Our songbird." Frances nods tentatively. Inside my head, I hear a name. *Kendall*. This is Kendall Farmer.

"Tate." Eyes on the ground, nervously lifts hand, bad skin, emotional disturbance he wears like a coat.

"Nell." Emily lifts her hand quickly, then drops it, not looking at us.

"Hank and Dan, the twins." Two boys looking nothing alike, raise their hands. They hate each other.

And then the flash comes again. Instead of Jonah, I see his father. In a dim, dark room, children are lined up on their knees. I see the bearded man mouth the names as Jonah does.

". . . Ruthanna, Maudie, Eli."

The twelve children are lined up in a row, oldest to youngest. Fear rises off their bodies like steam. None of them look at their father. As they rise, one of them — maybe it's Edwin, one of the older children — winces in pain, as though the act of rising hurt him. I think again about the boy I heard screaming in my vision.

And I'm back in the present, in the brightly lit room.

The two youngest, Maudie and Eli, have already started to eye the computers they've left.

Jonah spreads his arms. "Family."

The expressions on the faces of the kids tell me nothing except they want this over with.

I look at Eli, maybe eleven years old, but small and pale. He comes out of foster care. I see the house, crowded with kids. Foster parents who do it for the money. I see Eli sitting in a closet, making his own space there. He has a ball. He has three crayons.

Jonah continues. "Let's see, Lizbet is between Frances and Nell, so Frances, show Lizbet her bed and help her feel at home. I think she needs a sweatshirt; it was a cold ride. I'll see you all at supper." Jonah heads for the door.

I stand in the middle of the room in disbelief.

What now? The other kids drift away, but the girl and boy he called Susannah and Edwin come closer, close enough so that we are almost touching.

"That this group must somehow form a family," Edwin sings in my ear. He manages to make it sound nasty, threatening.

"Forget the names. I'm Torie," the girl says. "This is Jeff. Castle won't hurt you if you listen to us."

"Just do what he says," Jeff says. "And what we say, too. Then you'll be okay."

I look around at the other kids, who are deliberately ignoring me. They are afraid of Torie and Jeff. They are locked in their isolation. This isn't even close to the family ideal Jonah wants.

I know now why Emily has closed down. Nobody is leaving. Nobody is getting out of here.

There is no hope left in this room.

TWENTY-SIX

Frances-Kendall shows me the layout. The bedrooms are at both ends of the long room. The girls all sleep together in beds lined up like a dormitory. There are no windows, but there is a projection of a Webcam shot of the Sound.

"He checks on us," she says. "Sometimes five times a night. With a flashlight. So be here."

I remember the light in my vision, sweeping the bed, Emily shrinking from it, pretending to be asleep. The darkness, and then the light. I hadn't seen a lighthouse at all.

"If you're awake, he hates it," she says.

"Thank you, Kendall," I say.

She starts. "How did you know my name?"

"Your parents miss you," I say. "They found a girl who looks like you in San Diego, but it wasn't you, and they were crushed."

She works her mouth, sucking in her lip, biting it, letting it out. "Don't talk to me about my parents. Don't ever talk to me about them again," she hisses, and walks away.

★   ★   ★

Dinner. We line up on benches. Jonah has a chair. The girls had prepared the meal, me included. Jonah had brought fresh supplies from Seattle, and I recognize some of the stores, thanks to Shay. Fresh ravioli. Big loaves of bread from a designer bakery in Ballard. A chunk of parmesan that we grate over the ravioli. Bags of green beans so fresh they snap. It's easy for four of us to make the meal because the kitchen is huge. There are two ovens and a professional stove and every size pot you could want.

I think of how Shay would love this kitchen and feel something so new I can't identify it at first. I'm homesick.

Jonah takes a bite and pronounces it delicious. We all start to eat.

"We're finally all together," he says, looking around. "Now that Lizbet has joined us, the family is complete. Lizbet is our poet. Nell is our soul. Just like Frances is our voice, or Ruthanna makes us laugh."

Ruthanna keeps looking down at her plate and shoveling in ravioli. A less likely candidate for a laugh I've never seen. She's probably about thirteen. She doesn't meet anyone's eyes.

I see her suddenly, in the backseat of a black car, pulling away down a road. She's younger. I see gravestones behind her. Her mother is dead, but she can't understand why they're leaving her. I can feel her grief as keenly as I can feel mine.

She doesn't care what happens to her here. She is glad that the food is good.

Jonah smiles. His sleeves are rolled up, and he looks like any dad at a kitchen table.

"This is what my father believed, and I believe it, too," he says, and I realize that he's directing his remarks to me. "That the family can be a self-sufficient unit. Each of you has your own skill. We can entertain each other. We have artists and musicians and scientists here."

This gives me my opening. I need to unsettle him. I need to see what happens when I do.

"What we need is a cook," I say.

The rest of the kids freeze. Jonah blinks at me, as if my words are taking a long time to register.

He smiles tightly. "There is something wrong with the food?"

Torie gives me a murderous look.

"Well," I say, "it could be better."

His smile wobbles, then freezes. "I got this ravioli from the best place in Seattle."

"Really." I poke at my dish. "It tastes like glue."

Across the table, Torie mouths something at me. *You die.*

Jonah stands up. He is shaking with fury. Emily closes her eyes. "I bring you the best! I take care of you! You know that, Lizbet!" he shouts, his face red.

"My name is Gracie," I say.

"I know that!" he snaps. "Everyone else likes their new names!"

Torie gets up quickly. She removes my plate and takes it to the kitchen. As she moves, she jabs against me, hard, with her elbow.

Jonah's hand grips his fork. "Well. Supper is not about food. It is about communication and love. We love each other."

"We love each other," Jeff echoes. He shoots me a look that eloquently says, *shut up, idiot.*

Kendall bites her lip and pushes her food around. She is afraid and wants me to stop. She casts a quick look at Jeff, then looks away.

She's afraid of Jonah, yes. But she's also afraid of Torie and Jeff.

"Yes, Edwin. Let's eat." Jonah takes a bite of his dinner. Everyone starts to eat again.

I take a sip of my water. When Jonah stood up, I noticed something. In his front left pocket, I saw the tip of his swipe card. Of course, he probably keeps it on him at all times. The card works on the locks, but didn't he also say that he can control everything? Music, heating, security. There has to be a central control. It has to be in his wing of the house.

"This is all new to you," Jonah says suddenly, turning to me. His anger is gone. "You'll understand things in time. I was too harsh. I'm never harsh."

I see his father standing over a young Jonah, shouting, *This is what I do for you! I do this for you! Do you understand?*

"You do this for me," I say.

He shakes his head rapidly as if shaking out a mop full of dust. "Exactly."

I smell smoke suddenly. It is acrid, strong. Yet I don't cough, it doesn't fill my lungs, and I can't see it in the air. I look around, but everyone else is eating.

"I do this for all of you," Jonah mumbles.

I realize that the smoke is not in the air. It's in my head. And for the first time I wonder — what happened to the original house?

Jonah said that now we were complete. What came next? There was an end to this, and the only one who knows the ending is Jonah.

TWENTY-SEVEN

I wake up in the middle of the night. I hear the even breathing of the other girls. Jonah could come by at any time; I know he's already checked us at least once. His visits are random, so there is no way to avoid them.

But I can't wait any longer. I'll have to take a chance.

I slip out of bed. Emily's bed is right next to mine. I put my hand over her mouth. She tries to bolt up, terror in her eyes, but I speak quietly, rapidly, in her ear.

"It's Gracie. Don't worry. I just want to talk to you."

She shakes her head, her eyes fearful.

"Just for a minute."

"He'll come."

"I'm going to get you out of here."

She shakes her head. "No. Don't say that. It's dangerous."

"Why? Has he done anything to you?"

She turns away. "No, nothing. It's just that . . . he pays attention to me. Special attention. He watches me, all the time."

"I came to find you, Emily. Your mom, your dad . . . they're frantic. They miss you."

Emily starts to cry. I feel her shudders as she tries to keep her sobs inside. I'm actually glad to see her cry. It's so much better than that blankness.

"It's okay," I say, even though it's so obviously not.

I can see tears on her cheeks from the light cast from the watery reflection on the wall. "I'm glad you're here. But Gracie . . ."

"What?"

"Don't do it. Don't try to get away. Promise me." Her eyes are frantic.

"Shhh," I say, as if Emily were a little girl. "Go back to sleep."

Torie approaches me the next morning as I'm looking through the bookshelves. I can't imagine having enough concentration to read, but I don't know what else to do.

She stands a little too close for my personal comfort.

"Maybe I didn't make myself clear," she says. "Keep your mouth shut and you'll do okay here."

I shrug. Her gaze is so hostile. Why should I give her ammunition?

Her face is in my face. "Don't say your real name to him," she warns, spitting the words out. "Don't *ever* do it again."

Just what I need — to get snatched by a madman and then get bossed around by another girl. "Look," I say, exasperated, "I've been kidnapped by a psycho who makes up crazy rules according to some insane scenario in his head. I've got enough problems without having to listen to you, too. Don't you want to get out of here?"

"Listen up," she says. "This is a sweet spot compared to where I came from. Most of us here are the same. This is *better* than home. You're not going to take it away from us. One of these days, I'll figure out a way to leave, but until then, I have everything I want here. Just what do you want to send us back to? Our families?" She snorts. "The streets? Keep quiet and don't make him crack up."

I'm listening, but I'm also seeing her. Smoking a cigarette on a street corner. Crouching down in the cold. She had been homeless.

I see that things that have happened to her have made her capable of anything. Kendall is right to be afraid of her.

But I also know one thing. I can't show her my fear. "And what do you think will happen if he *does* crack up?" I ask. "It's scary inside his head."

"It's scary inside *my* head. Don't forget that."

I see a man, sitting in an armchair, smiling up at Torie. Her hair is shorter and blonder. Her smile is strained. He reaches up and, with his foot, rubs her leg.

The vision derails me for a moment.

"Look," I say to her, "There's no telling what he could do to us."

Torie snorts. "He's a millionaire. He's famous. What's he going to do?"

"He's kidnapped kids," I say. I can't believe that she is this stupid. "He committed about a thousand felonies. They can put him away for life. Do you know what that means? He has nothing left to lose."

Torie looks at me as though I'm the one who's stupid. "Rich people don't go to prison. Don't you know that?"

Jonah approaches us, his hands in his pockets, smiling. "I'm glad to see you're getting along already." He looks at me. "You know, there's a garden. We all planted it. Tomatoes, herbs, lettuce."

I don't know what he expects me to say, so I say the conventional thing. "That's nice."

"So we have fresh produce sometimes," he says. "I just wanted you to know that. Sometimes I overreact. That doesn't mean I don't love you."

A small boy lies in a bed, crying.

Sometimes I hurt you. That doesn't mean I don't love you. When you do bad things, that hurts me, too. But you still love me, right, Jonah?

"When I do bad things, that hurts you, too," I say.

Jonah blinks. "Exactly," he says. "Come and help me pick lettuce."

I follow Jonah out the kitchen door. It's good to be outside. The fog has lifted, and it's a bright summer day, warm enough to be in a T-shirt. I could almost feel hopeful on a day like this. If I weren't stuck on an island in the middle of nowhere with no way to get off.

Still, the sun is warm on the skin of my arms and my face, and it drains some of the anxiety from my muscles. We walk along the back of the house, and Jonah strikes off on a path between the trees. From here, you can't see the wall. Strangely, I am not afraid to be alone with him. Not now, anyway. Somehow I know he won't hurt me . . . at least, not yet.

"The garden is this way. I sited it so that it gets the most sun. Had to truck in some super-duper soil. You know, Lizbet was the sister I was closest to." He says this last part quickly, running into the discussion about topsoil, stripped of any emotion, just matter-of-fact.

"I mean, Nell was the special one. The rest of us . . . we didn't protect each other. We told on each other, as a matter of fact. But we all protected Nell. I was closest to Lizbet, though."

"Where is Lizbet now?"

"My father wasn't a monster." Jonah stops. We are in the middle of a glade, and it's cooler here. He picks up a pine branch and begins to strip the needles. "I don't want you to think that. He and my mother left San Francisco because they didn't like the atmosphere there. Everyone thought they were weird for having twelve kids. So they moved to the foothills of the Sierras for a while. I remember that. I was ten when we moved here. He said the family was the core of society, and if we made the perfect family, we could show the world how to live. He really believed that. Perfection was everything to him. He encouraged all of us to reach our potential. He shipped in my computer stuff. It wasn't like he didn't want us to succeed. He just wanted us to be special."

"Is your dad still alive?" I ask.

He looks around vaguely. He scratches his arm with the tree branch. His skin is pale, as if he never goes outside in the summer. He has a face people wouldn't remember. He's not handsome, but he's not bad-looking. There's no distinguishing feature in his face. Everything is in proportion, everything makes sense. But his eyes don't focus on the world.

"I don't see any of them now," he says.

Jonah is speaking to me now as an adult. I realize that this is why I felt such a disconnect with him. I remember him on the boat. *It's solar-powered! I'm glad you can come over!* Sometimes he speaks like a teenager. And sometimes he speaks like he is, like a man. He slips from one to the other.

"I just want you to have a nice meal," he says to me, with such simple directness I suddenly wonder if I'm the one who's crazy, and he's completely sane.

"You said you'd bring me back if I didn't want to stay." I figure I can at least try this when he seems so reasonable.

He cocks his head and smiles. "But you haven't given us a chance."

"I'm not Dora," I tell him. "I don't have an alcoholic mother. I'm not looking to be saved."

He nods. "But you belong here anyway. Don't you?" He takes a step closer to me, and I step back. "There's a hole in you," he says. He touches my collarbone, and I try to control my instinct, which is to shudder. But the touch is light and fleeting. "Here. Inside you. I can see it. You're like me. All of you, you're all like me."

"There's a lot of pain here," I say.

"That's why this will work. All it takes is time."

He starts walking again, and I follow as if tethered to him on a string. We break through the trees into a clearing.

The garden hasn't been weeded or watered. Some of the tomatoes have fallen off the vine and lie on the ground, split and rotten. Flies buzz over the pulp. Jonah stands, hands on his hips, looking at it. He begins to slap his thigh rhythmically.

"They were supposed to take care of this."

"It's not so bad," I say.

"We're all supposed to work together for each other."

"There's some nice tomatoes left."

"We're supposed to *help* each other."

His voice is strained and cracking. He is slapping his thigh harder now, slapping it with the branch he still holds in his hand. I start to back up.

"We're supposed to work *together*!" he screams. "How is this going to work if they don't *listen*! It's all their fault, and they won't try hard enough, and it's all about that, isn't it? We have to share. If only they could see that. How much harder can I try? They make me sick, they make me so mad!"

I have heard this voice before. I have heard this rant in my vision. I have seen this dark energy spill over in a torrent, and it is scarier in person.

He throws down the branch and picks up the hoe. He begins to hack at the garden, the tomato plants, the lettuces, the herbs, slamming the hoe into the ground, into the plants, over and over. Tears are running down his face. The hoe is flying in the air, a weapon now.

The rage came on so fast. How could I have not realized how dangerous he was? The danger was there, beneath the surface, beneath the khakis and the glasses and the smile.

I turn and run. I run through the forest, afraid

he is following me, but I am alone with the whispering trees. I hear my breathing, frantic, and my footsteps on the hard ground. My footsteps pound out what I already know:

I have to find a way out.

TWENTY-EIGHT

I run straight into Jeff. Literally. I bounce off him and fall.

"Where's the fire?" he says.

The fire . . . the fire! I *see* it then, I see the house burning. But is it in the past, or the future?

I can't tell.

"What's the matter with you?" he asks, crouching over me.

"He went crazy," I say. "In the garden. He's destroying it. You didn't take care of it while he was away."

Jeff shrugs. "It's hard to remember everything he wants us to do."

"You don't understand. He's out of control!"

"He gets like that." Jeff pulls me to my feet. "Then he sort of shuts down for a while and disappears into the woods. That's the good part. I think he's afraid he'll hurt us."

"But what if he *does*?"

His face hardens. "I'm not afraid of him."

"Why don't we all just jump him? Take that swipe card — I saw it in his pocket. We can get to the boat —"

"Shut up," he says.

"We can get out of here!"

"Shut up," he says. His gaze is flat and hard. "Shut your mouth and keep it shut and follow the rules. You don't know crap. We're in the middle of nowhere, man. We've got it good here."

"You're just as crazy as he is." I try to push around him, but he grabs me by the upper arm.

"I've lived in a lot of places," he says. His grip is tight. "My dad is an addict. So I get bounced around every time he's in rehab. Or jail. Jonah is a meal ticket, and this is five-star dining. Got it?"

"I've got news for you," I say. "You're the one who's in jail."

His face tightens. "He's not around all the time. When he's not, Torie and I are in charge. I'd think about that, if I were you." He squeezes my arm until it hurts, and then he keeps on squeezing. I try to twist away, but it just hurts more.

Finally, he drops my arm, but he keeps his eyes on my face. I'm trembling, and my arm is on fire. I walk past him, trying not to run.

Inside, I stop in the kitchen and splash water on my face. I take deep breaths, trying to get my focus back. Jeff's words return.

Then he sort of shuts down and disappears into the woods. . . .

He's out there now, roaming in the woods, trying to get his control back. It's now or never. I have to try it when Jonah is here, because if I can get out of the house and past the wall, I'll need the boat. I can't rescue everyone, but I can get Emily and maybe Kendall. Once we get to the police, they can save the rest.

For a second, I waver. I think of pudgy Ruthanna at the dinner table, shoveling ravioli into her mouth. There is a sadness in her that is total. And Eli, and Maudie. They're only eleven or twelve. How can I leave them?

I have to leave them. It's the only way to get out of here. It's the only way to save them.

There are no sharp knives in the kitchen, only butter knives, but I take one, along with a fork.

The other wing of the house is Jonah's. It's separated from the rest of the house down a long hallway. The door is locked, of course. I kneel, examining the lock, but I don't know why. I don't know anything about lock-breaking. I try to stick the blade of the knife in between the door and the lock. I push and push. Nothing.

A shadow looms behind me and my heart leaps into my throat.

"If you open it, an alarm will go off. The place is wired."

It's Hank, one of the twins who aren't twins.

I slump against the door. "Oh."

He's eating a carrot stick. He waves it at the door. "You'll never be able to break the lock that way, anyway. You can't use a butter knife to break a lock."

"You know this?"

"I'm handy. My dad is a carpenter."

The words cause him pain. I see a man in a room. Sitting in a chair. Dogs surround him, licking at empty bowls.

Hank shakes off the emotion. He crunches into the carrot. "Anyway, I've been in there. He needed help once, there was a busted pipe in his bathroom and he couldn't fix it by himself. He needed someone with small hands. I'm good with my hands. There's a control panel in his bedroom. I saw it. But you need his swipe card to get inside. There's controls for everything. The shutters, the main power switch. There's a generator and a backup generator. The swipe cards work on batteries, so even if the power goes out, the doors stay locked unless he opens them. He's thought of everything. Even if you got in that room, there's nothing you could do."

"There's got to be something. A phone . . ."

"He doesn't bring his cell inside. He keeps it in the boat."

"The wall . . ."

"It's electrified, didn't he tell you?"

"So help me break into the room, and we'll turn off the power."

Slowly, he shakes his head. "I'm not rocking the boat."

"I don't understand," I say. "I don't understand any of you."

"That must be because you come from a place you want to get back to," Hank says. He shrugs.

"What about the other kids?" I ask. "What about the young ones, like Eli and Maudie? Don't they deserve better than this?"

Hank pops the rest of the carrot in his mouth. "Don't you get it? We're all in this alone."

He hears a noise and he freezes in fear for a moment. It is the back door opening. Jeff coming back, maybe. I don't care. But Hank does, and he quickly and silently moves down the hall.

I lean against the door for a moment. I have felt pain before that made me rock and howl. And I have felt trapped in a deep hole of sorrow with no way out. But this is different. This is horror wrapped in a normal package. This is knowing that the worst isn't behind me. The worst is ahead.

And I'm the only one who cares.

TWENTY-NINE

That night it rains, a hard, steady rain that drums on the roof insistently. We eat our meat loaf in silence. Jonah is distracted, as though he is listening to voices from far away.

He is.

Every so often his fork drops to his plate with a clink, and he sits, staring into nowhere.

Torie and Jeff glare at all of us, keeping us in line. The threat of violence hangs over us, impossible to misinterpret. I'm not sure what they'd do, but I'm sure they'd do it. They are the most desperate of all of us. They've lived on the streets. They want this safe berth. They want the food, and the clothes, and the warm bed. For them, this place *is* their future. The only future they can see. It was no accident that Torie had mentioned Jonah's money right away to me. She would do anything to protect her status here.

Torie directs us to clear the table, moves us with shoves when Jonah isn't looking. Everyone is quieter tonight. They move fast and efficiently. Jeff hovers over us in the kitchen, watching us put food away, stick the dishes in the dishwasher. Jonah stays at the table.

As we're getting ready for bed, Kendall whispers to me, "He doesn't like the rain."

"Whoa, is he living in the wrong part of the country," I say.

She twists her mouth as if it's been so long since she smiled that she doesn't remember how.

We all go to bed, and the house is silent except for the clamor of rain. When I see the flashlight, I freeze. I'm remembering Jonah outside in the garden, slashing at the plants, the sharp edge of the hoe coming down and scoring the earth. But I slip out of bed. The flashlight tracks me as I move toward him.

"Go back to bed," he says. He looks glassy-eyed, and he's perspiring. His hair is matted to his forehead.

"I'm afraid of the rain," I say.

His gaze doesn't stop; it just keeps roaming.

"I needed to check on Nell. Is Nell all right?"

"She's fine," I say. The light rests on Emily. I know she is awake, but her eyes are closed. She has drawn herself up into a tight little ball underneath the covers.

"Go to sleep," he says to me, but there is no force behind his words. He's not aware of me, really. He's looking at Emily.

He looks with a hunger that frightens me. He looks capable of anything.

I sag with relief when he turns and leaves the room. What I want is to crawl back into bed.

What I do is follow him.

He passes through the dark playroom and into the living area. He sits on the couch and takes off his glasses. His head falls into his hands. I don't say anything. I don't try to hide. I stand in the darkness, watching him.

"My head hurts," he moans.

There is a flash, but it isn't lightning, it's another vision. I am so open to them now, it's like the boat locks in Seattle, the water rushing in, filling the compartment, and everything rising with it. Only here, it is the past. I think it is because Jonah lives with the past. I can pick it up so easily from him.

It is Nell, I see now.

Nell is sick, very sick.

The father stands in the doorway. He won't let the mother go in.

I can hear the voices, but nobody's mouth moves.

They are frozen like statues.

The human body is perfect, I hear. It is Jonah's voice. I am hearing the memory through Jonah. *She has received the right caloric input, the correct balance of nutrients. Her body will fight this without our help.*

The mother is crying silently. Her hands are tightly clasped, as if she thinks that by taking on the posture of begging but not speaking, he will somehow listen to her.

Jonah stands behind them, the oldest boy.

Father. Dad. We can use the radio.

She needs no help.

He closes the door.

The vision fades.

"You wanted to help her," I say to Jonah.

His head is still in his hands. "I wanted to."

"You wanted to call for help on the radio."

"I did want to!" He raises his head, and his face is streaked with tears. His pale skin is wet and glows in the darkness. I can smell him now. He is sweating. "I sneaked in to see her. She was so sick."

I see him again. It is Nell he is carrying in the rain.

He didn't kill her.

She was already dead.

"You tried to get help," I say. "You tried to get her to the boat."

"I thought . . . if I could get her to the mainland. To a hospital."

"It wasn't your fault she died, Jonah."

"It was her birthday. She was thirteen. She was excited about that. About being a teenager. Being one of the older ones. Every birthday we thought, I am closer to getting out."

He curls up in a ball, resting his head on his elbow. "You know how when someone you love dies? It's like running into a wall. You bang your fists against it because you can't believe it's *real*. You can't believe you won't see that face again. You can't believe you won't hear that voice. You *can't believe* it."

"I know," I say. I swallow against a throat suddenly dry.

He looks up at me without moving. "You do know." In the dim light, I can see only the gleam of his eyes.

"Tell me," he says, and I know immediately what he wants me to say.

It is like the storm outside is inside me, and if I open my mouth it will rush out in a flood. This is the moment, this is it, this is the time when I *must* say it, crazily enough, on this nowhere island, to this crazy man full of pain.

I open my mouth. I feel something crack inside me like ice. Then the words come. "My mother is dead."

"How?"

"A car crash. She got caught between a semi and a truck. The truck was carrying oranges."

I can taste it suddenly, orange in my mouth. Jonah rises to a sitting position, his eyes on my face, not leaving. I have never felt so listened to before. He is listening with his whole body. He is eager to hear. He wants to fill up on my pain, he wants to know it. He wants to share it.

No, he doesn't want to share it.

He wants to take it for himself. He wants to *own* it.

And I want to give it away.

"The oranges rolled all over the road. She was . . . she was choking to death. On her blood. The oranges . . . I can't see it. But I *smell* it. I smell it sometimes. I *taste* it. I can't eat oranges. I can't even smell them. The smell makes me sick."

My mouth still open, I start to cry. The tears run into my open mouth. I collapse on the couch across the room from him. My sobs are so strong they wrench my belly. I reach for a pillow and grab it, slam it on my knees and push my face into it to cry. I've done this before. I know what to do with this kind of tears.

I thought this kind of crying was over.

It will never be over.

I almost feel a kinship with him now. Jonah knows that the grief that marks you never leaves. What haunts you, haunts you. Just when you think it lets go, it comes back with teeth and claws.

"I asked her not to go," I say into the pillow.

"You couldn't have stopped her."

"That's what people say. But they don't know. I could have."

I lift my head. The pillow is wet. I am lying in a stain of my own tears.

I look at the damaged man across the room. I want to say, *I am damaged, too.*

I don't have to. He already knows it.

He crawls over to me. He lifts my chin so that we are at eye level. His gaze is tender.

Now I smell the burning again, and this time I see the house on fire and the children running. A window blows out, the glass flying into the night air.

His face is close. His eyes unfocus. His whisper is anguished and hushed and for my ears alone. "I don't want to do it, Lizbet. Help me."

THIRTY

Torie finds me the next morning as I'm brushing my teeth at the row of three sinks in the girls' bathroom. Kendall is next to me, washing her face. Ruthanna is just putting her toothbrush away.

"Hey," Torie says. "I saw you. Last night."

I shrug, brush, and spit. I'm leaning over the sink when she puts her hand on the back of my head and grabs my hair. She pushes me down hard. My teeth clunk against the faucet. I feel the impact shudder into the root.

"Oh, good," she says. "I have your attention."

Kendall backs up quickly, but hovers in the doorway. Ruthanna just vanishes.

Torie keeps my head against the faucet. She is amazingly strong. I have a feeling that if I try to resist, I'll lose my front teeth.

She leans over, close to my ear. "I was the first," she says, her words like bullets. Occasionally, for emphasis, she pushes me against the sink faucet. Not hard, just a bump, but it's enough. My lip is still healing from falling down the stairs on the boat, and every time it hits the chrome I wince.

"He found me first. I'm closest to him. I'm the

one he depends on. So don't think you can come here and work it."

"Hey, list —"

Bang. My face hits the faucet.

"Because I'm drawing the line."

Torie's words overlap with someone else's. I flash suddenly to a blond woman, tan and thin, well muscled, perfectly groomed. I hear a voice echo. "I know your tricks. I've never drawn the line enough with you. Now I'm drawing the line."

Torie leans in. "Let me remind you of something, *Lizbet.* You've already disappeared. Nobody's going to know if you do it again."

But I can't avoid him. Something has changed between us. He watches Emily, but he talks to me. He singles me out. He directs remarks to me. He asks me how I like the macaroni and cheese. He offers to order new DVDs.

He likes me.

I can feel Torie's and Jeff's eyes on me. I know they are wondering how to handle me. I know that they will not handle me with kid gloves. I am heading to a cliff and I don't know who's going to push me off.

He comes and gets me now, in the middle of the night. I follow him like a ghost in my T-shirt and Gap sweatpants, what we all sleep in. We are both barefoot. His feet are long and white and feminine-looking. It makes him seem fragile, even though I know he's not. He sits on the couch with his head in his hands. Sometimes he cries.

"I can't sleep," he says.

I get flashes, but they are confusing. I see him as a boy, running, breathing hard, barefoot on the oyster shells on the beach. I know someone is chasing him.

I see Nell, lying on the bed. I know she is dead. She is wet with rain. The wetness pools out on the sheets.

I'm tired during the day, from the nights spent with Jonah. And I'm holding on to what I can see and what I can touch, because I keep sliding into places that the kids hide deep inside their minds, places they don't want to go.

But they go all the time.

Eli. His older foster brother tied him up and flicked matches at him. For fun.

Maudie. Is clumsy. That's what her mother tells the doctor.

Ruthanna. Her mother died, and it was her fault. Her father told her so.

Dan. His father left him at his grandmother's to play one day. Never came back.

Hank. His father drinks. His mother works

two shifts. His brother died last year. He spends all his time alone.

Tate . . .

I am afraid of what's in Tate's head.

There is just too much pain in this house.

I can feel it. I can *see* it.

Everything parents can do, the world can do, to mess up a kid — it's all here. It lives in their heads.

They feel safe here because they don't know what safe is. This, they figure, is as close as they'll get.

He tells me about Nell. That from the first, she was the one they protected. That there was something special about her. Out of all of them, she was the one they all loved.

When she got sick, the fragile bonds fell apart. The family disintegrated. The panic was a string that vibrated at a pitch they could all hear. The children walked around with dread, fearing the inevitable. Fearing that what they knew would happen would happen: Their father would not give in.

"I can remember better when you're around," he says. "You help me remember." It's two o'clock in the morning. He is lying on one couch; I am lying on another.

"That's good," I say, trying not to yawn.

"I don't want to remember," he says.

"I'm sorry." A trickle of fear begins inside me. I feel him trying to push something away in his mind, something huge.

This is the thing he's blocked from me.

This is the thing he's blocked from himself.

"Her birthday is on Friday, you know. The birthday she never had. That's when it has to happen."

"What has to happen?"

"He was afraid it would all fall apart, that they would think he wasn't fit."

I smell burning. I smell the fire.

"He was afraid they'd take us away. He tried to save us."

I see the glass shatter, fall into blackness. I hear someone pounding on a door.

"I don't want to do it," Jonah says. "But I have to save us, too."

Friday. I try to remember what day it is.

I look out into the darkness. He is just a shape across the room. What he's saying doesn't make sense to me, but it doesn't have to. It makes sense to him.

There is urgency in his mind now. He is racing toward a goal. He has given up controlling this. He has given up analyzing it. He has given up changing it.

Whatever he is heading for, in his mind, he will have saved us. In his mind, he'll be able to rest.

Tomorrow is Thursday. I have to gather all the hazy ideas, the things I know, the things I guess, the things I'm thinking, and make a plan.

I only have one day to set it up.

One day to make it work.

THIRTY-ONE

The next morning, I find Emily in the laundry room, folding socks. There are two machines, two dryers, drying racks, a row of detergents and softeners. He makes it as easy as he can.

Emily has a row of white socks lined up. She is concentrating hard, as though it is the most difficult thing in the world to match up white socks. She smooths each sock as she places it on the long table used for folding.

"Emily," I say. "Are you okay?"

She isn't really here. I can feel that her focus on the socks is absolute. She likes the repetition of the motion, the smell of the bleach. She likes how white they are.

I put my hand over hers to stop her movement. She slips it out and keeps going.

"Do you know what I was afraid of when I was little?" she says, looking down at the socks. "Not monsters, or earthquakes. Infinity."

"Infinity?"

"I was in Sunday school. They taught us that in heaven, you just keep going on. Before I went to sleep, I'd think about that. I'd try to imagine going on and on, never being able to stop. I tried to imagine something never ending. And it used to terrify me. I'd run and get into my parents' bed. Dad would ask me what was wrong, and I'd say I was afraid of monsters, or the lion at the zoo. Whatever. I thought it was too weird to tell him that I was afraid of infinity."

She smoothes another sock, places one on top of it.

"Emily, we're all in danger. We have to get out of here."

She smoothes another sock.

"Emily, I'm thinking of a way. But it won't work if we all can't do it together."

She begins to hum.

"I need your help. We have to face this!"

"This isn't like you," she says primly. She takes another sock and rolls it up like a bandage.

"What are you talking about?"

"Nothing bothers you," she says. "You're a closed system."

She isn't making sense, and I'm scared. I watch her fold socks. And then the truth crashes down on my head so dizzily I want to fall on the floor and grab onto the floor to keep myself steady.

I had never asked myself the questions that were staring me in the face about our friendship. Why did Emily drop the friends she'd known all her life, the girls who'd known her since kindergarten, the boys who knew her parents, the group that hung together through long Saturday afternoons, through endless rainy February weeks, through crushes, through bad teachers, through pizza on Fridays?

Why had she picked me? It certainly wasn't because I was such a fun companion. It wasn't because we could share our sorrows.

It was because she knew that I wouldn't make her feel.

I would never ask her things. I would never push her. I would never make her cry.

She knew, with the cunning of the wounded, that I couldn't turn away from myself long enough to even *see* her. She could slowly close herself off. And no one would knock on the door.

Her abduction by Jonah was an example of the worst possible thing happening to her at the worst possible time. She had already begun to disengage. Now she was filling up her head with distance. And soon, no one would be able to reach her.

I'm still shaken by my encounter with Emily, but I'm more determined than ever to follow through on the plan that's forming in my mind. Kendall and I have the lunch dishes to do. She washes; I dry. We are only allowed to use the dishwasher at night. Too much power can blow the generator.

"I think we have a friend in common," I say. "Marcus Heffernan."

"Marcus?" Kendall looks surprised.

"He worked at the computer camp. I went there looking for Emily. She's met him, too."

"I've never really talked to Nell . . . Emily." Kendall smiles, sort of dreamily, and the muscles in her face relax. For the first time, I realize that she could be pretty. "I had a big crush on Marcus. He was so nice to me."

"You sang in that café he works in."

"Did he tell you about that? He talked me into entering that contest. I was so nervous, I thought I would die. And then I won second prize! That was a good day." Kendall puts away a dish. "Which was not the usual."

"You had a hard time with your parents."

"Yeah, How about you?"

"My mom is dead. I never really knew my dad."

"Oh. Yeah. Well."

A rather pathetic attempt at sympathy, but never mind.

"Have you ever seen Jonah have a meltdown?" I ask her, handing her a dish.

She looks around before answering me. "Yeah."

"Scary, huh?"

She doesn't answer.

She doesn't have to.

She reaches up to replace the dish on a shelf.

"Did you know that the original house burned down?" I ask.

"No." She takes a dish, glances at me, then back down at the dish.

"The children were trapped inside."

She doesn't look up, but the dish is dry, and she keeps rubbing.

"Don't you wonder what Jonah is trying to make up for?"

"It's none of my business," Kendall says. "It's none of yours, either."

"Kendall, it *is* my business. It's yours, too. The anniversary of the fire is this Friday. He's got something planned, and it's not a party. Where do you want to be?"

She puts the dish away. "There's nothing we can do."

"I *wish* everyone would stop saying that!"

"What are you saying, Lizbet? That —"

"My name is Gracie."

"Gracie, then. What are we supposed to do? Swim?"

"If I said I could get us out of here, would you come?"

"You can't —"

"Just answer the question."

Kendall hesitates, biting her lip. "I don't know."

"Okay," I say. "That's a start."

THIRTY-TWO

Jonah spends most of Thursday in his part of the house, but I see him from time to time. He pads out in his socks, looks us over, goes back again. There is none of the usual hearty encouragement. None of the beaming smiles. I come to know a particular muscle in his jaw that jumps and quivers, like a burrowing insect under his skin.

I am the one who sees that he is fighting something, and I am the one who knows that if he loses, we lose, too.

Kendall is a reluctant ally, but she is an ally. I move fast before she has a chance to change her mind. I tell her we have to talk to the other kids one by one. Except for Torie and Jeff. Kendall says darkly that they'll never agree, but I just tell her to leave them to me. I just wish I knew what I was going to say to them. The thing is, if they're against it, the plan won't work. They'll see what's up and stop us before I can get it rolling.

We get Dan and Hank to go along by tackling them separately and telling each of them the other one didn't want to go along with the plan. So they both agree. Hank is proud because he has the important role to play. Dan thinks maybe going back to live at his grandmother's house isn't so bad after all, because she has a pool.

I find Tate watching a DVD of some suspense movie. He keeps freezing a frame, then pressing PLAY, then freezing it again. I stop by his chair. Tate is the one boy here who gives off waves of disturbance. His gaze is brittle and hard. I see hurt in his past, deep hurt, starting with him in a crib, and a father standing over him, shouting. I don't want to see what else is there.

I don't want to see anything I've seen inside these kids. I don't want to see the misery and the neglect. I don't want to think about what I'm sending them back to. I just want them to live.

I tell Tate what I think is in Jonah's head. I don't know if he's listening, or if he cares. He stares at the movie, flicking the PAUSE button on and off.

I know better than to try to convince him. I just lay it out.

"Know what God does?" he says. "He sticks it to you. That's what my dad used to say. It's our job to take it and shut up."

I know something about Tate. I've seen how he watches Kendall. I don't want to know what he's thinking. It's another reason to get Kendall out of here. In the meantime, I'll use it.

"Kendall is with me on this," I say. "She thinks we can't do it without you."

I watch his thumb hover over the remote. It hits PLAY.

"Okay," he says.

Maudie and Eli agree because we're older and bigger and seem to know what we're talking about. Eli is used to being told what to do, and Maudie is afraid of being left behind.

It is Ruthanna who surprises me. When I tell her I have a plan to get us all out of here, I don't have to say another word. She lifts her head, her lank hair hanging in her eyes, and says, "My name is Erin. And I'll help."

It is Emily who is the problem. She listens to me lay out the plan, her face a blank.

"No," she says when I finish.

"But Emily . . ."

"He'll kill us," she says.

I exchange a look with Kendall.

"We'll protect you," I say.

"Easy to say. It's not you he wants."

Finally, I say the only thing I can say. "It's all decided. Everyone else has agreed. You'll be safer going along with us."

She looks at me, her face full of fear. But at least it isn't that blankness.

She doesn't say no.

So I take it as a yes.

THIRTY-THREE

Now it's time to tackle Torie and Jeff. If I can get one of them to agree, the other might cave. I decide Jeff will be first.

He flips around the music channels, MTV and BET, all afternoon. Usually with a plate of nachos or potato chips on his lap. The rest of them stay out of his way because if you get between him and the screen, you get yelled at or kicked at.

I sit down on the couch.

He looks over, surprised. No one except Torie ever joins him.

I watch TV with him for a while.

"Can you imagine what people would say if they knew about this?" I ask finally.

Jeff snorts. "Who cares?"

"Think about it. One billionaire, eleven kids, a house full of toys . . . They'd be killing each other to get camera crews in here."

"Yeah," he says. "It'd be wild."

"Katie Couric would be, like, salivating to get your number," I say. "Diane Sawyer would be sending you chocolates. Everybody wants an exclusive, right?"

Jeff doesn't say anything this time. It's a good sign.

"Geez, you think life is sweet in here, imagine what it would be like if you were on the cover of *People,* telling your story." I blow out a breath. "Sheesh."

"*People* magazine is lame," Jeff snorts.

"Of course, you wouldn't want to say too much, because there's the book deal, too. Or the TV movie. They always want to do a TV movie."

He looks at me. "What are you talking about?"

"Who do you think they're going to interview — weird Tate?" I say. "Eli? Ruthanna the mouse? No, they want the smart one. The one with charisma. The one who can tell the story so people will listen. The one who's telegenic."

This gets him thinking. He likes that he's telegenic. His gaze is shrewd now. "What's going on with you?"

"I have a way to get out," I tell him.

He laughs. "You have a death wish."

"It'll work. And once you're out, do you think you're going back on the streets? Into the system? I don't think so. You're going to be famous. The media can't leave this stuff alone. You'd have to play it right, not overexpose yourself. You'd have to be the spokesman of the group, say things right so that you're the one they want to interview. Do you know what a sound bite is?"

"Do you think I'm stupid? I know what it is."

"Sure you do. That's why you'll be the one they want. You know how to feed them the lines."

He drums his fingers on the couch. "What do you think you're going to do? Knock him out? Kill him?"

"We don't have to," I say. "We've got two things on our side. One: There's eleven of us and one of him. Two: He's crazy."

Jeff sniggers. "Tell me something I don't know."

Then he is quiet for a minute.

"So what's your big plan?" he asks casually, and I know I've got him.

Torie is flopped on a couch in the living area playing a Game Boy.

"Get lost," she tells me.

I sit. "I have a plan."

"Good for you. Get lost."

"I know how we can get out of here."

She slowly lowers the Game Boy. Her gaze is murderous. "You are so dead."

"Everyone else is in. Jeff, too," I say deliberately.

I see the tiniest vulnerability in her gaze. Jeff's defection hurts her.

"He wants to be on the cover of *People* magazine," I say.

She laughs. "Yeah. Good luck."

"Here's the insane part," I say. "He *will* be on the cover of *People*. So will you. If you want."

She returns her attention to the Game Boy.

"Everybody's scared," I say.

"Everybody's stupid."

"I think your mom was scared," I say.

Her thumbs stop.

"I think she'd finally found a safe place, and she couldn't give it up."

"What are you talking about?"

"Why she didn't support you when you said that about her boyfriend? About what he did. I think if you'd just hung around just a little more, she would have realized what was true."

She lowers the Game Boy. "I didn't tell anyone here about it. How . . ."

"I just know," I say. "I know the way I know that Jonah is cracking up. That Friday is the day he's been planning for a long time."

"What?"

"You didn't just leave your mom," I say. "You left a life. Friends. Your dad. You didn't even ask him to help."

"He's never helped me before," she mumbles.

"Maybe because you told him you hated him for leaving."

"How do you know this? Did you talk to my dad?"

I shrug. "I'm just telling you. He'll help you."

"What do you *know*?" she yells. Her eyes are dry, but I know the tears are there.

"Living on the street wasn't any better. And no matter what you think, living here isn't, either."

She looks away, biting her lip.

"There's one way to get through," I say. "Tell your story."

"I *told* my story. Nobody believed me."

"Tell it again," I say. "Till someone hears you."

"What if no one does, genius?"

"Someone will," I say. But that is something I can't see, no matter how hard I try.

THIRTY-FOUR

Thursday night is clear. I can see the stars overhead in the skylight. He is on what I've come to think of as his couch, looking through the photo album he's made of all of us. I am across the room on mine.

He passes his fingers across the photographs.

"I worked so hard," he says sadly. "The thing is, I can't let you go."

I take a beat, breathe. I wish like crazy for an adult to be here, someone who knows what they're doing. I have a sudden, immense respect for Dr. Julie Politsky. "I think you can," I say.

"They won't believe that I did a good job. That it all worked."

"We'll tell them," I say.

He brightens. "You'll explain?"

"Of course."

He considers this. Then he shakes his head. He shakes it over and over. "No. No. They still won't get it." He sits and clasps his hands.

"You ran onto the beach," I say, prompting him. "You were barefoot."

He looks up. The moon casts a bone-cold light on his face. "He wanted to bury Nell here. I couldn't let him do that. He wanted all of us, the children, to bury her. Even the little ones. To dig the grave. I couldn't let him do that. They were so scared. So I used the radio. I sent a distress signal."

"And he saw you."

"He chased me outside."

"Did he catch you?"

He looks up at the moon and doesn't answer. Then he reaches into his pocket, takes out his card, and enters something. Slowly, the skylights close. Now there is nothing but darkness. It's suddenly hard for me to breathe.

"I saw the flames from the beach," Jonah says dreamily. "I ran. When I got closer, I heard the pounding."

The pounding on the door. The father had locked them in.

"What did you do?"

"I broke the window. The ones in the front, they got out. It wasn't too bad yet. I was looking for you."

For Lizbet.

"Some of us got out. We all said it was an accident. To protect him. After that, we left the island. We moved up north, near the border."

He looks at me. "You understand, don't you? I had to show them how it's done. And they won't get it."

I see now. I thought the *they* he talked about had

been the public, the media, the world at large. But *they* are two particular people — his parents. He is trying to show his *parents* how to make a family.

"Here's the ironic thing," he says. "After all this, I see that he was right after all. I understand him now. I've lived his life. He couldn't bear to be separated from us. Isn't that the definition of a good father? I thought I could save you all by giving you love. But it's not enough. It won't keep us together. People grow up, you know. People disobey. People want to leave. Isn't that funny, that I forgot that? *I* was the one to disobey. *I* was the one who wanted to leave. I've come this far and I've made a circle. I've made a circle. But I can still make it right this time."

I understand it now. He blames himself for everything. For Nell's death, because he didn't send the distress signal soon enough. For the fire, because he sent the distress signal at all. He had pushed his father past desperation into madness. His father had set the fire and locked his family in, because he couldn't bear to have them taken away.

And now it's up to me. I've spent all day preparing for this moment.

"Nell never had a birthday party," I say.

"No."

"We should do that. We should give her a party this time. Do it right this time."

This catches him. He turns to me and his gaze is brighter.

"Yes," he says. "This time I'll get it right."

"She didn't want to say anything," I say. "You know how she is."

"Of course."

"We should do something."

"Well, of course, that's what we should do. We have to bake a cake!"

"Of course," I say.

"Frances will sing. And Tate will play guitar."

"Susannah and I will bake the cake."

"Cool!"

"And Eli and Maudie will make the decorations. A family celebration."

"I can't wait," he says. The look of childish anticipation on his face makes me turn away.

THIRTY-FIVE

Naturally, Torie is no help with baking the cake, but I find the recipe book and manage to do it. I even find birthday candles. Long ago, Jonah had stocked the closet with paper plates and party hats, but the kids say that they never celebrated birthdays before. If they remembered their birthdays, they kept it to themselves.

Tate sets up the projection screens in the dining room. Everything is ready to go.

Everyone has a job to do.

And now everything just has to go as planned.

This is our best shot.

Maybe our only shot.

Because if we fail . . . I don't want to think about if we fail.

It is four o'clock when we call the others to the table. It looks festive, with streamers and paper plates. Jonah has a party hat on. He pokes his head in the kitchen. "Is the cake ready?"

"Yes."

"Should I get Nell? I'll get her."

He ducks out again. He is sixteen again. He is

going to get his sister, to take her to the party she never had.

He is that far gone. He has no sense now of who we really are. He is in a place that is somewhere between the past and the present.

We turn out all the lights. Torie is ready in the kitchen, the others ready to run to the bedrooms and playroom. Hank is behind the door. Tate is ready by the computer.

Jonah leads her in. Emily looks terrified. Frozen.

"Come on," he says, urging her. "It's a surprise."

She shakes her head, not moving.

"Get in there," Torie hisses to me. "The wacko is going to blow it."

I burst in with the cake. We sing "Happy Birthday." I try to give Emily courage with my gaze, but hers keeps sliding away.

Tate flips on the projections. The screens light up with a summer rainstorm. The rain is rhythmic. It would be soothing, but Tate has pumped up the volume.

Jonah stops singing. "Stop it! Stop it!" he shouts. "Turn off the rain!"

Tate turns up the volume.

"No!" Jonah yells.

Emily is supposed to take his hand now. That was the plan. She doesn't do it.

Hank moves toward Jonah. Emily remains standing still. She covers her ears with her hands as Jonah yells to turn down the rainstorm.

"Now!" I yell, and we scatter.

We all count in our heads as we run. One. Two. Three. Four. Five. They are running to the computers, to the space heaters in the bathrooms. I run to the dishwasher, Torie to the two ovens. Six. Seven. Eight. Jonah is shouting, but it's just noise now. Nine. Ten.

At the same moment, we flip on everything we can. Torie cranks the oven to five hundred degrees and switches on all the burners. I switch on the dishwasher to its hottest setting. Maudie has started the three dryers. In the bathrooms, the heaters are on, the blow-dryers for the girls' hair. In the playrooms, the TVs, the computers, the stereo.

The generator blows.

We are plunged into darkness.

I push open the door to the dining area. I can see faintly by the light coming from the skylight in the living room. Jonah is whirling, shouting. Emily has dropped to the floor, out of sight, rolled into a ball. Hank is moving, dressed in black jeans and a black T-shirt, almost invisible. I see the gleam of his hand as he slips it into Jonah's front pocket. Emily was supposed to prevent Jonah from grabbing Hank by distracting him, but she didn't. Jonah turns, but he doesn't feel Hank's hand, he just sees him.

"What are you doing?" he says to Hank. "Where's Nell?"

Hank hands off the card to Jeff and they are running now, running toward the front door.

"Where are you going? It's her party! What's happening?" Jonah screams.

I run forward and drop to the floor. *"Go,"* I tell Emily.

She is frozen. She shakes her head.

"Emily, listen." I plead. I grab her face. *"We have something to go back to."*

Her expression changes slightly, but her arms are still locked around her legs. She ducks her head down.

I physically push down her legs, unwind her arms. I scream for Kendall. Together, we pull Emily out from under the table.

"Go," I say, pushing her.

And somehow her legs move, and she goes, Kendall half-pulling her.

The other kids are running to the front door, where Jeff is swiping the lock. There is a backup generator, but I know it takes a few minutes to kick on. Maybe five. Maybe more if we're lucky.

I run to the front door. Hank puts the card in my hand. Jeff is already out the door with Torie.

Hank looks hesitant. "I'll come with you."

"No. You have to get them on the boat. If I'm not there in five minutes, just go."

"Gracie . . ."

I can hear Jonah behind me, bellowing like an animal. He is tearing the house apart, looking for Emily. Looking for Nell in order to save her again.

I will be alone in the house with him. The fear of that is in my mouth, in my stomach. I've never felt so afraid.

"Go," I say to Hank, and push him out the door.

THIRTY-SIX

I run through the dark house, dodging the furniture. I race down the hallway toward the door to Jonah's wing. He is in the playroom. I tell myself I have time enough to do this.

My hands are shaking so badly that I can't swipe the card. I fumble and drop it. I hear him move from the playroom into the big living area. I swipe the card, and the light glows green. I push the door open.

I run down a short hallway. His bedroom door is open. There is a twin bed with a blanket, a chest of drawers, and a wall crammed with computer equipment. Hank has told me where the panel is. I race to it and swipe the card, getting it right the first time. The light shifts to green and I open the panel.

My fingers scrabble down the neatly lettered spaces.

SECURITY WALL. I turn the switch from ON to OFF.

BOATHOUSE SECURITY. OFF.

His arms are suddenly around me, around my waist, and he lifts me up as though I am a doll and throws me. I land hard on my knees. He drags me by one arm. I am screaming at him to stop, the pain is so bad in my arm, but he's not hearing me. His gaze is cloudy; his face is red with panic and rage.

Suddenly, he throws himself down on the rug next to me. I smell smoke again, but this time I know it's real.

"Lizbet," he says, curling up next to me, holding me down with one arm. "This time I won't leave you."

The generator kicks in, and the lights come on. I see his face, his unseeing eyes. I cringe when he strokes my hair.

I get a flash of his stroking his sister's hair. They are lying on the floor, waiting to die.

Smoke is in the room, and Lizbet is coughing.

Suddenly, Jonah raises his head.

He tries to pull Lizbet, but she slumps down.

He sees something — a light? He crawls toward it.

And I am back again here, with my head on the rug, and Jonah's hand on my head.

A moment ago, all that was in my mind was a scream. I couldn't focus or think. Now I know the only way out of this is to think.

"You left me last time," I say.

He ducks his head to my shoulder. "I'm sorry. I came back inside to get you. I didn't realize it would be so bad. I had to get out. This time I won't leave without you. This time I'll do it right."

That's it, I think. I have it now. This time, he won't be the one to get out. Getting it right means he'll stay with Lizbet. Stay in the fire.

"Let's go out together," I say. I can't see the fire, I can't feel it, but I can smell it and the panic is shivering up my legs.

He raises his head and looks into my face tenderly. "I won't leave you."

"Jonah, please," I beg. "Please."

"You are my family," he says. "Let's just go to sleep."

The smoke is in my lungs now.

I press my face down as far as I can, to find air.

I can't breathe.

I cough and cough. My lungs are filling up with blood.

My lungs are filling up with smoke.

Smoke and blood.

My mother is dying.

Lizbet is dying.

I am dying.

They burst back in the room then, all the kids, every one of them. My face is pushed into the carpet.

I'm coughing, but there is no smoke in the room.

But the smell is real. The fire is in another part of the house.

Torie grabs Jonah's arm, Hank grabs the other, Jeff grabs him by the neck, and all together they pull him off me. He kicks and screams like a child, bawling, his face red, but they manage to hold him back until I'm on my feet.

They drop him, and we run for the door. He's on his knees, struggling to get up.

Somehow we scramble through the door. Smoke is hanging in the living area. We run to the front door.

The fresh air is a relief. It is a surprise to me to see that the sun is shining. That seems the strangest thing of all.

The door is open in the wall, and we race through it. He is still running after us, running across the beach barefoot, as we reach the boat-house door. They've propped it open, they were smart. We race down the dock, jump into the boat.

Torie gets behind the wheel. "Does anyone know how to drive this thing?"

He's on the deck now, pounding toward us. "Don't go!" he roars. "Don't go! Please!"

Tate jumps into the pilot seat and turns the key that is dangling from the lock. He does something else and the boat begins to move. Jonah jumps from the deck, his arms whirling, his legs pumping. We feel his hands slap the boat and then the boat is moving and he goes under.

Jonah appears above the water. The wake of the boat slaps him in the face. His mouth is open, sucking in air, sobbing.

He howls.

His gaze locks on mine. "You're my *family*!" he shouts.

"I have a family," I whisper as the boat chugs out to the open sea.

THIRTY-SEVEN

This time, it is me who hears the footsteps, hears the sob that escapes despite the hand pressed against it, trying to hold it in. I lay awake, listening, as Shay moves down the hall. The door squeaks as she enters the kitchen. I can't hear the birds yet, but I can just make out the trees outside my window.

I've been back for a week now. A week of eating and sleeping and not answering the phone. Shay took the week off from work. It's the biggest story to hit Seattle since . . . well, since anyone can remember.

There was a compass on board, so we headed east, hoping we'd bump into land before we ran out of gas. We saw the ferry before they saw us, and we found the flares in the emergency kit. At first, it was just logistics. Calling parents, getting back to Seattle. Then the media storm broke on us the next day. We woke up famous.

Emily's parents took her away, down south to Rocky's sister in Portland. Torie and Jeff have been on *Good Morning America,* the *Today* show, and I hear they'll be on the cover of *People* next week. They are heroes. The oldest kids who protected the rest of us. They are getting everything they wanted, and I wish them well with celebrity. Somehow I doubt they'll be able to handle it.

All the rest of the kids have landed back at home — like Kendall — or in social services — like Tate.

They found Jonah waiting on the beach, sitting barefoot, staring out to sea, the house still smoking behind him.

He had started out with street kids. Maybe in the beginning he was really trying to help them. Torie and Jeff were the first. Then he started contacting kids on the Internet. He'd make sure they answered him in cyber-cafés and didn't tell their parents. When he found out that Emily had written him on her computer, he'd made her take it with her when she came to meet him. Because Beewick Island was so small, he wiped the library computers himself. Emily let him into Rocky's and he wiped Zed's computer, too, because Emily had used it. He had gotten sloppy with Emily, because she could be traced through the computer camp, and Kendall had already disappeared. So he asked his publicity department to remove her from the photos, just in case one got into the Seattle papers and triggered a link.

The board of Jonah's company has hired the best defense team in the country, and it looks like they'll plead the insanity defense.

I told Shay and Diego all about it, or about most of it. I couldn't tell them the way Jonah ate away at my insides, the way he made me hurt. But I think they knew. Diego got in about fifty pounds of trouble for taking me to the park that day. I don't think Shay had forgiven him until I came back.

I don't think Diego had forgiven himself, either. It turned out that one of those three-year-olds in the park had gotten lost and hysterical, and by the time Diego returned the little boy to one of the nature walk instructors, I was gone.

I think Shay must have lost ten pounds while I was away, and she doesn't even mention it. I'll never forget the look on her face when she walked into the room at the Seattle police station. I'll never forget how she held me, like I belonged to her, like losing me would have killed her. I didn't know she felt that way.

I swing my legs over the bed. I pad outside to the kitchen. Shay is sitting at the kitchen table with a wadded up tissue in her hand. She's staring out at the darkness. A pot of milk is on the stove on a low flame.

"So did you and Mom become blonds?" I ask, sitting down.

Shay's eyes are red-rimmed. Her mouth is taut from crying, from trying not to cry. I see raw grief on her face, and it stuns me. She's been hiding it from me, I realize. She didn't want to add to mine.

She had let me know, in a thousand ways, how much she missed my mom, but she never let me see her pain. I'm not sure if that was the right way to go, but I understand.

She clears her throat. "Carrie looked fantastic. Like she'd spent a month in the sun. I wanted to look just like her, so I left it on too long. It came out sort of platinum, and not in a good way. So we tried to dye it back, and it sort of looked greenish. So she looks at me, and she says, 'Maybe we should try on hats.' I just remember lying on the bathroom floor, laughing so hard. She could laugh so hard . . ."

"She would totally lose control."

Shay looks down at her hands. "You know, I just remembered this. I said something about how we'd have to learn to dye our own hair because we'd have to get rid of the gray when we got older, and Carrie said, 'I'll never have gray hair.' She said it totally seriously. I thought she meant she'd be lucky. But now I wonder if . . ."

"If she knew she'd never get old. If she was . . . like me."

"Maybe that's why she was always in such a hurry to live her life."

I absorb this. I wonder what it would be like, feeling that you wouldn't live long. I realize there are parts to my mom that I didn't know, deep parts, quirky parts. It's not just my memories that define her. Shay lost her, too. I want to hear those memories now. Now I'm ready to listen.

Shay gets up and pours out the hot milk. She's made enough for two, just in case.

"Do you ever . . . sense her?" she asks. I can tell this is hard for her to get out. And I can tell how badly she wants me to say yes.

"No," I say. "It doesn't work that way. There's absolutely nothing good about being psychic that I can see. It's a curse."

She takes a sharp, indrawn breath as she breaks up the chocolate into two mugs and brings them to the table. Then she pours in the milk. We stir, our spoons gently tinkling.

"You got ten kids out of hell because of it. That's good."

"It almost didn't happen that way."

"But it did." Shay blows on her drink. "You can use it. Not let it use you. That's all I'm saying."

We take a sip at the same moment, and swallow.

"Do you still get flashes of him?" Shay asks.

I shake my head firmly. "Not new ones." The memory of what he had done and seen is enough to keep me awake at night. The memories of the kids I tapped into gave me a glimpse into a world I didn't want to know, a place where love had withered at its root.

It's going to take me time.

"Loss can stretch you into a new shape," Shay

says. "Jonah was handed too much, and he didn't have the foundation to handle it. He couldn't find a way to live that made sense."

I take my first sip. I like it like this, when the chocolate has just started to melt, when I taste milk and just the beginning of the sweetness.

"You'll always be sad, Gracie," Shay says. "That doesn't mean you'll never be happy."

"Yeah," I say.

The light is changing. It is blue, bluer than blue. We hear the birds begin to squawk.

"By the way," I tell her, "Joe Fusilli has a crush on you."

A small smile curves her lips. "Yeah?"

She props her bare feet up on the sill. I put my feet next to hers. I remember the day I stared at her feet and transferred all my hatred onto her toes. Now I see how her foot is shaped like mine, how her toes are all almost the same size, like mine. I hold the warm cup cradled against my chest. In his loony way, Jonah was right about something.

You just can't get away from family.

DISAPPEARANCE

For Ric
rest in peace, baby

When she hands me my change,
I feel a pain that lives inside her,
a restlessness that won't go away.
Two days later, Susan Reilly abandons
her husband and children and runs
away to Las Vegas. For good.

When he takes my spaghetti order, I know
the waiter is worried that his wife is
cheating on him.
She is.

I can feel what people want . . . and
what they're willing to do to get it.

What if you could feel what other people
felt . . . and it was unbearable?

What if you saw what was going to
happen . . . and you couldn't stop it?
What if that something was murder?

ONE

I should have known that Saturday afternoon would turn out to be a disaster. And believe me, when I say I should have known, *I should have known*.

It all begins with a girl called Marigold. She's the inexplicable love object of my cousin Diego. I guess her gorgeousness makes up for a certain lack of charisma. For Diego, that is. For the rest of us, we just have to deal with trying to make conversation with someone with the personality of plankton. Diego has dated just about every pretty girl on the island of Beewick, and he's made inroads onto the mainland, even as far as Seattle. But Marigold, for some reason, knocked him stupid.

Well, she *is* a knockout, in that long-blond-hair, long-legged, blue-eyed category that makes other girls want to either be her best friend or poison her caffeine-free chai.

So when Diego asks me that Saturday afternoon in November if I want to hang with them and Marigold's brother, I should say no, considering that Marigold's conversation sends me into a coma and I consider her brother about as appetizing as brussels sprouts.

I look at Diego and Marigold for a minute while I make up my mind. I know I should be concentrating on answering, but I'm thinking about how beautiful people just naturally click together, like magnets. Maybe it's just as simple as that. Diego is tall and lean and so handsome that once I saw a waitress drop an entire tray of glasses when he walked into a restaurant.

Marigold is leaning against Diego, and she has a hand in the back pocket of his jeans. It's another thing that bugs me about her. She's always leaning against him, as though she can't stand up by herself.

Marigold flashes her halogen smile. "Come on, Gracie. This is Washington State. You've got to grab the sunshine while you can."

You see? Pick the most obvious thing, and she'll say it.

"Yeah," Diego says. "Pretty soon it will be January and the sun will be on semipermanent hiatus."

Marigold laughs as if that's the funniest thing she's ever heard.

"Okay," I say.

Well, what else was I going to do? Homework?

We take off in Diego's old VW, the one he bought with his landscaping money from the summer. The windows are open, because it's such an amazing day, so I can't hear the conversation in the front seat. Which is good, because Marigold is talking. The hum of tires on the road is far more riveting.

So I look at the scenery, which is not exactly a hardship. I moved from Maryland to the Pacific Northwest only last year, after my mother was killed in a car crash. My aunt Shay took me in. Now I live on an island off the coast of Washington State, in Puget Sound.

I hated Beewick Island when I first got here. It was February, and February is not the best month here. There's a permanent drizzle, and it's cold, yet you don't get the benefits of snow. But after about nine months here, I realize why, when you ask a Pacific Northwesterner the best thing about living here, they say "the weather." It's no joke. It's just our secret, that if you can get past the winter rain, the rest of the year is not too hot, not too cold. You can practically live outside.

Beewick is about an hour north of Seattle, if you drive really fast. The island is almost a hundred miles long but only a few miles wide, with wicked cliffs on the north end and gentle farmland on the south. The sky seems higher here, and bluer. Off to the west are the snowcapped Olympic Mountains. Sometimes they just seem like clouds on the horizon, and then on clear days they startle you with their presence. The Sound is the color of blueberries, and there are fields of farmland and lavender. It's a pretty nice place to live, and it is a tribute to my stubbornness that it took me close to six months to admit it.

We drive into Greystone Harbor, the closest town to us, and Diego pulls into a space outside the Harborside restaurant.

"We're going here?" I ask.

"They have the best fried clams," Marigold says.

Maybe he won't be here. Maybe it's his day off. But I see Zed's faded red Subaru parked in the lot, and I know he's here. It's hard facing the person you put in jail for kidnapping when he didn't do a thing. It really is.

Last summer, my friend Emily disappeared. I'd had a vision, and it had seemed to connect to Zed. By the time I'd figured out that the kidnapper wasn't Zed, the police had nailed him for tackling me and demanding why, exactly, I was going around saying he was guilty.

Oops is not up there on a list of acceptable apologies for this.

The thing I can't admit, hardly even to myself, is that I still think about the moment he tackled me and we rolled down the hill, how his chest felt so solid, how his breath felt against my skin. I was terrified at the time, but now I can look back and dissect every detail. Which I do. Frequently.

I am *so* glad there isn't another me around to see my thoughts.

I tag after Diego and Marigold into the

restaurant. Marigold's twin brother, Mason, is already here with a table full of his friends. They're all jocks, on the swimming team and the soccer team, and most of them aren't too awful. I just feel like I'm disappearing when I'm around them. I'm not the kind of girl they notice. I'm short, and I have brown hair and brown eyes and a devotion to gray sweaters. Not exactly a head turner.

Zed is waiting tables, and he looks up and sees me. This would be a lot easier if he weren't so good-looking. He has silvery-gray eyes and black hair he cut short over the summer. He looks startled to see me, as if he can't believe I have the nerve to show up in his father's place. Zed works here and in Seattle, at a glassblower's studio. We've seen each other since that whole thing last summer, of course — we live only a mile from Greystone Harbor, and it's a small town — but we've always managed to just nod at each other and look away.

Mason yells at us to hurry up, he wants to order, and Marigold and Diego head over.

"Hey, everybody, you know Gracie, Diego's cousin," Marigold says. "Gracie, everyone." The guys all look at me and say "hey," or slurp their sodas.

Marigold sits down on an empty chair next to Mason. Diego sits next to her. The only other chair is at the other end of the table, next to Dylan Brewer, one of Mason's friends. I go and sit there.

This is going to be fun, I can just feel it. All the thrills of a filling without novocaine.

They immediately launch into a discussion of some college football game that's going to be on tomorrow afternoon. That doesn't stop them from dissecting what is going to happen and who is going to totally rock.

It makes you think. Here I am, somebody who can occasionally see things that are going to happen. But when it comes to who's going to win a football game or have the winning lottery number, I'm totally useless.

I watch as Marigold takes a sip of her diet soda and offers the straw to Diego. Everyone orders fried clams, including me, even though I'm not crazy about fried clams. But I can't quite meet Zed's eyes when he takes the order. Still, he hesitates next to me. I stare at the silver ring he wears on his thumb.

"So, how've you been?" he says.

I look up. I feel ice crack and the earth turn. I realize, at that very moment, at long last, that Zed does not hold a grudge. Relief washes through me.

"Okay," I say.

"Good."

This dazzling display of conversational skill ends when Zed nods a good-bye. He tucks the order pad into the back waistband of his pants, which in my addled state I find an incredibly cool move. Then he heads into the kitchen.

The platters of food arrive quickly, which I'm happy about, because I haven't been able to think of a single thing to say while we were waiting. Nobody noticed, though. Mason and his friends have moved on from football to soccer. These kinds of guys can only talk about sports. I think it's a kind of primitive form of communication for guys, like gorillas making hand signals. Diego and Marigold are having an intense conversation by themselves. It looks like they could be arguing, but I try not to feel hopeful about the possibility.

I eat a couple of clams dunked in lots of cocktail sauce, and most of my fries, while sneaking glances at Zed waiting on tables. Occasionally, he'll smile at a customer, and it's worth waiting for.

Then Mason's friends start making fun of a couple at the next table. They're eating the Greystone oysters that Beewick Island is known for and looking out at the blue sweep of bay, and you can take one look at them and know they're from Seattle. Not that there's anything wrong with Seattle. But they look pretty rich and they're wearing pressed khakis and cashmere sweaters that are pretending to be sweatshirts, and Mason starts to goof on them.

"I'll have the plucky little Chardonnay, muffin, how about you?" he says.

Totally lame, but his buddies all guffaw.

Mason and his friends are the kind of goons

who think that because they're lucky enough to have lived all their lives on a beautiful island in Puget Sound they get to make fun of the weekenders. It's true that real estate prices have been zooming lately, and that more and more land is being gobbled up for development. But I don't think this couple from Seattle, out to have a nice seafood lunch on a Saturday, deserves to get heckled for it.

Meanwhile, Marigold is feeding Diego a French fry. I guess they made up.

I don't think the couple heard what Mason said, but somehow they know the snickers rolling across the room are directed at them. Zed turns, and I see his face darken. He strides over to our table. I wonder if I can assume the molecular structure of a chair and disappear completely. Zed thinks I'm friends with these cretins.

He rips the check off his pad.

"Whoa, dude," Mason says. "You didn't ask about dessert."

"You want dessert?" Zed asks. "There's a great ice cream parlor across the street. Our pies suck." He drops the check on the table and walks away.

"Whoa," Mason says. "Touchy Waiter Boy thinks we're rude."

"Yeah, you're upsetting the clientele, Patterson," Dylan says. Mason and his friends usually call each other by their last names, which is kind of funny because most of them have last names for first names anyway.

Andy Hassam pushes away his plate. "We should push their cars off the ferry, man. All we get from them is traffic and garbage. Pretty soon we won't be able to eat our own oysters. The water will be too polluted."

Everyone knows why Andy hates the weekenders and the new summer people. His family owns a farm. Last year they had to sell a chunk of their land to a developer, who built a whole bunch of houses on the site. Nobody is happy about it. Hassam's farm stand is a local institution. They have hayrides in the fall and a pumpkin field. Now, instead of overlooking fields of farmland and meadows, it's going to overlook a bunch of BMWs.

"What are you talking about? You don't even like oysters, man. You call them snot on a shell," Dylan says, hooting at Andy.

Andy flushes red. "And what are you talking about, Brewer? You've only lived on Beewick for five minutes."

"Try four years, dude," Dylan shoots back.

"Try all my life, dudette," Andy says.

"I didn't know this was a contest."

Mason's eyes gleam. "Whoa. Do you two need to take this outside?"

"Knock it off, Patterson," Andy mumbles.

"No, I mean *really* outside," Mason says. "On

the deck. Speaking of contests, I have a way to prove who's a true Beewick Islander."

Dylan looks intrigued, but Andy looks like he wants to go home and bond with his Game Cube. Marigold and Diego finally look up from their deep and boring conversation to notice what's going on around them.

"If you're really an islander, you know the tides," Mason says. "You should be able to gauge whether you can dive off the deck safely or not."

Andy looks green. "Dive off the deck?"

"Hey, Mason," Diego says. "Not such a great idea, dude."

"I think it's awesome," Brewer says. "My brother told me that guys used to dive off the decks of all the restaurants on this strip every Groundhog Day."

"It was extreme radical stuff," Mason says. "They called it The Gauntlet. You had to dive off at least three to be a member of the club."

"And they stopped doing it because it was too dangerous," Diego points out. "Somebody broke his leg."

"Which is, like, my point," Mason says. "If you're a real islander, you can figure out if you can do it by watching the water."

"Listen to Diego, Mason," Marigold says.

If Mason had been half-fooling before, now he's committed. You don't have to be psychic to see that he isn't about to let his sister's boyfriend tell him what to do.

"Let's go, dudes," Mason says, pushing back his chair.

Dylan stands up, and Andy has no choice. Diego shakes his head.

I look around for Zed, but he must be in the kitchen. By the time I turn around again, Mason, Dylan, and Andy are outside on the deck, and Dylan is kicking off his shoes.

Suddenly, the room whites out.

Water foaming, arms thrashing . . .

Panic. Fear. A heart bursting, everything bursting. Everything is red now and through the red I see a body falling through murky water.

When I return to where I am, I see that Dylan is looking over the railing. Diego is trying to talk to him. He puts a hand on his arm, but Dylan shakes it off.

I stand up so quickly, I knock my chair over. Across the room, Zed looks over.

"Zed!" I call. "You have to stop him!"

Zed looks out the window to the deck. He slams the tray onto the nearest table and starts to sprint across the dining room. The couple from Seattle look up from their wine.

I run behind Zed, but we're too late. Before we can get there, Dylan hoists himself up on the deck rail, balances for a split second, and dives. Diego shouts, and Mason laughs, and Marigold screams.

We all race to the railing and look over. I can see a white shape under the water, but then it's gone. Ripples are absorbed into the current. It was like Dylan was never even there.

"Diego," I whisper.

"Call 9-1-1," Diego tells Zed.

"Just wait a second," Mason says. "Brewer's laughing at us, man. He'll come up. He's on the swim team."

Diego gives Mason a look that says you-are-the-biggest-idiot-in-the-known-universe, but Mason doesn't see it.

"Come *up,* Dylan!" Marigold shouts.

And then Dylan shoots out of the water, screaming. His eyes are wild, and he strokes toward the beach, shouting. A wash of water hits him in the face, and he chokes.

At first we can't make it out. And then when we hear it, we can't believe what we hear.

"There's a body down there!"

TWO

"I touched it. I touched it."

Dylan sits shivering under a blanket Zed brought out from the restaurant. The police cars are parked in crazy angles on the street. A bunch of officers are talking behind the yellow POLICE LINE DO NOT CROSS tape. Dylan looks as gray as the water. Clouds have formed, blocking the sun, and the wind has picked up. Mason and his friends sit with him, but they don't know what to say for once. Every now and then, one of them mumbles, "Hang in there, dude."

The police divers are just beginning to search when a dark-blue sedan pulls into the Harborside parking lot. Joe Fusilli gets out. I am glad to see him. Joe is a police detective, and he dates my aunt Shay, and I totally believe he will make sense of this situation and demonstrate to Dylan that he touched an old beach ball, or a sunken buoy, not a dead body.

Because I don't want to remember the vision I saw.

Because now I know the vision hadn't been of Dylan Brewer. Deep inside, I know I saw the drowning of that poor body in the bay.

I know it's a man.

I know he fought to live. I know he fought very hard.

Joe looks annoyed to see that we're there. He raises his eyebrows at me for a hello and goes to talk to the police officers.

"Maybe we should leave," Diego says.

"Yeah," I say. We don't move.

I would have thought Marigold would go into hysterics — she definitely seems like a hysterics sort of girl — but she hasn't said much, just looked out at the bay and huddled close to Diego.

"Are you okay?" Diego asks her in a low voice.

She looks up at him and nods bravely, like she was the one who found the body.

A small crowd has gathered in the parking lot. In a small town, word travels fast.

Mason appoints himself the official spokesman. He fills in the passing pedestrians and the waiters from the Crab Shack next door, gradually adding more disgusting details about how the body felt when Dylan's foot hit it.

Most of the people have somewhere to get to and leave after a few minutes, but Joy Elliott, our town librarian, is hanging right in there, watching the cops and the divers in the water. It's clear that dead bodies don't spook her.

Franklin and Jefferson Ferris walk up. They are father and son and own Founders Realty in

Greystone Harbor. Franklin Ferris is about a hundred years old. He's wearing a suit, even though it's Saturday. Jeff is about Shay's age, and he looks like a Before picture of his dad, except in casual mode, wearing a tweed jacket and khakis. I think both Ferrises have an extreme case of If Only We Were Brits.

Joy sees them and jerks her head around, and Jeff makes the same maneuver, swiveling his head and looking straight at us, as if she isn't there. I remember that they dated for a while, and now they can't stand being around each other. Sometimes small towns can get really, really small.

"Look, son," Franklin says. "Ten of our fair town's citizens. Must be a parade."

"Hey, Dylan. Hey, Mason. Whatssup?" Jeff Ferris is one of those adults who thinks using slang is going to make us like them.

Mason fills him in on the police action. "Hey, coach," he says. Jeff also coaches part-time at Beewick High. "Dylan here did an awesome dive; you would have been proud. Except that he bumped into a dead body."

Jeff looks a little green. "Dead body?" He must be thinking how it will impact his real estate business. Diego and I joke about Jeff all the time, because he lives for his work. Every time he sees us, he says, "How's the house doing?" as though Shay's house is a person. He sold it to her when she first came to Beewick about twenty years ago. We always say, "Still standing," just like Shay does.

"A floater," Joy says. She pushes her red glasses up her nose as she looks out at the bay, watching the divers. "Even though it's not floating. That's what the police call a drowned body."

"Charming," Jeff says. "Thanks."

Joy's neck flushes red.

"What an excellent way to begin lunch," Franklin Ferris says. "Come on, Jeff. A dozen Greystones are waiting."

Jeff swallows, as if the thought of oysters at the moment is just about the most unappetizing thing he could imagine. I have to say I agree.

The Ferrises head into the Harborside, Jeff sneaking looks at the bay. Joy looks at her watch and heads off reluctantly.

Marigold shivers. "Imagine eating lunch while they drag the harbor for a body."

"They're not dragging it," I say. "They know where it is. And we were eating lunch while it was down there."

"We don't need the details, Gracie," Diego says to me.

The divers surface for the third time. There's a flurry of activity among the cops. They talk into radios. They walk from one group to another. Joe goes to his car and comes back again.

It seems to take forever, but Joe finally walks over to us.

"You kids should take off," he says.

"That's okay," Mason says. "We —"

Joe hits him with one of his level gazes. Joe isn't a handsome guy, although Shay probably thinks so. He has a thin, drawn face and a big nose, and he looks as though he might sleep two hours a night, if he's lucky. But he does have one terrific pair of brown eyes. They can warm you or slice you up like provolone. He used to be a detective in Seattle, and he's got a certain big-city coolness about him, like he's seen just about everything there is to see.

"You kids should take off," he says again. He looks down at Dylan. "Did you call your parents?"

Dylan is too freaked to even mind that he needs his parents called. He nods. "My dad is picking me up. Was it . . . was it . . ."

"It was a body," Joe says. He takes in Dylan's look of panic. "The first time is hard," he says to Dylan. It's the right approach, like Dylan is a cop, too. "I puked."

"You're not going to puke, are you, man?" Mason asks, taking a step back.

Dylan shakes his head. "I don't think so."

"Listen," Joe says, "I know this was hard. But the good part is that somewhere a wife or a mother or a brother is going to know what happened to someone they love. That's going to help."

"I didn't think of that," Dylan says.

"And you'll have so much cred at school," Mason says. "You touched a dead body, dude!"

Joe gives him a look of such withering scorn that even Mason is cowed. "Considering the circumstances, I'm not going to bust any of you today," Joe says. "But if I ever hear of someone diving off the deck of a restaurant again, I'm bypassing the ticket and throwing you in jail."

Just then, a pickup truck roars into the parking lot.

Dylan looks relieved. "That's my dad."

"I'll talk to him." Joe walks over and speaks quietly to Mr. Brewer, who just keeps nodding at Joe and shooting glances out to the gray bay and then back at his son. He looks totally freaked. Finally, Dylan hands the blanket back to Zed and goes off with his father. The rest of the guys get into Mason's car.

Zed stands, holding the blanket against his chest. "I really have to get inside."

"Thanks for everything," I say.

"I didn't do anything." Zed frowns. "I should have stopped him from diving."

"You can't stop that pea brain from anything," Diego says. "Come on, Gracie. Let's go home."

I say good-bye to Zed, and Joe walks us to the car.

"Are they . . . going to bring it up now?" I ask.

"Yeah," Joe says. "You really don't want to be here. Trust me."

Marigold shudders. "I just want to go home."

Diego and Marigold get in the car, but I hesitate, my hand on the door handle. "It's a man, isn't it?"

"How do you know?"

Because I saw him thrashing. Because I felt his fear.

"Because you said a wife would be worrying."

"He drowned, most likely. Got snagged on some old lobster traps on the bottom."

"But it's so late in the year to go swimming. We barely even swim in the summertime, the water is so cold."

"Some do, though. They underestimate the cold. Probably happened over on the beach and the tides took him."

Joe sighs deeply, and I know what he's thinking. He's going to have to bring the news to somebody, somewhere. Somebody who loved this man.

I hear his voice in my head, *I hope he doesn't have kids.*

"He doesn't have kids," I say.

Joe looks startled. Then he sighs. "I really wish," he says, "you wouldn't do that."

When it comes to Joe's belief in my psychic ability, the jury is out. He no longer thinks I'm a liar, thanks to the fact that I ended up following my visions straight to a kidnapper. Of course the crazy kidnapper kidnapped me, too, but it all worked out in the end. But Joe doesn't quite believe in me, either. He thinks I have "a special sensitivity" or "good instincts." He doesn't like to believe in something he can't understand. Can't blame him for that.

"See you later," I say. I get in the car. When I twist around in the seat, Joe is still standing there staring as we pull away.

"Call me later," Marigold says. She has already gotten out, but she walks over to Diego's side to talk to him through the window. She leans in and kisses him. Again. I look out the window the other way.

"I'm sorry about before," she whispers.

"We'll work it out," he says.

"'Bye, Gracie," Marigold calls. She walks into her house at last. Diego doesn't pull out until she stands at the open doorway and waves again, then closes the door.

"Should I check your pulse?" I say. "Do you think you can survive until you see her again?"

Diego doesn't even get irritated at me. He grins. "You'll know what it's like someday, Gracie, and then I'll be laughing at you."

"I doubt it." I try to imagine myself hanging on Zed's every word. I can't. I like him, but really, there are limits. "So what was she apologizing for?"

"We're having a difference of opinion," Diego says as he pulls out onto the main road. "She doesn't want me to go to Costa Rica."

Diego put off college for a year. He's working now, but he's going to quit in February and go to Costa Rica with a relief youth group that helps villagers build houses. He'll stay for four months. He's been looking forward to it since he signed up.

"Why not?" I ask, even though I can guess the answer.

He shrugs. "She thinks when you have something good, you ride it out. You don't bail."

"You're not bailing. You have a life."

"She knows that. It's just hard for her. I'll be leaving right when her senior year heats up. The prom and everything."

"Oh, now I see," I say. "Villagers should go homeless so Marigold Patterson can have the date she wants for her prom."

"That's not what I meant." Diego shoots me a look. "She's not an airhead, even though you try to pretend she is. And what do you think you're doing, flirting with Zed? He's too old for you."

"He's nineteen."

"Exactly. You're fifteen."

"I'm sixteen!"

"You're a young sixteen."

"You're dating Marigold, and she's still in high school."

"Yeah, but she's eighteen."

"If I were you, I'd concentrate on my own love life," I say. "I don't criticize Marigold to you."

"No, you just sigh and roll your eyes all the time. You make your opinion pretty clear."

"Well, you obviously need an intervention. She's culted you."

"That's not even a word."

"No, but it's a fact," I say. "It's just like you're in some kind of weird Marigold-worshipping cult. You can't admit that anything is wrong with her."

"You don't like her because she's beautiful," he says. "She can't help that."

"And her brother is an idiot," I grouse.

"I can't argue with that one. But she can't help that, either. Look, I'm not asking you to like her," Diego says sharply. "I'm just asking you to shut up."

"Then you can shut up about Zed, too," I say. This is a weird conversation. In a way, it makes me feel kind of good, because it's a step forward that we're close enough to tell each other to shut up. But in another way, we're still telling each other to shut up.

When I first moved in with Diego and Shay, I was an extremely unpleasant person to be around. I was scared and angry, and mostly afraid of trusting anyone, even my relatives. I thought that my grandparents, who had been taking care of me, just unloaded me on my aunt. What I didn't know was that my aunt had fought to have me.

I'm better now. Part of that is because Diego has been incredibly cool to me, and Shay has really made me feel at home. You know somewhere is home when you start trying to get out of doing the dishes and somebody says, "No way, weasel." The minute Diego started to tease me, I knew things would be okay.

Diego pulls into the driveway. Another car is parked there, a beige Volvo that I don't recognize.

"Did Shay say we were having a guest for dinner?" I ask.

"No, but you never know with her," Diego says. "She lives to feed."

The front door opens, as if someone has been waiting for us. A man walks out. He's tall and handsome, about Shay's age, with dark hair and eyes. I wonder if Shay is two-timing Joe, but I can't imagine that, because every time he leaves, she closes the door, leans against it, and says, "I'm smitten."

"Who's that?" I ask Diego.

"No idea."

I open the door and get out. The man walks toward me. There is something about his face that I know.

I begin to feel really, really nervous.

He stops a few yards away. Behind him, Shay

appears in the doorway. She lifts a hand like a traffic cop. Is she waving at us, or trying to stop him?

"Gracie?" he says.

"Yeah?" I say.

"It's Dad," he says.

"Whose dad?" I say. I'm trying to process what he's saying, and then I know, with a sick feeling in my stomach. It's *my* dad.

The dad who left when I was three years old. The dad who never wrote and never called. The dad I never wanted to see again.

The dad I had imagined was dead.

THREE

"Let's all go into the house," Shay says.

I notice that Shay and Diego have come up on either side of me. I can feel Shay's agitation, and I know she isn't happy to see Nate.

That's my father. A man called Nate.

"Do you want to go for a walk, Gracie?" Nate asks.

"No, Nate," Shay says sharply. "Give her some room."

"I'm giving her the whole outdoors, Shay," my dad says pleasantly.

I'm so confused. I feel dizzy, as if I can feel the earth's rotation.

"This is turning out to be quite a day," Diego says.

I look at Shay. "Can we just go inside?"

"Of course, sweetie." Shay puts her arm around me and keeps it there as we walk toward the house.

We sit in the living room. The house is small, but it has so many windows that it never feels dark or claustrophobic. To one side of the fireplace is a sofa with deep cushions, and facing it are two big, comfortable armchairs. In the middle is a table that we sometimes eat around on cold nights.

Nate picks the sofa and looks encouragingly at me, and I know he wants me to sit next to him. I sit in one of the armchairs. Shay sits in the other chair, and Diego leans against the wall.

"I apologize for not calling," Nate says to me. "I was going to. And then I was just going to drive by first, just to see . . . and Shay was outside, and she saw me."

"Why did you come?" I ask.

"I heard about your mother."

I shake my head. "It's been two years."

"I know. There was no way for me to know, Gracie. I would have come right away if I'd known."

"Let me get this straight," I say. "You don't come for my birthdays, you don't come when I'm sick, you don't come for thirteen years, but you would have shown up for a funeral?"

Nate shakes his head. "Okay, I deserved that."

"You're darn right you did," Shay murmurs.

"Oh, please," I say. "Listen, you didn't have to show up. You could have called. Or sent me an e-mail."

"There's so much to tell you," Nate says.

"Yeah, me, too," I say. "I was three years old when you left. A few things have happened."

I'm trying not to have it all come back to me, but it's flooding in, and I'm holding myself together because I just might fall apart. I am thinking of the years. The years before I was able to just wipe the notion of "father" out of my life. Watching other kids with their dads. Imagining him knocking on the door. Closing my eyes and picturing it. And mostly, seeing a three-year-old girl with her dad, seeing how the father holds her hand, or picks her up, or leans down to talk to her . . . and thinking, *How could he do it? How could he leave me?*

Mom had always said that Dad was a "complicated man." When I was little, she'd just say he loved me very much . . . and leave it at that. But later, she would tell me sometimes that she'd loved him despite the "better angels of my nature." When she quoted Abraham Lincoln, you knew it was serious stuff.

Nate stands up. "I know this must be a shock to you. Maybe it's better that the first visit be short, so you can process this."

Shay stands up quickly. "That's a good idea. What do you think, Gracie?"

I'm picking up so much turmoil from Shay. She hates having Nate in this house. I can feel it. Is she afraid of him? Afraid he'll snatch me away? Afraid I'll go with him?

"That might be best," I say.

"Will you walk me to the car?" Nate asks me.

I look at him, really look at him, for the first time. He's always been not quite a person to me.

Now I see . . . myself. I always thought I looked like my mom. She always told me I did, too. But now I know she was lying. Lying to protect me. Because I wouldn't have wanted to know how much I looked like him.

And that pulls me out the door with him, somehow.

The front door thuds behind us. It sends a shudder through me, as though it's cut me off from Shay and Diego forever. Since we've been sitting inside, dusk has fallen, and the light is deep blue and smudgy with shadows.

"My own dad was manic-depressive," Nate says. "Your grandfather. He died when I was in college. He killed himself. They didn't diagnose him correctly, I guess. He lived in terror for a lot of the time, and he tried not to take it out on us, but he did."

Well. Nate sure didn't believe in small talk.

"I never felt I was loved, growing up," Nate continues. "I mean, I don't want to boo-hoo all over you. That could get messy." He flashes an uneasy smile. "I'm just trying to explain a little bit of why it took me so long to get myself together. Only one person in my life really loved me as a child, and that was my aunt Jane. I was afraid I would grow up to be my father. After you were born, it all crashed down on me, all that fear. I was terrified I'd turn you into something you wouldn't want to be, Gracie."

I realize that I'm holding my breath so I won't miss a word.

"I was afraid I'd turn you into me," he says.

I don't look at him. I look at my shoes. I look at every individual blade of grass, because if this is an apology, it just isn't doing it for me.

"Some mornings I couldn't get out of bed," he says. "I thought — *It's happening to me. I'm going to ruin Carrie's life, and Gracie's life. They'll be better off without me.* I'll tell you. If you get to the place where you think the people you love most in the world are better off without you . . . well, it's a very bad place."

He starts walking again, and I walk beside him, listening now.

"I went to New Mexico because I didn't know anyone there and nobody knew me," he says. "I found a therapist. After some treatment — well, eventually, I got better. I found out I'm not manic-depressive. Just screwed up. And I worked on my problems, and when I got clear, I realized . . ." He swallows, and his voice cracks. "I'd blown it. It was too late. I couldn't just walk back into my own front door. It wasn't my home any longer. I lost any right to think that. And I was a coward, and so I kept . . . putting it off. *I'll call on her birthday,* I'd say. Or Christmas. Or summertime. And months went by, and years . . . and I remembered what a thera-pist had told me — *If you can't be there every day for her, don't do it. She'll be better off.*"

He stops, his hand on the car door. "I think you were better off without me. That's the honest truth."

"So what's different now?" I ask.

"I met someone. I got married. And she wants to have kids. And my track record . . . well, I just thought, I already have a kid. I don't want to be one of those dads who has a second family and forgets he ever had a first. And my wife . . . she's a good person. She's the one who pointed out to me that I couldn't be a father to a new child if I didn't try again with the child I had."

"So she told you to come here. You wouldn't have come otherwise." For some reason, that makes me furious.

He lets out a breath. "I'm not going to lie to you, Gracie. That's true. But what you have to know is, Rachel makes me do a lot of things I didn't think I was capable of doing. She makes me a better per-son. I want to live up to what she thinks I am." He pauses and then he says, "I'd like you to meet her sometime."

I hear in his voice a hopefulness that makes me angry . . . and sad, too. Does he really think that he can come here and make everything else go away?

"I don't think so," I say.

"Well." He clears his throat. "I'm going to hang around for a few more days. I'll call tomorrow and, if you want, I'd like to take you to lunch. Or anything."

"I'll see," I say. It's as much as I can give him, and it feels like too much.

FOUR

I let the door shut behind me when I walk back into the house. The living room is dark now. Shay and Diego are in the kitchen. I smell something funny, something I've never smelled in Shay's house. It's unpleasant. I wrinkle my nose.

Underneath my feet the hardwood floor feels spongy. I smell mildew and stale air and I want to cough, but I can't seem to catch a breath of pure air. . . .

And suddenly, I realize I'm having a vision, and I'm trapped in the vision, and I can't get out, and I can't breathe, and there's a roaring in my ears. . . .

Shay turns on the light, and the living room springs forward, all comfortable and warm. I feel my hammering heart.

"I thought I'd light a fire," she says.

"That would be good," I say. I tell my heart to slow down.

What had I seen? Was it Shay's house or another house?

Did it have to do with the drowned man? Or my father?

By the time Shay has placed the kindling and

wadded up newspapers and built her foolproof-fire system, my heart rate has returned to the normal range. I curl up on the couch and reach for the wool throw that's folded on the back. I pull it over my legs and sit back against the sofa arm so I can look at the flames.

Shay sits down opposite me. Her dark, curly hair is pulled back in a ponytail and she's in her floppy fleece pants, so I guess she's not seeing Joe tonight. Since she's been dating Joe, Shay's wardrobe has improved to an amazing degree. She's a little overweight, round and pretty, and she's started wearing filmy blouses and velvet pants instead of her denim shirts and jeans. She's even exchanged Chap Stick for lip gloss.

"You look pretty shaken," she says. "I know I was."

"I just don't get what he wants."

"He wants to know you, sweetie." Shay pats my leg. "Diego told me about Dylan Brewer. You poor baby, what a day. How do you feel?"

Here is the part where I'm supposed to share my feelings. Sometimes having a family is hard. What I want to do is look at the fire and zone out. I don't want to talk about my feelings. I just want to ignore them until they go away.

After my mother was killed in the car crash, I had to go to something called "grief counseling." I hated it at the time, but I came to have a great deal of respect for Dr. Julie Politsky. I learned that telling someone how you feel doesn't mean you'll fall apart and won't be able to put yourself back together again. I learned that it's possible to put yourself back together again, one piece at a time.

Dr. Politsky showed me the road map. Shay put me on the road.

So even though at this particular moment I don't want to talk about my father, I do.

"I feel angry and sad and confused and sick to my stomach," I say. "I feel like telling him to go away forever. But I know I should at least hear him out."

Shay squeezes my knee. "You don't have to do anything you don't want to do. I have his address. You can always contact him when you're ready. You don't have to be on his timetable."

That was true. I hadn't thought about it that way. "He wants to have lunch tomorrow."

"Do you want to?"

"I don't know."

"So sleep on it. I have an idea. Joe had to cancel, so it's just us for dinner tonight. I'm making black bean chili and cornbread for dinner. Then let's watch some really goofy DVD. Diego has a date with Marigold."

I groan, and Shay smacks me on the knee playfully. "Shhh," she warns.

"I just can't get used to her," I whisper.

"I know."

"I just don't understand him."

Shay shrugs. "What you need to know, honey, is that sometimes you can fall for someone you don't even like very much. I think that might have happened to Diego."

"But he defends her all the time."

"A little too much, I think. I think he's trying to convince himself, too."

There's a knock at the door. Shay and I both look at the door as if there's a werewolf behind it. We're both afraid that Nate has come back.

"Don't let him in," I say.

"We don't know it's him," she murmurs. She gets up and answers the door.

I hear Joe's voice saying hello.

"I thought you canceled," Shay says. "Because if you didn't, I'm busted. I'm wearing my very oldest sweatpants. Don't look."

"Gross," Joe says. "But I'm afraid I'm here in an official capacity. Is Diego around?"

"Is it about that poor drowned guy?"

"Shay," Joe says, "did you hear me say *official*?"

"Oh. Yeah."

"Then can you not kiss me when you say that?"

I smile, and a moment later Joe walks in. Shay hollers for Diego, and I say hello.

"How are you doing?" Joe comes closer to give me the once-over.

"I'm okay. It's not like I saw anything."

Diego walks in the room. "Hi, Joe."

"It's official business," Shay says.

"Hi, Detective Pasta," Diego says.

Before we knew Joe Fusilli, before he practically became a member of the family, we used to call him Detective Pasta. It must be hard to be named after a curly noodle, even though Joe claims an ancestor of his invented it.

"There was a break-in and some malicious mischief on a house down in the new development," Joe says.

Frowning, Shay moves a little closer to Diego.

"I don't think you did it, Diego," Joe says. "But did you hear any kids boasting about it? It seems like some kind of prank, and I know that crowd you hang with now doesn't like the weekend people."

"Look, Mason is a bit of a jerk, but he wouldn't do something like that," Diego says.

"Tempers are running high because of Hassam's Farm," Joe says.

Diego nods. "I know."

"Mason's best friend is Andy Hassam. Mason has worked at the farm stand."

"I've worked there, too," Diego says. "Practically every kid in this area has had a summer job there."

"Did anyone steal anything in the break-in?" Shay asks. I can tell she's trying to turn the conversation, because Diego is starting to look angry.

"No. The house is empty. It was just sold — or, at least, someone put a bid on it. A Seattle businessman," Joe says. "I'm just looking at the resentment factor. His name is Hank Hobbs."

I see Shay start at the name. Joe, who never misses anything, sees it, too.

"You know him?"

"Sure," Shay says. "He's a major contributor to the wetlands reclamation project. We almost had to shut it down last month until he pledged a million dollars."

Shay is a scientist with a special interest in wetlands. She works for an environmental company here on Beewick. Their major project for the past four years has been the restoration of this wetland area on Beewick, down near the ferry on the southern part of the island. Twenty years ago, a corporation, Monvor Industries, polluted and flooded the land. The final part of the restoration is scheduled for next week, when the last of the land will be drained.

"Maybe Hobbs was targeted," Shay says. "He was once vice president of Monvor. He's contributed to the reclamation project out of guilt, I imagine. But maybe somebody found out about his connection to the original pollution. It hasn't been publicized; he wanted to keep things quiet. Have you talked to him?"

"I've got a call in to him," Joe says.

The timer goes off in the kitchen. "That's my cornbread," Shay says. "Do you want to stay for dinner?"

Joe shakes his head wearily. "I'm still waiting for lab results. We still haven't IDed the body."

"I'll take out the cornbread," Diego says, and heads for the kitchen.

"I'll help," I say. I trail after Diego while Shay walks Joe to the door.

Diego puts on oven mittens and still manages to look fairly manly. He wrestles the cast-iron pan full of cornbread out of the oven and kicks the door shut with his foot. I start taking down plates to set the table.

"So?" I say.

"So, what?"

"So, did you tell Joe the truth, or do you know who vandalized the house?"

Diego is busy sliding the hot pan onto a trivet. He throws the oven mitts down.

"Of course I don't know," he says.

"Are you sure it wasn't Mason and his dinosaur pals? They definitely have it in for the weekenders."

"They're not idiots," Diego says. "They wouldn't do that."

Wouldn't they? Diego is so deluded that he thinks Marigold has an interesting mind. He's completely head over heels.

How far would he go to protect her brother?

FIVE

Sometimes just a question will rock a household, even if the answer is what you want to hear. I can tell that Shay is worried about the crowd Diego is hanging with. Diego is a pretty independent guy, so it's unusual that he's spending all this time with Marigold's brother.

The fact that my father has suddenly shown up hasn't made things any easier. When he calls on Sunday, I tell him I'm busy. I'm just not ready to deal with it. Not yet. Maybe not ever.

But even though I tell him I'm not ready, I still think about him all day, so what's the point? I can feel his presence on the island. I wonder what else he has to tell me. I wonder if I can ever ask the questions that burn me up inside. I know he's staying at the inn in Greystone Harbor, and so I stick close to home all afternoon. I don't want to run into him in town.

Shay has to work on Sunday afternoon, and Diego is off with Marigold, so I take out the photo album my mom made for me. I don't have that many photos of my dad in it, but I've memorized every one.

There is one I used to look at all the time, taken before they were married. He's at the beach, and he's wearing a dark T-shirt and loose khaki pants. They're rolled up at the ankles. He's sitting in the sand, his hands around his knees. The wind is blowing his hair, and he's laughing. Really laughing. This is the photograph that used to break me, because he looks so happy. So handsome. So much like a dad someone would want.

What is real? How much of what I see is influenced by how I feel? Do I want my father to be bad, or good?

I am a person who already has problems with reality. I see things that aren't there. But my psychic ability isn't going to help me figure out my own life — it doesn't work that way. It just confuses things more. I don't know if the feelings I'm picking up from him are true or not. I don't know if the yearning I felt in him the other night is real.

I flip through the pages of the album. When I was born, my mom and dad lived in a tiny house in Maryland, on the Eastern Shore. There's one photograph that my mom said my dad took of me. I'm probably about two, I guess. I'm sitting on the lawn, wearing my mom's hat, which makes me look like a baby version of the Cat in the Hat. My father picked the wrong place to stand, because the sun is casting his shadow on the lawn next to me. Some of his shadow lies over me.

It always has. It's all I ever had of him — a shadow. Now I have the real thing, the real man, the one I've hated. The one I've loved. The one who broke my life into two pieces.

I close the book. I'd rather have the pictures, have the shadow. The man is too real.

It's late when Shay struggles in the door, carrying grocery bags. I run forward to help her. We go toward the back of the house and put the grocery bags on the counter. Instead of unpacking them, Shay plops down in a kitchen chair, still in her coat.

"Founders Realty was vandalized last night," she says.

"What did the vandals do?"

"Threw some files on the floor, put trash on the desks, unplugged the little refrigerator, stuff like that," Shay says. "Joe says it's like they didn't want to do too much damage to push it into a serious crime, which sounds like —"

"Teenagers," I say. "Do you think it could be Mason?"

Shay shrugs out of her coat. "Diego has always been sort of idiot-proof," she says. "I mean, even as a kid, he knew what kids to avoid. He's got a good head on his shoulders. But he's in love. Sometimes you're looking so hard at who you love that . . . you miss things. Big things. Because you're trying to fit your love into the kind of thing you want it to be."

"Is he really in love with Marigold?" I ask.

Shay smiles gently. "Yeah. Look, Gracie, I'm as surprised as you are that it's this girl. But love is love. He's got to go through it. And we have to stay out of it."

She says this last part with meaning, and I nod slowly. "I guess I haven't been so nice about Marigold sometimes."

"So I hear. Let's just try to keep our mouths shut and support him, okay?"

"Okay."

"Joe will find out who's doing this. That's his job. Not ours. Your job is to do your homework, and my job is to get through this next few weeks with my job, and then we'll all be happy again. Right?"

"Absolutely." We smile at each other. We've been talking in the dark. It reminds me of the early mornings we once spent together, when I first moved here and wasn't talking to anyone. When I'd wake up in a panic, I'd sit in the kitchen, and somehow Shay would know I was awake, and come and join me. She wouldn't say a word, just pad around the kitchen warming up milk and cups until my crying stopped. She wouldn't even touch me. She knew if she'd touched me, I'd run back in my room. So she'd make hot chocolate, and we'd sit in silence, sipping the hot drink, and watching the light turn from navy to deep blue. And then, still without saying a word, I'd wash the cups and the milk pan, and we'd both go back to bed.

I have this, I think. *I don't need him. I have this.*

"Well, I'm going to take a shower, and then start dinner," Shay says. "Maybe trays in front of the fire tonight. I'm beat." She heads for her room, stretching as she goes.

I head to my room, which used to be a mudroom that Shay and Diego had fixed up for me. I reach out for the light switch, but for a moment, I get disoriented. I'm not seeing the room as it is, with glass panes. I see a broken screen, blowing. I see a door where a window is now.

And I smell that smell again, mildew and rot and staleness, as if the house had been shut up for years and years. I can't find the light switch, and my heart is pounding, and suddenly I feel terror well up in me, because the floor is sticky underneath my feet.

I see it in flashes. Footprints on floorboards, the outline smudged and rusty-looking.

Blood. Someone walked in the blood.

Clean it up clean it up clean it up . . .

A bloody towel.

The smell of it in the house.

"No!" I shout, and I step back, my hand desperately scrabbling for the light switch. Light floods the room, and it's just my room again, with the headboard painted yellow and the blue floor and the patterned curtains. I can hear Shay in the shower, singing a Joni Mitchell song.

I sink down on the bed and grab my pillow and squeeze it.

I don't want to see what I see.

I want it to go away.

I know that whatever it was that I saw — past or future — was murder.

SIX

It started when I was ten, when I almost drowned at the beach in Maryland. A lifeguard rescued me, and when I came to, I could hear what she was thinking.

I didn't tell anyone but my mom. She almost got me tested, but somehow we always found excuses not to. I think we just hoped it would go away. I know I did.

I could never read my mom, and I never got flashes about her, but the day she died was the worst day of my life, even before my grandparents showed up at the door to give me the news. I sat on the couch all day, knowing something was wrong. I stared at the phone and couldn't move.

I was smelling oranges that day, and I didn't know why. I felt like I couldn't breathe, and I didn't know why.

Then I heard she was hit by a truck carrying oranges. That she was choking on her own blood. And I knew why.

Even today, the smell of orange juice makes me sick.

Whatever this ability I have is, it's not

something I can shut off like a faucet. It sneaks up on me. It comes when I least expect it, when I'm eating ice cream or sitting in the car or listening to the principal read the school announcements. And then I know that the girl behind the ice cream counter is worried because her boss is hitting on her, or the man on the bike stopping to wipe his forehead at the stoplight is short of breath because there's something wrong with his heart, and the principal wants a divorce but is afraid of what would happen to her kids if she went through with it.

I don't want to know these things.

And I don't want to walk into my room and see a river of blood on the floor.

I don't want to walk through the house and feel spooked. But that's what happens. I see something out of the corner of my eye. Something I'll catch if I turn quickly enough. A shadow. An outflung hand. A spreading stain on the floor, a pool of blood.

I'm afraid of being alone in the house.

School is school. Some days it's not too bad, and other days it makes you want to run shrieking into the wilderness.

Beewick High squashes kids from three towns into one school, and it's still small. Everyone has known each other since preschool, so I felt a little left out at the beginning. I got befriended by Emily Carbonel, but she was kidnapped last year. I think what we went through together drove us apart instead of bringing us closer. I think I just remind her of what she went through. This year she's turned into a skittish, nervous geek who never takes off her earphones from her MP-3 player, which kind of reminds me of me last year, actually. Sometimes kids talk to me, and I have a few classroom friendships, but nobody is inviting me home for soda and pretzels.

My rep has not improved since everyone found out I get psychic flashes. You can break down reactions into three areas:

1. You're so weird. Are you reading my mind right now?
2. Can you see the questions on tomorrow's test in your mind?
3. Can you tell me if Jason really, really likes me?

You see, the thing is, when you're in high school, you have secrets. You have crushes, you have thoughts, you want things you shouldn't want. And if you're afraid someone can see inside you, you don't slide your tray next to hers at lunch.

I wish I could tell them that I can't see inside them. My flashes are unpredictable. The closer I am to someone, the murkier they are. For example, I can't tell what my aunt Shay is thinking just about one hundred percent of the time if she doesn't want me to. Diego is as much of a mystery to me as any boy.

And then there's dear old Dad. I won't even bother trying to figure him out.

After school, I stuff my books into my backpack, taking my time while I do it. I'm stalling for two reasons. One, I'm afraid to go home. Two, I always do. Everyone congregates outside on the steps after school. Plans are made, promises to call, running jokes. I don't want to have to walk through that, so I usually wait until kids have headed off to their cars or into town.

It's a gloomy, wet day. I decide to go to the town library and do my homework. If I stretch it out long enough, I can walk home and Shay will be just getting home from work. Diego works late on Mondays.

When I come out of school, Nate is sitting on the stone column at the bottom of the railing, just like kids do. He's got a paper cone of French fries from the Bluebay Drive-In, which has the best fries in the known universe.

He holds out the cone to me. "I thought you might need a ride home."

I ignore the French fries, even though the smell of them makes my stomach growl. "I'm not going home. I'm going to the library."

He jumps down. "The library, then."

"It's two blocks away."

"I think I can manage it." He swings into step beside me. "So. I have a proposal. We each get three questions we can ask each other. And we have to tell the truth."

"I don't want to —"

"Here's my first one. Do you want these or not?" He holds up the cone.

"No."

"Liar." He holds them out, but I refuse to take one. It will feel like some kind of surrender.

He shrugs. It is with some regret that I watch the full cone of fries sail into the garbage can.

"That was my best bribe," he says. He puts his hands in his pockets. "Okay, go ahead. Your turn."

"Are you still a lawyer?"

"No. I left the law when I left Maryland. I always hated it."

"What do you do now?"

"My last job was in commercial real estate. Before that . . . a bunch of things. I sold houses in Santa Fe. Wrote a newspaper column once. Oh, and I ran a surf shop in San Diego. That was fun."

Great. While he was having fun on the beach, I was growing up fatherless.

"Where do you live now?"

"Wallanan. It's right outside of Tacoma."

I stop. "Tacoma?" For almost a whole year, he's been less than two hours away.

He stops, too, and looks me full in the face. "I didn't know you were here, on Beewick, until last week."

We both breathe in and out, passing through the moment.

"Look," he continues. "I came here to tell you that if you want me to leave, I'll leave. But I also came here to tell you that even if I leave, I'll keep trying. Brace yourself for birthday cards, kiddo."

We continue down the hill into town. And I have such a weird moment of feeling normal. *Here is my dad, and we're walking into town.* As if all my heartbreak had never been.

And then the normal moment is gone, and I'm walking with the man who abandoned me and my mother. My whole body stiffens up again.

"The thing is," he says, "I have a lot to catch up on. So I thought I'd start with these." He hands me a stack of envelopes.

"What are these?" I ask, but I know what they are. Thirteen birthday cards. One for every year he missed.

He leaves me at the library steps without a word. I take out my books, but I spend most of my time there looking through the cards. He's chosen them carefully, I see. Each one is age-appropriate.

One after the other. Blues Clues. Dora the Explorer. Birthday cakes. Balloons. Sailboats. And then sentimental ones, near the end. Signed at the bottom of each is a message: *Love, Dad.*

There's something sort of goofy about the gesture. It should really piss me off, but it doesn't. And for some reason, it doesn't make me sad. Maybe it's because he chose such stupid cards. I can't help smiling.

The light is dimming outside, and I know it's time to leave. The other kids here have left long ago, and the moms with toddlers. Everyone wants to go home to dinner. And I'm still stalling.

Joy the librarian stands behind my chair, holding a stack of books. She leans in close to my ear.

"Murder will out."

Her breath on the back of my neck makes me start and pull away.

"What?" I ask, twisting around.

She nods significantly, except I don't know what the significance is. The fluorescent lights overhead shine in the frames of her glasses, and I can't see her eyes.

"Murderers get caught. He's on Beewick somewhere, with his normal face. But he'll be caught."

I realize now she's trying to reassure me. Because I was around when the body was found. But instead, she just creeps me out.

"Thanks," I say.

I walk home slowly in the dusk. When I open the door, I smell the fire and feel the warmth. I know the smell of this house now in my bones — of the beeswax Shay rubs on the wood floors, the floors she refinished herself when she bought the house, after tearing up the thick shag carpeting. Every house has a smell, and this house is starting to smell like home. I want to grab on to this feeling and ride it. I want to make it the one true thing I have. But I can't.

I wake up on Tuesday morning early. I hear noise in the kitchen, and when I walk out, Shay is already up. Papers are stacked on the kitchen table, and she's going through them, frowning.

"Work?" I ask as I pour myself some cereal.

"What? Oh. Problems, as usual," Shay groans. She looks at the clock and jumps up in a panic. "I have a meeting!"

"At seven in the morning?"

"Seven-thirty, and I haven't showered. . . . Oh, I'll be so glad when this project is over," Shay moans. She runs out, the belt of her bathrobe trailing behind her.

I chomp on my cereal. The papers are still spread out on the table, so I reach over to put them back in the file for Shay. She'll probably need them for the meeting, and in this state, she'll probably just run out the door without them if I don't remind her.

DEED OF SALE

I read the words upside down.

17 Fieldstone Lane.

This house. Why was Shay looking at the papers for this house? She bought it twenty years ago. I turn the deed around. I can't believe how cheap the house was, but Shay has told me what a wreck it was when she found it.

My eyes travel down to the bottom, where the owner's signature is.

SHAY MILLICENT KENZIE
NATHANIEL G. MILLAR

Nate? My father?

My father owns the house with Shay?

I can't believe what I'm reading. I look at the date. I know I was born about three years after my parents got married. That means that Shay knew my father before my mother did. Knew him well enough to buy a house with him.

I drop the spoon into the bowl. Milk splashes over the rim.

Shay has been hiding this from me.

Shay, who I thought was the most honest person I know.

Shay, who always told me that hiding your feelings can backfire.

Shay is as big a liar as dear old Dad.

SEVEN

When Shay comes out in her work clothes with her hair wet, I'm still sitting at the table. She starts hunting for her keys. "I hope they have bagels at this meeting. And coffee. Definitely coffee —"

She sees my face and stops. "What is it?" Her gaze travels to the papers on the table.

"You lied to me," I say.

"Not really," she says carefully.

I slam my hand down. "You *lied* to me!"

"Oh, honey, no, no. It just never . . . when I would bring up your dad, you would always just shut down. So I thought . . . one step at a time."

"So when were you going to tell me he owns half of this house? Is that why you took me in? Because you thought he'd come back and want the house, and if I was living here, he couldn't turn you out on the street?" I don't know where that idea came from, but suddenly it blazed across my brain. I feel tears sting my eyes, and I will them to go away.

Shay looks shocked. "No! No, of course not!" She puts her briefcase on the chair. "We need to talk about this."

"You have a meeting. It can wait." I turn away to go back into my room.

"No, it can't."

She picks up the phone and calls someone. I hear her murmur something about a family emergency.

"You're a pretty cool liar, Shay," I say after she hangs up. "I didn't think you could lie to save your life."

"That wasn't a lie. This *is* a family emergency. Will you sit down, Gracie?"

I don't want to sit. I want to run. I want to run and run and run until the blood pounding in my ears drives out every thought in my head.

But I also want answers, so I sit.

"Were you a couple?" I ask her. "You and Nate?"

"No, we were never a couple. We were friends. Let me start at the beginning," Shay says. "I met Nate a long time ago in Seattle, where I was living at the time. I had dropped out of grad school and was working as a waitress, and I joined this environmental group. We heard about what Monvor was doing up here, destroying the wetlands, and a bunch of us decided to come up here one summer and camp out for a month and do protests." Shay shrugs. "We were young. It seemed like a good idea at the time."

She pushes back her hair. "Well, we didn't

really accomplish anything. We did a few protests that made the papers. But mostly we sat around talking about the best way to shut down Monvor, then went hiking and swimming. Some of us were more committed than others. I'd say that Nate was our unofficial leader. He was so charismatic. We all looked up to him. He had these great ideas — but in the end, we all just drifted apart."

"What about the house?"

"I fell in love with Beewick Island that summer," Shay says. "I saw myself here. And real estate was really cheap. I had saved some money, and I thought if some of us chipped in and bought a house, we could all share it on weekends. Dumb idea, by the way. Two others in the group were interested. One dropped out, and that left me and Nate. We found this house, and we bought it. Carrie came out to help me with the sale — she had just graduated from law school. That's when she met Nate. I saw it happen the moment they met — they fell in love instantly. They were married six months later. So half of the house really belonged to your mother, too. She had a good career, and she didn't need the money, so even though I offered to buy her out a couple of times, she refused. She knew it was hard for me to come up with the money. And I wouldn't let her just give me half the house, either. It was just something between us, and we never thought . . . we never thought it would matter one way or another."

I absorb this. It makes sense. I knew my mother had met Nate out here. I'd never wanted the details.

This is what happens when you don't want details. They pile up and pile up, and then you get them all at once, and they knock you right over.

But I get the feeling that there are holes in this story. Things Shay isn't telling me. Usually, I can't read Shay. But somehow I'm picking up flashes.

"Apples," I say. "What is it about apples?"

"Apples?"

"And a . . . a gate?"

Shay goes pale.

The door has opened, but we haven't heard it. Joe is standing in the kitchen doorway.

"Yes, Shay," he says. "Tell us about William Applegate."

EIGHT

Shay looks up at Joe. Then she glances at me. I can tell this is something she doesn't want to talk about in front of me. Or maybe, I suddenly realize, she doesn't want to talk about it with Joe.

"Billy," she says, her voice faint. "We called him Billy. He was one of us. When we decided to disband the group, he disappeared. I don't know what happened to him. Neither did his family. They never discovered what happened."

"Imagine my surprise," Joe says, "when I ran Hank Hobbs through our computers and discovered that you tried to bring charges against him for the murder of William Applegate."

"It was a long time ago," Shay says.

"And six weeks ago, Hank Hobbs tried to get you fired from the wetlands project. Said he wouldn't give a contribution unless they fired you. There is a million dollars at stake."

Shay smiles faintly. "I guess he held a grudge."

"You never told me about it."

"It was a work problem."

I am watching both of them carefully. They are

speaking in low voices, but I can feel Joe's anger and Shay's fear.

"Why don't you tell me about it now," Joe says, and I realize with a chill that he has his professional voice on. Shay is no dummy; she feels it, too.

"Billy was always so intense," she says. "We all took our environmental work seriously, but for Billy, it was like life and death. He used to get so angry when anybody would goof off, when we'd go swimming or have a softball game. He used to browbeat us about our lack of commitment. So he wasn't exactly popular with the group."

Joe sits down at the table. "Go on."

"Then we had this breakthrough. Billy somehow got his hands on a secret file that showed that Monvor had falsified data regarding outflow pollutants. There was going to be an inquiry, and they decided to stonewall it by producing a false set of data. Billy had the file in his duffel. But then our campsite was burgled, and the evidence was stolen along with some personal items. We all had a huge argument. Billy basically accused someone — he didn't know who — in the group of betraying us and stealing the file. Everyone was furious, and that was the beginning of the end. The group just fell apart. We had no evidence to expose Monvor, and we weren't even friends anymore. Billy just . . . he went ballistic. This was the end of everything he'd worked for. That night, he took me aside. He told me he was going to Monvor's headquarters to confront Hank Hobbs. He believed that Hobbs had bribed one of us to destroy the file. He left. I never saw him again."

"And when the police investigated, you pointed them to Hobbs."

"Of course," Shay says. "That's where he was headed. But I don't know . . . it was soon after that I put everything together. I think Billy might have committed suicide. Or else he just took off. He was truly troubled, and his relations with his family . . . they weren't the greatest. I really don't think he was murdered. I don't think I believed it at the time. I was caught up in it all, and I don't think I was thinking straight. Now, I'm embarrassed at accusing Hank Hobbs. I think that's one reason I never told you about this, Joe."

The light has been growing for some time now, and sunshine is beginning to streak through the windows into the kitchen.

"Why did you come here, Joe?" Shay asks. "Why are you interested in Billy Applegate now?"

"Because the drowned body has been identified," Joe says. "It's Hank Hobbs."

NINE

Shay goes white. "Was he murdered?"

"We don't know," Joe says. "We know he couldn't swim. The Coast Guard found the boat out in the Sound."

"He has a boat, and he can't swim?" I ask.

"It happens," Joe says, in that way he has of showing that there isn't anything on earth he hasn't seen or heard about. "It looks like he slipped and fell, possibly sustaining a head injury. Or that could have happened after he'd been knocking around the rocks in the harbor."

Shay and I both wince.

"Anyway," Joe says briskly, "we'll know more after the autopsy."

"Was the dinghy missing?"

Joe turns to me. "No." He looks surprised that I would think of that, but it was the first question that popped into my head.

"But if he was murdered, how did the killer get away?"

"There could have been two boats," Joe says. "Or the killer could have swum to shore. It's possible. The tides are tricky, but you can do it."

Shay has gone very still. "Am I a suspect, Joe?" she asks.

"Nobody's a suspect," he says. "I don't know if he was murdered. I'm just looking for background."

"Oh. Because you're acting like I'm a suspect."

"I'm just gathering information."

"You could be nicer about it."

Joe looks annoyed. "I'm on a case, Shay. I don't have time to hold your hand."

She's furious. He catches her anger, and chooses to ignore it. I'm watching them like a tennis match.

He turns to me. "Speaking of the case, I hear your father is in town. Why did he come?"

"He heard that my mother died," I say.

"That was two years ago."

"He was out of touch."

He turns to Shay. "Nathaniel Millard was one of the group that summer."

"He was a friend before he became my brother-in-law," Shay says in a small, tight voice that isn't like hers. "I haven't seen him since Gracie was a baby."

"Do you know where he's staying?"

"The inn in Greystone Harbor," I say. "Why?"

Joe stands. "Just gathering information," he says.

I know why Joe is going to talk to Nate. Is it just a coincidence that he's shown up, and Joe has a murdered guy on his hands?

Is this a reunion or a crime scene?

Shay drives me to school. She's gripping the steering wheel and grinding her teeth. Once, she pops out with, "'I don't have time to hold your *hand*,' he says!" Detective that I am, I get that she's thinking about Joe.

She stops in the parking lot and turns to me.

"Look," she says, "I know you feel I should have told you all this. You have to believe I was going to. I wanted to find your father first. I hired a private detective to find him."

"Why?" I couldn't believe that it was *Shay* who'd started all this.

"Because he was always out there!" Shay bursts out. "I don't know what he'd want. And the fact that this man owns half my house and could take you away from me — I couldn't sleep at night, thinking of that. I had to do something. I offered to buy him out, and he said yes. But he had to see you first."

"Buy him out?"

"Of the house," she says. "I don't want his name on the deed."

I'm just sitting there, clutching the door handle, trying to make sense of all this.

"I can't believe you didn't tell me!"

"I didn't know if I'd find him."

"Well, you found him." I can't even look at her. I'm too confused and angry. "Happy now?"

"You have every reason in the world to hate him," Shay says. "Of course. But he's just a man, Gracie. A screw-up, sure. But someone who wants to know you. Do you know, the private detective told me that when he told Nate that Carrie was dead, he broke down. He really didn't know, Gracie. Nate called me soon after. I told him not to come up, that I wanted to talk to you first, but he couldn't wait. I was shocked when he drove by. I thought I'd have time to prepare you."

"Did he know Hank Hobbs?" I ask.

"What?" Shay is startled.

"You were all there that summer. Did he know him?"

"You think he could have killed Hank Hobbs?"

"I'm just asking."

"I don't think he ever met him," Shay says. "I know I didn't. We were protesting against a company; we didn't target any individuals. Nate isn't a murderer, Gracie. I know he isn't."

"You haven't seen him in twenty years."

"I don't care. I knew him pretty well back then. He was irresponsible, obviously. Maybe not the most truthful person I ever met. But he wouldn't commit cold-blooded murder. He couldn't."

How can she be so sure? I'm not.

"I wish I hadn't started this." She blows out a breath and rests her forehead on the steering wheel for a moment. "I know I just made a mess of every-thing. But I was thinking of you the whole time."

"Maybe . . . maybe you should have thought a little harder," I say.

I see Shay's hands tighten on the steering wheel. "Good point," she says.

TEN

After school, I head into town. I don't want to go home yet. It has nothing to do with the fact that I happen to know that Zed works the lunch shift on Tuesdays and then has the rest of the day off. It has nothing to do with the fact that I know his shift is over right about now.

I walk slowly past the Harborside, and I hear him call my name.

He's sitting outside, one leg over his bike. He leans the bike against the railing and comes over. I wish, I wish, I wouldn't immediately go blank when I see him. I wish I could manage a witty hello. Something more interesting than "hi."

"Hi," I say.

"I'm glad I ran into you," Zed says. "That was one weird afternoon. I was wondering if you were okay."

"I'm okay," I say. "Did you hear that they identified the . . . the guy?"

"Hank Hobbs, yeah," Zed says. "It's funny, because he just had lunch at the restaurant last week. I waited on him. Creepy. Not him, but knowing that he died, like, maybe later that day."

"Who was he having lunch with?"

"Jeff Ferris. They were talking about some house he's buying in that new development over by Hassam's Farm."

"Hobbs was buying a house there?"

Zed nods. "He was buying Jeff's house. He has one on Larch Lane — prime spot, right on the water. He bought right at the beginning, before they were even built, and now he'll make a killing. Smart."

"I guess. Did Hobbs seem upset or anything?"

"No. I already talked to the police. So did Jeff. Neither of us picked up anything from Mr. Hobbs. It was a beautiful day, though. You know how the weather was so nice last week. I guess he decided to take a boat ride after lunch."

This is the most Zed has ever said to me, and I want to savor the moment, but I have an idea. The new development isn't too far; I can make it on my bike in twenty minutes. I could go out to the house on Larch Lane and poke around.

Something is pulling at me. An image of a body falling through water, sinking, spiraling down from sunlit green water into the black depths of the bay. I know now that the body I saw is Hank Hobbs.

I try to get a picture of my dad on that boat, but I can't. It's a blank.

Zed is looking at me curiously. He looks a bit spooked, as a matter of fact. Of course, like all the kids I know, he's a little freaked out because he knows I see things.

Suddenly, I'm tired of it all. I'm tired of trying to appear normal. Tired of striving not to freak people out.

Especially to Zed. I didn't want to have to do that with him.

I want to say "boo!" But instead I just say "see ya," and take off.

It's an easy ride past Hassam's to the development. The farm stand is open, and Mr. Hassam waves as I spin by. I turn the corner and ride toward the new road into the development, cruising past the evergreens and the fields.

The new development is a shock. It hasn't been landscaped yet, and the empty houses look naked on their dirt lots. Most of the houses on Beewick were built in the early part of the last century, and they've tried to follow that model, but they've blown up the farmhouses into huge monsters with oversize windows and double doors. Their garages are thrust forward. I imagine all those garage doors open, and it would be like gaping mouths facing the streets, ready to chomp on anyone strolling by.

I can see signs of vandalism. One garage is splattered with red paint. Another one's yard is littered with refuse.

It's easy to find the house that Zed was talking

about. It's at the end of Larch Lane, and it's the only one on that road with full access to the bay. I bump my bike over the dirt and walk it, avoiding the trash in the front yard. I park it behind the house.

This house has a private dock at the bottom of a hill that leads down from the back deck. One day, this will be a lawn. One day, I guess, it will be beautiful, but I just don't have the imagination to see it.

I prowl around the house, peeking in the windows. Everything is shut tight. One window is boarded up, so I guess it had been smashed in the break-in. The house is totally empty inside. There's nothing to see. I start to wonder why I came. There are no clues here. There is nothing to pick up on.

I sit down on the steps of the back deck. There's a bag crumpled up underneath, shoved down behind the stairs. I reach down and pick it up. Just garbage, a bag from Starbucks with two empty coffee cups inside. I look at the sides of the cups, where they mark them. One was a cappuccino. The other was a tall nonfat latte, double shot. The bag feels heavy, which is weird, because the cups are empty. I feel a wave of sadness that makes no sense.

And then I feel it. A shudder inside me. The bag feels warm and heavy, as if the coffee cups are full.

Surprise floods me. But it isn't my surprise. I am feeling *someone else's* surprise. I hear a different heartbeat thud in my ears, hammering in panic.

The shock of the cold water takes my breath away. My head, my head . . .

I flail, while fireworks explode behind my eyes.

My heart is going to burst inside my chest. It is going to bloom like a rose.

It's him. It's Hank Hobbs. I can feel him, see him.

And someone is watching him drown.

And that someone feels nothing but impatience. No panic. No sorrow.

I hear footsteps against gravel.

Gravel?

I open my eyes. I am on the deck again. I am covered in sweat.

And the footsteps are real.

ELEVEN

I must be truly spooked in general, because I'm ready to pick up a stray beam and swing it at whoever appears. So it's kind of good that I don't, considering that Jeff Ferris appears with his father. They're both wearing suits, but they've tucked their pants into knee-high rubber boots. The sight of that is so silly that my fear drains away immediately. Anyway, since Jeff still owns the house, it makes perfect sense that he would be visiting it.

The reason for my presence, on the other hand, is not so clear.

"Gracie Kenzie," Jeff says. "What are you doing out here?"

"I hear so much about these houses," I say. "I just wanted to see for myself how great they are."

"Yeah. Look at that view." Jeff turns toward the cove and clicks into realtor mode. "It's one of the prime spots on the island."

His dad's gaze roams over the back of the house. "Looks all right. We'd better check the inside, though. Kids. That Fusilli should throw them in jail."

"He doesn't know who they are, Dad."

"Are you going to move in here?" I ask.

Jeff shakes his head. "I bought it for an investment, but man, it hurts to let it go."

"They vandalized our office," Franklin Ferris says. "They turned off the refrigerator so everything would spoil. Somebody smeared peanut butter all over my desk. I'm allergic to peanut butter! What kind of a person would do something like that?"

I just catch a hint of a smile as Jeff bends down to knock some dirt off the rubber boots he's wearing. Could it be that Jeff is amused at the thought of his prissy father getting hives? He slides a look at me. "You know Mason Patterson, right?"

"My cousin goes out with his sister, so yeah, I guess so."

"He's a good kid," Jeff says neutrally. He doesn't fool me. He's wondering if I'm in with the crowd who's vandalizing the development. So is his dad, who clears his throat and looks away. "So. How's the house?"

"Still standing. Did you hear about Hank Hobbs?"

Jeff nods. "Freaky, huh? My loss — he'd just gone to contract on this house. I had lunch with him right before he died. I mean, I guess I did. They found him the next day."

"I don't know why," Franklin Ferris says, "everywhere I go, I have to discuss this."

"Dad sold Hobbs his first house on Beewick. A big sale for us, back then."

"Did he seem depressed or weird or anything?" I ask Jeff.

"No. Why? Do they think he committed suicide?"

"They don't know."

"Well, neither do I. He seemed fine. But you never know what's in someone's head."

Jeff doesn't look too thrilled at discussing a former client with a teenager. I have a feeling I'm at the end of my conversational rope with him. His dad has decided to ignore me. He's wandering over to look in the windows.

We hear the noise of a car door slamming. Footsteps head toward us. This time I'm not scared. I have a feeling I know who it is.

Joe Fusilli heads toward us. He steps in an enormous mud puddle on the way, which really pisses him off. He should have worn a pair of rubber boots. He shakes off some of the mud and keeps on coming.

"Gracie. What are you doing out here?"

"Checking out the view," I say.

He gives me that Joe-probe, the look that's supposed to make me squirm, but I don't react, so he turns to Jeff and his father. "Hi, Jeff, Franklin. Glad I ran into you — I left a message on your cell. I wanted to look around a bit."

"Sure. No problem."

Joe notices that I'm still holding the Starbucks bag. "What's that?"

"I found it here," I say, pointing to the stairs. "I think Hank Hobbs left it here."

"Why do you say that?" Joe asks.

I shrug. Joe sighs.

He whips out a pair of latex gloves from his pocket and takes the bag from me. He lifts out first one cup, then the other. He bends down to look. "Lipstick stain," he says.

He turns to Jeff. "Did Hobbs come here with his wife?"

Jeff looks uncomfortable. "You know, a realtor is like a psychiatrist, in a way. We know everybody's secrets."

"Like who's getting divorced?"

Jeff shoves his hands in his pockets. "I heard him talking to a Betsy on the phone. His wife's name is Pam."

"Jeff, that's gossip," Franklin Ferris says disapprovingly.

"Actually, it's not," Joe says. "I'm investigating a death. Go on, Jeff."

"I was struck by the conversation, because I thought he was talking to his wife. He had that tone in his voice. And whenever we talked about this house, he never mentioned her. So I just kind of assumed that maybe," Jeff looks at his father nervously, "there was someone else. But of course I don't know anything for sure."

Joe is writing in his notepad. "There's no Starbucks on the island," he says. "Whoever this Betsy is, she could be from the mainland."

"Well, Hank Hobbs lived in Seattle," Jeff says. "I mean, you know that, of course. I'm just trying to be helpful."

Joe puts the cups and the bag into a plastic bag and seals it. "Can you show me around?" he asks Jeff.

"Sure."

Nobody pays attention to me, so I tag behind them as Jeff opens the door and punches a code into the keypad to turn off the alarm.

"Never thought I'd have to use an alarm on Beewick," Jeff says. "That's a sad thing."

"We sold houses with alarms twenty years ago," Franklin Ferris says. "I hate this false sentimentality."

"These days, we have to remember so many codes and passwords, it's a wonder our heads don't explode," Joe says as he pokes around the empty kitchen. "My secret system is to code everything on my dog's birthday."

"You remember your dog's birthday?" Jeff asks, amused.

"No. That's the problem," Joe says, bending down to open the cabinet under the sink.

"Ha," Jeff chortles appreciatively.

We follow Joe around the house. I can tell he's disappointed by the lack of clues. The house is not only empty, it's clean. There are amazing views from all the bedrooms, and each bedroom has its own bathroom. That would sure cut down on arguments in Shay's house, let me tell you.

"Let's take a look at the dock," Joe says when he's finished.

"I was hoping we could get back to town," Franklin Ferris says.

"Just another few minutes," Joe says. It's clear they can't say no.

Franklin Ferris's face is flushed as we walk out the door. He doesn't like being told what to do, that's for sure.

I'm keeping very quiet, hoping they'll just forget I'm there. Nobody suggests it's time for me to get lost, so I trail behind them down the incline to the dock. Jeff punches another keypad, and the gate swings open. Our footsteps thud along the wooden dock as we walk down toward the end.

Joe stops at the pilings and runs his fingers along one. "Someone tied up a boat here."

"I'm not surprised," Jeff says. "Folks like to come into this cove to fish. Some of them probably use the dock, even though they're not supposed to."

"Did Hobbs ever come to the house by water?" Joe asks.

"He never mentioned it."

Suddenly, I notice Joe's body stiffen. He's seen something. He squats and plucks something that had been wedged into the dock boards. He holds it up. It's a small capsule.

"Vitamin?" Jeff asks.

Joe slips it into a ziplock bag. "We'll see."

Joe looks around some more, but the light is fading. Franklin Ferris looks at his watch in an obvious way.

"Well, I guess it's time to shove off. Thanks for your time," Joe says. "Gracie, I'll give you a ride home. We'll throw your bike in the trunk."

We walk back down the dock and up the hill to the house, then tromp through the mud back to the driveway. Joe looks mournfully at the state of his shoes. While Joe puts my bike in the trunk, I watch as Jeff and his dad sit in his car with the doors open. Together, they take off their rubber boots and put on their shoes. Jeff takes the boots and puts them in the trunk. He waves as he drives off. Franklin Ferris stares straight ahead.

I slide into the front seat. Joe just drives for a while.

As he hits the main road back toward Shay's, he nods a couple of times, as if to give himself courage.

"I spoke to your dad."

Somehow I don't like hearing the word *dad* associated with him. "Nate," I say.

"I think I scared him when I showed up. He seemed to want to defend himself from me, as if I was going to arrest him for being a deadbeat dad. I could have. I wanted to."

I have to admit I get some pleasure out of that.

"I didn't think that's what you or Shay would want."

"No. I don't want him in jail. Mom never cared about the child support payments. She was lucky she didn't have to. She just divorced him and never tried to find him."

"I just want you to know that I'll do whatever I can for you, Gracie. That's all. That includes running him out of town if you want me to."

Well, here it is. I could make him disappear. All I have to do is say a word.

"That's okay," I say.

"There's nothing wrong with spending a bit of time with him, and then sending him on his way."

I twist in my seat to face Joe. His expression is stern as he drives. "You don't like him," I say.

"Men who abandon their children are the worst sort."

"He was sick. He thought we were better off without him."

Joe's mouth twists. "They all say that, honey."

"Is he a suspect?"

"Well, he didn't know Hank Hobbs. Never met him, he said. Shay backed him up."

You might think Joe is finished, but I know something else is coming. He pulls into my driveway.

"Are you coming in?" I ask. "I'm sure Shay wants to see you. Even if she's still mad at you."

He shakes his head. "Stay out of the Hobbs case," he says.

"I *am* out of it."

"I mean it, Gracie," Joe says. "Don't forget what happened last time. You started poking around, and the next thing you knew, you were kidnapped by a seriously disturbed guy. We're talking about a murderer here."

"But you don't know Hank Hobbs was murdered for sure."

"I know he was."

"You got the autopsy reports?"

"He was smashed on the head and pushed into that water when he was still alive," Joe says. "Whoever did it is dangerous. Are you getting this now?"

"It's just hard," I say, "when I see things . . ."

"What do you see?"

I shake my head. "Nothing that would help you."

I get out of the car and lean in the open door for a minute. "Thanks for looking out for me," I say.

"Just doing my job," Joe tells me. "Now do yours. Be a kid. Not a detective."

Once I get my bike from his trunk, he pulls out

and drives away. The evergreens look black, with spiky tips brushing the darkening sky. I shiver, thinking of what I saw. I had stood behind a killer's eyes and watched him kill.

I wish I could stay out of it. I wish I could. I wish I could turn off the visions.

If only.

TWELVE

After my mom was killed, after I got over the shock of it, I discovered parts of me I wish I hadn't. I didn't know I had it in me to be mean. I didn't know that I could turn away from someone trying to help me, and not even care. I didn't know I was capable of so much anger at the world.

I look back on that time, when I shut the door in my grandmother's face, when I told my best friend in Maryland that she was stupid, when I hated Shay whenever she smiled or laughed, hated her for breathing when her sister was dead. . . . Well. I'm just grateful that everyone forgave me.

Of course my friend Jessie back in Maryland may have forgiven me, but our friendship will never be the same. Still, I'm grateful to her for trying. Grateful to her for sending me e-mails, photographs of the friends I used to have, so I don't feel completely lost in the world.

A river of pain still cuts a path through me. Sometimes I get pulled under. When the people who love me say "it's okay," I feel lucky.

I stare down at the thirteen birthday cards I've laid out on my bed.

I get that my father did a very bad thing. But part of me remembers that time in my own life, and part of me wonders: When everyone has forgiven me, why can't I take even one tiny step toward forgiving him?

He waits for me again after school. Hands in the pockets of his jacket, looking like another teacher, a new history teacher who all the girls have secret crushes on. I notice how the other students are trying not to watch as I come up and we fall into step together.

There is no problem with rhythm. Even though his legs are long, he matches my stride. I look down at us, our legs, both in jeans, walking. Is there a secret rhythm that fathers and daughters have, no matter what?

"Want me to carry your backpack?"

"I've managed to do it myself since I was seven."

He breathes in and out. "I just have to make a personal observation," he says. "When you've screwed up as badly as I have, there's about a million minefields in every ordinary conversation. And I keep triggering every single one. Pow."

"I've noticed that," I say.

"Do you admire me at least for trying?"

"Actually, no."

"Pow. There goes another one."

We're quiet for a while, but it's a better silence.

"I thought I'd leave," Nate says. "I think it's better for now. You have my address and phone numbers and e-mail. Can I write you once in a while?"

"I guess so."

"Gracie." Nate stops, so I stop, too. On him, my unruly hair makes sense. He looks so ordinary, a handsome guy who's just a little careworn, who's seen a little too much sun and hard times. I see that his eyes aren't quite as dark as mine. They aren't the same color, after all. I note a thousand details of his face in one small moment, and the living reality of him makes me feel disoriented, as though I'd made him up and he suddenly appeared. "What I would really, really like is to take you to dinner tonight."

Everything I've been thinking, everything I've been feeling, tugs me into different directions. But there is one through line: I'm hungry to know him. If he leaves tomorrow and I don't do this, I'll regret it.

He sees the answer on my face, and he smiles.

"It occurs to me that I didn't tell you that I loved your mother," Nate says. "I should say those words out loud. Just because they hurt doesn't mean I shouldn't say them. I let her down so badly. But she was the love of my life."

We're sitting in the restaurant that's in the Greystone Inn. We have a quiet table against a wall. Candles are lit. The potato-leek soup was awesome. My dad is nursing a glass of wine. We both have ordered the lasagna.

Just a father-daughter dinner.

"It was love at first sight," Nate says. "That old corny thing. I was about to back out of the deal to buy the house with Shay, to tell you the truth. I don't know why I agreed to go in on it in the first place. I inherited some money from my aunt, and I was afraid if I didn't invest it, I'd blow it, I guess. I was regretting it until Carrie walked through the door. I even remember what she was wearing, that sweater . . . the color of cornflowers."

He isn't here anymore. He's back in the past. His eyes suddenly have a light in them.

"What was it like, that summer?" I ask.

"Crazy fun. I have to admit, I went to Beewick because it would be free. The group back in Seattle was picking up expenses, and we were camping out in summer. We'd swim at midnight — man, it was cold. I'm not much of a swimmer, so splashing around made sense, just to keep warm. We had some wicked softball games. One night, I crashed a big society party at the country club. One of the locals sneaked me in. It was all such a blast. And then it all went bad. Billy disappeared, and we were all worried about him. Shay thought Hobbs had done something to him, but I thought it was more likely that Hobbs paid him off. Billy hated his family — I wouldn't blame him for disappearing."

"You think that's a solution? Disappearing?"

He comes back to the present and looks at me across the table. He doesn't flinch. "Honey, I didn't hate you. I didn't hate your mom. Sometimes you leave because you love your family so much. You don't want to keep hurting them."

I push my food around, not answering. It's not enough, and he knows it.

"Ohh-kay, maybe I should stick with the past. Shay just couldn't believe that Billy would run out on her without a word. She was in love with him, after all."

"Shay was in love with Billy?"

"Well, sure. They were a couple. They came up to Beewick together. Then she broke up with him, and he was destroyed. I guess Billy thought he didn't have anything to lose, confronting Hobbs."

This was news to me. Shay had never mentioned being in love with Billy. What else was she concealing?

Nate doesn't notice my surprise.

"Did you ever meet Hank Hobbs?" I ask him.

He shakes his head. "We were fighting this abstraction — the Big Evil Corporation. We didn't know any of the executives. Billy was the one who found out somehow that Hank Hobbs was leading the cover-up — or that's what he thought, anyway. Then, for a brief period, Shay herself was under suspicion," he says. "That's why Carrie came out. It wasn't just to help with the house. She wanted to protect Shay. When Carrie and I fell in love, Shay wasn't crazy about it. I guessed at the time that she had feelings for me. She was upset about Billy, maybe she was looking for something to help her . . . maybe she wanted something to happen with us, and I fell for her sister instead." Nate shrugs. "She didn't come to the wedding. Carrie was devastated. They were very close, and Shay's disapproval really hurt her."

"Of course," I point out, "it turned out that Shay was right."

"Yeah, that's the irony, isn't it? Shay was right. Maybe I suspected that she was, even then. I never felt good enough for Carrie."

"You *weren't* good enough for her."

"Believe me, muffin, I know."

He keeps talking, but I'm not there anymore. The word *muffin* spirals me out, away from the table, into a past. His past. Or is it his present? His future?

The light is so bright, summer light. I see him handing something to a little girl, a stuffed rabbit. "There you go, muffin," he says. "Good as new."

The girl is blond and wearing a white dress. I am her negative image. I am a dark spot and she is shining light.

When I return to the now, he's talking, and I

struggle to focus. "I'm betting that Shay wasn't dev-astated when I left. I'm sure she thought you two were better off. I'm not good enough for Rachel, either. I'm just lucky she sticks around." Nate grins. "The woman loves a project."

He leans over the table. "I look at you, my beautiful daughter, and I think — everything you are is perfect."

I'm not about to buy that. I'm still thinking of the pale little girl. "You don't even know me."

"But I know it's true. I want you to know that I told Shay that I'm signing over my half of the house to her as long as you can inherit it."

I guess I'm supposed to gasp and say thanks. But it means so little to me. Half a house? Is that payback? Is that what it's all worth to him?

I think he realizes what I'm thinking, because he leans back, and suddenly, it's like, pull up a chair, because sadness just walked in the door.

There isn't anything he can say, anything he can give me, that will make up for not having him. He knows it. I know it.

I just don't know what to do with it.

Nate drives me home. I get out. He gets out. I wonder if we're supposed to hug when we say good-bye, and if I want us to.

But suddenly, a shadow moves across the lawn and forms into a person, rushing at us, and I gasp.

It's Mason. He looks bigger in the dark.

Nate moves in front of me so quickly, I don't have time to think.

Mason points a finger at me. "Stay out of my business, Kenzie, or you'll be sorry!"

"What are you talking about?" I ask. "I'm not in your business."

"Just keep your freaky nose out of it, freak!"

"Hey!" Nate moves smoothly forward and puts his hand on Mason's shoulder. He must have applied a nice amount of pressure, because Mason steps back as though he's propelled.

"Good night, friend," Nate says. "That's enough."

Mason shoots me a dirty look as he goes.

"What was he talking about?" Nate asks.

"I don't know."

"Do you want me to stick around?"

What a question. Another wrong step in the minefield. Of course I want him to stick around. I've wanted him to stick around since I was three years old.

I say what I always told myself on all those days I missed him, on all those times I wondered about him, on all those nights I dreamed of him.

"I'll be fine."

THIRTEEN

The next day, we have off for a teachers' conference, which is a gift. I don't want to have to face Mason at school. I don't know why he's angry at me, but I'm sure it has something to do with Hank Hobbs.

I'm still spooked to be in the house, but I decide to be brave and hit Diego's computer after he leaves for work.

I plug *Hank Hobbs* into a search engine. Even Joe couldn't be angry with me about that. I can't believe the flood of information that comes up. He had some career going, and he was on the boards of a bunch of companies. It makes for rough going. I can't get through the information overload, and after spending over an hour scrolling through corporate newsletters and articles about "synergistic strategies," I feel like my brain cells are going to fuse.

Time for my own personal computer geek.

I met Ryan last summer, when I was nosing around trying to find out what had happened to Emily. He had a bit of a crush on her, and a bit of a crush on me, but now he has a girlfriend, Tobie, so we're able to be friends. Whenever I have a glitch I can't solve, I call Ryan, and he leads me through a fix-it strategy while blasting my ear with his newest obsessions — last time it was polka-rock (yes, really), the mating habits of polar bears, and Turkish food.

"Gracie! Awesome!" Ryan also has a tendency to speak in exclamation points. "What brings you to call me on my landline?"

"I've got a sleuthing problem."

"Talk on, Nancy Drew."

I explain my information deluge, and what I'm looking for.

"No worries!" Ryan says. "I can devise the right string to find the info. Can you hang on for a few?"

I hang on. I hear the clackety-clack of computer keys.

"Got something!" Ryan says. "Hang on. . . . Yeah, the newspaper on Beewick back there in the ice age was called the *Beacon,* not the *Star.* And they totally rock, because their archives are all online. Some sort of historical record project. I'm going to e-mail this to you."

A moment later, Ryan's e-mail pops up. I click on the URL.

"ACCUSATIONS LEVELED AT MONVOR FOLLOWING DISAPPEARANCE"

I read the article quickly. Shay is quoted saying that Billy Applegate went off to see Hank Hobbs. She makes it clear that she suspects him of hiding something and challenges him in print to "tell the truth about what happened that night."

No wonder Hank Hobbs tried to get her fired.

At the end of the article, it notes, "Ms. Kenzie has also been questioned regarding Mr. Applegate's disappearance."

So Nate was right.

"Here's something interesting," Ryan says, breaking into my thoughts.

My little flag pops up, and I click on Ryan's e-mail. He's included a paragraph from another article that mentions that Hank Hobbs's house was broken into twenty years ago. The police investigated and "concluded that it has no connection to the Applegate disappearance." A few things were stolen, including a briefcase. "I was certain I'd set the alarm, but I guess I didn't," Hobbs said.

A briefcase was stolen. Could it have contained the documents that Billy Applegate had claimed to have, the ones that proved that Monvor had falsified data? The break-in had happened just a few days before he disappeared. Just around the time he told the group that he had the goods on Monvor.

"It's got to be it," I whisper.

"Hey, this is weird," Ryan says. "This guy Hobbs was married to a woman named Pam. But back then, he got engaged to someone else."

"Who?"

"An Elizabeth Anne Dunwoody. I love these

announcements, they are so *incredibly* cornball. Elizabeth, known as Betsy, has attended the Heath School in Seattle and is currently —"

"Known as Betsy!" Jeff Ferris had heard Hank talking to a Betsy on the phone.

"Is that something? Did I find something?"

"You are an incredible genius."

"I have to inform you, Gracie, that I am taken. Tobie is the axis around which I revolve. So even though I worship your completely awesome personhood, we must remain attached on only a spiritual plane —"

"Can you find out if Betsy Dunwoody is still living around here?"

"Does a chicken have lips?" I hear keys clacking again. "Betsy Dunwoody married someone else. She is now Mrs. Elizabeth Dunwoody Wheeler, and she lives in Bellevue, Washington. Let me see . . . museum trustee, country club, chair of Save the Parklands committee . . . yeah, we're talking major Betsy bucks."

Bellevue is a swanky suburb of Seattle. It's only an hour south of here. And Diego has a car.

FOURTEEN

"You're kidding, right? Because if you're not kidding, you're nuts." Diego sits at the kitchen table, his spoon halfway to his mouth. He'd just been about to dive into a tempting bowl of Shay's granola. I like to hit him up in the mornings, before he's made plans. Marigold sleeps late on Saturdays, but Diego is an early riser. He always wakes up in a good mood, too.

That is, if I don't spoil it.

By my silence Diego correctly assumes that I'm not kidding.

"You're nuts," he says again. "Do you happen to remember what happened the last time I drove you into Seattle on the trail of a kidnapper? And do you happen to remember that you yourself were kidnapped while I stood around in the park half out of my mind? Do you remember that my mother has still never forgiven me?"

"All of this is true," I say. "But this is different. I'm not investigating a suspect. I just want to talk to —"

"That's what you said last time!"

It's clear I have to tell Diego everything. I pull

out a chair and sit down. "Joe thinks Shay is a suspect in the murder of Hank Hobbs," I say.

"That's ridiculous."

"Of course it is. He also thinks it might have been my father."

Diego blinks. "Not so ridiculous," he says. "I mean, he just shows up on the same weekend that someone is found dead. . . ."

"Yeah. Exactly. So I'm going to go from the weird girl who sees things to the weird girl who sees things whose father is a murderer. Can't wait."

"It doesn't matter what your father is, or does. Anyone who knows you knows —"

"Diego, you sound like a guidance counselor. Come on."

"Well, it's true. I never knew my father. He could be a murderer."

"But he isn't, is he?"

Diego takes a sip of juice. His father is something we never talk about in this house. Nineteen years ago, Shay went on a trip to Spain and came back pregnant. She simply told her family that she was having the baby and raising it, and his father would never be discussed. Somehow, she pulled it off.

I've asked Diego about his father. He's told me that he knows some things, but it's obviously difficult for Shay to talk about, so he doesn't ask her about it. And when I press him for details, he fixes me with his beautiful liquid eyes and tells me to ask Shay.

I still haven't worked up the nerve.

"My granola's getting soggy," Diego says.

"So's your logic. And if those two candidates for the slammer aren't enough, the other suspect is Mason Patterson. Do you want Marigold's brother to go to jail?"

Diego doesn't say anything. He's thinking.

"This woman was engaged to Hank Hobbs twenty years ago. Maybe they reconnected. Maybe she knows something. Maybe if we just go down there and talk to her, we'll be able to go to Joe and give him a new suspect. Just think how grateful Marigold would be if you took the heat off Mason. You'd be the man."

"When you start talking like a bad TV show, I know you're desperate," Diego says. "I don't care about being a hero to Marigold. I just want to bask in her lovelight."

"Oh, gross!"

Diego grins. "But I'll take you."

Diego may give me a hard time, but secretly, he loves surveillance. We sat outside Betsy Dunwoody Wheeler's McMansion in Bellevue in Diego's old Saab, watching the house.

"What if she doesn't come out?"

"It's Saturday morning. Everybody goes out on Saturday morning sometime."

"Wait, I see the side door opening —"

"It's her! Duck!"

"Why?" Diego asks me. "She doesn't know us."

"Oh. Right." I peer through the windshield as Betsy gets into a Mercedes SUV.

"Looking good for a mom," Diego notes approvingly.

It's true. Betsy has a trim body, and her chin-length blond hair is glossy and full. From behind, you could mistake her for a teenager, especially for the jeans and tiny jacket she wears. She starts the car and drives down the long driveway toward us.

She turns into the street and we follow, winding through the neighborhood and then out onto the main road. When she turns at the light, we turn. When she picks up speed, we pick up speed.

"You're loving this, aren't you?" I say to Diego.

"Don't push it," he says.

Suddenly, Betsy pulls over.

"She's going to that Starbucks!" I yell. "Pull over!"

"Why, do you want a latte?"

Betsy gets out of the car and goes into Starbucks.

"Wait here," I say to Diego.

"Bring me a cookie!" Diego yells after me as I scoot out.

I follow Betsy into the Starbucks. I maneuver close to her, pretending to study the muffin selection.

"A tall two-shot nonfat latte," Betsy says.

Bingo.

I race back to the car.

"Where's my cookie?"

"She ordered a double-shot nonfat latte," I say. "Just like the cup on Beewick. That was definitely her!"

"What now?" Diego asks. "Should we go in and talk to her?"

I shake my head. "She's leaving. We have to keep following her."

Diego pulls out after Betsy. We follow her through the hills, up and down the twisting roads, trying to keep at least one car behind her. Finally, she pulls into the long, curving drive of the Conifer Country Club.

We drive in. Diego parks the car an aisle away from her.

"We're going to have to talk to her quickly," he says. "We can get busted if we don't. We're not members."

It occurs to me at this moment that I have no idea what I'm going to say. But it's too late now. I get out of the car and we walk toward Betsy. She's grabbed a tote bag and is heading for the front door of the club, swinging the bag as she walks. She reaches the front door before we can catch up and disappears inside.

"Now or never," Diego says.

I push open the door. My foot hits a deep rug on a bleached wood floor. A huge orange glass object is spotlit on a shelf, looking like a giant clam. I see paintings. What Shay would call window treatments, not curtains. The whole place screams "tasteful."

"Go," Diego says. He gives me a small push in the middle of my back.

I need it. I'm intimidated.

"Betsy!" I cry. My voice sounds like a croak.

I try again. "Betsy?"

She hears me this time. She turns, already smiling, thinking I'm a daughter of a friend, perhaps. I see her searching her memory banks.

So I blurt out the thing I shouldn't say, the only thing I can say.

"Isn't it sad about Hank Hobbs?"

Her smile disappears. I see panic in her eyes now. And the panic opens her up to me like a picture book.

I see . . . a small, empty room with a raised platform and a view outside to the tops of trees. Skylight overhead. I hear a woman crying.

. . . a white carnation, its petals brown and crumbling.

. . . an ache somewhere, something hurting, a knee.

"Yes. I haven't seen him in years, though." She backs away a step and then the smile is there again, a practiced smile.

"That's not exactly true," I say.

Her eyes flick from me to Diego, and suddenly, she looks hard. "Who are you?"

"We live on Beewick Island," I say. "We —"

"I don't know you."

"We just wanted to ask you a few questions," Diego says. "That's all. We're not here to harass you." He smiles at her in a friendly way.

Usually, when Diego turns on his charm to any female with a pulse, he gets results. But not with Betsy.

"You're not members here, are you?" she says in a glacial tone. Her gaze roams the hallway behind us. "I'll find someone to escort you back to the parking lot."

"How's your knee?" I ask.

"My knee?" She looks confused again.

"I know it's still bothering you."

"An old ski injury. How do . . ."

"And that room you built at the top of your house, where you go to be alone . . . you were going to do yoga there, but all you do is cry. Alone. Where no one can hear you."

"H-h-how do you know these things?"

"You wonder if your whole life is a mistake, but then you look at your children and you think, *How could I think that?* But you keep thinking it."

"Who are you?" she whispers.

"The carnation that means so much to you . . ."

Now she gives a cry and steps back, her hand at her throat.

Diego puts a hand under her elbow. There's a fireplace at one end of the long hallway, with some armchairs around it. He walks her all the way there, gently places her in one, then draws the others closer. We sit.

"What is this?" Betsy asks. "What's going on? Who *are* you?"

"My cousin is a psychic," Diego says. "She sees things."

"And you were drawn to me for some reason?" Betsy's green eyes are wide. I can tell that this excites her. Betsy's not a skeptic. She's eager to believe.

"Yes." I pitch my voice low, trying to sound more mature, like someone she'd listen to . . . and give answers to. "Hank's death left disturbances behind."

"Oh." The word is a cry, and Betsy presses her hand against her heart. "It did."

"You loved Hank Hobbs," I say, because I'm picking this up most of all. "You met him on

Beewick Island. You saw his new house, the house he was buying so that you could be together."

She bites her lower lip and looks up at me. "How did you know about the carnation?"

"The carnation?" Diego asks.

I nod to give Betsy encouragement. I know what I saw, but I don't know why I saw it, or what it means to her.

"It was . . . a joke," Betsy says. "From one afternoon when Hank and I were together . . . after he found me again. He couldn't remember my favorite flowers, and I teased him, because he remembered everything else. The day we met. The song that was playing the night we got engaged. What I wore, the things I said . . . it was amazing. So I reminded him that I didn't have a favorite flower, but the only flower I couldn't stand was a carnation. That night, when I got home, I opened my purse . . . and there was a carnation." She smiled. "I don't know how he found one and sneaked it in there, but he made me laugh. That was the day I knew I still loved him."

"So he looked you up," I say.

"It had been so long. Twenty years. And he e-mailed me out of the blue — *Are you the Betsy Dunwoody with eyes the color of sea glass?* We started writing, and then we met, and then . . ." She looked at the fire. "We didn't have an affair. We just wanted to be friends. We didn't want to fall in love." She looks down at the rings on her left hand, a band with three large diamonds, and, above it, a square-shaped diamond.

"You were thinking of leaving your husband."

"Yes," she whispers. "How do you know these things? Do you . . . see things in me? Things you want to tell me? Because there is so much I want to know."

I see bottomless need in her eyes. Here is a woman in need of so many things — reassurance, direction. I don't really have any for her. I can't tell her about her life. I can't tell her if she made the right choices. She doesn't understand that even though I can pick up flashes from her, I can't validate her. But that's what she wants.

I'm not sure what to do. I search in my mind for the right tone, the right words. And then I think of a role model. The person we look up to more than anyone, the person who spells it out for us, the person who asks the right questions in the right way.

Oprah.

"Tell me more about Hank," I say. "He seems to be a key for you."

She gives a sad smile. "A key to a different past. A past I should have had. I met him at a dance at the Beewick Club. I drove up to Beewick that weekend with some friends. There was a dance on Bastille Day. We were all dressed like French revolutionaries and royalty. It was silly, but we had fun. Hank just kept coming over to ask me to dance until my escort wanted to take him outside. I didn't care. I left with Hank. He drove me all the way home that night — all the way back to Seattle. A month later, he asked me to marry him. I didn't have one single doubt. And then . . ."

"And then?" Diego asks.

"There was that business with the missing young man."

"Billy Applegate."

"Was that his name? I don't remember. It was all so ridiculous — of course Hank didn't have anything to do with it. But some horrible woman accused him."

Diego and I exchange a look. That was Shay.

"His name got in the papers. And then apparently, there were some other things about his company, what they were doing on Beewick . . ."

"Polluting it," Diego says.

"Well, that's what they said. Hank didn't have anything to do with that, either — he was just a vice president." Betsy pushes at her hair, managing to brush it out of her eyes without ruffling it. "But with my parents, you just don't get your name in the papers. Once when you're married, once when you die, but that's it. My dad played golf with the chairman of the board of Monvor, and the chairman hinted that maybe Hank would lose his job. The chairman said he was careless — but Hank was the most careful man! He had enemies at that company. But my parents didn't understand. They never liked Hank anyway, and they were totally against the engagement, so they started pressuring me."

Betsy looks at the fire again. "It was so hard for me. I didn't know what to do. I was young, only twenty-one. Hank was more than ten years older than I was. . . . I was just a kid. I couldn't go against my parents. And Hank lived full-time on Beewick then. Nobody lived on Beewick. It's not like it is now. So my parents . . . they just thought, here's our daughter, marrying this guy, maybe he's a criminal, maybe he'll get fired, and he's taking her to this island in the middle of Puget Sound. So I broke it off."

Wow. Was this story for real?

Her hands twist in her lap. "Hank was so upset. He said I had to believe in him. That he was taking care of everything, that there was no way in the world they would fire him. But I didn't listen. I thought maybe my parents were right. Maybe my first love wasn't my real love." She looks up at us, tears swimming in her green eyes. "But it was. It was!"

"And he never got over you," I say.

"That's what he said. He wanted to leave his wife and start over, start living the life he said he was meant to live. And now he can't. And neither can I." Betsy ends on a sob. A couple passing by looks over, but Diego's stare tells them to butt out.

She lifts her head from her hands. Mascara has smudged underneath her eyes. "Can you tell me how he is?" she whispers. "You can feel him still, can't you? Can you tell him I'm sorry for what I did?"

"Sorry?" I repeat. My heartbeat quickens. What will Betsy reveal?

"I should have told him that last day I would go with him. We drove up together and he showed me that house and said he was buying it for me. He laid out his whole life, his whole plan on how we would live, where we would travel. . . . And I could see it. But I didn't tell him yes. I told him I needed more time. But I would have gone with him! Can you tell him that?"

"I'm not in touch with Hank," I say. "But I feel he knew that you loved him."

Diego nudges me with his foot. He knows I'm giving her a line. But it's not just that I want more information. I want to make her feel better.

"Betsy, did you know Nathaniel Millard?" I ask. I know time is running out. In another minute, Betsy will come to herself and realize she's unburdening herself of memories to two strangers. She'll feel uncomfortable, and she'll split.

She looks blank and shakes her head.

"Shay Kenzie?"

"No idea."

"They spent the summer on Beewick twenty years ago, along with Billy Applegate."

"I only went to Beewick one time back then," she says. "The night I met Hank. Hank always came to Seattle to see me. He drove in every weekend, and it wasn't as fast a trip then, either. He was so devoted. And I never, never truly appreciated it. And now I've lost him!"

Now Diego rolls his eyes when Betsy isn't looking. I agree with him — there's sincerity in what Betsy is saying, but also just a little too much drama.

She looks at Diego. "Would you mind? Can I . . . talk to her alone?"

"Of course." Diego rises and drifts off. He pretends to study a case full of medals and trophies against one wall.

"Can you tell me anything else?" she asks me. "Anything I should know about me?"

Huh? Betsy is looking at me hungrily. I have to come up with something. "Keep up with the yoga," I say.

She nods, as though this is precious information. "And what about my husband? Should I leave him?"

What a question. How would I know?

I wonder what a psychic would say.

"You must move through your grief for Hank," I improvise. "Grief distorts your intention. Only when you move on can you see your path."

She nods again. "Thank you. Thank you."

She wipes at her eyes carefully, then gathers up her things and walks down the hall. I wander over to Diego.

"That was a bust," I say. "Hank was planning on leaving his wife, though. Joe should know that."

"He should know this, too," Diego says. He points to the wall. Betsy Wheeler has won the gold medal in her age class in every swim meet since the year 2000.

The significance clicks in.

"She could have swum to shore easily," I say.

FIFTEEN

Usually, Shay and Joe try to see each other three or four times a week, and Joe eats dinner at our house on Fridays. So I'm surprised when Shay suggests pizza night on Friday. She always likes to cook for Joe. She looks exhausted, and I suddenly realize that Joe hasn't exactly been burning up the phone lines, either.

"Joe's not coming?" I ask.

Shay has her back to me. She's getting out the phone book, even though pizza delivery is on speed dial. That's how addled she is.

"No, he's working," she says. I can't see her face, but I can see by her shoulders that she's sad. Or angry. Or both.

I wish I could see into my aunt's head. Normally, I don't have to. Shay is just out there. She tells you what's on her mind. I never get flashes about her, and I think it's not only because we're close, but because she's so clear, so direct. There is no secret engine driving her, the way it is with the others I can pick up things from.

Or so I thought. I never thought she could keep a secret from me, either.

Does everyone have a secret engine? I know what mine is — grief. The loss of my mother fuels me. What I want more than anything is for that grief to stop driving the bus.

What about Betsy Dunwoody? She's made a secret engine out of her confusion. She seems like an unlikely murder suspect, but I have to wonder if someone capable of that much ego and sadness could funnel it into rage. Could she have pushed Hank off that boat?

Shay seems unreachable right now, and that's weird. She's the one who keeps this house running, who keeps us together at the dinner table, who lights the fires, who cooks the meals, who looks up the weather every morning so she can tell us to wear our gloves. Even though she knows it drives Diego crazy to be told what to do like a kid.

Is it just the thing with Joe that's making her so withdrawn? Or is she worried about something else?

I know lots of things about Joe Fusilli, and one of the things I know is that every morning he goes to this bakery near his house and buys his mother a carrot muffin. She has Alzheimer's, and she lives with him. She has a caregiver who comes in during the day, and Joe's sister comes over on the nights Joe is out. It's hard on the family, but Joe is going to do it as long as he can, because that's the kind of guy he is.

Anyway, I don't know if Joe's mother remembers from one day to the next if she even likes carrot muffins, but he knows she does, and it makes her happy, so he buys a muffin and coffee for himself every morning at the BlueBay Diner. Which happens to be on my way to school.

I see his car parked in the lot, so I park my bike and walk in. Joe is sipping his coffee at the end of the counter, and an egg-white omelette sits in front of him. He's not really eating it. He looks as bummed as Shay.

"That's not much of a breakfast," I say, sliding onto the stool next to him. "Where's the toast?"

"I'm on a diet. Can I buy you something and watch you eat it? A muffin? Toast with butter? Chocolate cake?"

"No, thanks. I just stopped by when I saw your car. We haven't seen you."

"Yeah." Joe looks down into his coffee cup. "This case has me pretty busy."

"Did you and Shay have a fight?"

He puts the mug down on the counter. "No. Not really. But until this case is over, I have to watch out how things look."

"Because Shay is a suspect."

"Not to me, Gracie," Joe says. "Shay doesn't seem to get that." Sometimes his dark eyes seem to hold all the misery in the world. This is one of those times. "Of course I know that Shay couldn't have done anything like that — she doesn't have a homicidal bone in her body. But she does have motive, and she doesn't have an alibi for that evening. She was out at the wetlands site, alone."

"Oh. But she's probably really mad at you for asking her for an alibi."

"Let's say," Joe says, sipping his coffee, "it was not the most pleasant conversation."

"Well, I have something that might help you," I say. "A clue."

He raises his eyebrows at me. "This better involve a hunch, and nothing else. No more poking around."

"I found Betsy."

"You found Betsy."

"Betsy Dunwoody Wheeler. She was engaged to Hank Hobbs twenty years ago, and they were having an affair when he died. Well, she says they weren't, but I don't think she'd tell a couple of kids the truth, do you?"

"A couple of kids?"

Oops. I was supposed to leave Diego out of it. "Diego took me to see her." Joe's stare tells me to go on. "In Bellevue. We talked to her at the country club. And she's a champion swimmer, Joe! She could have whacked Hank with an oar or something, pushed him off the boat, waited for him to go down, and then swam back to shore, no problem."

Is that steam rising from the coffee, or is it coming out of Joe's ears?

"Gracie, I told you not to get involved."

"But what I did was, I —"

"I told you to stay out of this. It could be dangerous."

"I just thought if I talked to her, I could pick up something you couldn't."

Double oops. Definitely the wrong thing to say.

"I'm a trained *investigator*, Gracie."

"Right. And you are supreme. But I thought maybe I'd get a flash or two from her, and I did. Nothing about the murder. Just some other stuff that made her open up. She admitted that she'd been out to Beewick with him, Joe! And she had a double-shot latte —"

Joe groans and puts his head in his hands. "Stop." He pushes his coffee mug away and picks up the bag with the muffin in it. He stands up. "I will investigate Betsy Dunwoody Wheeler, and you will stay home and never — ever — do this again. I'm going to talk to Shay about this, Gracie. I mean it. Come on, I'll walk you out."

We walk out together. Joe is still fuming. I know he's mostly concerned about me getting myself into trouble again. What he doesn't realize is that I'm already in trouble. I'm already involved. Shay is a suspect. My father is a suspect. I can't just sit there and do nothing.

I have to know.

Joe pauses by my bike. "You going to school?"

I nod. Obviously, I'm going to school. Joe is leading up to something.

"Do me a favor. Don't start investigating Mason Patterson. Keep your distance, okay?"

"Why?"

"Just do it."

"But why?"

Joe sighs. He knows I'm not going to give up.

"We tested that capsule I found at the dock. It's andro."

"Andro?"

"Androstenedione. It's a steroid precursor popular among bodybuilders and athletes. We searched Mason's house last night and the identical brand was found in his room."

"So he was there. At Hank Hobbs's house."

"Could be. Could be he's involved somehow."

"Do you think he killed Hobbs?" I ask breathlessly.

"I don't know who killed Hobbs, and I don't discuss my cases with anyone," Joe says sternly. "The only reason I'm telling you this, Gracie, is that you might hear it at school today, and I don't want you asking Mason any questions. I want your nose out of it, do you hear me?"

"I'm out of it," I say. "I promise." And I mean it. Mostly because I don't want to cross Joe. But also because the last thing I want to do is tangle with Mason.

I'm hanging up my jacket in my locker when I see Marigold heading toward me. Sometimes she makes an effort to seek me out, but I think it's just to get points from Diego. Our conversations never really go anywhere, and I can tell she's relieved when she trills her "'bye now!"

But this morning is different.

This morning, Marigold finally gets real.

She is followed by her best friends, Ashley Hull and Kelly Farnsworth, and I suddenly get a sinking feeling. With teenage girls, the presence of a posse usually signals an ambush.

Marigold closes my locker door with a bang. "You've got a lot of nerve, Gracie Kenzie," she says.

I don't say anything, because I know there is no stopping her. Behind her, Kelly and Ashley glare at me.

"Stay away from my family," Marigold hisses. "I know you got Detective Fusilli to search our house. It was humiliating!"

"First of all, I had nothing to do with it," I say. "Second, didn't the police find something?"

Marigold's face flushes. "Mason is innocent! He doesn't take steroids! That was left there by somebody else. And now the police think he might have killed that guy!"

"Marigold, I have nothing to do with this," I say. "I don't know why you think I do."

"I know that your aunt dates Detective Fusilli. And I know you're a psychic weirdo," Marigold says. There are tears in her eyes. She's not just being mean. She's scared.

Scared of what?

That her brother will get arrested for something he didn't do? Or that he's guilty?

"You told the police that he was guilty," Marigold goes on.

"And Mason is totally innocent," Ashley Hull says. "He's the greatest guy, and now everyone will think he killed somebody."

I know that Ashley has a wicked crush on Mason. She seems particularly overheated.

"It is *so* irresponsible of you," Kelly says.

Kids are gathering around us. I want to open my locker and crawl back inside. I know that nothing I say to Marigold and her friends will make any difference. But I'm also angry at them for jumping to conclusions. For attacking me. I can feel my anger rush up from my feet to my head, and I feel words crowding my throat, things I shouldn't say.

"My mother won't come out of her room," Marigold says. "We had to hire a lawyer and everything, thanks to you. And I know why you did it, too. Diego told me."

My stomach drops to the floor, and I feel sick. "What did Diego tell you?"

"That your long-lost father is in town. That he suddenly shows up, and Hank Hobbs is dead. You don't want your dad to be a murderer, so you point the finger at my brother!"

Everything balls up inside me. Fear and anger and, most of all, loneliness. I have never felt so alone.

Except for one person. One person I never expected to think was on my side.

My dad.

Hearing someone else attack him does something to me. I feel blind rage, something black and ancient roars up from inside me.

"Marigold, I know it's hard for you to concentrate, especially in school," I say. "But make an effort. Get those brain cells to cooperate. I didn't say anything to Joe about Mason. If he's in trouble, it has nothing to do with me."

Marigold takes a breath. I see all the angry words bottled up in her, too, and now they come rushing out. "You don't have to insult me," she says. "I know you never liked me. I know you're jealous of me."

"Jealous of you?"

"Don't even try to deny it. And not only are you a weird freak, you're a liar, too. Weren't you at

Hank Hobbs's house with Detective Fusilli? Andy saw you go by the other day."

"But what does that have to do with —"

Marigold's eyes glitter with tears. "Just leave us alone," she says. "Leave all of us alone. Go back where you came from, I don't care. Just get lost."

Crying, she stumbles away. With last looks of death at me, her girlfriends follow.

Now I realize that the hallway is silent. No one is slamming a locker door. No one is chanting a rap song. No one is hooting with laughter at something someone else said.

They are all looking at me.

One of them is Andy Hassam. He stares at me from his open locker. The stare is anything but friendly.

It is instantly clear to me that my less-than-stellar social standing at Beewick High has now bottomed out. I am less than zero. I am finished.

And it's only ten after nine.

SIXTEEN

I get through the day. I don't know how. But time passes, and you have to go to class, and take your French quiz, and hide in the bathroom next to the gym during lunch period, and scurry to your classes while kids whisper about you, and then, boom, after about twelve thousand hours of agony, school is over and you can go home.

There are cliques in my high school, like all high schools, but it's small, so everyone sort of hangs together in a crisis, and Mason was having a crisis, and if Marigold's blaming me for it, well, kids just kind of go along with that. Nobody's mean to me or trips me on purpose or writes *SKANKY FREAK* on my locker, but nobody gives me a "hang in there" sign, either.

That feeling I had at my locker, that feeling of being completely alone in the world — it's still there. It's like I'm standing still, and Diego and Shay are moving away. What I thought was family is just three people living in a house.

I make my way home on my bike. The cool wind hits my face and feels good. I wish it were colder. I wish it were freezing. I wish that every time I start to cry, the wind would freeze my tears and they would break like glass.

Shay isn't home from work yet, and neither is Diego, so I'm on my own. It's only four o'clock, and it's close to dark. I turn on some lights and I still feel spooked. Even though I don't want to see them right now, I wish they were here.

"This is ridiculous," I say out loud.

What is it about this house that is spooking me?

And do I really want to know?

What I need is some hot-water therapy, I decide. I turn on the shower and wait for the water to get hot, then climb in. I let the water pound my back, sluice down my short hair. I scrub with Shay's special oatmeal soap, the kind that has little nubby pieces of oatmeal in it, the soap Diego swears has twigs in it, it hurts so much. I like how it feels, like I'm washing the whole day off my skin. I scrub until my skin is pink, and then I turn off the water and pull back the shower curtain and the light dims and there is blood on the curtain.

There is blood on the curtain and the curtain is on the floor and the body is lying on it.

When I wrap the curtain around the body, it makes a crackling plastic noise that makes me jump.

At least it covers his face.

It's a body. It's not a person. Not anymore. Don't think of it as a person. That's how you'll get through this.

It is so heavy to drag. But it's not far to the door. The smell is so awful.

I don't want to see this, I don't want to know this, I don't want to feel this. . . .

And I am myself again, my eyes wide open, standing in the bathtub. My hand is clutching the curtain.

I am shaking with cold, shaking with terror. I reach for the towel.

And then I hear it.

Footsteps.

Now, I know the footsteps in this house. Shay's quick step. Diego's work boots.

These are stranger's footsteps. I am not having a vision. I am hearing them.

I look over at the door. I can't seem to swallow, can't seem to move.

The doors in the house were shaved on the bottoms years ago, before Shay had the house, to make way for the horrible shag carpeting that Shay tore up. There's a good two or three inches of space at the bottom of the door.

So when someone moves, I see the shadow.

SEVENTEEN

I look around the bathroom for some kind of weapon. There isn't much damage you can inflict with a loofah.

I hear the footsteps, so soft outside the door. I hear them stop. I see the shadow. I know if I kneel down and look underneath the door, I could probably see shoes, but I'm too scared to move.

And what if I bend down to look, and someone is bending down at the other side of the door, looking at me?

That thought sends such terror through me that it makes me move. I lunge toward my pants hanging on the hook on the back of the door. My cell phone is in the pocket.

I punch out Joe's number. Why didn't I ever put him on speed dial?

Because I never thought I'd need him so fast.

I get his voice mail, but I pretend he picks up. If I can hear the person's footsteps, the person can hear me.

"Joe! Joe! There's someone in the house. I hear them. Come right away! You're already on your way over? Oh, hurry. Don't use the siren, maybe you can catch them. . . ."

I hear the footsteps retreating. Fast.

That's when my knees give way, and I fall on the floor. I feel myself shaking and I can't stop.

I can't get up. The floor is so cold.

The phone rings next to my hand. "Gracie! Gracie!"

It's Joe. He must have picked up on his voice mail.

"Joe, someone is here. Please, hurry."

"I'm on my way. I'm close. Is the intruder still there?"

"I . . . I don't know —"

It is as long as forever, but I hear footsteps in the house, and I know it's Joe. I realize I'm lying on the floor in a towel, and I struggle to my feet and get into my clothes as fast as I can.

Joe knocks on the door. "Gracie, open it. It's me. No one's here."

I open the door. My knees are shaking, and I fall into his arms while he fires questions at me, and I'm trying to talk, and he's gently sitting me down on the hall floor.

"This is where he died, Joe," I tell him. "This is where Billy was killed."

He frowns, not wanting to believe me. "Are you sure someone was here? There's no sign that someone broke in —"

"I didn't lock the door. I never lock the door. I didn't imagine it, Joe!"

"No, I don't think you did."

Joe is looking past my shoulder. It is clear in the light from the living room lamp. A muddy footprint outside the bathroom door.

EIGHTEEN

It doesn't take the police long to figure out the brand of the shoe, an athletic shoe in a size that pretty much rules out the intruder being a woman. Within half a day, they discover that a pair was sold to Mason Patterson at the Athletic Aerie over in Ardsley. Then the police search the school, and the shoes are found dumped in the waste can in the gym. Way to go, Beewick Police Department.

There's only one problem — Mason has an alibi. He was hanging with two of his buddies, Andy and Dylan, goofing off in the woods outside school.

Or so they say.

I ask Joe what he thinks Mason's motive was, and for once he lets me in on what he's thinking. He's come over to give us the news, and he and Shay have a truly awkward conversation, and I offer to walk him to his car. We stand by his car in the driveway. Joe must be distracted, because he doesn't seem to mind answering my questions.

"He might have broken into your house just to scare you because he's got it in his head that you're a pipeline to me," Joe says. "The Pattersons are furious that I'm including their son in the investigation.

So just because he broke in doesn't mean he killed Hank Hobbs."

"Why *would* he kill Hank Hobbs?"

"Maybe Hobbs caught them at the house, they were in the middle of some prank, and he tried to stop them, and things went bad." Joe's hands are in his pockets, and he stares back at the house. Behind the lighted windows, Shay is moving around, preparing for evening, switching on lamps, bringing a wool throw to the sofa. She was wearing her work clothes, but she disappears and comes back in sweats. The woman can't bear to wear a piece of clothing with a zipper, I swear.

"Maybe Hobbs had his boat at the dock, and Mason was aboard, and pushed him or something, and he fell off into the water," I say. "So they take the boat out to sea and just hope the body never turns up."

"Not quite, Gracie," Joe says. "Leave the detecting to me, remember?"

Joe turns and opens his car door. He looks back at me. "Go back inside. I'll wait."

"You're going to wait for me to go back inside? It's right across the lawn!"

But the shadows are lengthening, and I suddenly do feel spooked. Joe just looks at me. So I turn obediently and start back across the lawn, secretly glad he is there to watch me.

★　　★　　★

125

I'm just waking up the next morning when I hear it. *Dah doh din daa do.* In my head, it's a familiar tune. But then I'm fully awake, and I realize it's not a tune, not really. It's a series of notes. Like something out of that movie *Close Encounters of the Third Kind,* when they communicate with the alien spaceship through this giant synthesizer.

Dah doh din daa do.

The tune is still in my head as I stumble into the kitchen for my morning cereal. Diego is chomping on some toast. We haven't really talked since the Marigold incident, or since Joe told us the footprint belonged to Mason's shoe.

"How're you doing?" he asks.

"Okay."

"Mom says I should take you to school today. She'll pick you up."

I look up, surprised. "Why?"

"Because she's worried about you, spook doozy."

Diego calls me spook doozy sometimes, and I don't mind. It's kind of cool to have a nickname, and he says it with affection. But this morning, it hits me wrong.

"I don't want to interfere with your morning plans," I say huffily.

"I talked to Marigold," Diego says. "She's sorry about what happened. She was upset. Her parents are freaking out."

"You told her that my father could be the

killer," I say, looking down into my cereal bowl. "You told her all about him."

I sneak a look at Diego. He doesn't look guilty, and that makes me more angry at him.

"But your father *could* be the murderer," he says. "You think that, too. And why shouldn't I tell Marigold that your father came to see you? She's my girlfriend."

"She told the whole *school* that he could be a murderer!"

"The whole school thinks that *Mason* could be a murderer. Looks like you're even."

He's not on my side. He's on Marigold's side.

What is family? It's people there to catch you when you fall. What happens when they step back, when they're looking at someone else so hard, they don't notice that you're falling?

Dah doh din daa do.

The music in my head sends a shudder through me. I am afraid of this house.

Diego gets up. "Let me know when you're ready to leave," he says.

Dah doh din daa do.

I realize something, something I picked up in my vision, and I didn't even register it.

The killer is thinking about killing someone again.

He is thinking about killing me.

NINETEEN

It is a cold Saturday morning before Thanksgiving. Nate and Shay meet at the lawyer's office so that Nate can sign over the house to Shay for me. I watch them sign about a million papers, and the whole time I'm thinking, *After this he'll leave.*

I'll never know him.

I'll never know what he really is.

They finish signing the papers. They shake hands.

"Can I talk to Gracie?" Nate asks Shay.

He has to ask permission. My own father has to ask permission to talk to me. This is one seriously screwed-up situation.

"Of course," Shay says.

We go outside. Shay's lawyer, Debra Peterson, has an office in her house, an old white frame farmhouse. We go out into the backyard. Nate climbs up on the picnic table and puts his feet on the bench. He motions for me to join him.

We look out at Debra's son's wooden swing set. Nate doesn't say anything for a moment. We just listen to the wind.

"How's this for an insane proposition?" he says. "You, me, and a turkey."

"What?"

"Why don't you come with me today for Thanksgiving vacation? You'd have to miss three days of school."

I shrug. Missing school is not exactly a hardship.

"I could drive you back on Sunday. Rachel would love to meet you. I'm under this delusion that we'd get along, all of us."

I'm so surprised, I don't know what to say.

"I'd really like you to come," he says in a very gentle voice.

I breathe in and breathe out. I stare at Deborah's son's playground set. I babysit for him sometimes. Jared.

There's a red ball on the grass. There's a green pail. A blue train car left underneath the swing. Here is a kid who is loved. You can just see it. You can see it in the living room, in the basket of toys. In the kitchen, stocked with granola bars and fruit and oatmeal cookies. You can see it in the framed photograph on Deborah's desk, of her son and her husband on the beach.

I can open my heart and feel how much he's loved.

I was loved. My mom loved me. But there was

always a shadow there, a shadow where a father should be.

I don't know if I can love my own father. But I do want to know him. I *need* to know him.

Nate peeks at me, but he bursts out laughing when he sees my face.

"Oh, man," he says. "It's not a root canal. It's a nice house in the 'burbs." He nudges me with his shoulder. "Who knows, maybe you'll even like it."

And I think — *Where is home?* Beewick Island started to feel like home. Shay's house started to feel like home.

But people like Mason don't want me to feel at home here. And Shay and Diego are a unit, woven as strong as steel mesh. Shay has invited all my confidences, but kept so much of herself secret from me. Maybe the oppression I feel in that house now has more to do with how I feel about the people in it.

My father is a stranger. I don't know what sports he likes, or music. I don't know if he's grumpy in the morning. I don't know if he likes Christmas, or knows how to cook. I don't know any of the million details you're supposed to know about your father.

But something vibrates between us. We can pick up on a rhythm together. We can be silent together. We can hook on to a feeling and ride it, even if it's sadness.

It's something to go on. And it's somewhere to get to.

TWENTY

Shay sits with her mouth open for at least five seconds.

Then she shakes her head. "I can't let you."

"It's just Thanksgiving."

"But . . . we don't really know him, Gracie. We don't know anything about him, what he's been doing."

"He's been working. He got married."

"We only know what he's told us. And there was a murder here."

"If Joe thought he was a suspect, he wouldn't let him leave."

Shay shakes her head again. "I can't let you go."

"He's my father. I have a right to make this decision."

"I'm your guardian and I love you. I have a right to forbid you."

We stare at each other.

"I just want to know him, Shay," I say.

"I need to talk to him first," she says.

Shay talks to Nate. Shay calls Rachel. They talk for a long time. When she gets off, Shay finds me in my bedroom, where I'm lying down reading a book. "She sounds nice," she says. "I already called Nate and told him to pick you up. Go ahead and pack."

I've already packed. I point to my suitcase. She gives me this sad little grin.

"And wear your gloves," she says.

Nate pulls up and honks. I go outside. First Diego gives me a quick hug, and then Shay gathers me up into one of her enfolding extravaganzas.

"Just come back to us," she whispers in my ear.

I feel surprisingly throat-lumpy about this, as if Shay's fear is right, as if I'm leaving forever.

We don't say much as we drive to the ferry. Nate pulls in back of the line. I look a few cars ahead to see who else is in line. I realize that it's a Beewick Islander thing to do. You usually know at least one person in the ferry line if you've lived here long enough.

And sure enough, I see Zed's Subaru up ahead. We still have a few minutes left before the ferry, so I tell Nate I'll be right back.

Zed is reading a book behind the wheel when I approach. I have to tap on his window to get his attention. He looks up at me and I get the gift of his smile, which just about knocks me backward. For a moody, complicated individual, Zed can sell the simple stuff.

He gets out, even though it's started to rain. It's a Pacific Northwest rain, a mist that nobody would dream of carrying an umbrella for.

"Hey, heading to the city?" Zed asks.

I tilt my head toward Nate's car. "I'm going away for Thanksgiving. With my father."

"Oh, cool. You're coming back, though, right?"

Why is everyone asking me that? "I guess," I say.

"You guess?"

"Well. Things haven't been going so well here," I say. "Ever since Hank Hobbs got murdered, things are so screwy. School is completely wrong."

"I heard what happened," Zed says. "Marigold went ballistic on you. She and Mason are tight."

"Everybody keeps saying that, as though that's an excuse," I say angrily. "You islanders really hang together."

"Not really," Zed says mildly.

"I'm just so tired of not belonging anywhere," I say in a sudden rush. "I mean, I really feel tired, you know? Tired of making an effort all the time. School. Home." I wave around at the trees. "Here. And with Shay and Diego. Everyone of us tries so hard, and should we have to? Should a family have to try so hard?" Suddenly, the lump in my throat is back. I don't know why I've chosen this day to finally talk to Zed, and when I do, I blurt out my feelings like an idiot.

Zed's silver-moon eyes regard me carefully. I

wonder what he's thinking. I can't read him. Once, when I first met him, I read his sadness. His mother is dead, just like mine, and that's something you don't get over. His dad is an okay guy, but he works all the time, so Zed was basically raised by his dad's succession of live-in girlfriends. No wonder Zed seems remote. Here's a guy who's used to being left.

"What's a family?" Zed asks with a shrug. "A couple of people who lurch from crisis to crisis together. Maybe you just have to hang, Gracie. I don't know your dad. I just know Shay and Diego. If they were dealt to me as a new family, I'd be all over it. If I had to work it like work, I would."

The cars have left the ferry that just came in, and I hear the car engines start in the line. We're ready to board.

"Well, good-bye," I say.

"Have a good Thanksgiving," Zed says. "I'll see you when you get back."

I start back toward Nate's car. Everything seems to shimmer, the mist, the trees, the clouds, the sky. I feel as though I'm walking in a dream. A dream I've had forever. I'm walking toward my father, and he waits for me.

TWENTY-ONE

Nate lives in a town called Wallanan. It's one of those anywhere towns, neighborhoods made up of strip malls and developments, but it's plopped down in a beautiful area in the shadow of Mt. Rainier. If Rainier ever blows, the town will probably get swept all the way to Seattle.

I'm surprised as the streets we drive down become progressively more posh. The houses get bigger, the streets wider, the landscaping more lush. Finally, Nate pulls into the driveway of a huge pile of wood and glass. Three stories of fine living.

"Wow," I say. "What do you know. You're loaded. If I'd known, I would have made up with you sooner."

"Ha. We're not really loaded — Rachel just has a nose for real estate."

We haven't really talked much on the way down. We'd been content to let the silences ease us into each other's space. Now he smiles at me.

"I'm glad you came."

I see movement at the front window, and a moment later the front door opens and a woman comes running as we get out of the car. She grabs me and hugs me, something I wasn't expecting, and then steps back.

"Let me look at you," she says, so I feel I have permission to check her out, too.

For some reason I feel surprise, as if I'd been expecting to recognize her, even though Nate has never shown me a photograph of her. She's not really pretty, but she has thick dark-blond hair and nice hazel eyes. Her face is very long and thin, as though it's been stretched out an extra couple of inches. She's one of those women who give the illusion of being pretty until you look harder and start judging the length of a nose or the thinness of an upper lip. Attractive, I guess you'd say. She's dressed in jeans and a white sweater, and a pair of battered leather boots. When she hugs and kisses Nate, I get a good feeling from her. She really loves him. She wants this to work, all of it.

She wants a family.

"Come on, come in, you must be famished," Rachel says, which is something people always say to people after car trips.

The house is full of overstuffed furniture. Sofas and armchairs and window seats and love seats. Everywhere you look, there's a place to sink into. There are pillows and wool throws and footstools, magazines and books and flowers. I want to make fun of it, but I can't. So much effort went into it, so much time picking rugs and fabrics.

"I love decorating," Rachel says. "I had this catering business, and I sold it, and, boy, did I have time on my hands. Suddenly, I had time to shop. I used to have, like, a futon and a bookshelf and my cooking knives. That was it." She crosses her arms and squints at the house, as if she's seeing it through my eyes. "Sometimes I think I went a little overboard."

"No way," I say.

Rachel has made ham sandwiches and cheese sandwiches — "in case you're a vegetarian" — and an avocado sandwich — "in case you're a vegan." She has bottled iced tea and soda and water and milk. The refrigerator is crammed with food, and she has four kinds of cookies for dessert. I begin to sense that overboard might be a way of life for her.

Nate tells her about Beewick, and she listens, but she's noticing me the whole time, refilling my glass, getting up to fetch another napkin, pushing the plate of sandwiches over when I finish what I have. She gives me little smiles of encouragement, too.

I have never seen somebody so glad to see me in my life.

It doesn't take a psychic to figure her out. I am the cement to hold her and my father together. That, and the baby she wants so much.

"How about a tour?" Rachel asks when I'm done.

Nate heads off to do some business in the study, and Rachel and I wind through the house, through the pretty dining room with yellow walls, through the master bedroom suite, through the little "sewing room" that she uses for her office. "I gave Nate the office downstairs," she says. "He's going to handle the business end of things for our new venture."

"New venture?"

"We'll show it to you tomorrow." She waves her hand at her office. "I've mostly used this for my scrapbooking. I do stuff for me, and for friends. This will be the baby's room soon. We'd want her on the same floor for a while. I think it's bad luck to decorate ahead of time, but I have so many ideas. I think I'm going to paint clouds on the ceiling."

"That sounds pretty," I say.

"Come on, let me show you your room."

The guest room is about five times the size of my room at Shay's, with big windows that flood the room with the gray light of the afternoon. It has its own bathroom with a huge tub. Rachel has laid out lots of bath oils and bubble baths. There is a stack of thick blue towels resting on a little stool.

"I'll let you get settled," she says. "Then I can give a tour of the town, if you like."

I take a shower in a stall as big as a room. There's plenty of hot water, and the pipes don't knock. I don't have to worry about anybody else needing to use the bathroom. I get out and use two big towels to dry myself.

I get dressed again and start downstairs. I stop on the stairs when I hear Rachel and Nate talking in the living room.

"You just have to be patient, sweetheart," Nate says. "Something could come through any day now."

"It's just so hard, waiting . . ."

"Let's focus on the new business. There's a lot to do."

I enter the room, and they look up. Rachel looks teary, and I start to back out again, suddenly feeling like an intruder.

"No, it's okay, honey," Rachel says. She wipes at her cheeks and gives me a big smile. "We were just talking about the adoption."

"Adoption?" I knew they wanted to start a family, but I'd assumed that Rachel was trying to get pregnant.

"We're adopting a baby," Rachel says. "From Russia. Some days are just hard, that's all. You get your hopes up, and it turns out you have to keep waiting."

"Oh," I say. So I'll have a half-Spanish cousin and a Russian brother or sister. The thought fills me up, makes me smile. It sounds like a pretty cool family. "I'm sure everything will turn out okay," I say.

"Thank you, honey." Rachel springs up. "How

about a tour of the town? We can stop for ice cream or Starbucks or something."

"Sounds great," I say.

Nate says he'll stay home, and Rachel and I take off. She's a good driver, zipping around the streets in her little sports car.

"I had a business in Seattle, and I sold it to my partner," she says. "A big catering firm. I moved to Seattle from Ohio, and I didn't know a soul. Then all I did was work. I needed a break. So I took the money and put it into my house, and I have enough to live on for a bit until I figure out my next direction. I feel so lucky. I met Nate at the right time, and he's been so incredibly supportive of the adoption. What do you think of the name Sonia?"

"I like it."

"I want something that will connect her to her heritage. We asked for a girl."

She shows me the high school, the library, the places where the kids hang. Everything looks bigger than it does on Beewick. Bigger and newer. Everything is landscaped and lovely. I've landed in Pleasant Town.

"Who knows?" she says. "Maybe you'll want to stay." She reaches over and gently pats my hand for a second. "I want you to know that you're welcome, Gracie. Nate and I talked about it. We'd love to have you live with us. Summers, holidays, or all the time, if that's what you want. I mean, I wouldn't want to take you away from your aunt Shay. I'm just saying that we're here for you. I know your father wasn't there for you. But now he is." She takes her eyes off the road so she can look directly at me. "I promise you that."

But can one person promise another person that? I want to believe Rachel. I want to believe in her comfortable house, her vision of a family, her towels. It's all there for me to sink into. And I almost believe I can. Because somehow I know that she believes every word she says to me is true.

Yet there's some notes in my head that won't go away. Even as I talk to Rachel, even as I drive through a life that could be mine, I hear it:

Dah doh din daa do . . .

But what it's really saying is: *Be careful.*

TWENTY-TWO

The next day, Rachel and Nate take me to the building they're going to rent for their new business.

"Nate had the idea," Rachel tells me as she pulls into the parking lot of an upscale strip mall. "A café with a play-care area. There are tons of young kids in Wallanan. Lots of moms and dads. Nate thought, with my experience in food and his in business, we could really have something. We'd start out with only breakfast and lunch and coffee and snacks, and then we could eventually phase it into a kid-friendly dinner place. I was even thinking of calling it Kid Friendly, but Nate wants to call it Rachel's."

"I think it sounds more personal," Nate says. "Plus, the place is going to have Rachel's heart. It might as well have her name."

Rachel laces her fingers through his. "We just signed a lease on the space," she tells me. "See, there's a great kids clothing store here, and a day spa. Places moms come all the time. We need to do some renovation work on it. We want to open by February." She squeezes Nate's hand in her excitement. "Nate will handle most of the business end. And I'll be testing recipes for the next couple of months and over Christmas. It would be a fun time to be a houseguest, hint hint!"

We get out of the car. Rachel gets the keys out and opens the door. I guess I don't have much imagination, because all I see is a big empty space.

Rachel taps a heel on the floor. "We're putting in a new floor; this carpet has to go. And our idea is to have a little raised platform over here — kids love that — with chutes they can climb up and down on. You can sit here and have your coffee, or your salad, and watch your kid play. . . . And here is the kitchen, and we're going to redo the bathrooms. We've got the best contractor in town. You have to give him a hefty deposit, but we've nailed him for December. . . ." Rachel spins around. "You could be a waitress, Gracie! And go to school here, and live with us. . . ."

And I can see it. I can see going to that gleaming school, and biking over here and tying an apron over my jeans, and bringing nice moms like Rachel their chicken salads and their balsamic vinaigrettes. I can see living in that third-floor bedroom, getting to know my dad, starting all over in a new place, with the person who should have been at my side from the beginning.

Nate smiles at Rachel and turns to me. "No

pressure, Gracie. Of course we want you here, but we know you have a life on Beewick."

"Of course," Rachel says. "I just want her to know that she's welcome."

Nate slings an arm around my shoulders. "I hope she knows that already."

I feel his arm on my shoulders, and for once, I don't flinch. I like feeling the weight of it.

We head for the door, but a balding middle-aged man is coming in, a ring of keys dangling from his fist. "Rachel, Nate, how are you?"

"Howard, it's nice to see you," Rachel says. "We were just doing some planning of the space."

"Good, good. Listen, I just thought I'd speak to you, because I didn't get your check. I'm sure it's an oversight, but . . ."

"But we mailed it last week," Rachel says, frowning.

"Uh, no, we didn't, honey," Nate says. "Totally my fault, Howard. I had it in my pocket and I forgot to do it. I found it this morning and dropped it off at your office. I left it with your secretary. It should be there."

"Okay, I'm sure Monique forgot to tell me. Enjoy your day, folks."

Rachel and Nate start out, and we wait while she locks the door.

He lied.

I know it. I can feel it. I can feel the lie.

Things tumble in my brain, things I don't want to face.

You don't know him. Don't make him into something that you want him to be.

Something here isn't right. And I have to find out what it is.

TWENTY-THREE

The next morning, I watch from upstairs as a delivery truck from an office supply store drops off several bags at the front door. Nate signs for them. Rachel is out at the gym. I don't want to see Nate this morning, so I'm pretending to sleep late.

He glances up at my window, and I jump back.

One lie isn't much to go on, I tell myself. And I don't know for sure it's a lie.

But doubt has a way of spreading, until all you're doing is watching someone and wondering . . . *What else about you isn't true?*

If Nate lied about dropping off the check, he was just buying time. But for what? Had he spent the money already? The questions pound in my brain, until I can't think.

So I decide to start with what I know is true.

He grew up in Bristol, Rhode Island.

He was able to buy the house on Beewick because of an inheritance from his aunt.

He got through law school, but hated practicing law. He quit when he left D.C.

He worked as a realtor in New Mexico.

He lived in San Diego for a while and ran a surf shop.

He wrote a newspaper column somewhere in Pennsylvania.

He met Rachel in Seattle, where he worked in commercial real estate.

He loved my mother.

He loved me.

How much is true?

I decide to leave out feelings. I'll start with the simple stuff.

Nate is just leaving when I come downstairs. He kisses me on the top of my head. "Got to get up earlier if you want to catch the worms. Or something like that."

"Who wants to eat worms?" I say.

Rachel comes in the door, still dressed in her gym clothes. She stops when she sees the bags of office supplies. "You went to the store for me! Thank you!"

He leans over and kisses her. "Don't mention it. You do enough."

It's a small lie. Taking credit for something he didn't do. *Not such a big deal,* I tell myself as I grab a bagel and some juice.

Or is it? Do you tell one lie, and that makes it easier to tell the next one, and the next?

Nate leaves, and Rachel plops down in a kitchen chair and begins to leaf through a catalog of chairs. Every so often, she sticks a little Post-it flag on a page.

"We've got to order the chairs soon," she tells me. "They've got to be comfortable, but not too comfortable. You don't want people to stay forever. You need turnover. What do you think of these?"

She flips the catalog over so I can see. "Nice."

She puts a little Post-it strip on the page, but she suddenly looks up at me. "I hope you're not bored. Let me narrow down some choices here, and we can go shopping or something. Your dad won't be back until dinner."

"Sounds good," I say. "He's been out a lot since I've been here."

"Oh, honey, are you disappointed? It's just that things are coming together for the business, and there's a million details."

"No, it's fine, it's just that . . . I think of these questions I want to ask, because I don't really know that much about him, and then by the time I see him, I forget what they are."

Rachel closes the catalog. "Well, try me. When we first met, all we did was talk and talk. I know everything about him." She grins. "Well, almost everything. I asked him not to tell me about old girlfriends. I'm the jealous type. As a matter of fact,

I'm planning a surprise for him for Christmas — a scrapbook. I've got plenty of photos and mementos from our time together, of course, but whew, I never met anyone who could stick all his photographs into one envelope. It's like the man doesn't have a past." Rachel's hand flies to her mouth. "Oh, honey, I didn't mean . . . I mean, of course he does, of course he has a past. Most of the photographs he saved were of you. I just mean, he moved around a lot, and . . ."

"It's okay," I say. "I know you didn't mean it." I want to keep her talking about Nate. "I know he grew up in Rhode Island, but I don't know much about my grandparents. I never met them, and neither did my mother. They died before she met my father."

"William and Eleanor," Rachel says, nodding. "William died of cancer quite young."

Ding. He died of cancer? Nate told me that he killed himself.

"Nate's mom died of a heart attack when he was in high school. So tragic." She leans forward and puts her hands on my hands. "So you see, you have so much in common. He doesn't like to talk about it, and I know you don't, either. But there are so many things you can share."

But I'm not interested in sharing grief. "What about his aunt, the one that left him money?"

"Jane," Rachel says. "She left him a bundle, I guess. He was able to buy that house on Beewick — which I'm so glad will be yours one day — and pay for law school, too."

Ding. I'd always heard from my mom that she put my dad through law school.

Two lies in about three seconds.

But they aren't just lies. They're someplace to start. Someplace to begin to figure out who Nathaniel Millard really is.

I tell Rachel and Nate that I made a date to see a friend in Seattle on Wednesday, so they drop me at the bus. I've already called Ryan, who told me he was "awesomely available" to help.

I meet him at his "office," a cyber café somewhere on the outskirts of Belltown, this very cool neighborhood in Seattle. I recognize his red hair and geek glasses as soon as I walk in. He's sitting at a back table with a supersize soda and a table littered with *People* and *US Weekly* magazines. He pushes them aside to make room for me.

"Celebrity worship is my life," he says. "Have a seat. Can I get you a soda or coffee or something? My treat, as long as it's under three dollars."

I stand back up. "I'll get it. And I'll bring back some food, too. Cookies or muffins?"

"Cookies, for sure."

I order a cup of tea and pick up two fudge cook-ies as big as salad plates.

"Awesome!" he says approvingly as he accepts the cookie. "I work better with a massive sugar rush." He flips open his laptop and cracks his knuckles. "Now, let us begin to reveal the real Nate Millard. Tell me what you need, and I'll open the portals of cybertown."

I take a bite of cookie and push over a piece of paper. I've written the names of Nate's parents, his aunt, and his full name. "Everything there is to know about them."

Ryan's fingers fly over the keyboard. He's an astute Googler, but he also belongs to this subscrip-tion newsnet site that allows him to search more efficiently and faster than I can.

He finds Eleanor Millard's death notice in the Providence paper, and the funeral notice about my grandfather. So far Nate's stories check out, at least about when they died. But Ryan frowns as he searches for Jane Millard.

"Millard bequest," he murmurs. "Wait, let me go back a few years. . . ."

"What?"

"Here we go. Jane Grace Millard. She was on the board of the local animal shelter."

"Grace?" Had I been named after my father's aunt? I never knew that.

"Yeah, wait . . . it's a family name. There are Graces and Millards all over the place in that part of Rhode Island. Looks like you might have a couple hundred second and third cousins once removed. Here we go — Jane Grace Millard died June second, 1988."

"What? That doesn't make sense." I quickly do the math. That means she died *after* Shay had bought the house.

"Newspapers don't lie. Well, scratch that — they lie all the time, I guess, but not about death notices. Yeah, and look, her whole estate went to the animal hospital."

So there was no inheritance.

So where did Nate get the money?

He put himself through school. He said. His father left him nothing. He said. The only money he ever had came from his Aunt Jane, who was the only one, he said, who really loved him.

"All right, let's get cracking on Nathaniel," Ryan says. "Not much coming up here. Nothing, in fact."

I watch Ryan chew his cookie and type and mouse-click. "Whoa. Whoa, whoa, whoa."

"What?"

I can see by his face that he doesn't want to show me. But he pushes the laptop over so I can see.

It's a Web site called *DEADBEAT DADS*. Women who have been abandoned post their husbands' names and photos on the site. And there he is, Nate, smiling, by a backyard grill.

"Tampa, Florida?" I ask. "Nathaniel Grace Millard, missing since 1998. Two kids?"

"Bunny and Ben," Ryan says. "Aw."

Ryan takes the laptop back as I sit, stunned.

Bunny. The pale blond girl with the stuffed rabbit. His daughter.

"Searching under the name Nate Grace now. Sometimes dudes on the run use variants on their names to . . . uh-oh."

I look over. It's a Web site created by Cheryl Anne Hinker from Factoryville, Pennsylvania.

HAVE YOU SEEN THIS MAN?

It's Nate.

He owes her money. He left town with it — and their wedding album.

"Whoa, serial sleazebag," Ryan says. He peers at me anxiously. "Some cold water or something? You look sort of green."

"Who is he?" I ask. "Who's my dad?"

"I'm going to have to break it to you gently, goddess Gracie," Ryan says. "He's a crook."

TWENTY-FOUR

A crook.

I've waited all my life to meet him. Even while I told myself I didn't need him, I did. Even while I told myself it didn't matter what he was or wasn't, it did.

Why had he come to Beewick Island? I no longer believed he had come there for me. Someone who lied his way through his life had to be lying now. Someone who always had an ulterior motive had to have one now.

I stare out at the highway and listen to the sound of the bus wheels whining on the wet road. It's raining, a true hard rain, not a Northwest mist. When I lean against my window, my breath fogs the glass. I keep wiping it with my hand. The window fogs and clears, fogs and clears. The road disappears and appears again. All the way back to him.

Nate is waiting in the car at the bus stop. I walk over to the car and get in.

"Have a good time with your friend?"

"Awesome," I say.

But he knows me now. He gives me a look, as if

he knows something is wrong. I look out the window and slump in my seat, teenage body language for "don't ask." He doesn't. He thinks I'm bummed because of a boy. Good.

"You should see what Rachel is cooking for tomorrow," he says, pulling out into traffic. "It'll just be the three of us, but she's making enough for a truck stop."

I suddenly feel enormously sorry for Rachel. She loves him. She does everything she can to please him. *Ask me. I know everything about him.* I remember her confidence, the love in her eyes. I'm so furious at him now, I could kick him out the car door into traffic.

"Rachel's great," I say. "You're lucky."

He gives me another sharp look, because he hears the acid in my tone. He coasts to a stop at a traffic light. He taps my knee. "Don't sweat it, kiddo. Teenage guys don't know anything."

"Oh," I say, "and when they're adults, they're so much smarter?"

"Ouch," he says. "Good point."

I watch his hands on the wheel, and I wonder if they could have murdered someone. Could he have hit Hank Hobbs and pushed him off a boat, then stood by and waited until he drowned?

The money.

I suddenly realize where he got the money for the down payment. I can't believe it's taken me so long to put it together.

Billy Applegate had gotten secret documents that would expose Monvor. But something happened. They disappeared. Billy believed that someone in the group had stolen them. Someone had sold them out for money.

How much money? Enough for half a down payment on a rundown house?

Why not?

But the question still hammers at me. If all this is true, I still don't know why Nate would come back to Beewick. If it wasn't for me, then why? Did he come back to kill Hank Hobbs?

That night, I set my alarm for three A.M. When it goes off, I almost catapult out of bed. My heart slams in my chest, and I have to force myself to calm down.

If I'm going to do this, I have to be careful. At this rate, my heart is hammering so loudly it will wake up the house.

I tiptoe to the stairs and pause on the second-floor landing. I listen carefully, but behind the door of the master bedroom, there is no sound, even of snoring. I keep going downstairs.

I have to move slowly in the unfamiliar house. It's so dark, and there's so much furniture. I shuffle my feet along, peering as the shadowy forms turn into end tables and ottomans in the huge living room.

I push open the door to the study. I'm going to

have to risk a light. If I get caught, I can say I couldn't sleep and I came down to surf the Web.

The desk is pretty neat. There are piles of folders on the top. I go through them quickly: the lease on the restaurant space, different kitchen catalogs, permit applications. There's one file marked ADOPTION. Another says MENU PLANS. Nothing I didn't know about. No secrets.

But secrets wouldn't be on top of the desk.

I start going through the drawers. I get out a big checkbook, a binder for the business checks. MILLARD/TOBIN ENTERPRISES. I leaf back through the record and see a check to the landlord made out for six thousand dollars. I flip back to see the running balance in the register. I pull out a bank statement and study that. I'm no accountant, so what do I know? It looks fine to me. But I'm sure Nate never delivered that check.

Then I see some numbers written in a small hand on the first page of the register. I'm guessing, but I bet the numbers are a password.

I boot up the computer. I go to the bank's Web site. There's a box for entering a password and one for a user name. Under PASSWORD, I type in the numbers I saw.

USER NAME. I try *RACHEL*. I can't get in.

NATE. Still can't. *NATHANIEL*.

I try their full names. I try Rachel's maiden name. Nothing.

I hesitate, then type in *SONIA*.

I'm in.

I look at the bank balance, then back at the register. There's a twelve thousand dollar difference.

He's been writing the checks. He just hasn't been mailing them.

He was busted by the landlord. But I bet he's stalling him. I bet he gave him another story, and the landlord is giving him another day or so.

I feel sick, sick at heart. I know what he's planning now. He's going to leave her, and soon, before his lies are discovered. How could he be so heartless?

And then I think of Cheryl Ann in Pennsylvania.

The family in Tampa.

Me.

I go through the drawers, but there's nothing left to find. Rachel has left the business to Nate. She won't find out until he leaves, when she has to look up her own bank balance and discover the truth.

What I need to find out is more personal things. If only there were something I could get a reading off of. I usually run away from visions, but now I need one. I need to see the way to the truth.

As a matter of fact, I'm planning a surprise for him for Christmas — a scrapbook.

She has photographs. Old photographs.

If I search Rachel's office and get caught, what excuse could I give for being there?

I just can't get caught.

I switch off the lamp in the office and climb the stairs. I listen on the landing. Nothing.

I tiptoe into Rachel's office. I close the door, glad it doesn't squeak. I switch on the lamp on her worktable.

Rachel is very organized. There are photos, pieces of nice paper, calligraphic pens, glue sticks, paste-on lettering, different kinds of scissors, those little black corners people put on photographs. There are files labeled HOUSE and VACATIONS and BABY. I look in the baby file. She's already collecting things to put in the scrapbook — a line drawing of baby shoes. Samples of birth announcements. Pink labels.

I search through the files until I find it. NATE.

I open the accordion file. I thumb through the things that look current — photographs of Nate and Rachel, restaurant menus, ticket stubs. There is a separate envelope inside and I slip it out. It's full of old photographs.

The first one is of me.

I'm a baby. My mom is holding me in the hospital. A pink balloon rises above her head. Her blond hair is sticking up in a funny way, but who has a good hair day after giving birth? What you really notice is her smile. Her big, generous, goofy smile.

I swallow and blink. It just tears me, how grief never stops. It hits you when you're not looking, it spins your head around. It makes you gasp with the shock of it.

I put that photograph aside and keep looking.

There is a photograph of Nate as a boy standing in front of a brick house with a porch. He has dark hair and his hands are shoved into the pockets of his jeans. I am shocked to see how much he looks like me.

And then there are the photographs I'm hoping for. Beewick Island. I recognize it immediately. It's a shot of kids swimming at what the kids on Beewick call Fishstick Cove, since you can see the restaurants across the bay. It's a popular place to swim in the summertime because the water is fairly warm. I recognize Nate immediately, then Shay. She is dressed in cutoffs and a white T-shirt and is about fifteen pounds thinner. I touch her image, but I don't get an image from that smiling girl. And then I look at the young man by her side and get a chill, and I know that this is Billy Applegate.

He's got a cherubic face with round cheeks. Not what I expected. He's thin and wiry and good-looking. One of his hands rests on Shay's ankle.

A few days, or weeks, from when this picture is taken, he'll be murdered.

I don't even know him, and I feel sorrow for him. Because he died young. Because he didn't deserve to die.

I push the photograph to one side.

The next photograph is of Nate and Shay and my mother. It takes me a moment to recognize where it was taken. It's Shay's house. I recognize the windows of the back room, the mudroom that Diego and Shay turned into a bedroom for me. It's filled with trash, and two of the windowpanes are cracked. The three of them are holding up cans of soda in a toast and grinning for the camera.

The third photograph is taken from the hallway looking toward the bathroom. On the floor is an awful pinky-orangey shag carpet. Shay hadn't exaggerated the horror.

Shay and Nate are standing in the bathtub. Shay is holding her nose and making a comical face. Nate is waving a sponge. A mildewy shower curtain is pushed all the way to one side.

I recognize the curtain. Clear, with palm trees on it.

The body through the curtain.

The blood on the plastic.

Someone breathing, hard. Someone trying not to panic.

The last photograph is an old Polaroid, a snapshot. It is of Nate and a man it takes me a long second to realize is Jeff Ferris. They are wearing kerchiefs tied around their heads, and they've painted on fake curly mustaches. They're at a party. People in costume swirl around them, dancing. The women are wearing long dresses, some with aprons, others with big petticoats. Some of them are wearing white wigs with long curls. Some of the men are wearing knickers and white stockings.

This must be the party Nate told me about. The local who had sneaked him in had been Jeff Ferris. That made sense. Jeff was his realtor.

We met at a Bastille Day party at the Beewick Club. . . .

I look at the other faces. I don't need to see him. I know Hank Hobbs was there.

Which means Nate could have met him.

Which means Nate could have lied.

Then I remember something else. The surf shop he owned in San Diego. Would someone who couldn't swim run a surf shop? You have to be a pretty good swimmer to surf.

I'm not much of a swimmer. He lied about that, too. Why would someone lie about that if they didn't have something to hide?

I hear footsteps outside in the hall. They are heavy. It's Nate.

I lunge for the lamp, almost knock it over. I turn

out the light and hold it before it crashes to the floor. Then I quickly stuff the photographs back into the envelope and shove it all back where I found it.

I run to the door and listen.

I hear a toilet flush. Footsteps start back toward the bedroom.

I run back to my room. I hug my knees and wait until first light. Until I can call Shay.

TWENTY-FIVE

"Gracie!" The relief and pleasure in Shay's voice sends warmth through me. "I was just sitting here with my coffee, thinking of you. I'm so glad you called."

I close my eyes and think of Shay's tiny dining room, the room that sticks out from the side of the house, that's big enough only for her long farm table and chairs. When we have people over for dinner, they have to crawl over each other to get to the bathroom. Shay's tiny house is so different from Rachel's. Shay doesn't have near the amount of sofas and pillows and room, but her house is always crammed full of guests and laughter and conversations. Rachel has a house that's filled with furniture but no people.

"Wait a minute, why are you calling? Is everything okay?"

"I just wanted to wish you Happy Thanksgiving."

"It's six-thirty in the morning. Tell me another one."

I flop over in bed and cradle the receiver. I keep

my voice low, even though I'm pretty sure Rachel and Nate are still sleeping.

"I guess I'm homesick."

She gives a laugh of pleasure. "Good. I mean, I hope you're having a good time with your father. But that makes me feel good."

"I was thinking about your house."

"*Our* house."

"Our house. I saw some pictures of it last night. When you first bought it. There was this really hideous carpet —"

"Hoo, I'll say. That color! Like a bruised cantaloupe."

"Nate is in the pictures. And my mom is in one of them. Do you remember who took them?"

"I don't remember. . . . I don't have copies of them. I think those were taken on closing day. We went over to celebrate. The house was a mess, but we felt like we'd just bought the Taj Mahal. Well, I did. But the work ahead of us was enormous. Nate started that night. He took out that carpet and the curtains and cleaned the floors, for a surprise for me and Carrie. It smelled a little better after that. But only a little. We threw open all the windows for weeks."

Nate took up the carpet and cleaned? He hasn't rinsed a dish since I've been here.

I'm scared, I want to tell Shay. *I want to come home.*

But I have one more thing to do here. So instead, I say "Happy Thanksgiving" again and hang up.

Look, I'm not good with holidays anyway. I've had two serious crashes on Christmas since mom died, and my birthday just makes me sad. But I didn't know how bad it could get until I was spending Thanksgiving with two strangers, one of whom could be my dad the murderer.

Rachel has gone all out. Butternut squash soup. Turkey, stuffing, creamed onions. Mashed potatoes and sweet potato casserole. Carrots. String beans. And two kinds of pie.

It's all good, but I can't eat. Every bite sticks in my throat. I have to pretend to eat, pretend to join in the conversation, but I can't stop thinking of what happened to Billy Applegate and Hank Hobbs.

And Rachel. Is she in danger, too?

In the middle of the pumpkin and the apple pies, the phone rings. Rachel gets up, a smile on her face. "That's probably my parents. I left a message before."

We hear her say hello in the kitchen.

Nate looks at me. "What's up, kiddo?"

"What?"

"You're not yourself."

"I'm in a food coma."

"You hardly touched your food."

"It's just weird, being here, I guess."

He puts his fork down. "You must miss her on holidays."

"I miss her every day."

"But it's worse on holidays, isn't it? It's like you're running on empty."

Yes, that's exactly what it's like.

"I always hated holidays myself," he says.

Suddenly, we hear Rachel sob.

We push our chairs back and hurry into the kitchen.

"Honey, what it is it?"

Rachel looks up him, tears streaming down her face, her hand still on the phone in its cradle. But she's smiling. "Our baby. Sonia. Our baby is ready for us. She's ready to come home."

Nate rushes to gather Rachel in his arms. "That's great, honey. That's great."

Does he mean it? If he doesn't, he's a great actor.

But isn't that the point? That he's a great actor? A con man?

Rachel swipes at her tears. "We have to leave for Moscow within a few days, they said. There's so much to do, I can't think. . . ."

"I'll take care of everything," Nate says. "Our passports are ready, you have baby clothes for Sonia, you even have diapers! Don't worry, sweetie, we're set. I'll buy the tickets."

Rachel holds out her hand to me. "Gracie. Gracie, I'm so sorry to cut your visit short. It's just that, they said we'd have very little notice —"

"I understand," I say. "It's okay. I can take the bus back."

"No," Nate says. "I'll drive you. I can do the trip in a day, then swing back here for the flight."

But he won't come back, I know. He'll take me back, but he'll keep going. He'll have her money, probably all the money she was going to use to pay for Sonia, the money for the tickets, everything. He'll clean out the business account. And he'll keep driving, maybe to Canada. I know it.

He'll leave her, just like he left all the others.

TWENTY-SIX

Rachel starts to call her family in Ohio to tell them the news. The kitchen is full of her voice, her laughter. Nate and I do the dishes. As he scrapes, I rinse and put things in the dishwasher, carefully choosing the right slots for the serving pieces, the pitchers, the gravy boat. He scrubs the pots while I wipe down the counters. He puts away the leftovers while I dry the crystal. We do all this half-listening to Rachel.

Yes, they just called me. . . .

I don't know, we haven't looked up flights yet, but maybe Saturday. . . .

Lots of paperwork and things, but we'll maybe be back in two weeks. . . .

I know, it will be cold, we have plenty of warm things for the baby. . . .

You will? Oh, you doll, you, thank you. . . .

Isn't it strange, I think, *that Nate has no one to call? He's about to be a father, after all.*

Every so often, he puts his hand on Rachel's shoulder as he goes by. There is so much trust in the way she covers his hand with her own. He leans over and kisses the top of her head.

My hands shake, and I can't see for a moment, as rage fills me up. These are things he did with mom. He touched her gently. He smiled at her. He listened to her plans. And all the time, he was waiting to leave us. Wanting to leave us.

Did he steal from mom, too? I don't know. It's not something she would have told me, I realize. She would rather me think of my dad as a flake than a crook.

After all the dishes are done and the leftovers put away, Nate sits at the kitchen table with Rachel to make plans. I go upstairs. On the way, I sneak back into Rachel's office. I slip out the photograph of Nate at the Bastille Day party. I tuck it in my pocket. I need something to show Joe, proof that Nate had known Hank Hobbs.

Turn my own dad in? You betcha.

Here is what I think happened twenty years ago.

Billy Applegate broke into Hank Hobbs's house and stole the incriminating memo. But somehow Nate got hold of it — stole it from Billy and gave it back to Hank Hobbs — for a price. That's how he got the money for the down payment. Maybe he never expected to go through with the house, but he did.

Billy suspected Nate and confronted him at the house. Nate killed him.

And then, years later, Nate bumps into Hank

Hobbs somewhere, probably in Seattle. Hobbs remembers him as the guy he'd bribed all those years ago. Maybe something happened, maybe something clicked, maybe Hank Hobbs suddenly realized that Nate had killed Billy. So Nate killed Hank Hobbs. Nate pushed him off the boat and watched him drown.

It all makes sense, but I feel like I'm missing something.

I toss and turn for a long time, but I finally fall asleep. I fall into a dream so deep, I can't wake up.

I dream that I'm breathing dirt. There's mud in my mouth and nose, and I can't get it out.

I'm being sucked down through the bed. Things are sliding against my skin, dragging against me. I feel oozy mud between my fingers, between my toes, in my mouth. I am drowning in a swamp.

Spiky branches are above me, and I try to grab them. Ferns crumble in my fingers.

It seems to take an enormous effort to wake myself up. I spring up from the bed and run to the bathroom. I switch on the light and splash my face with cold water. Over and over until I can breathe again.

When I come up, pushing my wet hair behind my ears, I suddenly know, with a blazing certainty, why Nate was on Beewick. It wasn't just to kill Hank Hobbs.

The wetlands reclamation project.

The land is being drained. On Saturday.

And the body of Billy Applegate will surface.

Did he hope the killing of Hank Hobbs would delay it? Stop that last-minute million-dollar grant? He was wrong.

Did he hope to find out more, to find out exactly when the draining would happen? Did Shay tell him? Is that why he's planning to leave Rachel, before the body is found and a murder investigation is reopened?

I need to get back. I need to find out. I need to know where Billy Applegate lies.

The next day, I wait in my room until he leaves on an errand. I pull on my jacket and make sure the photograph is still in my pocket. I can't let them know I'm leaving, because I'm afraid he'll track me down.

She's sitting at the kitchen table, a teapot next to her elbow and a mug of tea in one hand, while she writes a list with the other.

"Hey, sleepyhead," she says. "There's so much to remember, I'm making lists like crazy. Can I get you breakfast? Lunch?"

"I thought I'd go for a run."

"A run? But it's raining."

"It's always raining."

She laughs. "True. Seize the day, I guess — I'll

stick with hot tea. I'll have some breakfast for you when you get back."

I can't tell her. I can't tip him off. But I can't leave her like this, either.

"You've been really nice to me," I say. "I just wanted to tell you — I'm really glad about Sonia. She couldn't have a better mother."

Her eyes fill with tears. "That means a lot."

I go to the door and open it. "Just . . . be careful."

I shut the door on her puzzled frown. And then I start to run.

I catch the bus to Seattle. I have to wait another hour to catch the next bus, the one that will take me to the ferry. It's late. By the time I board, it's past two o'clock.

The bus lets me off at the ferry. I am so glad when my feet hit the deck. I stand at the railing, my back to the line of cars driving aboard. I face the island in the distance.

The ferry ride is so short that most people don't get out of their cars. Just the pedestrians, like me, and the bicyclists, and a few people wanting to stretch their legs before we dock.

I am lucky. I see Nate racing up the stairs before he sees me. I see him searching the deck, his head swiveling. I feel his urgency and his anger.

I duck down the left stairway, down to the deck

where the cars are. I keep my head low. He'll have to get back into his car in three minutes, when the ferry docks. I am so glad it's only a twelve-minute trip.

I don't see him again. I stay hidden. The ferry begins its docking maneuvers. Car engines start up. The slow exodus begins, people patiently lining up and driving off.

I see his Volvo bump off the ferry and zoom away.

I don't have much time.

TWENTY-SEVEN

It's almost dusk when I reach the swamp. I check the shadows and realize I don't have much daylight left. Just enough time to go in, see what I can pick up, and leave. If I can pinpoint the area where I think Billy Applegate's body lies, I'll have more leverage with Joe. It's a big area, and I want to be sure. I know the final drainage will take place early tomorrow, and I need more than hunches to get Joe out here.

The first place Nate will go will be Shay's. She'll probably freak, and he'll have to stay while she calls Rachel, calls Joe, calls everybody she can think of. I hate to put her through another disappearance of mine, but I can be home within the hour, or even sooner, if I'm lucky. I've made sure my cell phone is off, so I won't have to feel guilty about ignoring the calls for a while. I'm not ready to talk to anyone yet.

I know the wetlands area well, thanks to Shay. She actually enjoys hiking around in this stuff. The reclamation project has used narrow wood decking to build a trail through the swampy area to make it easier for the scientists to gather information over the past years. I know the way, since Shay has brought me out here many times. I used to think Shay's work was boring when I first got here. Well, I still think it's boring, but I sure have learned a lot about wetlands.

I hadn't counted on how the trees would block the remaining light in the sky. I wish I'd thought to bring a flashlight. I decide I'll only go another couple of hundred yards and then try to get a sense of what I'm looking for. I remember my vision — I remember the way the branches hung, and the ferns that lay like a blanket nearby.

The only trouble is, I don't know if the vision was of the present or the past. If it was the past, then things have changed since then — trees have died, have grown, ferns have given way to bushes and scrub.

But the landscape is looking familiar now, and I can feel the back of my neck prickle, and it isn't from the falling mist. I'm close. I know it.

There was once a pond here. The water has been draining for weeks. I put one foot out and sink, but not too deeply. I know if I walk through these trees, I will find a dry area to stand on. I know there will be ferns and dead leaves. I know because I saw it.

The ground sucks at my shoes, and I have to drag my feet out while I walk, a creepy sensation. Something is pulling me onward, and I could no more resist it than I could a cold drink on a hot day. It will bring me relief, somehow. I will *know*. I will know everything that happened. I will know my father. I will know what is broken and can never be fixed, and I will know how to go on.

The land is firm, just as I'd seen. It used to be underwater. The light is fading, but I can see something shine ahead. A glint.

I go closer. Mud-smeared, filthy, but still intact. The edge of a shower curtain.

And unmistakably, a human hand.

I want to run, but I can't, the mud is too thick. But the panic inside me is rising, and I can't seem to make headway. The trail is just yards away, but it might as well be a mile.

I fumble for my cell phone in the pocket of my jacket. I stab out Joe's number.

I hear the tones chime.

And I understand at last what I've been hearing in my head.

Dah doh din daa do . . .

It wasn't a tune. It was the electronic tones of numbers on a keypad.

I disconnect the call before it rings. Slowly, I punch out numbers, trying to match the tones. It takes me a while, but I get it at last. 7 1 4 8 6.

It's not a phone number. What is it? I play the tones once, twice. I close my eyes and feel the keypad, concentrating as I listen.

I see fingers stabbing a keypad.

I see Jefferson Ferris pushing the alarm code at his house.

Seven. One. Four. Eight. Six.

And behind my closed eyes, those numbers form a date. July 14, 1986.

July fourteenth. Bastille Day.

We met at a Bastille Day party.

The photograph of Nate at the party.

What am I missing? What is there that I can't see?

"These days we have to remember so many codes and passwords, it's a wonder our heads don't explode. My secret system is to code everything on my dog's birthday."

"You remember your dog's birthday?"

"No. That's the problem."

People pick codes that mean something to them. Wedding anniversaries. Their children's birth dates. Jeff Ferris's code was the same date that Hank Hobbs met Betsy Dunwoody. But why?

And then I remember something. When Hobbs's house was broken into twenty years ago, the alarm didn't go off. He'd told the police that he thought he'd set it. What if he had? What if the thief knew the code?

What if Hobbs used the date he had met his fiancée for his code? What if someone knew that?

Someone like Nate? He'd been at the dance.

He'd been at the dance with Jeff Ferris.

Dad sold Hobbs his first house on Beewick. A big sale for us, back then.

If Jeff Ferris knew Hank Hobbs's alarm code, he could have been the one to steal the file and pass it along to Billy. But why?

So many whys, and it all happened so long ago. I'm confused now. Confused by things I've seen, confused by what people say and what they don't say. Confused by facts that jumble together in my head. Confused by all my visions. Everything seemed to point in one direction, but now it feels as though they point in so many directions, sending me spinning like a top, bouncing from one thought to another.

Nate and Jeff at the Bastille Day dance.

I was never a great swimmer. . . .

Jeff Ferris is a great guy. He coaches at the high school. He knows Mason and Dylan, who are both on the swim team. . . .

I can't untangle this. All I can do is go straight to Joe and dump it on him.

I turn my back on the shower curtain, but suddenly, I see it again.

The shower curtain rips off the rod. It falls to the bathroom floor. He drags the body onto it. The carpet is soaked with blood. He rolls the shower curtain around the body. It is hard to do because his hands are shaking so badly. He rolls the body into the curtain. Beads of sweat roll down his nose and drop, drop, drop onto the curtain. He secures the curtain with twine. It is no longer Billy he sees. He just sees . . . a body. Soon he will forget this. He will move on. After he lays Billy to rest. Not Billy. The body. The body.

Hobbs treads water. Blood trickles into the water. He's getting tired. The boat circles him, chugging. Circling. Circling. Waiting . . .

I feel the fear of Hank Hobbs as the cold water locks him into a paralysis that is pure terror.

He doesn't have the strength to scream, or the breath. The scream is inside his head. It is inside my head, and it is so loud that at first I don't hear the sound of someone tramping through the marsh and dragging something behind him.

TWENTY-EIGHT

I look down as I drop the phone. It seems to fall in slow motion as I bend to catch it. It disappears into the murky water.

I sink into the muck as I drop to my knees to search. My hands are in the muddy water and I'm crying now, crying hard, as Jeff Ferris appears, dragging a sled. Something a kid would use on a snowy day, flat on the bottom, curled in front. A coil of rope is slung around his shoulder. He's carrying a shovel.

He looks surprised and dismayed to see me. "Is that you, Gracie? What are you doing here?"

"I'm here . . . looking," I say, stammering, "with Shay and Joe."

His eyes shift. "Where are they? I didn't see a car."

"No? Oh, they're around," I say. "Shay wanted to do a few things before tomorrow. . . . You know, the last draining will take place. . . ."

I can feel something shift. He narrows his eyes, and he smiles. "You're lying." He takes a step closer to me. "Why are you lying, Gracie?"

"I'm not," I say, taking a step back. I can't help it.

"You look afraid. If one were paranoid, one might think that you suspected me of something."

I search for something to say, but there is nothing to say. He knows I suspect him. He knows Shay and Joe aren't here.

"It's really a drag, having a psychic girl around," Jeff says, hitching the rope higher on his arm. "You gave me some sleepless nights, especially after I caught you at my house."

"I don't know what you mean —"

"Yeah, you do."

"It was you," I say. "You're the one who broke into Shay's house."

"I didn't break in. The door was open. Get your facts straight." Jeff's face turns nasty for a minute. "I wasn't going to hurt you. I just wanted to scare you off, that's all. And make you think it was Mason."

"The shoes . . ."

"I got them from Mason's locker — he always leaves it open. Beewick is such a friendly place. That's one of the reasons I like it."

"You wore his shoes. And then you threw them away at school so the police would find them."

"So you see, I didn't want to kill you." Jeff looks at me sadly. "And now it looks like I have to. I don't want to, mind you. But I just want you to know — I can. I turned this corner when I killed Billy. I didn't know it at the time. At the time, I just thought, oh boy, I'll never do *this* again. Have I learned *my* lesson. Hoo boy. But then, when I killed Hank Hobbs, it wasn't so hard. Gets easier all the time."

I'm so cold. I'm so very cold.

"Hate to do it to Shay. She's a nice lady. But you haven't been here very long. It's not like you're her kid or anything."

Is he crazy? He's saying these things in a totally normal tone of voice. Yet he means them. I know he's capable of killing me. I can see it in the odd, glassy way he's looking at me. His bland features are suddenly ugly. I wish I could go back to teasing him behind his back with Diego. I wish he'd ask me "How's the house?"

I wish I hadn't been so stupid.

I wish I wasn't here.

"And this is great, in a way, because you can help me move Billy's body."

"*What?*"

"I've got the place all picked out. Nobody will find it. Up on the north end of the island, where the tides will take him all the way to Canada. That was my mistake last time — I didn't know the island well enough. The whole thing will be real quick, I promise."

"You're crazy."

"No, I'm not. I just have a job to do."

I have to do what they do in the movies. Get him talking.

"Why did you do it?" I ask. "Why did you kill Billy?"

He looks annoyed. "Well, I didn't mean to. That's the whole point."

"What happened?"

It's getting darker by the second, but I can read his sneer. "Why don't you tell *me*? You're the one who's psychic."

"I don't know. It has something to do with that Monvor file."

"Gold star. Of course it does. Shay and Nate and Billy and their crowd — they were so cool. I just wanted to hang out with them. We went swimming, played softball, I sneaked them into the country club. . . . They liked me! And I agreed with what they were doing, too. I mean, what Monvor was doing was destroying real estate values. Of course my dad couldn't see that. He was too busy selling houses to the executives."

He pronounces the word *ex-EC-yoo-tives* in a deep, prissy voice, just like Franklin Ferris would. *He hates his father,* I realize. He had vandalized his own office. That peanut butter on his father's desk was *personal*.

"I wanted to help them. Why not? So in August, when they were getting set to maybe leave, I told Billy I could find him evidence. And I broke into Hank's house. I knew his code — he told me it was the day he met his fiancée, and I knew it, I was there at that party, I remembered. I got Nate into that party. That's where he met Hank. Hank hardly noticed us, so when he told me how he picked his code, he had no idea I knew it was July fourteenth. It was so easy."

"So you were friends with Nate and Billy."

"I was friends with all of them! Now Shay treats me like I'm only the person who sold her the house. She forgets." Jeff scowls.

"So what happened next?" I ask.

"I thought I did a great thing. Look at what Monvor was doing back then — destroying the land, lying about it — they deserved it. And Hank Hobbs deserved it, too. What a snob. He looked down on my dad and me, treated us like rubes who didn't know anything. He didn't care about Beewick. He'd just work here and use it for what he could, then move on to somewhere else."

"But what happened, Jeff?" I ask. "After you stole the file and gave it to Billy?"

"My dad guessed who stole it," Jeff said. His mouth became a thin line. "He told me I was stupid. That I couldn't alienate Monvor, it was half our business — what if they found out? He practically kicked me down the stairs. He said" — and again, Jeff uses that same deep, caricature of a voice — "'Get it back, boy! Or I'll turn you in myself, and you'll go to jail!' So I went back to Billy and said, hey, sorry, I need it back. And he said no."

"And that made you mad."

"No, I expected that. So I offered him money. Some of the money I'd saved for college, because my old man didn't believe in college — it's like, you need a diploma to sell houses? — and Billy just laughed at me. He said, 'Who do you think I am? I'm not going to sell out my friends.'"

"So you found someone who would sell out his friends. Nate."

"Not only did he take the money, he negotiated a better price." Jeff laughs hollowly. "All my college money. And he uses it for the down payment. And he says to me, 'At least you'll make your commission, Jeff.' Ha. And I never did go to college, thank you very much."

"And Billy suspected."

"Yeah. He didn't know who sold him out, but he called me, threatened to go to the papers, tell them what was in the file and let the chips fall. Well, I couldn't let that happen. I told him to meet me at the house. I knew it would be empty. I still had the keys, and Shay hadn't changed the locks yet. So we talked, and he made me so mad. I tried to explain about my father, about *jail,* and he told me I had no commitment, I was a hypocrite. 'You pretend to love this place and then the first chance you get, you sell out. . . .' And I hit him, and he came after me, so I hit him with a log from the fireplace, and he cracked his head on the mantel. Wow, he was tall. I still remember his head hitting — *crack* — and the way he went down. And the blood."

"You wrapped him in the shower curtain and dragged him out. And then you tore up the carpet. You pretended you did it as a favor." And Nate took the credit. He told Shay he'd done it. It was typical of him.

"It took me a long time to be able to sleep at night," Jeff said. His voice was close to a whine. "I'm not a monster."

"What happened with Hank Hobbs? Did he know you killed Billy?"

"He walks into the realty office twenty years later and doesn't remember me. But he's looking for a major property, so I show him the house I bought for an investment. He flips for it. Has to have it. Everything is going great, and then, that last day . . ." Jeff shakes his head. "I do such a stupid thing. We go out to the house together for a last walk-through, and my hands are full of papers and my briefcase and my cell, and so I say to him, just punch in my code, and I tell him the numbers, and he punches it in, and I see him looking at me, and I realize that he knows that I have the same code as he does, and how could that be?"

"But why would you use it, too, all those years later?"

"To remind myself of what I'm fighting for." Jeff's face is harsh. "I'm not content to be a townie.

I want to be bigger than that. Every single day I punch in my code, my password, I remember that I can do the hard stuff. I can win."

"What did he do?"

"Yeah, Hank. He's just looking at me, and I see that something clicks for him. Maybe he's already living in the past, seeing the girl again, that Betsy. I know he's thinking — *Here's the guy who broke into my house, all those years ago.* And I even see the moment when he makes the leap — *And what happened to that kid, that Billy Applegate? Could that be connected?* And meanwhile we're going through the house, talking about this and that, and I'm being totally cool, but I can read him like a book. So here's what I do. I think of the plan right on the spot. I say, 'Hey, you need to see the house from the water,' and he's not that interested, but I push it, in a nice way, and he says, 'Okay, yeah, we can go on my boat.' I manipulate him, see, so that he'd be hurting my feelings if he put me off. And then, once we're on the boat, the rest is easy."

The rest is easy? Murdering someone, watching them drown, that's easy?

"I know what you're thinking. You're disgusted, right? But listen to me, Hobbs wasn't a nice man. He cheated on his wife. He covered up what his company did, and then he tried to pay blood money to fix it, just because he wanted to retire here. And he tried to get your aunt fired, don't forget that!"

I feel the edge of my cell phone with my foot. I nudge it, trying to get it closer to the surface. I only succeed in pushing it deeper. But at least I know where it is.

"Yeah, old Hank wasn't a great loss to anyone. Whereas I'm a part of the island's history. I buy houses and renovate them. I run the annual Chamber of Commerce drive to help needy kids. I coach the high school swim team for free. . . ."

"The andro," I say. "That was yours."

"I only give them what they ask for," Jeff says. "You don't think the other kids are doing it, the kids from the rich communities on the mainland? Come on! And it's not a steroid, you know. It's a precursor. There's a difference." Jeff looks annoyed now. "You know, we're wasting time. It's dark now, I don't have to wait anymore. You can help me load Billy onto the sled."

"No."

"It's not far. I pulled up real close. I have a four-wheel drive."

"I'm not helping you."

Jeff laughs. "What, you think you have a choice?"

I can't feel the cell phone with my foot anymore. It doesn't matter — he'd never give me a chance to call anyone. But I've noticed something else. He's dropped his hand, the one holding the coiled rope. The rope has uncoiled, and his foot is tangled in it.

"Okay," he says, handing over the shovel. "You dig, I'll haul."

He's not kidding. I am not the strongest person. But I have my surprise on my side and, if I'm lucky, a certain lack of balance going on with him.

I grab the shovel and push it right back at him, hard, in the stomach. He is surprised. It wouldn't work, except he has to step back, and his foot gets caught in the rope. I give the shovel another push, and he goes over.

TWENTY-NINE

Now the nightmare is real. Crashing through the underbrush in a blind panic, not remembering where the trail is, the swamp sucking at me like a breathing monster, trying to bring me down. He's behind me, panting, not yelling, just running, and I know my head start is going to dissolve.

The cover of the trees helps. He can't see me. I run as quietly as I can, but it's hard not to make noise in a swamp. Things snap and rustle, and I hear him change direction and come after me again.

I burst through a thicket. Brambles tear at my skin. I push through, fall, get up, run around a tree, and almost bump into Nate.

He jumps and catches me. "What are you doing?" he practically shouts.

"Shhh!" I start to sob.

"Gracie, what's going on? I followed you from the ferry, and let Shay know. I just want to talk to you, I've been looking . . ."

"Let her go, Nate."

Jeff stands with the shovel. Casually. Dead-eyed.

"What are you talking about, Jeff? Gracie . . ."

"I know about you," Jeff says. "When you

reappeared on the island, I looked you up. Your life played out just the way I thought it would."

"He killed Billy," I tell my father. "And Hank Hobbs."

"You killed Billy? What? Why? You hardly knew him!"

"Didn't you suspect it?" Jeff asks. "Come on, Nate. Did you really think he just disappeared?"

"Yes!"

"I don't believe you. You knew I did it and you walked away, with money in your pocket and the girl, right? You know what it looks like? It looks like you were an accessory. I can say you even helped me hide the body, and who's going to doubt me?"

"What do you want, Jeff?" Nate asks. I hear him swallow. He's just beginning to understand what he's walked in on.

"I want you to let her go and walk away. Find another one of your identities and get lost. Get lost for good."

"She's my daughter."

"Yeah, that meant so much to you."

I feel Nate's fingers loosen on my arm. Feel his muscles relax.

And then a strange thing happens, stranger than maybe anything that's ever happened to me, and that's saying a lot. I know what he's going to do before he does it. And it isn't because I sense it, it isn't a psychic thing. It's a connection. One I didn't even realize we had.

So I move when he moves. I bend my knees just as he pushes me down. I tuck and roll as he catapults forward and slams Jeff Ferris with a fist on the side of the head, a blow I can hear, knuckles against skull, and then kicks him somewhere in his midsection and pushes him down.

But Jeff grabs his legs and yanks, and Nate topples. They grapple in the mud. I hear the blows and hear my father grunt.

I crawl toward the shovel. I stand, but I'm weaving, and I can't get a good shot at Jeff. I can't imagine I can slow him down. They are charged with adrenaline, and I see Jeff's fingers tighten on Nate's throat.

I feel a hand on my shoulder. I haven't even heard him come up.

"No need for that, Gracie." Joe's voice is calm. It's easier to be calm when you're holding a gun. "Jeff, get up. It's over."

THIRTY

I meet Nate at the inn, where he's spent the night. He and I had stayed over an hour at the police station last night, talking about what happened. In another room, Jeff Ferris had confessed to everything he'd done.

The venom of years had spilled out. How he had done so much for the island, and no one appreciated it. How he knew Mason and his friends had vandalized his house, so he got back at them by framing Mason for breaking into my house, and maybe for the Hobbs murder. He even trashed his own office so Joe would think the kids did it.

And his envy spilled out, too. How much he hated Hank Hobbs, who could so easily buy the house Jeff had bought but couldn't afford to live in.

His father refused to hire a lawyer for him. Jeff was on his own.

And Joe had suspected Jeff from the beginning. He'd been quietly gathering evidence while I was running around trying to pin it on everybody else.

Now, Nate leans against his car. "I'm sorry I can't stay longer, but Rachel wants me home. She's so glad you're okay."

"You're not going to Russia, are you?" I say. "You're leaving again."

He shakes his head. "I know you see things. Don't *imagine* them, too."

I fix him with my gaze. I pin him down. "Tell me the truth, for once."

He looks away, then looks back again. "Well," he says, "I guess I am leaving her, then."

"You're a real piece of work, Dad," I say.

His mouth twists in a way I haven't seen. "Yeah. I really thought I was ready to stick this time. Look, Gracie, everything you think about me is probably true. I've bounced from family to family. I don't mean to leave. But I do."

"It's just so weird and awful, having brothers and sisters I don't even know about."

He looks startled. "What brothers and sisters?"

"The kids in Tampa — Bunny and Ben."

"How do you know about Bunny and Ben? Okay, never mind. They weren't mine. I was married for less than a year. They were my stepkids. I'm a deadbeat dad on a technicality. I didn't owe Leslie child support. I mean, except in her own mind."

"What about Cheryl Ann? You stole her money and her wedding album?"

"Her wedding album?" He laughs. "I'm sorry, it's just that . . . I didn't take her wedding album. We weren't even married. We only had a 'commitment ceremony' — her idea, I assure you. That

album is probably kicking around the house, I bet —
the house was always a mess. I might have lifted a
few bucks when I left, though."

"Like you'll do with Rachel."

"Serves me right, I guess," he says. "I came here
so you *wouldn't* find out these things. When Shay
sent that private eye after me, I was afraid of what
he'd dig up. So I came here to talk to her, to see you.
I'm glad I came, even though now you know what
a crook your old man is."

"You're not just a crook, you're a sociopath. I
don't know if anything you told me is true."

"Well, now is your chance to ask."

"Did you suspect that Jeff killed Billy
Applegate?"

"No," he says, shaking his head. "I never
dreamed that Billy was murdered. Of course I
didn't think Jeff killed him."

"Did you really think you were manic-
depressive? Is that really why you left?"

He hesitates. "No."

I think back to the way he told the story, how
sincere he was, how, even though I was resisting
him, I was listening the whole time. The hurt of it
takes my breath away. What a good liar he is.

"You're sure good at telling stories," I say. I hear
the bitterness in my voice. "It's a wonder you're not
a millionaire."

He steps toward me and curves his whole body

toward me, lowering his head so that he can speak softly. "I wasn't afraid of losing my mind. But the rest of it is true. I did think I was hurting you. I know I was hurting your mom. I wasn't cut out for marriage."

"Did your father really commit suicide?"

"Yes."

"He had cancer! You're still lying!"

"And he took his own life when it got really bad."

"Oh." Suddenly, I feel deflated. I realize that the facts don't really matter. He lied to me once, and now I'll never quite believe him, even at his most sincere. "So why did you ask me to come back to Rachel's, then?" I ask. "You knew you were going to leave her."

"I was trying to stay," he says. "I always want to stay, kiddo."

"You know, I thought it might have started here, when you took the bribe and betrayed your friends. But it probably started way before that, didn't it? People don't matter to you. Nothing matters to you. I bet you gave away your *dog* when you were little."

"How'd you know?" He grins, but I don't smile.

But suddenly, to my surprise, his face changes and he steps forward and hugs me, really hugs me. He lifts me off my feet.

"This matters to me," he says in my ear. "This is the one true thing I know."

For a moment, I just sink into it. The feeling of being loved.

He pulls away. His hands dangle by his sides now.

"If you love me, then try," I urge him. "Try with Rachel. Get the baby. Start again. Do it right this time."

"Oh, Gracie. I don't think I can. She expects too much of me."

"Well, I do, too, and you love me," I say. "You've got a two-hour trip to consider your options. I'll call at eleven A.M. and if you're not there, I'll put Joe Fusilli on your tail."

"You'd do that to me?"

"In a heartbeat."

He cocks his head and looks at me. "You know, sweetie, that you can't make someone stick. You just can't. No matter what you hold over their head."

He's right, of course. I can't reform him.

"Just go with her, then. Help her get Sonia. Don't take that away from her, too. You can leave later."

"I'm afraid the die might be cast."

"You mean the money? For the rent and the airline tickets and things?"

He shakes his head in a marveling way. "You know that, too?" He sighs and gets in the car. "I guess I've got some thinking to do. I'll be in touch."

I watch him drive away. I don't know where

he's going. I think he'll go back to Rachel, just because he doesn't want Joe Fusilli on his trail. But I really don't know.

I stand there, watching, until I can't see his car anymore. I feel so tired. Tired of looking at all the cracks in love, all the imperfections. Tired of him. I don't want him in my life.

But there he is.

THIRTY-ONE

When I turn, Shay is waiting. She is always waiting. She waited for me to grieve for my mom. She waited for me to accept her. She waited for me to love her. She'll never stop waiting.

"Can I buy you breakfast?" she asks.

We start walking toward the diner.

"He's a real creep," I say.

"Yeah," she says. She hands me a tissue, and I wipe my tears.

"Did you make up with Joe yet?"

She stretches her arms above her head and smiles. "Not yet. But I feel a thaw coming."

We walk up the hill silently for a minute. "I thought you weren't coming back," Shay says. "I was so scared you weren't coming back."

"I want this to feel like home," I say. I want to be honest with her. "And sometimes it does. But in a way, I'm still looking for whatever that is."

She lets out a breath. "Okay."

"And I can't get over that you lied to me."

She stops and faces me. Her hair blows crazily in her face, the way it does. She's not wearing makeup, and everything looks naked on her face, all her emotion, all her feeling.

"Well, you're just going to have to get over it," she says.

I laugh at her fierceness. I can't help it.

"And stop saying that I lied," she goes on. "You know darn well what the circumstances were. You can't expect to know every detail of my past."

"Did you ever have a crush on Nate?"

She's startled. "Nate? No. I left that to Carrie."

"Did you like him?"

"Sure. Everyone liked Nate. But I guess maybe there was something about him I didn't trust . . . some instinct, because when Carrie fell for him, I was worried. Something . . . something seemed to be missing in him. But she loved him, so there was nothing more to say."

"You didn't go to the wedding."

"I was in Spain."

Shay opens the door to the diner. She smiles at Josie, the waitress, and holds up a finger, which means this morning she wants coffee. I know her routine as well as Josie does.

"Tea, Gracie?" Josie calls.

I nod.

Shay slides into a booth. Josie brings the coffee, and Shay takes the first sip with great appreciation, sniffing it first, curling her fingers around the thick mug. She smiles her thanks at Josie, asks her how her son is doing.

I am beginning to realize, as Zed told me, how lucky I am. And if making this work takes work, I'll work it.

"I don't expect to know everything," I say to her. "Just the important things. It's just that . . . there were secrets in my family. Things my mom couldn't tell me. And my dad is obviously one major liar. So I think I'm making a decision in my life to live differently. And I'd like it to start with you."

"Fair enough." Shay puts down her mug. "Fire away."

"Who was Diego's father?"

Shay takes a sharp breath. "Well, you certainly cut to the chase."

She doesn't want to do this. I see that. I see something there so deep, it hurts just to probe it.

She takes a sip of coffee and nods again.

"His name was Pablo," she says, and our long morning together begins.